PASS
THROUGH
MANHATTAN

PASS
THROUGH
MANHATTAN

BY RICHARD WORMSER

19 40

New York

WILLIAM MORROW AND COMPANY

To my father
LOUIS WORMSER

PASS

THROUGH

MANHATTAN

PART ONE

It had been a mild winter in New York, and now it was March. Two weeks ago a haberdasher at 85th and Broadway—The London Tophatter—had put a sign in his window —Winter Overcoats, 33 1/3 off. Promptly The Princeton Toggery on 88th had countered with save 40% on ulsters. By the time the bear market had reached The Elite Eton Haberdashers on 97th, a wise shopper could get a Heavy Topcoat for Half or Less and there seemed no bottom to the decline.

But now, in the second week of March, a blizzard had hit the Northeast, was concentrating on Manhattan Island.

Don Morton lay flat on his back on the couch and crossed one knee over the other raised one. He swung his foot five times, reversed his legs, and swung the other foot five times. Then he got up, pulled the couch a little farther away from the hissing radiator, lit a cigarette, took two puffs on it, and tapped it out again.

Pass Through Manhattan

From the bedroom came his father's stertorous snoring; the deep-throated gurgle of a man who was in his early fifties, had always smoked and drunk too much, and now had a bad cold.

Don yawned and slouched over to the desk. He pushed aside a pile of his father's junk—old clippings, announcements of friends' weddings, book catalogues, letters, and the beginnings of various articles for the national weeklies.

From a drawer he took a neat canvas letter-case, zipped open its binding. He extracted his slide rule, paper, a pencil and a sharpener. Then he delved again and came up with a copy of *Principles of Steam Engineering*.

In neat firm letters—printing—he inscribed a sheet of paper: THE PROBLEM. If, in the All's Fair Mine, gravel is running at $14, and movement charges, gravel bank to shipment box, are $7, how much heat can economically be applied to the wash?

He began to figure, marking his findings. The subject was purely theoretical; the operation would not open up again until the bank melted of its own accord; the owners saw no need for haste. It was now the second week in March; he should receive the call to start back for Colorado in two weeks.

Nevertheless, he went on figuring, the mental exercise seeming to bring him that much closer to Colorado and the open air, that much farther from steam heat and his father—and this city which he did not like.

He came to the conclusion that operations could commence when the seven A.M. temperature on the surface of the gravel was 28° F.

But—wait. This left out an additional operating factor. Opening that much sooner would involve more heat being supplied to the bunkhouses and offices. This must, properly

4

speaking, be added to movement charges, sub-division "labor."

From the big bottom drawer of the desk he took out a canvas portable book case matching the letter-case. He unzipped this, took out *Insulation Factors of Building Materials*, and laid it on the desk alongside *Principles of Steam Engineering*. The bunkhouses were board and batten, one-inch fir and—

Mr. Daniel Flynn, an inspector for the Department of Parks, had tried to get through the winter without buying a heavy coat, despite the Broadway bargains. At twenty-nine he considered himself lucky to have a good political job under Robert Moses, though his cronies, buying each other beers in Shea's Bar & Grill under the L tracks on Columbus, assured him that the Fusionists could not stay in forever, and some Tammany man would have his position come the next election.

Still, he liked his job, and the pay was not bad. But Mary had two children and a third on the way, and with a good muffler a man could get by in his spring coat. On the first day of the blizzard, Mr. Flynn made his patrol—the 96th Street Transverse and one block north and south—in the topcoat, muffler, a heavy blue sweater, and rubbers over his shoes. Halfway through the day he felt himself sneezing, and at lunch took an extra amount of mulligan in his beer, but it didn't do any good; his throat got dry, and his nose ran.

Mary made him soak his feet in mustard and water and put him to bed; and the next morning she wrapped herself up as warm as possible, went to the drugstore and phoned the office, in the old Arsenal across the Park, that Dan had a bad cold.

5

Pass Through Manhattan

The super in the office checked Daniel Flynn without looking to see the beat. With the snow coming down the way it was, no one would be using the Park, anyway. No kids would be swinging on the swings, the walks wouldn't have to be kept clear, it didn't much matter. No use sending a relief.

Don's head whirled, he felt a weight that was almost physical pressing down on his chest. This damned steam heat. A mist like damp in a coal mine covered the paper, obscured the figures on the paper.

Got to get out of here. I am an outdoor man, a mining engineer, this sort of thing is not for me.

He got his overcoat out of the closet, slammed on a hat. But as he opened the front door his father turned over, groaned. The blurry voice called: "Don?"

Don let the overcoat drop, went into the bedroom. "Yes, Joe?" His father objected to being called Father.

"Get me glass water."

Don ran the water into a dusty glass, threw it away, ran a clean glass and carried it to the bedside. Joe Morton tried to grin. "Can't tell how much this is hangover," he said, after the water had eased his tongue, "and how much cold."

"You get some rest now, Joe," Don said. Back in the living room he hung up the overcoat, put the hat away. If he went out, Joe might get some idea of going after a drink.

But what would he do if I weren't here?

Unfortunately, the answer to that was plain enough. Ray would send Ron or Brawley up to look after him. And Don owed them too much now. Too many loans, too much counsel, too much kindness.

So long as it was not business or necessity that took him

out, his place was here. He couldn't get more indebted to the three friends his father had.

I've got four fathers, Don thought, dragging me down.

But I'll be in Colorado soon. Visions of pines and mountains and placer streams filled his head, and he went back to the desk.

Mrs. George Victor, Third Avenue at 94th, looked out on a fire-escape that carried two feet of snow. Really white snow. "Do you have to work today?" she asked.

Mr. Victor, WPA foreman, shook his head from the drowsy comfort of the creaking bed. "Naw. That pile of wood we cut'll be ten feet under snow. Reminds me of when I was a boy on the farm. Seems like a pile of wood," said Mr. Victor, "will make a bigger snowdrift than anything else."

"Where were you cutting?"

"Just north of the transverse, over near the Central Park end," Mr. Victor said. He slept. . . .

Mr. Horace Cohen, of the Bureau of Streets, beat his hands together before dropping a nickel into the slot of the public phone at 93rd and Broadway. It was cold out there. He got the office downtown. "Lissen," he said. "If we don't get a crew up here at 93, the whole upper West Side's gonna jam. The snow's packin' down into the slot on the street-car tracks, an' two cars is stalled already. That big conveyor truck you sent me broke an axle and . . . O.K. All the men you can spare. . . . Naw. . . . Soon's I get this straightened, I'll go over the rest of my territory. The cops'll let me know if anything too bad happens."

The snow had continued to fall, covering the gray and black city with a white frosting. When it stopped falling, the city would embrace it, turn it the color of everything else, and it would cease to be snow as Mr. Victor had known it on his father's farm, would become merely an annoying problem for taxi drivers, milk companies, and the Department of Sanitation, who would use their own garbage trucks, Mr. Cohen's road-building machinery, and the brawn of Mr. Victor's indifferent crew to bundle the dirty gray stuff through streets and down manholes to sewage systems until it reached the North and East rivers. There it would become an annoyance and a menace to ferryboat and tugboat captains, it might mean near starvation to the little licensed junk-boats that make a living picking up flotsam in the harbor.

In the meantime, it fell, white and soft, on such odd things as Joan of Arc's head at 93rd and Riverside and the pigeon coops of a little Italian boy who lived in a tenement at 98th and Second. Internes in the Harlem Hospital regarded it, picturesque and clean in their courtyard, and knew that it meant work for them; Negroes in New York die of pneumonia like flies when it snows. The snow fell here and there, paying no attention to Mayor LaGuardia, bumping downtown in his limousine and wondering if he should have bought more snowplows. But, dammit, you don't get a snow like this once in ten years, and there are a thousand better things to do with the money.

At 97th and Fifth, the Mayor told his chauffeur to cut west through the transverse and see if it was open. Yes, all right. That was a big drift there near the Central Park end, hanging over the transverse wall. The Mayor, who wished he could be God and know where each sparrow fell in his five boroughs, made a prodigious effort and remembered that the WPA had been cutting up dead wood there to distribute to the poor. Call up the Federal people when it

stopped snowing, and ask if they needed any help digging
that wood out; the poor would be cold and want the fuel.

The Mayor told his driver to go South on Amsterdam.

*   *   *

JUST WEST of Broadway on 96th the street is very wide, and
quite steep as it slopes down to the old coal pockets and the
Naval Reserve training ship. Not so very many years ago
the big Burns Bros. coal trucks needed an extra team to
help their four big horses up 96th to Broadway; the company kept two pairs of their best grays there, just to get
the coal started up from the pocket to Broadway. But now
the old coal yards are a park, and even before that the
trucks marked Burns COAL Burns were motor-powered,
with heavy compound gears that made the hill surely, if
slowly.

The 96th Street buses turn around just past Broadway.

If, at the moment Don went from the couch to the desk,
he had chosen to look out the window, he would have seen
a driver named Arthur Kreutzler come in westbound and
be told by a cop that he was to make the swing in 96th
Street, instead of going to West End and then around the
block. "Jam on 93rd and Broadway; we're sendin' Broadway traffic up West End," said the cop, and went away.

Arthur Kreutzler brought his bus into the corner and
discharged two passengers. There was another bus ahead of
him, not making the turn, and he shut the door and climbed
out.

He didn't know the driver of the other bus by any other
name but Slim. Not that he cared; he didn't like associat-
ing with the other drivers. A bunch of roughnecks. Arthur
lit a cigarette and looked at Slim, standing there.

Pass Through Manhattan

Slim said: "How was the transverse?"

Arthur shrugged. "Rough. The snow has packed down and it makes bumps."

"It was bad when I come through," Slim said. "It ain't going to get no better."

"That is quite evident," Arthur said, sharply.

Slim looked at him. Then he shrugged. "Let's get us some sand and fix the track. Me, I don't wanna go skidding down the hill into the river; 's too cold."

"You could always stop the car by turning it sidewise," Arthur said. "If it skids, merely turn the wheels in the direction towards which you are skidding." But he went back to the bus and got the bucket thoughtfully provided by the despatcher; he filled it at the D. of S. box on the corner and followed Slim along the parabola the buses would have to describe to make their turns and take their places in the eastbound schedule.

The tracks of the bus ahead of Slim's were plain, slick under a light coat of snow, the flakes not joining yet. There were two places where the big car, for all its slow speed, had skidded.

Arthur sprinkled sand, twisting his hand from the wrist. It should have been he and not Slim who thought of the sand. He was a graduate engineer, Columbia School of Mines, '32, whereas Slim was nothing but a dirty-talking bus driver who had the picture of a naked woman pasted inside the door of his locker.

When the buckets were empty, the two drivers went back to their stations. Arthur looked at his wrist watch. "You had better start. You're scheduled to leave in ninety-three seconds."

Slim said: "You sure are a pippin, Doc," and climbed into his bus. Arthur, taking over his own wheel, winced as

Pass Through Manhattan

Slim raced the motor, sending clouds of blue and white smoke out the exhaust; waste, non-efficient waste.

Then he followed Slim around the curve, and parked pointed east. He would wait six minutes after Slim left and then he would leave. Some of the drivers waited a few seconds, if there was a subway train discharging underground and a crowd of people coming up, but he did not believe in that. That sort of thing caused drivers to take unsafe chances in order to make up time further along. And it was inefficient.

Slim left.

Arthur wished the drivers would not call him Doc. He was not a Ph.D., though some day he might be; he had the credits, was just finishing the thesis that might earn him his M.A. With that, perhaps he might get a position at Columbia teaching, though they gave the preference to men who had had actual experience in the mines.

But how could he do that? There was a prejudice—oh, they concealed it, but there was a prejudice, all right—in the mining industries. One of his race was discriminated against. The only positions he had been offered on graduating were completely and finally beneath him. Timekeeper. Blaster's helper.

That was all right with Gentile boys, who could hope for quick advancement, but it would not do for him. To be passed over in favor of stupid Goyim who—

Arthur Kreutzler glanced at his watch, and gently eased away from the curb without any passengers. It was 1:42 P.M., Saturday, in the second week of March.

There were two passengers waiting on the far corner, next to the uptown local subway station. Arthur kept the door open while the white man took the second seat back of him, while the Negro automatically went to the broad seat on the very back which was, tacitly, the best place to go.

Arthur Kreutzler, when he thought about this at all, thought maybe it was a habit, from the Jim Crow cars he had read about in the South.

He shut the door, and instantly the snow that had blown in on him began to melt. He piloted the bus up the hill towards Amsterdam.

*   *   *

SWINGING THE BRIEFCASE marked W. Gordon Maxwell, Gordie got out of the express train at 96th Street, stamping his feet on the platform because it was cold. Like most of the other passengers who had ridden the express north, he waited for a local; because the 96th Street West Side station is peculiarly constructed. You can walk through the local trains to the platforms on the side that lead up to the street; this is the only station in Manhattan where this is true. Passengers who hurry down the central stairs, only to find that they have to hurry up again to the local platforms, are regarded with scorn by the experienced 96th Streeters.

A 137th Street local came in, and Gordie walked through it, first allowing the local people to get off. He was cold; the long ride up from 14th Street had melted the snow that had fallen on his almost-tweed overcoat in the two blocks from the office to the subway.

But he stamped his feet automatically, not thinking about it. Because he had an idea. An idea for a story. An idea for a story that would sell to the *Saturday Evening Post* for five hundred dollars.

Why not? He was a writer, wasn't he? He had been writing since before those boys up at Popular got out of college.

Pass Through Manhattan

They regarded him as an authority on the pulps, and yet two of them sold the *Post* with some regularity, and he had never hit the slicks at all.

And he, W. Gordon Maxwell, was a good writer. He had sold, he figured, a half million words in his life. Mostly, of course, to the magazines he edited, fillers and blurbs and little puzzles that started off: "First Grade Detective Joe O'Reilly looked at the body of—"

But he had sold stories in the open market, too. In between jobs as an assistant editor at Popular, Munsey's, Street & Smith and the old Fiction House, he had kept himself and Elsie alive selling short stories to—Popular, Munsey's, Street & Smith and the old Fiction House.

True, the returns had never been so opulent that he could afford to turn down the next assistant editorship that offered. But—

Waiting on the street corner for the eastbound bus, he forced his mind back to his story. He would go home, get out the card table and the portable and knock out a first draft this afternoon. Maybe he could polish it tomorrow, Sunday, and mail it to Philadelphia tomorrow night.

This cop, see, has been shot arresting a crook. Shot in the shoulder, and also creased in the head. Well, he gets out of the hospital and the other cops give a big banquet for him. But they don't know, nobody knows but this cop, that the crease has left him slug-nutty, like a prizefighter. He—

The bus was pulling to a stop in front of him. Gordie beat snow off his shoulders, and waited for the other man to precede him up the steps. But the other man waited too, and Gordie, peering near-sightedly through snow-damped glasses that should have been readjusted, saw the other man was colored. So he went first, embarrassed, and the colored man followed him into the bus.

Pass Through Manhattan

Gordie chose a seat near the front. Now, the cop ought to have a girl. You had to have a girl for the slicks. But wouldn't a girl know he was slug-nutty? And—

Say, this would make a good filler for the mag. They needed a short short, and it was the editor's privilege to write it himself and sell it to the magazine at a cent a word, since thousand-word detective stories cannot be bought in the open market.

No. Sell this for ten dollars when the *Post* would pay five hundred? Put a girl in and a decision—

The colored man stumbled into Gordie's knee, walking to the back of the crowded bus, and Gordie mumbled "Excuse me." Put a girl in and—

Buck Ranulph was cold. Wonder if white folks get as cold as we do? Certainly doesn't look like it, there's Malincovich guiding traffic right smack in the middle of Broadway, and not even bothering to stamp the snow off his shoes. And here, thank the Lord, was the bus.

As he dropped his nickel down the little box, Buck fumbled for the papers. Pages 1207 to 1248 of the *Book of Torts.*

He had had to cut the binding off his textbook and split the book up into little pamphlets for two reasons: (a) the law books were too big to carry around on duty, and (b) it made the white detectives sore to see a colored man studying to be a lawyer, when they were perfectly content to be policemen all their lives.

He sat down in the back of the bus, bracing himself against the bouncing. Now—

In the case of Adams *v.* McNeil, 104 Ala. 271.

Ala. Alabama. The state courts of Alabama where a colored man had the same chance of getting justice that he had of being made John D. Rockefeller's sole heir. Scottsboro, Ala.

Two pictures of Alabama crossed Buckingham Ranulph's mind. The popular picture of homesick old colored people in Harlem slums—persimmons ready to drop, a cow in every yard, fat back and turnip greens melting in your mouth. And the picture of the Communists whom Buck—as a cop—could not join, or even listen to, except when he was ordered to report their meetings. Bare red clay and exhausted soil, and white store keepers grinding the black share-croppers down into a slavery worse than the one Lincoln ended.

Man ought to see the South. A Negro—Buck did not like the term colored—ought to see his homeland, even though he had been born on a truck farm on Long Island. A competent colored lawyer who was probably going to graduate in the first tenth of his N.Y.U. night class ought to go South and serve his people instead of carrying the badge of a third-class detective of the New York Police Department.

Because a colored detective was really nothing but a stool pigeon. The white men ran the cases, and when they were stuck they said: "Buck, go hang around that nigger barber shop and see if they'll talk to you. They shut up like clams when they see a white face. . . ."

Read your law, boy. Adams *v.* McNeil, Ala. Sup. Ct., 37—

Two thirds up the long, sloping block from Broadway to Amsterdam, Arthur Kreutzler saw a girl start out of the door of a beauty shop and start racing his bus for the corner. She slipped and slid on the packed-down snow, and her skirt flashed over her knee for a moment, making him go hot and tense with longing.

Automatically he slowed the bus down so the girl—and

her knee—could make it. There was a fat kike waiting for the bus, and Arthur fussed around with the door, opening it slowly, as though the snow had jammed it. The fat kike bustled in, threw his nickel into the glass box, and sat down directly behind Arthur. A middle-aged woman—looked like a cook they used to have—stumbled in after him. Oh, Lord, one of those who carried her change in a little purse, inside of a big handbag, and stood on the platform fumbling while you kept the door open and the snow blew against your legs.

The girl came in fast, after the woman, and opened her own pretty handbag, black patent leather with red trimming. But she was not very tall, and when she opened the bag Arthur could see into it, and he saw the beads and cross of a rosary.

Crossly he let the clutch out and the door slam shut so fast that the bus started with a lurch, and the girl was nearly knocked off her feet.

The fat Jewish-looking man sitting right behind the driver was the kind that twisted around in his seat and looked to see if your knees showed when the bus went over a bump. The one behind him was all right, though. Kind of a bookish-looking boy. The poor thing looked like he didn't get enough to eat.

If you sat further back than the second row behind the driver it was too bumpy, so Peggy Reilly sat down opposite Gordie Maxwell. She looked at her big wrist watch, the one with the second hand that had been Dad's. Ten minutes of—

A voice behind her said: "Please, have you got the time?"

Peggy twisted her head to smile at the lined face of the German woman on the seat behind her. "Ten minutes to two."

Pass Through Manhattan

"Thank you very—"

The bus went over a mound of packed-down snow that had drifted over a box some kids had left in the street. The German woman was bounced and nearly had her breath knocked out. "Ach, iss rough."

Peggy said, kindly: "Sit up here next to me. The further forward you get the less you feel it." She put out a hand to help the woman forward.

The German lady sat heavily down beside Peggy. "I have such a pain here," she said. "It is going from the heat in the bakery out into the cold of the snow, I think. The bouncing of the bus, it always hurts me, going home."

Peggy said: "You should sit up forward."

"I remember that. Thank you. This is bad snow, no? Like we have in the Rhine country."

"It *is* a bad storm. I hope we aren't held up in the transverse; I have to be at Fifth Avenue by quarter past two."

"A date with your young man? American girls, they have fun."

"No. Not me. I have to be up at the hospital and in uniform by two-thirty."

"Oh, you are a nurse. I used to go to the hospital, to the clinic, for my pain. But Artur—"

Peggy was glad to talk about the hospital, and about sick people. "You ought to come back. I'm graduating next week, and I think I'm going to get a job in the out-patients clinic. I'd look after you."

"Mount Sinai?"

"Yes," Peggy said. "We have the biggest clinic—"

"You are not Jewish?"

"No. Most of the nurses are Irish, you know. I don't know why, except I guess Jewish girls don't want to be nurses."

"Oh. Artur, he made me stop going. He said I couldn't go by a Jewish doctor. . . ."

"Oh, yes, I see." Well, of all the nerve. It was pretty decent, Peggy thought, of Jewish people to run a clinic and take in German and Porto Rican and colored patients, anybody. If Mount Sinai didn't mind looking after Hitler's people she would think— Not wanting to start anything, her Irish blood rose the way it used to do and make Dad laugh, and she said: "I'm pretty fond of Mount Sinai. It's the second finest nurses' school in the country, and they take in Catholics and Protestants just like their own girls. We have some of the finest surgeons in the world, doctors who had to leave Austria and Germany—"

"Please, I do not feel that way. It is just Artur."

Startled, Peggy saw that the old woman was going to cry, and put a hand on her gnarled one. "I didn't mean to scold you. . . . Look, Fifth Avenue isn't Jewish. Why don't you go there?"

"Maybe I could come to see you, and tell Artur I go to Fifth Avenue. The doctors at Mount Sinai, they helped me so much."

"Well, ask if I'm in the clinic. My name is Miss Reilly."

"I am Mrs. Lempe, Mrs. Artur Lempe. . . ."

The building was going to be all right. Maybe he had been a fool to start steel going up this early in the year, but there was nothing up but the girders and they hadn't caught enough snow to bother them. And this would be the last storm of the year, they could start the masons off next week, or as soon as the snow melted.

He'd have her open for the fall rental season. Hitting his clenched fist on his knee, Jack Firstin saw her open and the people coming in to look at apartments. Too bad he couldn't have a sign out, Jack Firstin, Inc., or Firstin Properties Corp., but maybe after those two bankruptcies he'd better keep his name off it. . . .

But next year he'd run up a real house, maybe down south of the park, he'd made the grade from 96th Street down to the big money twice and he'd make it again. Have to look around the office for those old lease forms. A lot of stuff had been lost while he was in jail for alimony that time.

But Jack Firstin, sitting right behind the driver, and urging the heavy bus over the rutted snow so he could get to Lexington Avenue and catch a downtown subway to his office, Jack Firstin beating his fist on his knee with exultation because his steel work had stood, he wasn't thinking of the old times, the bad times, he was looking ahead to next winter, when he'd run up a real house, a Fifty-Seventh Street house, with penthouses. Make it an apartment hotel, and rent out the restaurant to some swell operator.

If his lawyer couldn't see any way to float the bonds, he'd get a new lawyer. Hell, if you just sold them in one state, the SEC couldn't touch you. Or could it? Ask his lawyer—

Columbus Avenue was going to be soupy under the L tracks. The snow had not had a good chance under there, and it had melted, then frozen again. There was ice under the new, powdery snow. Two passengers waiting for him. A dinge gal and a sailor. Wonder if they're together? Those sailors sure don't draw the color line. You see them—

Sure enough, the bus skidded. Some damn fool woman screeched, and Arthur swore under his breath as he turned the wheels into the skid, manipulated across the ice and the steel car tracks.

Pass Through Manhattan

He got her under control again, and drew up as near to the curb as the snow would let him, opened the door to make two more nickels for the boss. No, they weren't together. The sailor got on first, dropped in his nickel, and slouched towards the back of the bus; then the dinge girl scrambled across the snow, and gave him five pennies. As his cold fingers got a nickel out of the change rack to give her, he sniffed. Boy, ten cents' worth of Woolworth's best perfume on her.

Seeing nothing but humor in the gaudy clothes, the feathery furpiece of the colored girl, Arthur wondered if she looked like a knockout to that big colored guy on the back seat there. The one studying the book. Or did he want white women? Up in college, they used to sit around the library steps and talk about—

There were enough people in the bus now to have fogged up the air. Arthur wiped the inside of his windshield, but it promptly clouded again, and he had to open the little window to cool the glass from the inside. A draft hit his right ear. He was going to catch a cold.

The fat kike sitting behind him said: "Close that window, driver."

"Sorry, mister, but I can't see if I do."

"It's an outrage. They ought to equip these buses properly."

"Write a letter to the company, mister."

Arthur started the bus up. Central Park West, and then into the transverse. It seemed to him that it was, if anything, snowing harder.

Marlene Smith sat down on the back seat of the bus, next to the big young fellow reading the book. She held herself poised and when the bus went over a bump she slid into him. "I hope you'll excuse me," she said, in her very best accent. She and Fifi Lawrence, next door, had been practicing talking the way the swells in Harlem did. Southern, but not too much. Like your parents talked Southern at home, but you'd been born in New York.

But it didn't seem to work on this one. For all he knew she'd spoken, she might have used monkey-chaser talk, like Mama and Papa did. She'd corrected them and corrected them, but Papa wouldn't give up saying "look-out" for look, and he wouldn't take up saying "you-all" for you.

Sometimes it seemed like it wasn't any use. You'd think anybody would want to move from West 99th up to Harlem, especially when your very own daughter had gone to all the trouble of finding a flat. But they'd just looked at it and said it was dirty. They said Harlem was dirty.

The bus bumped her into the big fellow again, and he smiled at her: "I hope I'm not crowding you, miss."

Oh, gee. Didn't he talk swell? Marlene started practicing an entirely new way of talking, in which you pronounced your rs. She didn't even notice that the big fellow was reading again. When he had spoken, she saw he was older than she had thought. Maybe thirty or more. Too old for her.

She would use her new way of talking on Dinky when she met him on the street corner of Lexington and 96th. "I beg yourrrr parrrdon, Dinky," she would say. Then she realized that she had spoken aloud, and blushed, the rise of blood painting her cheeks faintly pink under their natural beige.

But no one noticed her.

Cowboy Connors wondered if he had been smart to take this bus. Maybe he should have stayed over there on the West Side and eaten kosher. That hot pastrami sandwich he'd had in the delicatessen between Broadway and Amsterdam had sure been wonderful.

But he'd heard about a Gypsy joint on 95th near Third where you could get chicken paprika with dumplings, and maybe some imported beer to go with it.

He looked at the watch on his cold wrist, under the marks that designated him Boatswain's Mate Second Class. Not two yet. He'd have plenty of time to chow up before he had to meet Bo Cavanaw down at Lexington and 85th to take the two dames Bo was going to round up to dinner at the Turnhall.

Sure, it was no mistake to take the bus across town. You *always* got swell chow in Yorkville. . . .

And now the bus was nearing Central Park West, where it would turn uptown for a block, because the 96th Street transverse actually enters the park on 97th.

Arthur bet he was the only person who rode his bus in a whole day who knew why the transverse was where it was. He'd had it in geology at school. "Manhattan is a solid rock, composed of a material known as Manhattan schist. There are three faults in it, one at 96th Street, one at 79th, and the largest at 125th. In early times these were the only points in uptown Manhattan where access could be had to the North River waterfront, and in this way the natural geology of the island made these streets main thoroughfares, passes through the island to the Hudson River."

Two people waiting by the Independent subway entrance. He skidded into the curb, and opened the door, automatically dropping his eyes to catch any leg-shows he might be offered when the girl got on.

But when her camel's hair coat fell open he saw that she had riding boots on. So did the guy with her. Golly! Were

22

they going to take a couple of horses out in the Park on a day—

Naw. They were probably going to ride indoors at Squadron A, the big armory that ran from 94 to 95th, from Park to Lex. Make a bet with himself. He often did this, making little bets where passengers would get off.

He'd bet from the snooty look on the guy's face they were going to Squadron A.

Did the Squadron take in Jews? . . .

John Tenbruye helped Eleanor Castron to the fourth seat back, and they sat down together. He was glad he didn't have his uniform on, when he saw that sailor sitting there. On drill nights, sometimes when he changed his uniform downtown and wore it in the subway, common soldiers and sailors spoke to him, not realizing that there was a difference between the Squadron and ordinary National Guard.

Once when he had been bringing Anne Davidson to the Armory a man in the uniform of a corporal, regular Army, had even winked and nudged him, saying: "Some baby!"

He remembered how embarrassed he had been. And for what? Anne Davidson! Who had turned out not to be one of the Suffolk County Davidsons at all.

He was sure Eleanor Castron was all right. He had even seen the house in Brooklyn Heights where she and her mother lived. Captain Castron of Orange Street was mentioned in several old New York histories he had taken the trouble to examine at the library.

And he was making time with her, too. She didn't have that nasty prying attitude of—say—Dot Harriman. When he spoke airily of going to school and college in Jersey, she seemed to assume he meant Lawrenceville and Princeton instead of Peddie and Rutgers. And—

Pass Through Manhattan

If Tenny apologized once more for taking a bus, she'd scream. The insufferable snipe. As though anybody cared why his particular branch of the Tenbruyes was not in the Social Register. Probably, she thought maliciously, it was because their name had not started out as Tenbruye at all.

And making a fuss about being in Squadron A. Anybody could join the Squadron who could stick on a horse, or so she'd always thought.

But—and this was the truth, Elly, and face it—she shouldn't have been so snooty about making her own living three or four years ago, when she could have married two or three times. Nice boys with money or jobs, and one nice boy with money and a job which, God knows, was rare enough these days.

But not for little Elly. She was going to be dependent upon no man. And now her commissions for bringing customers into stores had been exactly twelve dollars last month.

And while it was true that the bank couldn't find a tenant or a buyer for their house, and let them live there, a sucker might show up. And then Mom and she—

And so, under the guidance of Arthur Kreutzler, the bus ran up its one short block of Central Park West and made a right turn into the Park. It carried nine passengers: Buck Ranulph and W. Gordon Maxwell; Jack Firstin; Peggy Reilly and Mrs. Artur Lempe; Cowboy Connors and Marlene Smith; John Tenbruye and his date, Eleanor Castron.

Ten, counting the driver: two Jews, two Negroes, and six of the ordinary mongrel American breed. Or maybe—if you take the view of Artur Lempe and his Fuehrer—five Americans and Mrs. Lempe.

But Mrs. Lempe would not thank you for the distinction.

Pass Through Manhattan

She had married Artur so her children could be born in the America he was going to, a free country. She wanted to be American.

And neither Jack Firstin nor Arthur Kreutzler would enjoy being lumped together. Firstin hated nothing so much as failure, and a guy driving a bus was a flop, wasn't he? Whereas Artur, hating his own subtle Teutonic Jewishness, scorned even more the frank Polish Jewishness of Jack Firstin.

And what did Marlene Smith and Buck Ranulph have in common, except for color?

Cowboy Connors, Bos'n's Mate, 2nd, *U.S.S. Oregon*, and Sgt. John Tenbruye, Squadron A, 101st Cav., N.Y.N.G., were both in the service of their country, in a manner of speaking, but if they had sat down to dinner together, the only one who would have enjoyed himself would have been Cowboy, who had never regretted a meal in his life.

Peggy Reilly and Eleanor Castron. Two girls trying to get along, but not on the same path. Peggy wanted to be a nurse, and she was pretty close to getting her cap; and Eleanor wanted to make a living, and she might even go so far as marry Tenny to get it.

Which leaves us W. Gordon Maxwell, ass't editor of a group of pulp magazines. But everything left Gordie, pretty much. He was born to be left. . . .

Into the transverse, then. A long ditch through the Park, stone-walled to keep the park from falling into it, tunneling under Park drives and walks. Following the natural contours of one of three streaks of softness in a hard, tough rock.

And, two-tenths of a mile from the Central Park end, waited the snow, piled high on Mr. Victor's crew's woodpile. Because Daniel Flynn, who should have inspected along there for the Department of Parks, was in bed with a cold, and Mr. Cohen, whose job it was to keep the streets in that area clear, was still struggling with the block on 93rd and Broadway.

The phone rang as he was deep in a treatise on the amount of heat a full-sized man could reasonably be expected to contribute towards his sleeping chamber's temperature.

Darting quickly across the living room he had straightened three times that morning—quickly so that the phone would not wake his father—Don thought that the diet of the miners should affect this. Men fed on vegetable protein— by which he meant beans—instead of animal protein, steaks, should put out a different amount of heat. More or less?

"Hello."

"Don? Is Joe there?"

"Is it very important, Ray?" Don asked his father's city editor. "He's got a foul cold and he's sleeping just now."

"Cold or hangover, kid?"

Don gulped. But then, Ray had been one of the several people from whom he had borrowed money to finish his college career. "Joe's really got a fierce cold," Don said. "I had a doctor for him. Dr. Goldstein, 322 West 9—"

"O.K., kid. I believe you." Implying that he would not believe Don's father. "S'too— Say." The voice was rising in excitement. "Say, I got it. Now, listen carefully. Go get Joe's press card, see. . . . You got any cash?"

"About twenty dollars between us. I can cash a check at the deli."

"Twenty's ample. Go over to the transverse, the 96th Street one, just inside the Park from your end. Don't bother with names or addresses. I have the legman on it already.

Pass Through Manhattan

What I want, see, from you is the story from a mining engineer's viewpoint. Mine Disaster in Manhattan, get it? You're a natural, kid. You did some correspondence for us from summer school and you know your mining."

It was something to do. And the good Lord knew that anybody but Ray would have fired Father a long time ago. "O.K. Just one thing . . ."

"Yeah?"

"What's the story I'm supposed to cover?"

"Oh, did I forget? Snow drift or a landslide or something —the legman wasn't clear—fell on a crosstown bus. They're trying to get it out, now. . . ."

*   *   *

JUST INSIDE THE GLOOM caused by the high stone walls of the transverse, the bus hit a bump. Arthur Kreutzler went high in the driver's seat, nearly lost hold of the wheel. Behind him, Jack Firstin muttered: "Be careful, I'll report you," but Arthur, terrified, was too busy driving to be angry.

This was going to be bad. Every little piece of rubbish on the street had caught a tiny snowdrift in the night, when traffic was light; these had been growing all day, exactly as snowballs grow, and every car that passed over them packed these bumps down harder and harder, made them more dangerous.

Peggy Reilly, holding on to the back of Jack Firstin's seat, said: "Oh, dear, we'll be late." But it didn't really matter, she could hurry into her uniform, and her hair would show that she had really been to a beauty shop. And she had a clean record for her whole course. Just so there was no question of morals, no investigation of her past, they would surely give her her pin.

Pass Through Manhattan

Mrs. Lempe said: "Ach, I hope not. Artur will be angry. Tonight is Bund meeting, and I have to press his uniform. He will be angry with die kinder if I do not hurry. . . ."

Marlene Smith, on the back seat, bounced high, showing a lavender garter where sepia flesh met pink stocking. Buck Ranulph, seeing it, thought angrily, what was he studying for? What could you do for a race that dressed like—like monkeys?

Gordie Maxwell thought: "So, in the end, the mob is driving this slug-nutty copper, taking him for a ride, and they hit a bump and his head clears when it hits the top of the car. Boy, what an ending. What—"

Cowboy Connors, asleep, dreamed of trying to eat split pea soup in a Force Nine storm on the boat deck.

That same first bump threw Eleanor Castron hard into John Tenbruye, her riding boot scraping his with the sharp squeak of well-polished leather. He caught her around the waist to steady her, his fingers firmly touching her through the camel's hair coat and the tailored riding jacket and her blouse; the next jolt slid his hand up and Eleanor Castron knew that if they had to sleep in the subway, beg coffee on the street corners, she couldn't marry Tenny.

"Rough," he said. "This is a rough trip."

She looked at him scornfully, amused to notice that his lips were tight, his eyes a little glassy from touching her. He was, she enumerated, a cheap, underbred, whiny pipsqueak of a social upstart. Unfairly—for the paving of the transverse was really rough—she classed him and dismissed him with the sort of men who brush up against you in the subway.

"Reminds me of once we were out on Johnny's yacht and a storm came up—"

"I didn't know you were a sailor," she said. "I think I'll

call you Bilgy instead of Tenny." She began to giggle in a high shrill voice, unable to stop, aware that she was attracting attention, ashamed of herself.

Bump followed bump. Arthur Kreutzler thought, they'll have to shut the line down, send us home for the day. It isn't safe to carry passengers across here, someone will break his head open against the roof.

Behind him one of the women started to get hysterics. He called out: "There is nothing to be afraid of, the bus is under control," but another bump nearly sent his teeth through his tongue and he shut up.

The worst blizzard since '88, he'd bet.

And then, with all of his mind that was not on the wheel he began to hope that there would be a dispatcher or someone at the Hell Gate end to tell him to put his bus up. Because it was his duty to his passengers and to his employers to report that the transverse was impassable—and—

And supposing they laughed. That laugh that meant: "We shouldn't have let a Jewboy drive for us. Jews haven't any guts."

But surely Slim, ahead of him, had already reached Fifth Avenue, was getting ready to report. Slim wouldn't have to be afraid they'd call him yellow. Tough Slim, with that picture inside his locker, with his hair grease and his slant-mouth talk, didn't have to worry.

Oh, please God, let Slim or the westbound driver make the report and not me. Please. . . .

A bump worse than any of the others sent him up the narrow sidewalk. He skidded, trying to get back into the roadway, and his bumper hit the heavy stone wall. But the recoil gave him the leeway to the street, and there was no damage done until a huge pile of snow, loosened or started by the tap the bus had given the wall, came hurtling down almost on his radiator cap. He kicked the brakes, pulled up the emergency, stalling the motor—and stopped with the radiator melting a hole in the snow pile.

God had heard him, he thought wildly. Now he wouldn't have to say anything, they could see for themselves that he, Arthur Kreutzler, had driven his bus right up to the last moment, when it became impossible to do anything but wait for the snow plows to come and get him out. Or maybe he could turn and go—

A loud slushy noise made him turn as the bus shook. But he could see nothing, did not realize that more of the snow drift had fallen square on the roof of the bus.

And then the windows which had been translucent white became solid black as more snow fell, and with it a four-foot piece of firewood that cracked through the slate-and-canvas roof of the bus and caught Arthur Kreutzler square on top of the head that had won him a B.S. and nearly an M.E. The end of the piece of wood did not stop until it was even with Arthur Kreutzler's slightly stooped shoulders.

By which time the glass in the back window had snapped, and cut—as neatly as a surgeon might have—Marlene Smith's throat.

*　　　*　　　*

BY THE TIME Don got out of the taxi at the police line established on Central Park West and 97th, there was a small crowd collected. He showed his father's card to one of the two cops guarding the entrance to the transverse, and went through, beginning to run, sliding on the slick snow.

The snow was still falling, it swirled into his face, got between his coat collar and his neck. He was a fool to come out. He was a mining engineer, Superintendent of Operations of the All's Fair Mine, and not a reporter.

Pass Through Manhattan

No wonder his father drank so much, doing this sort of work. Let's see, he's fifty-one, I guess, though he surely doesn't look it—and he got his first newspaper job when he was fifteen. Cub reporter up in Boston.

An image of his fifteen-year-old father chasing trivial news along Boston's waterfront in a blizzard came across his mind and made him feel startlingly, crazily tender. Poor Dad. Poor Joe, with his beautiful waxed mustache, his distinguished gray temples, his natty clothes and—his appalling, destroying thirst.

There she was. You couldn't see the bus; it was nearly covered. Up there on the transverse wall, timbers stuck up blackly out of the snow, their ends beginning to frost. Two cops and a man in civilian clothes were down between the wall and the bus, trying to dig. A man in a police lieutenant's uniform was directing operations.

But Don's trained eye saw that they were getting nowhere. They couldn't throw the snow far enough to keep it from sliding back.

A piece of wire cable dangled down from where the timbers had been piled. Don caught it and clambered clumsily up to stand next to the lieutenant. He showed his press card. "What happened?"

The cop said: "A woodpile made a snow drift too close to the wall. Fell on a bus."

"Anyone in the bus?"

"Yeah. Man on the corner of 97th says he saw it go by, tried to stop it, but the driver didn't see him. Looked about half— Hey! Whyn't you guys make a chain, throw the snow from one to the other, get it out that way?"

One of the cops shoveling called back: "We're just trying to get air into 'em. They'll smother in there."

"Yeah. But—"

Pass Through Manhattan

A thin man with a face almost as copper as an Indian's came up the wire cable with the ease of a monkey. "How's about a job digging, cap?"

"We got only three shovels. When one of the guys gives out, take his. Only I don't know who'll pay you. Maybe you can pass the hat among the passengers if—"

"That's all right, cap."

Don said suddenly, excitedly: "Say, lieutenant. I've got it. Take those timbers there—"

"Huh? Oh, you mean the firewood?"

"And drive them down through the snow. Make a caisson right opposite the door of the bus, and throw the snow over the wall, just like digging a—"

"What does a newspaperman know about it?" the cop asked disgustedly.

"I'm a mining engineer. The *Mail* sent me up here to make a special story."

"Oh—hello, Father."

A priest with his robes showing under a black Chesterfield overcoat panted: "Any rescues yet? I was conducting a special— Anyway, I hurried as much as I could, Barker."

The cop said, "You're in time, Father. We haven't gotten anybody out yet. I'm afraid it won't do much good when we do, you couldn't live under there very— Father Cardovic, this is a man from the *Mail*. Mr.—"

"All right," Don yelled. "Listen, we can't let those people die, I tell you. My plan would work." He slid over to the snow, grabbed the snow-wet end of a piece of wood. It wouldn't come loose.

The thin man was alongside. "They're all bolloxed up under the snow there, mister," he said mildly. "You can see from the way they're pointing." He put his hands—remarkable, muscular, smooth hands—over Don's and pulled. The timber moved a fraction of an inch, and snow five feet away buckled.

"See. This is the key log. You pull this one out, see, and the others'll lie right in your fist. Be pretty—"

They were completely absorbed now, the cop and the priest forgotten, even the bus shoved to the backs of their minds. There was the unknown leverage under the snow that transmitted an eighth-inch movement of this log into a five-inch movement over there. The position and inter-relation of the invisible logs under the snow was unknown.

"If we fastened that cable there to this log," Don said, "and applied power to the other end of the cable, it should do the trick."

"You know your business, mister," the dark man said. "I'll secure the cable. You go down with the other end and see if you can get that cop car to pull it." He began to bend the cable around the log. "Guess they were going to use this to pike the firewood up with," he murmured. As he bent the stiff, unwieldy wire, unlaced the end, began splicing with a pocket knife, he began to sing:

> Wire pricks my poor hands till they bleed,
> This job's the worst that I have ever seed.
> Just got sneakers on mah feet,
> Workin' in the snow and sleet and—

He had a clear, almost vibrant tenor. For some reason Don found himself laughing. "Knew you were a sailor when I saw you come up here. We'll get 'em out, boy."

The dark man smiled slowly, still humming. "We will, mister."

Don had never been so happy in his life as when he slid down to the cops. "We'll make your rescue for you," he cried. "Copper there and I. Just let me tie one end of the cable to the axle of your car."

The lieutenant was staring down at the snow. His men had made no progress. "Sure wish they'd get some equipment up here. City's got plows, derricks, all kinds of stuff, except when you need it. O.K., mister. You can't lose. If you hurt the car—"

"The *Mail*'ll pay for it," Don said, still laughing, and dropped down to the floor of the transverse, aiming for and landing on a loose pile of snow. He ran out into the middle of the roadway where he could see Copper-face, and waved. "Send me the cable."

"Comin' right up, sir!" The dark man took the rope in his hand; he shook it and a wave walked down it, brought the end to life, jerking like a snake. Copper twisted his wrist, and the cable flew through the air, and into Don's hand over the twenty feet of snowy air.

Don walked to the axle of the cop's car. The dark man called in his beautiful voice: "Pull her straight but don't strain her!" Don waved to show that he'd heard.

His own clumsy bend around the axle would hold. The motor was running, but there were no cops around; Don moved her ahead in low gear till the wire rope was nearly straight. He climbed onto the running board: "Ready!" he called, through cupped hands.

"And take her—awaaay," called Copper.

There, Don thought as he got behind the wheel, was one sailor who was going to swallow the anchor. Come thaw in the mountains, Copper was going to find himself working at the All's Fair Mine.

Slowly bringing his foot up on the clutch, Don wondered how he had known the stranger's name was Copper?

Nothing else would fit him. He'd be Copper to **Don** as long—

The car began to move forward, the chained wheels straining a little. Then she went ahead, fast, too fast, and Don stalled her, pulled on the brake and climbed out.

Timbers were lying all over God's acre. Lots of them were graduated, too. Be easy to drive them down through unpacked snow and—

"Ho, Copper!" There was no answer.

He ran back to where the cop had been. But the lieutenant had his back turned to the accident, was watching the priest who knelt in the snow, his hands busy. While Don watched, Father Cardovic intoned: "and the Holy Ghost," and made the sign of the cross on Copper's forehead.

"What—"

"That first hunk of firewood caught him square in the chest," the lieutenant snapped. "Never knew what hit him, it musta got his heart. Now, for Gawd's sake—sorry, Father—do whatever you was gonna do with them sticks, so's we won't all be investigated for killing this guy!"

Don said: "All right," in a voice he didn't know. Then he heard his own Superintendent's tones ordering the cops, the lieutenant, the bystanders to put the timbers down, hammer them home with car tools, rocks, smaller pieces of wood, anything. The bulwark sank and the shovels flew, and then they could see the top of the bus door.

But when they got that door smashed away and the cops were helping the passengers out—live passengers, rescued passengers—Don climbed up the wall to where Copper lay, forgotten.

Falling snow had drifted and caught on his eyebrows,

35

making them bushy and white as though he had, in the few minutes he lay there, lived out a life, from black-haired strength to white maturity.

"I wish I could pray. I wish I knew what there was about him— Not just a good man with a cable. Thousands of sailors—and not because he was lithe and graceful to watch in his clumsy, cheap clothing. Nor because he had a voice or—"

He had never seen a man so very much alive. That was it, his life, his—

The priest's voice, barely avoiding unctuousness, said: "Son, they have already taken seven people from that bus. Three women. And they're not through. At least seven lives for one; you mustn't blame yourself."

Don shook his head. "You can't keep books on lives. Who was he? Who are the people in the bus? They—"

"It does not matter to God. A human being is a human being, son. A life is a life. Seven—more than seven—for one man. You must—"

The lieutenant's voice came to them through the snow. "Hey, Father, this way!"

Father Cardovic took Don's arm, led him to the transverse. They slid down. The police officer's face was gray and shiny. "The driver was killed, Father."

"Catholic?"

The cop said: "I didn't find no rosary or capulet or nothing. Head taken— He was croaked when it hit, I guess. Here's his papers."

The priest took them, handed them to Don. "Look through them, will you, my son? I left my glasses at the church."

Don took the papers, thumbed through them. Driver's license, card to the St. Nicholas Tennis Club, Columbia

Library. "I know this chap," he said. "Arthur Kreutzler. He was a classmate of mine at Columbia School of Mines."

He tried to remember Arthur Kreutzler. A brilliant student, a greasy grind, depending on your point of view. And here he'd been driving a bus, and Don, who'd never made the first tenth, was superintendent of a good mine. "I didn't know him well."

"Was he a Catholic?" Father Cardovic asked.

Don considered.

"I don't know," he said. "But Kreutzler, Kreutzler, that sounds German. Maybe he was a Lutheran, but I'm not sure."

"Could be Jewish," the lieutenant said, speculatively.

"He didn't look it," Don said.

*   *   *

THE PRIEST JOINED HIM by Copper's body. "Son, don't brood. You have a duty to your newspaper to interview the passengers, at least."

And Don: "I'm not a newspaperman. Just substituting for my father."

"Then, surely, you'll want your father to be proud of the job you do."

"Sure." His feet were heavy through the snow, and he sneezed twice before he got to the group of passengers. An ambulance marked Mount Sinai Hospital was waiting, chugging, and from some place someone had produced a bucket of coffee

A cop said: "This is the guy who directed your rescue. 'Cept fer him—" he shrugged, throwing his shoulders wide.

Eight pairs of grateful eyes turned to him. Don said: "If I could have your names—" And then wrote busily. Ray had said not to bother with names, addresses, but he had to do something.

There was a pretty big crowd now, as he wrote down names. Firstin, Castron, Ranulph—not Randolph, Ranulph— Lempe. He was grateful for the easy spelling of Reilly, looked up. A very pretty girl. Wide-spaced eyes, snub nose, brown hair, strangely lacquered to her head. He smiled. Tenbruye, and then an easy run: Connors, Maxwell.

He said briskly: "What do you all do? Mr. Firstin?"

Firstin was heavy-set, about forty-five. Cruel-looking mug, but somehow competent. "I am a builder. The great Greenwich Square was my building. I have constructed several great hotels and apartment hotels. The office building at—"

"I won't keep you standing in the snow for that," Don said, laughing. "The files at the newspaper will have it all." The Reilly girl gasped, and he looked at her curiously: "But what are you working on now, Mr. Firstin?"

"An apartment house between Amsterdam and Broadway, sir. All the most modern building factors applied to middle-class rentals. I had just been inspecting the steelwork to see how it stood the blizzard. Perfect, sir, perfect!"

But why did he look at Don with such hatred in his eyes? Why?

It didn't matter. You're a reporter for the moment. Remember the tricks Father taught you when you corresponded with him— "No doubt, when the snow slide came down, you wished the buses had modern cantilever construction, eh, Mr. Firstin?"

"Yes, yes." Which made a good line for the paper, and now—

A flashlight went off behind him. He turned, jumping. "You're Joe Morton's kid, aren't you?" the photographer said. "For some reason we're the only paper here. Snap it up, and we'll go to press—"

When he looked back, Miss Reilly had covered her face with her hands. He stepped forward but the German woman, Mrs. Lempe, was there. "So brave," Mrs. Lempe said. "She iss nurse from Mount Sinai. When the snow fell, she takes my hand, she talks to everyone, so calm, so good."

"Ah, yes." That covered Miss Reilly. Make a good story if he could just remember how to pull a story together. Oh, it didn't matter, there were rewrite men for that. "And you, Mrs. Lempe, and then—"

Miss Reilly dropped her hands. He didn't know much, but he knew she hadn't been sick. Faking, for some strange, obscure— "Mrs. Lempe is ill," Miss Reilly said. "She had a pain on the bus, before we hit. I'd like to take her to the ambulance."

"No," Mrs. Lempe cried. "Iss late. I must go home. Artur he wants me to press his Bund-suit, and die kinder—"

"How many children have you?" Don interposed, rapidly. "Two? Thanks, Mrs. Lempe, and all right, Miss Reilly. You're a nurse at Mount Sinai, is that right?"

"I graduate next week," she whispered. Hell, why didn't she say what she wanted, and stop looking at him in that beseeching, dumb way? The flashlight went off again, and she cried out: "Oh, no," then dropped her voice and her eyes as the blue-coated interne shoved through to her, saying, "Hi, Reilly—"

"Dr. Jacobs, this lady here used to be an out-patient and—" They moved out of earshot towards the ambulance.

Lieutenant Barker stuck his head in, said: "Traffic'll be cleared in a few minutes, folks, and we'll send you home." He turned to Don. "My first name is J. C., there's another Lieutenant Barker downtown."

39

"O.K." Don had the feeling this was taking too long, a better newsman would have finished his interviewing. The cameraman nudged him. "How about you, Miss Castron, what do you do?"

"Oh. Eleanor Castron, Orange Street, Brooklyn Heights." She looked down at her riding boots. "I was on my way to go riding at the Armory with Mr. Tenbruye here."

"Yes, but what do you do for a living?"

She said: "Why—nothing." Don scribbled débutante and left it up to the rewrite man. "And Mr. Tenbruye?"

"I'm in Wall Street. Corning and Seligmann, Brokers."

"Quite so. And what did you two think when the snow came down?"

Eleanor Castron said, in her well-bred, considered tones: "I thought it was better than a desert island," and then began to giggle wildly. Tenbruye helped her towards the ambulance.

The photographer said: "Snap it up, Morton." Don nodded. "Connors, no use asking what you do for a living. You're not, or haven't been, in the submarine service, by any chance?"

From over the rim of a coffee cup the sailor said: "Naw. I'm on the deck of the *Oregon*."

Which left the colored man and the thin mousy guy who didn't seem to know where he was. "How about you two?" Don asked. The two men looked at each other, the colored man as if he were waiting permission to speak.

Don asked him, "What do you do?"

"I'm a detective out of the 104th Street Station. I'm on my way to work."

Don felt a flicker of interest. This should be news material. "What did you think of, Detective Ranulph?"

Pass Through Manhattan

"Mister," said the cop, "I was in a fog. I'm studying law. I go up for my bar examination in two months, and I was reading. My first feeling was that the light was gone, I couldn't study, and then—"

Lieutenant Barker said: "All right, Ranulph." The detective subsided and Barker took his arm. "Detective Ranulph kept things under control and took charge of the rescue from the inside while I superintended from the outside," Barker said.

Don grinned, and the lieutenant growled: "We'd been working ten minutes before you showed up."

A patrolman swung up to them, his face purple with the cold. "Another one for the dead wagon, l'tenant. S'wartzer."

"My God," Detective Ranulph said. "I forgot. A little girl, she was sitting next to me."

Don turned to the colored man. "Didn't you notice anything?" He held his pencil poised. "How was she killed?"

The patrolman said: "Flying glass got her in the neck. The doc's—"

Ranulph had turned a peculiar green shade.

Lieutenant Barker said: "Get on with your interview, or you'll have all these people dead of exposure. Ranulph, come help." He grabbed the colored man's arm and hurried him away.

Don looked after them a moment. That Ranulph hadn't showed up too well. He probably ought to turn in something about that to Ray. But then, that was a matter of newspaper policy, no business of a special report. "Mr. Maxwell? Didn't mean to keep you waiting. What do you do for a living?"

W. Gordon Maxwell, Fifth Avenue, at 97th, blinked. "I? Oh—I'm an author. I was—thinking about a story. But, you know, this is a great yarn, people buried under the snow, course of lives changed. Unless you plan to use it yourself, sir?"

"I'm not an—author," Don said. "You go ahead."

"Thank you. And I certainly want to thank you for rescuing us." Mr. Maxwell hurried away, walking. Barker yelled after him: "We'll have a ride for you in a minute," but Maxwell disappeared in the swirling snow.

"That's all," the photographer said. "Let's get out of here, Morton, and—"

"No," Don said. "There was a man killed in the rescue, you know."

"Yeah, the driver, Kreutzler. He—"

"Another one. Volunteer. A— Oh, Barker?"

The lieutenant bustled up, stamping snow off his shoes. "Yeah? Lissen, you going to give me a pan on this? Cop's not supposed to know about engineering and that kinda stuff."

"No pan," Don said. "None at all. I just wanted to know what did you find out about the man I—about the man who was killed."

"The driver or the other?"

"The other."

"Unemployed seaman," Barker said. "Name Ringgold. Address, The Seaman's Union. 'At'sall we could get."

"O.K." He turned away, the photographer at his side. They walked west in the transverse, through the lines of police, thick now. A voice behind them called: "Wait, oh, wait—"

It was Father Cardovic. Don stood waiting, snow hitting him.

The priest said: "You're not a communicant?"

"I'm not a Catholic, no. I'm not very religious."

Pass Through Manhattan

"I'd like your address, if you don't think I'm impertinent. I'd like to talk to your father, tell him what a fine thing—"

"He's not very religious, either," Don said.

But the Father wouldn't be insulted. "I'm not proselytizing. I just—you know, I was listening. A writer. And a nurse, an angel of mercy. A great builder. I've seen Greenwich Square, a beautiful edifice. And a colored policeman, you have no idea what a fine thing it is for a Negro to raise himself—"

Don said: "I guess I'm worrying more about the one than the ninety-and-nine."

The priest reddened, dropped his head. "Still, I'd like your address."

Don gave it, turned away. The photographer said: "What was that all about?"

Don shook his head. "Boy, I'll be glad to get out of this city. Where can we find a phone?"

"Columbus'll be closest, I guess. You're a lumberman or something out West, aren't you?"

"Miner. . . ."

* * *

RAY PUT HIS INITIALS on the front page marked Five Star Sports Final, and tossed it over his shoulder to the Chief. He had already shoved his pencils into a little pile, reached in the desk for his soap and towel when the Chief said: "O.K., let a hundred thousand go."

Ray rose stiffly, the towel and soap in his hand. "Another day, another dollar."

The Chief said: "Not a bad day," his pinkish jowls crinkling. "Not bad." He was about thirty-eight. A helluva newspaperman, Ray thought. Wait'll he's been at it as long as I have. "Morton's kid turned in a good job. How's about letting the old soak go, hiring the son?"

Ray's voice had a flat ring. "When Joe Morton's in there pitching there's no better. If he averages six sober days a month, he does this paper more good than any three of your seven-to-four, punch-the-clock, white-tie-or-black, mama-wipe-my-nose cubs you're so proud of."

The Chief said: "Sounds like you're planning to go on a bat yourself."

Ray said: "It's not a bad idea. You run the paper a while. You're the M.E."

"That's right. I am. Joe Morton wouldn't last twenty-four hours on the *Sun* or the *World-Telegram*. Why—"

"The *Sun* can afford five men for each street-car derailed. The *World-Telegram* has the features, the national coverage. We've got to use brilliance to cover the fact that we only report a tenth of the important news, that we haven't any names on our op ed or our one-two. Joe Morton's got the brilliance. So have Levine and Smith."

"Lame ducks and drunkards."

Ray said: "Fire them. It's no skin off my back. I'll get a job in a minute on the *Times* or the *Trib*. And you'll have a lot of newsprint and a puzzle contest."

He walked swiftly to the washroom, through the rows of cubs bent over their desks, politely disregarding the fight between the managing editor and his city editor. Gawd, he was stiff. Between the cold and snow and that bad tooth, and sitting at a desk from seven in the morning till four in the afternoon, his rheumatism got worse and worse.

Well, he was fifty-two. It took a Joe Morton to be young and spruce at that age. Preserved in alcohol.

He dried his face and hands carefully, making sure that

no trace of water was left for the blizzard to touch, and went back to the desk for his coat and hat. The Chief was still sitting there. Oh, you snotnose. The metropolitan agreement permitted the paper to run extras for a couple of hours more, when it became the morning sheets' privilege, and the Chief would sit there, hoping . . .

"I'll be downstairs if you really need me," Ray said. "Just tell them to look behind the old-fashioned glass."

"I didn't mean all that," the Chief said. "It's been, as you say, a hard day."

"Don't worry," Ray told him. "I'm not off on a bat. Just the usual two before I take the subway for Brooklyn. I'll be on deck tomorrow."

"Good," the Chief said heartily. "You know, the old sheet depends on you."

"What old sheet?" Ray asked, and lumbered towards the elevator, carrying the last word with him. Two of the Chief's cubs, waiting for the car, politely stepped aside to let him get in first. Wonder what they really think of me? Do they know I'm a failure, that being city editor of the fourth largest metropolitan evening newspaper is not success at fifty? Or do they think I'm a tin Jesus, like I did my first city ed?

The elevator came, and he got in, the two cubs standing on the other side to give him plenty of room. The operator was reading the front page of the last edition. The Irish face of that nurse caught in Don Morton's bus was prominent between the deb's slick, posed portrait, a picture of Jack Firstin—hat over face—going to jail two years ago on the alimony charge.

"I'd sure like to get caught in a bus wit' dat," the operator said.

A young stereotyper from the top floor leaned over.

Tough, defiant in the presence of the editorial department—wasn't he a union man?—he sneered: "Y'd be too scairt to even take a feel, Mickey."

One of the reporters, trying to be a good scout in spite of the Columbia School of Journalism, said: "You can't be too sure. Psychologists say the last impulse of a dying man is to propagate his kind."

The stereotyper said: "G'wan! Is that a fact?", impressed, and the elevator reached the ground floor. Grunting, Ray followed the stereotyper but preceded the reporters out of the car. The slick, imitation marble corridor downstairs was being washed; one of the efficiency experts the boss was always hiring ought to point out that it would be smarter to wait an hour till the building cleared.

He stepped outdoors on the wet sidewalk where the heat from the pressroom kept the snow from sticking. Twenty feet to the right, and the window of the bar-room, decorated with the red neon Schaefer's Beer sign, was even with his shoulder. He turned left and the double doors yielded to his shove, one after another.

His place was right smack in the middle, directly between the two brass grills set in the mahogany to drain away suds. Jake O'Hara, the Sports Editor, and Wilcox, one of his writers, moved over for him.

"Nice story on that bus, Ray."

"Joe Morton's boy wrote it, Jake. He's a mining man."

The bartender slid the first of Ray's two old-fashioneds into his waiting curved fingers, placed a bowl of cheese sticks conveniently, and said "Good evening" politely.

Ray took the first swallow, that wonderful first swallow of the day, then waited until the bitters-enforced whisky slid through the arteries to joints, limbering the rheumatism, washing from his mouth the dirty taste of printers' ink and paste and brass polish.

He took a second swallow and ate a cheese stick.

"Joe on a bat?" Jake asked.

Ray nodded.

"He oughta watch himself," the Sports Editor said. "You're the last guy in the world'll hire him."

"I had a fight with the Chief this evening over him."

Jake made a derisive noise with his lips. "I heard the bank's taking the paper over. That'll be the end of the Chief."

"It may be the end of us, too," Ray said.

He finished his old-fashioned, nodded at the bartender. "Joe's a friend of yours, isn't he?" he asked the sports writer. "See if you can straighten him out. With this blizzard this time of year, those punks in the news department will be coming down with colds, and I'll need every—"

"Tell him yourself," the sports writer said. He jerked his head over his shoulder. "C'mon, Jake. Like to see the basketball tonight, Ray?"

Ray shook his head. "No, thanks. . . ." His head turned, he gave a warning look at the bartender. The barman nodded, moved away to serve a group of the punks down the bar. Their somewhat shrill voices discussed "leads" and "angles" and "methods of attack," and they thought they were newspapermen. But what could you expect in a day when the old *Tribune* supported Luscious Beebe?

Ray said: "Hi, Joe."

Joe Morton put his two hands on the bar, the knuckles white, and said: "Nothing for me," though he had not been asked. Around the broken veins of his cheek bones the skin was white, taut. The points of his mustache quivered.

"What the hell was the idea of sending my boy out on that bus story?" he asked, without preliminaries.

"Now, Joe—"

"Goddammit," Joe Morton said, bitterly, "isn't it enough ruining my life? Can't you lousy big-circulation bugs leave anybody happy, can't you—" He broke off. "Hey. Bourbon and a beer chaser."

The bartender slid deftly up, looked at Ray, and kept on moving. Ray nodded, and he stopped, swooped whisky glass and bottle on the bar, fixed the chaser, and then poured the whisky. Joe Morton's hand closed around the drink. He was facing the bar, but he must have caught Ray's smile, because he relinquished his hold, said: "You think this is just a dodge to get a drink?"

Ray didn't answer him; but he kept his eyes steady on the back bar. The bar glass and the whisky just missed his left ear by a fraction of an inch.

He said: "Get out of here, Joe." The fury restrained under his quiet voice would have frightened anyone but a drunk. "If you've got anything to say to me, wait'll you sober up."

"Fire me, you bastard, fire me."

"Why? I'd just have to loan you the money to live on. Now get out of here. I've had a hard day, I don't want to fool with you. You can have a drink before you go."

Joe Morton put both hands on the bar, leaned on them. He mumbled: "I'm sorry, Ray. You've been a good friend . . . no drink, thanks. I'll drink the chaser. Try and taper off on beer. . . ." He sagged, caught himself. "Believe it or not, Ray, I'm going to try and straighten myself out."

"You ought to go home, son. Don said you had a bad cold."

"Forget it. Good night, Ray."

Pass Through Manhattan

Ray sighed, watched Joe's tired back go away. No rest for the weary. . . . "Joe!"

Morton came back. "Yeah?"

"What is it about Don?"

"Oh, I don't know." Joe shook his head. "He engineered the rescue, you know . . . Oh, of course you know. You ran the story— It was the man who was killed."

"The driver?"

"No. The bum, sailor, whatever he was. You see, Don had the idea for the rescue. The man—Ringgold, is that right?—wouldn't have been killed if Don hadn't been there."

Ray nodded. "I see—let me think this over. But Joe, the kid's crazy. He saved seven people, the ambulance surgeon and the cops said they would have suffocated if they'd stayed there much longer."

"Seven for one. That's what I told him. . . . But it was all that crap you ran about Firstin."

Ray laughed. "Well, Firstin had it coming. You can't down that rat. Crawls out of an accident and starts giving a sales talk about his new building. And the testimony about his two bankruptcies—people who had committed suicide when his bonds defaulted and wiped out their savings—all that testimony was court record and privileged. So we ran it. Made a good twist to the story."

"You've ruined my son's life to put a good twist to your story."

"Nuts. Stop pitying yourself. Pull yourself together and go home and tell the boy about the nurse. She ought to save as many lives in her career as Firstin ruins. Wasn't one of the women a mother? Tell him about that. Christ, man. Don's—how old—twenty-six, seven—and you've never done a damn thing for him. Pull yourself together. If thirty years in the newspaper business—"

"Thirty-seven—"

"If being a newspaperman has taught you anything, it's the gift of blarney. Go use it for some good for once."

"You don't understand. There was something special about this sailor."

"What could there have been? Don hardly saw him. All right, then, go down to the Seaman's Union, get the dope on him, show him up. Just an unemployed sailor." Ray took a deep breath. His chest ached. Probably getting pleurisy. "Have a drink?"

Joe shook his head. "I'm going to sober up. You don't understand." He walked to the door to the street, went out, letting a gust of snowy air into the smoky atmosphere.

Ray watched him go, turned to the bartender. "Give me three aspirins and another whisky—"

Outside, Joe Morton walked slowly towards the subway. Ray didn't understand. Old men didn't have any children. Didn't know what it did to a father to see his son sitting around, thinking he was a murderer. More than flesh and blood could stand. . . .

His fingers, thrust deep into his ulster pockets encountered a coin. Working his hand loose from his glove, he felt its milled edge. A quarter he had forgotten all about. He turned into a gaudy hot-dog spread on the edge of Times Square, made his way automatically to the bar, laid his quarter down. "Bourbon, beer chaser."

Hot tears pushed up under his creased eyelids. Nobody understood him, or cared about how hard it was, seeing your boy—

*   *   *

FIVE-THIRTY. Somewhere down in the bottom of the apartment house the janitor threw on more coal, or turned an oil valve, and the steam came up harder, thumping in the pipes. Don swung his legs off the couch, went to the window. The sun must be going down some place behind all this snow, it was getting dark out, and cheap, gaudy stores down on Broadway were turning on their signs, painting the flakes weird neon colors.

Through the snow he could read the names of the pictures showing at the Riverside. He'd seen both of them.

Don turned back into the stuffy, stale-smelling room. He gathered up the scattered pages of the paper with his story spread across the front page, and rolled them into a ball which he carried into the kitchen, shoved down the incinerator shute.

Coming back, he looked without interest at a quarter-bottle of cheap bourbon his father had left on the kitchen table. Then his interest rose. It was a way, a means of solace that seemed to satisfy a number of people. Others have found satisfaction, why not you? He poured himself a stiff drink, took a swallow, and set the glass down. It was unfortunate that he didn't like the taste.

The second Saturday in March. By April first at the earliest—

The phone rang. Probably his father..Stuck in a bar, and couldn't pay the check. "Hello, Don Morton speaking."

A half-familiar voice said: "Morton, this is Mr. Makin, of Armstrong and Grainger. Have you a date for dinner tonight?"

"Well, no, Mr. Makin."

"Some of us have been having a conference about the All's Fair this afternoon, it just broke up and—"

"I'd have been glad to come down." Panic raced through his mind, to be replaced with cold thought. He knew all about this sort of thing. If the banking firm that owned

All's Fair had an all-afternoon conference—on Saturday afternoon, too—and did not invite the engineer in charge, it meant that he was getting the knife. Well, he knew how to handle all that. He knew where the gold was, he knew the quirks of the machinery, and he knew the men. If they tried to supplant him, they'd find themselves with a gold mine running at a loss.

"This was not about engineering, as it were. More political. But I'll tell you when I see you. Got any preference about dinner?"

"No, sir."

"Well, a chilly night like this heavy food's the best. Yorkville would be convenient for both of us. What's a good place, you live near there?"

"I've heard of the Tsigany. On 95th."

"I'll meet you there then, in the bar at—say quarter to seven. Oh, and by the way, that was a remarkable piece of work you did this afternoon. I didn't know Joseph Kolk Morton was your father."

"Yes."

"I've been reading his newspaper work for years. Remember his reporting of the Democratic convention in '24. Like to meet him sometime."

"He's not home now."

"Well, I'll see you in about an hour."

Now, why the devil did Makin have to bring up the bus? Copper's face swam, dizzily against the wall, his musical voice was clear in the room. Poor Copper. So much more alive than that bunch of dudes they had hauled out of the bus. Stiff and cold in their bulky heavy clothing. Stay with their feet on concrete, their heads in the steam heat all their lives, and never really live at all. While Copper—

Ray ran a bath, shaved. He concentrated on the All's Fair.

Pass Through Manhattan

Maybe they weren't getting enough return on their money. Just a hundred percent. He wished he owned her. As good a placer operation as you'd find in the Alma-Fairplay district. And if he owned it, he could live there through the winter, run a trap line, there was good hunting in the hills. Venison. Get another man to stay with him through the freeze.

And there he was back to Copper again. Around and around and back to something you couldn't do anything about. You couldn't add up figures and solve a problem of ethics, this is right, this is wrong. The bus slide was an act of God, and he had tampered—

No. The flash in his mind that had shown him about the timbers was—according to the ministers—as much of an act of God as the original disaster. To have let the seven people smother would have been denying the brain God gave him.

Or you could take it the other way. Why should God let a Firstin live? An embezzler, a preyer on widows and orphans, to use an old hackneyed phrase. Because Don had kept him from smothering, Jack Firstin would float one more deal, find one more loophole in the law.

Hey. Maybe Firstin would know how to raise the money to buy the All's Fair if Armstrong and Grainger no longer considered it a good risk. Firstin ought to be grateful to the man who had saved his—

As he slid under the water, his eyes closed. Copper's face came across his eyelids, Copper's face laughing at him, saying: Guys like you and me don't do business with the Firstins. Copper, Copper—

*   *   *

Pass Through Manhattan

PEGGY WAS THE HERO of the student nurses' dining room. Every table had three or four copies of the story Donald D. Morton had written about her, with her picture, and all the others. The girl next to her at the table said: "Were you sitting near John Tenbruye, Peg? Did he ask for your phone number?"

"Call him up, Peggy," Nan Shane called down the table. "This is Miss Reilly. I just hoped you didn't suffer from shock, Mr. Tenbruye."

"Mr. Tenbruye, do you need a nurse?"

A probationer asked: "Is that the Tenbruye house down Fifth? With the stone deer?"

"He doesn't live there, according to the papers," an older girl told her. "What does he have, Peggy, a bachelor apartment?"

"A pied-à-terre, with etchings," Lucy Farley suggested. "Boy, I'd like a look at that one's etchings." She moved her big shoulders under her white uniform. She was the girl they always sent for to work on the 185-pounders.

But their voices faded away. All that Peggy could hear was a girl behind her: "Don't crumble that picture, I want to send it to my mother," and another girl saying: "It'll be in the St. Louis papers, they send these all over the country."

It would appear in the Cincinnati papers. She could see Miss Ager's sharp eyes, beady under her pulled-back hair. "Why, that's the Reilly girl who—" and then pressing her bell for her secretary, "Take a letter to the superintendent of nurses, Mount Sinai Hospital, New York. Dear Madam: I think you ought to know that the Margaret Reilly who is a student nurse in your school, and who was involved in the bus accident last week, was once enrolled as a student in—"

Pass Through Manhattan

Peggy could see those sharp eyes, those thin lips, shaping the words: "Nursing is a sacred profession, Miss Reilly, a profession for serious-minded women who can behave like ladies. There is no room in it for girls like you."

The superintendent here was not like that, she was remote and cool, Peggy hardly knew her, but she didn't seem the dried-up vindictive type of Miss Ager. But false registration in the school and a scandalous past did not merit a Mount Sinai cap. The least that would be done would be to send Peggy before the Advisory Board. And men could be worse than women about that sort of thing, doctors worst of all, doctors wrapped up in their tight ethics.

There wasn't enough left in her to try a third time. Maybe she could get a job as an office nurse, answering the switchboard for some doctor. Maybe they wouldn't send out her picture, just the story. Margaret Reilly was the most common sort of name. She—

The waitress said: "You're wanted in the office, Miss Reilly."

Peggy gulped, nodded. She pushed away her half-finished dessert, stood up. Just inside the door of the dining room there was a mirror; she straightened her ribbonless cap, patted her pinless collar. Just a few days more and she would have—

And then, walking down the long composition-floored corridors to the assistant superintendent's office, she suddenly remembered a face. The young reporter who had—according to the police and the newspapers—rescued her. Donald D. Morton. She would call him up, ask his help.

Reporters were notoriously good sports, nice boys. She wouldn't even have to tell him what sort of trouble she had been in in Cincinnati. Tell him it was a prank. She had poured water through the super's transom at night. Or—

She began to giggle, pleased with herself. He could ask the other reporters, and—

She had read only the part of the bus story that applied to herself, had skipped the rest in the eagerness to get to the next printing of the words "passenger" or "nurse" or "Reilly." Now she began to remember, vaguely, that there had been a little story off to one side, in a box, about Donald D. Morton not being a regular reporter or something. Or—

She opened the door of the assistant super's office and walked in, stood in front of the desk, straight and demure, as a student nurse should.

"Oh, Miss Reilly. This is Mr. Morton, of the *Mail*. He wants to interview you about the accident you were in." The super was all honey and cream. Publicity for the nursing school, for the hospital, for the profession.

She turned to Mr. Morton, then stopped. It was not the boy.

The handsome old duck shook his head. There was an odor of peppermint around him. "I'm the father of the boy you were saved by. He was relieving me. I've had a terrible cold for the last day or so."

"You oughtn't to be out on a night like this." Peggy looked at the window. But it would be all right. Old boys like this were easy. You sort of patted their hands and looked up at them from under your eyelashes. All you had to do was bring out the—the father in them. She shivered with hatred of herself for having to use devices, but she wasn't going to throw away three years of nursing school for a scruple. She hated herself, staring at the cold, clean snow through the window, but what could you do? She had promised Dad—

The assistant super said: "Why don't you take Mr. Morton in the Superintendent's office, Reilly? You don't want to interview me, Mr. Morton."

"Business before pleasure, madame," the old boy said gallantly. He followed Peggy into the big, dark room next door, waited while she turned on the light. She said: "Yes, Mr. Morton?"

"I want to know about your plans for the rest of your life, as it were," he said. He pulled a crumbled package of cigarettes out of his pocket, nodded questioningly towards the closed door.

Peggy grinned mischievously, came close to him to whisper: "You light one and I'll puff off it. If I'm caught—"

The schoolgirl note. Oh, Peggy—

But she couldn't just let it go, let the dead past be raked up again, for all the fool she'd made of herself in Cincinnati.

A picture of herself, making opportunities to see Dr. Bush, hoping she would see Dr. Bush, trying so hard to let Dr. Bush know she liked him, crossed her memory. Fool, little cheap fool of a Peggy Reilly.

She moved away from Mr. Morton. "That's enough cigarette. I don't understand, I'm going to be a nurse, of course. I graduate—"

"Yes, my son got that." He was older than she had thought at first. He looked tired. "I mean—well, what sort of a nurse?"

"I hope to get an appointment to a clinic."

"Ah." He brightened. "I see. Serve the poor. You want to be a sort of—of er—philanthropist, giving yourself, your youth instead of money?"

"I want to be a nurse." And then, almost despite herself, as though from outside, her own personality asserted itself. She'd get out of this on the level, or not at all. Go down honestly, but stay Peggy Reilly.

"That's a terrible cold you've got." Spoken like a nurse, and not like a schoolgirl.

"Yes, yes. A nurse. Hm, a nurse— Who do you think was the greatest nurse of all time, Miss Reilly? Nightingale, or—"

"I don't know about that." She studied him for a moment. "Have you been a reporter long, Mr. Morton?"

He jumped. "Eh? I— Thirty-seven years, Miss Reilly. Since I was fifteen years old. Why?"

"You seem so nervous. Do you always get so excited about a story?"

He sat on the edge of the holy desk and swung his leg. The cigarette glowed bright under his pointed mustache. She didn't like the yellowish whites of his eyes, the shaking of his large-veined hand. Kidney trouble, possibly.

Joe Morton said: "I'll be frank with you. You look like a nice kid. My boy—Don—he's a fine boy. He's the only worthwhile thing I've done in a life of working like hell all day to produce something to wrap tomorrow night's garbage in. No, don't laugh. Don's going places. Only twenty-seven, and head of one of the biggest gold mines in Colorado."

"He's a fine-looking boy, Mr. Morton."

Joe said: "Yea. Smart boy, too. Well—the truth is—I was drunk today. Been on a bat since yesterday morning. Don went out on that story to cover for me. And—it stands a good chance of wrecking him."

"You mean the people who own his gold mine don't like his working for a—"

"No. It was that man who was killed, Ringgold. My boy Don's apparently brooding about killing him. There was something special about this man, I don't know. I

58

talked to Lieutenant Barker, he said he just looked like another bum to him."

"I don't see—"

"Where you come in? But you do. Beautiful girl, life of service, that sort of thing. If you—if he—"

"I'll be glad to meet Don, or anything you say. He saved my life."

Joe Morton stared at the floor. "Yes, I hadn't thought of that. My whole mind runs on one track, you see. I figured on a Sunday story about the total number of years of useful life he's saved, something like that. Or maybe, I hoped I could sell a feature to the *American Weekly*. Something about how you and maybe a couple of the other passengers were the sort who made America. That colored detective's a good angle. Success story."

Peggy nodded, slowly. "I wouldn't know— This seems to mean a lot to you, Mr. Morton. So maybe you ought to know. I was discharged from a hospital out West once."

"Cincinnati?"

"You knew?" Then it was all over, all finished. Tell a reporter and cut your throat.

"I knew you had come from Cincinnati. Second edition after the accident ran it. I suppose a legman got it from the hospital here."

"Well. This—this accident was the worst sort of bad luck for me. It—if the old witch out there sees my picture. They won't give me my pin. I'll never be a nurse."

"So?"

"I—I wish to God your son had left me in the bus. To smother. If I can't be a nurse I don't want to live. You hear me? I don't want to—"

He said: "What the hell? The picture's already gone

59

out, probably. Airmail and telephoto. But—" brightly "—newspaper pictures are notoriously bad. Maybe she won't recognize it. Margaret Reilly."

"She will," Peggy said dully. "She— My luck's run out. Gone, Mr. Morton. I'd have graduated in a few days. I went over to get my hair done so I'd look nice for graduation. I—"

"Listen. If they try and kick you out of here over this, my paper'll blow Mount Sinai Hospital off the map. We'll—"

Peggy shook her head. "You'd be licked before you start. There's no place in the nursing profession for a girl who had an affair with a resident doctor and had to have an—had to have a—"

"An operation?" Joe Morton asked.

The girl nodded.

Joe Morton picked up his hat and went to the door. "You're a hell of a lot of use to me," he said bitterly, and left.

*　　*　　*

ARTUR LEMPE SAT STIFFLY on a kitchen chair. He had on a brown shirt, a brown jacket with an armband, a Sam Browne belt, and a pair of old-fashioned long woolen drawers. He said: "Hurry, woman, mach schnell. The Bundfuehrer himself addresses us this evening." He spoke, as was his habit, in German.

Mrs. Lempe answered, as was her habit, in English. "You do not want your trousers to burn, Artur? Such expensive trousers."

But Herr Lempe was not to be tricked into a discussion of the cost of his uniform pants. "What an hour to be coming home. These women!"

Pass Through Manhattan

"I was in a bus accident. The snow, it has fallen from the wall in the park and—"

Herr Lempe grunted, not to show disbelief, but to indicate a complete disregard of any accidents his wife had been in. The grunt indicated first that such an accident would be womanly, trivial, and second that it could have been avoided if she had asked him. Good German men did not ride in buses that had accidents.

George Washington Lempe said: "Pop, when was Lincoln shot?"

"Deutsche sprechen, Georg!" His son's name was a constant annoyance, but it had been the occasion of one of Marie's two revolts. The other was when he wanted to go to the German consulate and make German citizens out of the children.

George Washington stared at his father a moment, his lips working. Apparently the question was too difficult to translate. He said, in his badly accented Yorkville German: "I remember, Papa," and went on writing. His sister, Grace Coolidge Lempe washed dishes in the corner.

Artur did not believe that his son remembered. He believed that the boy was unable to speak good German. Well, that would be repaired. They would not stay in this—this amateurish country forever. In the bank was nearly three thousand dollars. This would be good money in Germany, the Tourist Bureau told him. The State was paying good premiums in rate of exchange to Germans who returned to the Fatherland. And he would get a good job, once home. Sixteen years of American engineering methods, that would count. The Fatherland must study, so that it could do everything better than other countries. It must—

Marie was a fool. Marie said that the Korps-Hauptmann, and the Tourist Bureau too, they told lies. She said that the

Fatherland was soon going to war and that it wanted Georg back, and Artur too, to fight.

But this was foolishness, womanly foolishness. Who was there for the Fatherland to fight? Cowardly France, indecisive England, Red Russia? A new day was opening in the old country, a day as bright as had been the America of sixty years ago, when the frontier was open—

Once he had been a fool, too. He remembered himself in Württemberg, sixteen years ago. What sort of a doltish picture had his mind drawn? Himself and Marie—lovely Marie, the belle of the little Rheinpfalz town from which they had both come—making a new home in the American West which he had seen in the cinema. Snowed in together on the range, all winter together, not minding because they had the sort of love which—he knew now—existed only in the films.

Marie had finished the trousers. He pulled them on, stepping on the heels of his drawers to keep them from making lumps under the uniform; he put on his shiny black boots. Well, he had been successful in this country. He had worked all through the depression, even though he had to do the work of three men for a while. And being chief heating engineer of a forty-story office building, that was not exactly the position of a janitor!

Marie was looking at him. "Thanks for ironing the trousers," he said, gruffly. "They look fine!" Then, as she still gave them that sad, patient look, he added, in English: "So long, keed!" He smiled at the children, and went out, his boots stamping down the stairs.

The trouble was, Marie had never loved him. She had said so when she married him. She had said she liked him, and she wanted to go to America, she wanted to have children who would be like her brothers, only without military conscription. Her brothers had died in the war.

And he, romantic young fool, had had his head full of motion pictures. She would grow to love him. Like the actresses grew to love William S. Hart. Only—

He pulled his civilian overcoat up around his throat, pulled down his fedora hat. This was a good snow, like they had in the Rhine country, a man's snow.

Behind him, Marie Vogel Lempe looked at her children. She said: "Lincoln was shot in 1865, Washington. He was a very brave and good man, who freed the slaves and saved the country from division. He stopped the war, and then a crazy man with his head filled with wild speeches shot him."

"Well, gee, maw, I knew all that. Except the date."

Mrs. Lempe watched him make the correction on his history paper. She got her purse out from the cupboard. The bakery had paid her that day, and Artur let her keep her wages, he would not touch them. He thought she ought to stay home all day, but what was there to do with both children in school?

"Grace, why don't you take Washington to the movies, it is not snowing so hard."

"What's playing, Ma?" Washington asked.

"*Union Pacific*," said Mrs. Lempe, "and *Dodge City*. Two pictures from the West of the old days, before Mama and Papa came to this country. You will like them. In the *Daily News* it says—"

"All righty," Grace said. "Don't care if I do. Go get your hat, kid." When the boy was out of the room she turned to her mother. "Ma, was it a bad accident? You feel all right, don't you?"

"Fine, fine. I was not hurt."

"Maybe it'll be in the papers."

"There were men there took pictures and asked questions. Maybe, yes, it will be in the papers."

"I'll look when I come out of the movies."

Mrs. Lempe nodded, and sat down. "Do that. I think I will go to bed."

"I'll keep the brat quiet when we come in."

"Now, Grace, you must not call Washington a brat."

"Aw, Ma, I was just teasing. You want us to be so American, and then when we are, you scold us."

"I am sure that Mrs. Boettiger never calls young Curtis a brat." . . .

In the doorway of the Turnhall Artur stopped and wiped his boots with a rag which he carried in his hip pocket for that purpose. Then he hurried to the cloakroom, and blossomed forth from a man in a last year's ulster and slouch hat to a full-fledged S. A. Mann. He took his cap from his locker and put it on.

There was no one else in the cloakroom. He trotted down the corridor, saluted the black-coated S. S. Mann on the door, hurried in. Ach. Already they were inspecting the guard. That must be the national Bundfuehrer, that strange, powerful man in glasses. He had not been to this Korps meeting since Artur joined six months ago. He had been on the Coast, they said.

Luckily the inspection party had not yet reached Artur's place in line. He edged in, and his squad members made room for him.

But the captain had seen him. As the inspection party reached Artur, the captain growled: "You are late, Lempe." The national Bundfuehrer stood in the background, looking stern at the idea of anyone being late when *he* was going to speak.

"My wife was in a bus accident, she was—"

"That is no excuse. In our cause, all must come after devotion to the State."

"Wait a minute," the Bundfuehrer said. "Lempe, did you say?"

Artur, standing at attention, was surprised that he spoke in English.

"Yes, Lempe," the captain said.

"I saw that in the papers. Mrs. Artur Lempe was one of those people trapped in that crosstown bus. Was your wife injured, Lempe?"

"Well, sir, she cooked dinner—"

"But shock, she was suffering from shock, nicht wahr?"

Since the Fuehrer said it, it must be so. Glad that the interest of the accident was saving him from further criticism, Artur said: "Yes, sir."

"See me after the meeting. Perhaps we can make some money for you and for the cause some propaganda. . . ." The Bundfuehrer smiled. "The driver was named Kreutzler, a Jew. Incompetent to drive a bus, no doubt." . . .

Grace C. Lempe and her brother, G. Washington Lempe, stood in a doorway at 95th and First. First Grace pressed the third button in the second row of buttons communicating with the flats upstairs; then Wash pressed. But there was no answer.

"I guess Rita's already gone to the show," Grace said.

"Aw, come on. Can't you get along without Rita for one night, Gracie?"

"You sound like Papa."

"No, you know I don't mind Rita being a— I don't mind, Rita, only every night and every night . . ."

Pass Through Manhattan

Grace pressed the button again. When there was no answer, the Lempe girl sighed, and she and her brother went on down First, towards the movies.

At the corner, Grace collided with another girl, both their heads bent away from the snow. "Gracie!"

"Rita!" Grace cried, kissing the girl. "C'mon, ma gave us a dollar to go to the movies."

Her joy at meeting Rita Cohen was—though she did not, of course, know it—exactly that of a diabetic eating cake, a Catholic reading a book from the *Index Expurgatorius*, a Prohibitionist taking a drink.

*   *   *

ELEANOR CASTRON stood on the edge of the tanbark riding hall of Squadron A Armory and watched Tenny go around and around the ring on the back of a bay gelding. She was freezing to death, and she wanted a drink. But first it was necessary for Tenny to ride the horse around the ring and thus demonstrate that he was a gentleman and a soldier, and that his nerves had not been undermined by the accident.

Well, hers had. And she was cold. She had never been so cold in her life. The drink of brandy that the ambulance surgeon had pressed on her was dead now, and—

Tenny had stopped the bay in front of her. "Don't you want to try him, Eleanor? Warm you up."

She heard herself saying all right. Then he had swung down, and she was up. His hand brushed her thigh as he adjusted the stirrups for her, and she said, irritably: "Stop pawing me!"

"Come, Eleanor, there is no need to be insulting. I was merely—"

Pass Through Manhattan

She kicked the gelding, hard, and the horse bounced away from Tenny. She went halfway around the ring with one stirrup too long, tugging at the strap. She got it adjusted herself, settled back to posting, the hoofs banging softly, steadily, on the tanbark. She began to feel better, the second time around she even smiled at Tenny, and the third time she called out: "Oh, this is a lovely nag."

"I'll get another horse and join you," Tenny said, and trotted towards the ramp that went down to the stalls.

She raised the reins and the bay cantered. Settling back in her saddle, Eleanor thought, this is fun, this is what I like, I was never so happy as when we had the place on the Island and I used to ride Nancy every day down to the beach. Dear little Nancy, I wonder who owns her now. Maybe she's dead, let's see, she was ten years old when we had to sell her in '32, after Dad laid the Castron fortune on the bottom of the market and then found out there was a hole in the bottom.

Around and around the ring. What is it horses' hoofs say —Property, property, property. Tenny would be rich some day. He had success written all over him. A man to remember. Property, property, property. That was in a poem they had learned in Miss Finch's. "You don't have to marry money, but go where money is," or something. Perfectly awful dialect that the English teacher had said was North of England.

I want money and Tenny is going to have it. And what does Tenny want? Not my pretty little body bouncing up and down on this horse. Oh, no, not Tenny. He wants me because my grandfather's father did what Tenny is going to do, start out poor and end up rich. This makes me something Tenny would like to share his bed and board.

Pass Through Manhattan

Eleanor! You ought to be ashamed of yourself. Nice little girls—

Get off this horse and make Tenny take you home, right now. You were tired when you started out, and nearly getting smothered in a bus didn't help any, and if you go on getting more tired you'll wear yourself all out. You'll do something you'll be sorry for.

Tenny came up the ramp on a chestnut just the color of little Nancy. Oh, I was such a nice, simple girl when I had Nancy. When I was thirteen years old and used to ride Nancy down Goat's Neck outside Southampton and ride behind the sand dunes to go swimming. I used to feel so daring, swimming without any clothes on, though nobody ever came out there, and if they had I could have seen them coming down the spot five miles away.

Maybe if I was just a little better rider I could get a job showing horses for some parvenu. I love that word, parvenu.

"Having a good time, Eleanor?"

"I'm getting warmed up, anyway, Parvy."

"Why Parvy?"

"I don't know, it fits you."

The trouble with Tenny, he never knows when to shut up. If he'd just keep quiet and let me ride this darling horse around the ring, I might get so I like him. Yes, Tenny. No, Tenny. Yes, Tenny. Yes, Tenny. Yes, Ten—

Now what? Tenny had stopped his horse back there. She turned and rode back to him. His eyes were all funny, he was sort of shaking.

"What's the matter, Tenny?"

"Let's get out of here where I can— Oh, Eleanor!"

Good God! It suddenly dawned on her what she had been saying yes to. She had promised to marry Tenny, John Tenbruye the Stinker. She—

68

Pass Through Manhattan

Then, suddenly she was quiet. She had started out the day not knowing which way to turn, playing with the idea of marrying Tenny because there wasn't anybody else and the grocer was getting mean.

All right, Fate had decided for her. The bus accident and the drink of brandy had worn her down till she was so tired she didn't know what she was saying and she had said she would marry him. So why not?

But she kept thinking of how she used to ride Nancy down Goat's Neck in the hot summer sun with the fine smell of salt water and sand and seaweed. One time she had found an oyster in the rushes, in the shallow water off Goat's Neck, and she had eaten it and then been afraid she was going to die because it was July without an R in the month.

But now it was March and snow was blowing down her neck where she hadn't tucked her scarf in right, and Tenny was holding her by the arm, walking through the snow. If winter comes can spring be far behind, but behind or before, spring wasn't going to bring back all the money Dad had dropped through the hole in the market before he put the hole through his head that the relatives and the doctor and all had been so clever about, not letting the newspapers know.

And now they were going up in an automatic elevator like the one in Dr. Latham's building when she used to have to go every Saturday to have the braces adjusted, because my little girl must have nice straight teeth.

Except in summer when they went out on the Island and Dr. Latham used to put on a permanent brace that was supposed to last the summer only it never did because Eleanor would take it out with a buttonhook when she went to bed, and sooner or later that broke it, always, and she had to go into town on the Long Island Railroad, and Mother said if you take that brace out once more I'll get Dad to sell Nancy.

And she would never love any man as much as she had loved Nancy who had been a purebred hackney pony while Tenny wasn't a purebred anything.

"It's just a little place but it's convenient to the Armory," Tenny said. Then: "Oh, Eleanor, you're shivering. I hope I haven't let you overdo it, darling."

In a minute he would be kissing her, and she couldn't stand that, not yet. "I've got snow in my boots," she said, in a little girl voice that she hardly recognized as her own.

"Oh, well, look, why don't you go in the bedroom and take them off? I could give you some heavy woolen socks to—"

"Do you want to compromise me, Tenny?" Oh, stop giggling, Eleanor Castron.

"But if we're engaged, surely you trust—"

"Oh, I was just making a joke. Which is the bedroom, here?"

He followed her in and fished a pair of heavy woolen socks out of a bureau drawer and gave them to her. Then, walking on tiptoe like a stage butler, he went out, shut the door.

Eleanor sat down on the floor and tugged at the wet heels of her boots. You can't take boots off sitting any place but on the floor, no matter who tells you that ladies don't sit on floors. You can't—

The first boot came off with a rush, and she went over backwards. She lay on her back, staring at the ceiling while her head went around and around. My little girl overdid it today, all right, she certainly did, darling, go to bed and I'll send up a nice cup of hot milk with seltzer in it.

The second boot was a snap. She lay on her back again, though, because it had been so restful the first time, and put her feet into the air. Oh, dear. She had worn old silk stockings, ones all runnered under boots, because she didn't have or couldn't find any proper riding socks. Tenny mustn't see that. He'd be shocked, the right clothes for every occasion mean so much to Tenny he—

She had to unbutton the pants legs to get the stockings off, and after that it seemed the most natural thing in the world to take the rest of her clothes off, warm as the good steam heat touched her skin the way the sun used to do out on Goat's Neck with no one to watch but little Nancy.

When she had all her clothes off she opened the door and walked into the living room. "Oh, Tenny," she called. "Come see me, I'm just a little girl."

*   *   *

DON WAS ALREADY THROUGH the park in the taxicab before he realized that he should have been afraid going through the transverse. It was the driver reminded him, turning his head away from the wheel to say: "Notice there wasn't no traffic coming through the cut? I hadda think twicet before I went in there, there was a bad accident in 'ere today. Mosta the cars is goin' around tonight."

"Yes, I know," Don said. There was undeveloped land down the creek bed about three miles from the All's Fair that would probably pan about as well as the present location. The catch was in getting the machinery in; unless you had or could buy second-hand machinery in the neighborhood, fourteen-dollar sand wouldn't pay back in less than five years. And with capital scared of inflation and revolutions and things, five years was too long.

Though, maybe with gold . . . At least it was an argument he could use. If the country undergoes inflation, the

71

gold will be worth just that more, you ought to go into this as a hedge to cover your other, commodity, investments.

The trouble was, most investment bankers apparently didn't know the basic economics of investment, as taught in the sophomore year at any good college. You couldn't give them scientific arguments, they'd just look down their noses and say: "There are factors in the present market that make that no longer true."

Thank God for engineering. Given time and an unlimited access to good textbooks and a slide rule—though even the latter was not necessary—and you could get the answer to anything. Anything physical, that is—

No slide rule would solve the equation you could make out of this afternoon. One mother, plus one nurse, minus one embezzling contractor, plus the square of a good citizen—

No, you couldn't tell whether it equaled a Copper or not. A—

All he knew about Copper was the way they worked together. That must have been it, he had pushed it around his head till it ached, that must have been it. They could read each other's minds, they—

"This is the joint," the driver said. "I guess. How'd you say you pronounced it?"

"Tsigany's my guess."

"These Bohemians," the driver sighed, pocketing his fare and a tip.

The clock at the entrance said exactly quarter to seven, but when Don came into the barroom, Mr. Makin was already waiting. Which was all the proof that Don needed that he was *not* there to raise Don's salary. When an investment banker is ahead of time for a date with an employee, Duck.

Pass Through Manhattan

"Hello, Morton," Mr. Makin said, brightly. "Have a cocktail. Josef here has been introducing me to the Gypsy Kiss, it's wonderful."

"What's a Gypsy Kiss?" Don asked.

"First, in a very cold bar glass put slivowitz one ounce. Then, with care, t'ree drops from Pernod, one, two, t'ree. From eggs, one white and—"

"Make mine a Vermouth Cassis," Don said. Old Ron Levine, his father's sidekick, had taught him that: sounds sophisticated, looks like a drink, and hasn't much more alcohol in it than a glass of good, strong, vanilla soda.

"Yes, sir," Josef turned to his blackboard, "and another Kiss for the shentleman."

"The well-kissed banker," Don said. He was perfectly aware of Mr. Makin's surprise without bothering to look at Makin; employees of mining outfits—even employees with contracts that have two more years to run—do not talk to the operations manager of the bank in that tone.

"Josef," said Makin, "ask the headwaiter to step in. We can order here and then it will be ready when we sit down."

"Very good, sir."

After they had ordered chicken dumpling soup, chicken paprikash with spetzler, beet salad and a bottle of Tokay with seltzer, there was a big, cold pause in the conversation.

Makin said: "The worst blizzard in years, I hear."

"Yes."

"Though that was a terrible one about four years ago. Our garage was snowed in for two days."

"It must have been bad."

"It was. We live out in Port Washington, you know."

"Oh, do you?"

"Yes. You must come visit us sometime. We're staying at a hotel in town just now. The snow, you know."

"I don't," Don said carefully, "expect to be in town much longer. This is the last snow of the season, the placer beds ought to thaw out in a couple of weeks."

"Well—er—yes. Ah, dinner ready, captain?" Makin led the way to the table, being determinedly gay. Don felt a wicked, cold pleasure in tormenting the banker. Hell, if the job fell through he'd move down the bed and build himself a hand rocker. Man could clear about five bucks a day that way. It would be a come-down, from superintendent of a fifty-man hydraulic operation to a one-man rocker, but after what he'd seen today, those things didn't seem important.

Wonder what Makin—down whose chin a little drop of chicken soup is crawling—would say if I told him I'd seen a better man than him wiped out today, and he could take his banking firm and—

"Good soup," Makin said.

"Yes."

"Have some wine— I say, do you know anyone in the Navy very well?"

This took Don completely by surprise. "No, why?"

"There's a sailor over in that corner been trying to get your attention ever since we came in."

"A sailor?" Don looked. "Oh, of course. You know, ever since you asked me over the phone if I knew a good restaurant up here, I've been trying to remember where I heard of this one. It was that sailor who said he was on his way here. In that bus." Don waved at the sailor, who beamed a little drunkenly.

"Oh, stupid of me," Makin said. "Have I congratulated

you on what must have been a really superb piece of engineering?"

"Yes, over the phone," Don said absently. "Hey, I'm sorry, but my nautical pal is on his way over here."

"Well, a hero has to expect a certain amount of adulation."

Cowboy Connors tacked across the big, barnlike dining room. His face was shiny and red, there was a spot of paprika sauce on his neckerchief. "Mr. Morton."

Don said: "Yes," coldly.

"I guess you don't remember me," Cowboy said. "Connors, Bosun's Mate Second, *U.S.S. Oregon.* You saved my life today." He belched and reeled a little without moving his feet. He giggled foolishly. "Not much of a life but 's only one I got."

"I save so many lives," Don said. "I can't keep them all straight." He thought he was going to throw up, lose his dinner. Or maybe throw the chicken soup in Connors' drunken face, the wine in Makin's smug one. Oh, I saved your life, Connors. Sure. No trouble at all. Saved your life so you could overeat and overdrink and go to bed with that cheap whore you're feeding up at your table. And a better man than you lies down in the Morgue, with snow on his dark face. A better man than Makin.

"Well," Cowboy said. "You saved my life. Just a hick from Idaho, Cowboy Connors, never amount to anything, allatime hungry, but it's my life and you, by God, sir, excuse me, it. Lemme buy your dinner?"

"No, thanks," Don said. "I'm eating with this gentleman here."

"Oh. Guess I'm 'ntruding. Well, I sure do thank you, and —and any time you need 'nthing 'n I'm in port, just you—"

"O.K., Cowboy. I'll remember that."

75

Pass Through Manhattan

The sailor wandered away, back to his table and his friend and his cheap woman. A dirty, lousy, unfair deal, all the way around and—

Makin said: "I guess it isn't every gold miner gets to dig up as priceless a cargo as eight human lives."

"More priceless than gold? Come, come, Mr. Makin, what would Wall Street say?"

Makin said, sharply, laying down his spoon: "What's the matter with you, Morton, are you drunk? I must say, you are acting very strangely."

"Mr. Makin, you didn't stay in town Saturday night to discuss the future of Cowboy Connors or the best way to make a Gypsy Kiss. What's on Armstrong and Grainger's mind?"

Makin cleared his throat. He said, earnestly: "I really wanted to have dinner, a pleasant social occasion, with you. But what do you say, we get the business over with first?"

"Fine."

"The government—er—I won't ask you your views on the present administration. Our employees' politics are their own. However. The government has some dam-fool project of dropping a dam in the hills behind our All's Fair operation. Which would mean the end of All's Fair; I don't need to tell you that."

"Sure. If they dry up the stream, we're through. It wouldn't pay to pipe water to the bed."

"Precisely. And so— You have found traces of iridium in the gold, haven't you, Morton?"

"Of scientific interest only. Yes, iridium color shows in the spectroscope. I doubt if you could extract it."

"But certainly if there is that trace—hardly more than a suspicion—on the surface of the bed, at the present levels, there is a possibility that more will turn up deeper down?"

Pass Through Manhattan

Don said: "Iridium, like other metals, is where you find it. It might turn up any place. In the schist of Manhattan as likely as in our bed. It's rarer than hell, there are only about three places in the world where it can be mined and—"

"Rare, and of great value both in time of war and in peace. National importance. A new iridium deposit would be an important thing to the Army, for in—"

"What are you getting at?"

"The government—we have been given a week to present a report showing why the water shouldn't be dammed away from All's Fair. If we can't, we'll be paid the cost of moving our machinery elsewhere."

"And you want me to testify that I expect iridium down in the bank. But I don't."

"Damn it, man, you're being rather dense. Your job depends on—"

"I have a two-year contract."

"With the All's Fair Corporation. Which will go into bankruptcy if—"

"If I don't perjure myself before some committee in Washington."

Makin stared at him for a moment, his eyes as shiny and expressionless as the fat bodies of a pair of oysters, while the orchestra leader tapped on his music stand and then led the piano player and the mandolins into wild, wailing gypsy music, the leader's violin always leading, climbing, screaming.

"I am unaware," Makin puffed, raising his voice over the music, "of ever asking an employee to violate his moral code in the interests of my employers." He called the waiter, who was staring raptly at the orchestra, his head nodding to the music. "Waiter!" he had to say it twice. "Waiter! Bring us the check, please."

"But please, sir, the dinner it is all ordered, we are sorry for delay, but each order is cooked fresh, we—"

"I'll pay for what we ordered."

The waiter shuffled away, mumbling, looking as though he were going to cry. I ought to be uncomfortable, but I'm not. Let Makin worry.

Two minutes went by, three. The violinist finished, bowing, tossing his curly black hair. Makin patted his fat palms together, perfunctorily.

"After all," Don said, "I'm a field engineer." He was surprised at his own voice, cool, almost dreamy. "My job is to get metal out of the ground as cheaply, quickly and safely as possible. Like the guy who watered horses."

Makin gave up craning his neck, looking for the flat-footed waiter. "Horses?"

> He waters horses for a living,
> A pail of water kindly giving.
> He knows not malice, nor remorse,
> Or monetary forces.
> But he knows the thirst of a thirsty horse
> And how to water horses.

Makin smiled a little. The waiter arrived, breathless, followed by the man in the Hungarian peasant or gypsy costume who had let Don in at the front door. "There is trouble, please?"

"No, we just—"

"Anything that iss wrong, we fix. Saturday night, iss crowded, sometimes—"

"Oh, bring the dinner," Makin said, beginning to laugh.

Pass Through Manhattan

"My friend and I were having a business argument, but I guess it's ended."

Then, suddenly: "I think we can solve our difficulties, Don. I'll talk to Mr. Grainger Monday. He's not the ogre you field men think. . . ."

The music had started up again. It was not the same piece, but it had the same defiant cry underlying all its chords, a thin shriek thrown at the world, and to hell with it. The shrieks of a spring wind coming down off Steamboat Pass, or of a gale in the wire rigging of a freighter.

The sort of noise he and Copper knew, and that meant nothing to Makin, starting on his chicken paprikash. Fatly absorbing fat food.

"Where'd you hear that poem, Don?" Makin asked with his mouth full. "Your father's?"

"A friend of his, Herb Lewis, a newspaperman."

"Joseph Kolk Morton is a brilliant man, a marvelous newspaperman. I might have known his son wouldn't be a fool."

Don, watching Cowboy Connors' face across the room, just raised an eyebrow. Something had happened, but he didn't know what.

Cowboy turned and gave him a fatuous smile.

*   *   *

BUCK RANULPH SAT IN ONE CORNER of the detectives' room of the 104th Street Station and read his law book. Over in the middle of the room, under the green-shaded light, five other detectives played a desultory, perpetual game of poker.

It was held in the case of the Tennessee Coal and Iron Company *v.* the Southern Railway, 114 Tenn., that—

Pass Through Manhattan

The words swung around and around in his mind. He had missed an opportunity that day. Lieutenant Barker had been annoyed with him, and that would swing around through the devious meshes of department politics, and do him no good. He was very likely to find himself directing traffic or walking a beat in Harlem if he was not careful.

On the other hand, he could have made something out of that bus accident. If just one of the passengers—that Mr. Firstin, he had looked important—had told the reporters that panic was prevented by the presence of a police officer, he, Buckingham Ranulph, would stand a good chance of being a second-class detective pretty soon.

But it had all happened so quick, and there hadn't been anything to do. That nurse had spoken up all right, she had sung out: "Is anyone hurt, I'm a nurse?"

And he should have answered right then. He should have said: "I'll go through the bus and check up, lady. I'm a policeman." But before he'd had a chance, somebody'd struck a match, and you could see that no one was hurt except the driver, and no cop, no nurse or doctor was going to help him. When the glass broke, he must have jumped forward, because he had never seen the little Smith girl, with a jag of glass in her jugular vein.

It hadn't been fear that kept him quiet. Just slow thinking. Just— Aw, what difference did it make? He wasn't going to stay a cop. He was going to pass his bar examinations and be a colored defender. He was going to throw away his nice three thousand a year and get out there and work for his own race, for the dimes and quarters of poor Negroes who couldn't afford a good white lawyer. He'd be a famous man, invited to speak at race meetings, maybe even given an LL.D. from Howard or Tuskegee, but he'd be a poor man.

Pass Through Manhattan

Still, he'd walk in pride and—

A thin man, a white man, stood in the door of the room, squinting at the poker game. Snow on his shoulders and his shoes. Seen him before some place, maybe a reporter.

The thin man coughed, and said: "Is Mr. Ranulph here? They told me downstairs it was all right just to come up and—"

Detective Sergeant Villier looked up from his hand. "Two for me," he told the dealer. He stared hard at the thin man for a minute. "Right in that corner," he said.

The stranger stepped nearer the light, and then saw Buck over in the dark corner, the book still in his hand. He came over and put out his hand in the sort of self-conscious way white people do when they shake hands with a Negro.

"Mr. Ranulph, my name is Maxwell, W. Gordon Maxwell. I was in the bus today."

"Oh, yes, sir. I've been trying to place your face. Won't you have a chair?"

Buck went and got another chair from the table, brought it over to the corner. He had a little flash of resentment at the white cops, not offering him a place in the light when he had a visitor, a gentleman, too. You could tell this was an educated man.

Gordie Maxwell sat down. "As soon as I read in the paper about your being a detective, a policeman, I began thinking. You see, I'm a writer, I write detective stories. You don't think I'm presuming on an accident, do you?"

"Of course not, Mr. Maxwell. Glad to have you drop around. I've read many of your stories." And that's a lie, Buck Ranulph.

"Oh, do you read *Nightstick Stories?*"

"All the time. I am, you might say, a constant reader."

Maxwell said: "Well, I am writing a story which I hope

to sell to the *Saturday Evening Post*. Being in some doubt about a couple of technical points, I thought you might be willing to help me out."

"Surely."

"Well, now, for one thing, do policemen, detectives, call a blackjack a sap or a socker?"

"Gee, now. Well, sir, I guess they would call it a blackjack, but you would be correct in referring to it as a sap."

"Now, as to the difference between a mobster and a gangster. Do you feel there is any—or do the two words mean the same?"

"I would say," said Buck Ranulph, "that they had the same denotation, but a slightly different connotation. A gangster would employ mobsters; or he might employ other gangsters. But a mobster would never employ anyone."

"That's very clear," Maxwell said, stroking his thin mustache. "Yes. Have a cigarette, Mr. Ranulph?"

Buck accepted one, struck a match to light the two cigarettes. "Well," Maxwell said. "I think that's all. Interesting room you have here. This is a pretty active district, I suppose?"

"It is a cross-section of the city," Buck told him. "We've got some really fine people living in our district, over on Fifth. Then the Italian district, and the Porto Ricans, they are middle class, you might say. And over on 99th and 100th, between the two Ls, that's about as tough a stretch as you will find on Manhattan."

"I'd like to go see it sometime."

"If you just mind your own business, you'll be quite safe. But I'd be glad to accompany you."

"Oh, thanks. But I mustn't take up any more of your time."

"Not at all."

Pass Through Manhattan

Mr. Maxwell rose, looked around for an ashtray, finally dropped his cigarette in the spittoon, and shook hands again. He took a couple of steps towards the door. "By the way, Mr. Ranulph. I'm giving you a little writeup in the next issue of *Nightstick*. And would you consider writing us·a few of your experiences? We couldn't pay much, but—"

"I'm afraid I'd have to ask my superiors for permission. But thanks for the writeup."

"It's a real honor to know you. Good-bye."

When the noise of his heavy shoes was gone down the stairs, Sergeant Villiers said: "Who was your friend, Buck?"

"An editor. Of a magazine."

"Yeah?"

"He sounded like a white nigger to me," Gregori said. The other cops laughed and Buck with them. "Never heard so many long words outa no white man."

The phone rang, and Villiers got it. "Yeah? Yeah? White or—? Yeah." He hung up the phone. "Nigger wench over on 99th just sliced the guts outa her boy friend—another monkey-chaser. Patrolman conked her and they're bringing her in, but they wanta plainclothesman to pick up the razor, and so on. I guess you're elected, Buck."

"Yes, sir." Buck got his overcoat and hat from the tree, put them on. He turned up the collar of his coat.

"They took the pimp to Mount Sinai, and if he dies homicide'll send her up. You better wait there till you get a call, Buck."

"Yes, sir." Buck picked up his pamphlet, and put it in his pocket. He tramped downstairs, through the muster room, remembering to salute the desk. Then he started the long cold walk to 99th and Second. Be no cabs in this district at this hour. A nasty night ahead. Those Porto Rican girls knew how to use a blade, and the man would die, and he would have to spend the night sitting in a 99th Street prostitute's flat.

Passing a cigar store, he swung in and got a package of cigarettes and a copy of *Nightstick Stories*. He stood in the store a moment and examined it. There was a story, the last in the book, by W. Gordon Maxwell. It was called "Revenge Trail," and it began: "The underworld had killed his brother. But the Big Cop said no shooting, and Patrolman Joe Devine was loyal to his badge."

Buck put that in his pocket over the law pamphlet, and tramped through the snow on his grisly errand.

*　　　*　　　*

GO SOUTH FROM WALL AND BROAD and turn to the left, and you come to South Street. It starts some place in the mad scramble of L tracks and open space to the east of Battery Park; Water Street runs up on the edge of the Park, and to it face the offices of the big shipping companies. Their backs are turned to south, and south, in turn, faces the "Farm" that bounds the East River docks.

You can get a shot of pretty active whisky for a dime on South Street. A glass of beer is only a nickel, and hamburgers—well diluted with bread, but covered with a thick, peppery, flavory gravy—are a nickel, too. A man can fill his stomach for a quarter, get good and drunk for fifty cents; in fact, if you want to spend more than four bits for any of South Street's luxuries, you have to buy a woman, some of whom run all the way up to two dollars—plus, of course, anything they can find in your clothes.

Such reasonable prices should attract all the semi-employed single men in the city, the dishwashers and gandy dancers, the reliefers, the junkmen. But they don't. South

Pass Through Manhattan

Street—for its first mile, before it gets into the Fulton Fish Market and the domain of the pressmen from the Hearst papers—is seagoing.

First mates of tugs, wearing greenish derbies, wipers and ordinary seamen off the banana boats—these wear flat caps —A.B.s, oilers, watertenders, carpenters, bos'ns, storekeepers, all go to South Street when they are between boats, and sometimes when they are just loading. The Seaman's Institute is down there, and the Seaman's Union.

Nightly they gather in the brilliantly lighted, washroom-architecture-styled open-face joints that opened up after repeal to take the place of the old cozy hideaway shock joints of prohibition. And these places smell of the sea, which is amazing until you realize that one of the favorite dishes is steamed clams.

Joe Morton shoved open the glass door of Honest Ikie's and shut it quickly behind him. He sneezed twice, and pushed up to the bar. "Bourbon and beer," he said. The bartender waited, looking him over suspiciously, and Joe put a quarter down. He had tapped Ron Levine for five bucks.

The bartender gave him his drink and fifteen cents change. Joe drank. "Know a guy named Cronin?" he asked.

"I don't ask the customers' names."

"They told me over at the Seaman's Union he'd probably be in here."

"Yeah? Well, look aroun'. Lotsa sailors in here."

This was how he had spent thirty-seven years. This was easy for Joe Morton. "I'm a newspaperman," he said. He exhibited his police card, the one from last month; he hadn't been able to find the current one when he dressed. "I understand this Cronin is a pal of a man named Ringgold who was killed today up—"

Pass Through Manhattan

The bartender's rag stopped wiping the bar. His chin went up, then dropped. "Injun killed? Ya mean to say Injun was—"

"Didn't you see it in the evening papers?" Joe asked. He looked around the room. There was a somewhat soiled *Mail* lying on an imitation black-glass table. He went over and got it, but when he came back two sets of blue-reefered shoulders had closed in, absorbed his place. The bartender reached out: "Make room for this guy. . . ."

Joe folded the paper over so the front page could be seen, handed it over. "There he is. Three casualties, the driver, a colored girl, and Ringgold."

The bartender had to read the whole story, down to where it announced Ringgold's name and his address, the Seaman's Union. Then he looked up. " 'At's too bad," he said. "Too damn bad. He was a good guy, Injun Ringgold." He went on reading. "Give his life for that son of a bitch Firstin," he said. "Huh! When I was steward on th' *J. L. Luckenbach*, the captain sunk his dough into Greenwich Square. Lost it," said the bartender, and went on reading. "Poor ol' Injun," he finished, and carefully folded the paper, handed it back.

"That's all right," Joe said. "I don't want it." He watched the bartender put the paper on the backbar, in front of the cut glass bowl of hardboiled eggs, and said: "Have a drink with me?"

"Not on duty," the bartender said. But he poured Joe another, picked up a dime.

Someone had put a nickel in the phonograph, and it said: "Hello, Joe!" in a clear, vibrant voice. Joe Morton jumped, then smiled a little as a group of colored people some place inside the machine began shouting, All Right, All *Right* at each other.

Pass Through Manhattan

Joe said: "Why did they call him Injun?"

"You're from a newspaper?"

All right, well all *right*, all right, well all *right*.

"That's right." Now they have me doing it too. That's the longest nickel's worth of music I ever did hear. Bartender's saying something.

"Looked like an Indian. I wouldn't want to say he had Indian blood in him, mind you; that ain't a nice thing to say about a fella's dead."

"No, no, of course. We want to fix up a good story about him."

"An obituary," said the bartender. "If ever a guy deserved an obituary, Injun was the guy. Pardon me, I gotta go wait on a customer."

Joe Morton took a pull of bourbon, pushed it down with a little beer. His head felt tight and stuffy from the cold, and from the incessant noise of the phonograph. It stopped for a moment, someone put another nickel in, and it said: "Hello, Joe." Then it started assuring itself it was doing all right.

The man next to Joe said: "Pass me the mulligan, willya, mister?"

Joe reached for the bottle of pepper sauce, missed by two inches, and tried again. He got it, and passed it to the man next to him.

The man said: "Rough weather, pal."

"I have a bad cold," Joe said.

"Oh. You oughta be home then. I heard you telling Slops you're a reporter."

"*Evening Mail.*"

"Newspaper Guild?"

"Yes," Joe said. "Sure."

"Let's see your card."

Pass Through Manhattan

The bartender came back. "Cronin just come in," he said. "I told him to come over. He—"

"Le's see your Guild card," the man next to Joe said.

"G'wan," Slops said, "no rough stuff in here, Larry."

"I got a right to ask to see his Newspaper Guild card, ain't I? I'm the delegate off the *Lucy Zweig*, and when we had our strike—"

"This gentleman is a friend of mine, writing an obituary for a friend of mine who died, and I won't have him insulted in my place."

"So now it's an insult to be asked if you're a union man, huh? How about you, Slops, are you—"

Slops jerked a fat thumb over his shoulder at the sign hung on the mirror. "Union House. Union of Bartenders, Waiters and Countermen, Local No. 1. You see the sign."

"How about your dues? Your dues paid up, Slops?"

Joe said: "I don't mind showing my Guild card. Always carry it—" He fumbled around in his pocket.

"Don't you bother, Mister," Slops said. "And you, Larry, lay off."

Larry said: "I don't drink in fink joints," and then he was gone.

Slops was saying: "Cronin, this is a gentleman who is writing an obituary for poor Injun."

Cronin was a short, fat, bald man with a day or so's stubble of beard. "I read about Injun," he said. "It was a too-bad thing. Injun was O.K."

Joe Morton pressed his fingers on the curve of the mahogany rail until the tension in them went through to his brain, stopped his head from going around.

He said: "What was there about him? Anything special?"

"I dunno. He was just like anybody else, except—"

Pass Through Manhattan

"He made up songs," Slops said. "Tell him about the songs."

Cronin's whirling head split into a grin. "Yes, sir. Any time the going got tough Injun usta start singin'. Make up songs just as good as Bing Crosby. On the radio, you know. You remember, Slops, in the *Gulf of Tehuantepec?*"

Slops said: "Sure do. I was in the galley, see, mister, and it's maybe two hundred and twelve on the thermometer. And Injun comes by for a mug-up, see, and starts singing. He sings something about Old Slops is just a grease spot on the deck, and the first thing you know, I'm laughing so I don't mind the heat."

"He sung us out of a limey jail oncet in Jamaica," Cronin said. "He sang about Look at the Sergeant Dressed in Red, and the nigger cops let us out."

Joe Morton mumbled: "Can't you remember any of the songs all the way through?"

"Naw. He never would write them down."

"Where was he from? Drunk or sober, I'm as good a newspaperman as you need. Keep right on working when my knees give out."

"Say," Cronin said. "That's something maybe would look good in an obituary. He was a cowboy."

"What?" The mist cleared away, and Joe Morton looked around the steamy, gaudy bar. Sure he knew where he was. South Street. Bunch of sailors playing a pin game over there, lotta guys eating at the lunch counter, bet I could count them if I wanted to.

"Came into town with a carload of horses, he told us. We were berthed over in Brooklyn then, down at the end of 25th. He comes walking down, and he comes aboard, easy as anything. Says he'd always wanted to see the ocean.

89

Got to singing about Every Cowboy Likes the Water, and me—I was watchman—I got him some coffee, and when the skipper came aboard he hired him. You was visiting your wife out in Cedarhurst, remember, Slops?"

"My second wife," Slops said.

"Well— Have another drink?" Joe asked.

"It ain't necessary, Mister. We're glad to help the fella's writing poor Injun's obituary."

"All right. Well, good night then."

When he let go of the bar, the hot, food-sticky, humid air of the joint hit him. He was going to be sick if he didn't get out of here. He started for the glass double doors.

Cronin said: "Say, funny thing. Injun come in this morning when he started up town—he thought he might get a job on a barge, y' know—an' he says he wants me to have a pitcher of him and me was took once. Maybe he knew, or—"

"Fella on a tanker I was on onct comes into the galley and hands me a five spot. 'Take the fin an' keep it for me,' he says. Then he goes for'ard on lookout, slips on a spot of grease and goes off the turtle-deck. We never did find him," Slops said.

"What you talkin' 'bout?" Going to lose my dinner, all right, all *right*, all—

"Ya might 's well take this pitcher, Mister. Mebbe you can put it in the obituary."

Joe Morton shoved something into his pocket, and made it outside. It had stopped snowing. But there was plenty of snow, slick and hard, on the pavement, packed down by heavy feet getting out of the night and into the joint, and he slipped halfway across the pavement. He caught hold of a parcel-post box, steadied himself, took deep breaths of the cold air coming up the harbor.

Pass Through Manhattan

He began to cough, and then was violently sick into the gutter. His hands slipped off the mail box, scraped in the snow.

An arm came from no place to catch him around the waist. straightened him up, and he was walked around the corner. It was darker there, the lights didn't hurt his eyes. "Wanta go to sleep."

A hard, somewhat drunken voice said: "Now let's see your card. Orders is no reporters kin talk to sailors without a Guild card."

"What card? I haven't got no—got any card. Whatta I need a card for?"

Something hit him on the jaw. He stumbled back into the snow.

The sailor off the *Lucy Zweig* bent over quickly, started fumbling in Joe Morton's pockets. He found three dollar bills and some change. He held these in his hand a minute, considering. Then he looked further. In Joe Morton's upper left-hand vest pocket he found a Newspaper Guild membership card, with the neat little stamps indicating that he was paid up through March.

Larry carefully put the card, the bills and the change back in Joe's pockets. Then, slipping and sliding on the snow—because he was drunk, too—he guided Joe Morton up South Street. He helped him through a doorway between two ship's uniform stores and up a flight of stairs. At the top of the flight there were a light and a desk.

The man at the desk said: "Hello, Larry. Who's your friend?"

"Union man," said Larry. "My guest."

"Yeah? That'll be a buck for the two of you."

Larry reached into the pocket of his blue reefer, extracted a fifty-cent piece. He rested Joe Morton on the desk, and

91

fumbled around. In the pockets of his pants he found a quarter, a dime, and seven pennies. "Trust me for eight cents?" he asked, after adding things up in his head for a while.

The desk man said: "No."

Larry thought a long while. Then he borrowed a pencil from the desk man, wrote: "I had too boro 8¢" on a slip of paper. He put this in Joe's vest pocket, along with two pennies, and extracted a dime.

He and the desk man half dragged, half carried Joe to a two-cot cubicle, and put him on the bed. The desk man went away, and Larry took off Joe's shoes, covered the news-paperman with the blankets off both cots, and lay down on the other cot, turning his reefer collar up around his ears, pulling his knees up to his chest.

*   *   *

JACK FIRSTIN LOOKED OUT THE WINDOW of his office. Still snowing. He shrugged. Inside here, it was warm enough, it was all right. He ought to eat, though. Eight o'clock. He hadn't had a bite since breakfast.

He counted the money in his pocket. Two dollars and a quarter. There was an Automat down the block where he could get plenty of food for thirty-five cents. Yes, he ought to eat, keep his strength up.

He laughed. That was a good one, keep his strength up. Forty-five years old, and like a bull, that's what he was, like a bull.

Plenty of time to eat in the fall, when the new house began to rent.

He hunched his big shoulders over the desk, pulled the papers near him. Now, the contractor figured he could put in a restaurant and kitchen for eight thousand dollars.

Pass Through Manhattan

Or, in the same space, you could get two doctors or dentists all equipped with water connections and everything. That would only cost three grand.

Interest on the five-thousand difference was not so much. But he hated to lose it, the rent from those doctors. Good payers, 96th Street doctors were. Young ones, with their wives' families paying the rent so they could say: "I was over by my son-in-law the doctor's yesterday," or old ones with a steady practice of nice fat mammas from the Steam-heated Ghetto over on West End.

And a restaurant, nothing but grief comes from a restaurant. If you stick the concessionaire enough rent to pay the interest even, he goes broke and you have to go get you another sucker. If you don't, you get some cheap slob in that doesn't keep his kitchen clean, and upstairs comes complaints about bugs.

But without a restaurant, you could not hold furniture and clothes for the rent. You could not get it an apartment-hotel license, but it had to be a straight apartment house. "So I'm going to move out, so sue me."

With an apartment hotel comes sure rent to put up at the bank for a loan. But comes also bugs. With an apartment house comes no bugs, only what the tenants bring, but comes lawsuits, and the bank holding up the loan on the next house. . . .

His mind went flying away with that phrase. The next house. Maybe 57th Street this time. Or maybe back downtown, not another Greenwich Square yet, but a big place and pictures in the real estate section.

They had thought they had him pushed back with the *nebs*, the poor guys who ate in Automats and rode in buses. Like that busful today.

Pass Through Manhattan

That was a close one. But what the hell. Just when they rescued him he had figured it out. He had a way for getting out of there. He could get out of anything.

You couldn't kill Jack Firstin. Say Greenwich Square, and all those other beautiful 1930 properties, say they had taken them away from him. Say the bond house had had to close its doors.

Say even Rena had put him in jail for alimony.

So what? He was coming back, wasn't he? Three cheap houses on West End he had remodeled for doctors. One taxpayer he had built. Now a twelve-story job on 96th.

And next something with class, something for which he would hire the best architect money could buy. Modern. Lots of glass and steel. Nothing fancy, no gingerbread on this one. Gingerbread was out.

It was worth everything he had been through. It was worth two years in jail, even, for one year of living at the Ritz or in the penthouse on a real good Firstin job.

The best or nothing for Jack Firstin. And he'd had the nothing. Now—

He took his belt up a couple of notches and went back to his problem. Lawsuits or cockroaches, cockroaches or lawsuits.

Better three years with a blonde and two years in alimony jail, than five years with fat Rena.

He wondered what had happened to his second wife, the blonde Molly.

Cockroaches. Lawsuits. An exterminator fifty, a hundred, a month, and you had to have a lawyer anyway. But by the doctors' rent, by the restaurant grief—

Cooking smells in the lobby or yells in the court.

*   *   *

Pass Through Manhattan

THE SNOW MUST HAVE STOPPED FALLING early in the night, for it was already black out in Brooklyn when Ray walked to the subway at a little after six. Must have stopped falling around two.

Before he started his work, looking through the morning papers on the subway, Ray gave a thought to that lonesome hour or two. That grim hour when the world stands still for a fraction of a second, when your resistance is lowest, when people die in hospitals and release the waiting reporters outside, when single, lonely men bemoan their womanless state, and drunkards drive themselves into the final frenzy before the pass-out.

If he told the Chief to go to hell, he would, with ease, get a job on the *Trib* or the *Times*. For various reasons he had poor prospects of getting on the *World-Telegram* or the *Sun*. Go back to being a morning newspaperman. Which would mean working through that two-o'clock hour. Exposing himself to the drag of night work.

The only difference between him and Ron or Joe or Brawley Smith was that he knew how to protect himself in the clinches. He would not tell the Chief to go to hell.

He opened the *Times*, and began scanning it for items to rewrite. It was cold in the subway.

Later he leaned back in his chair, the rewriting handed out, the paper running, and looked over his city room. Two out of three of his lame ducks and drunkards on deck. Ron and Brawley Smith. Brawley, as usual, going out to the can every few minutes to take little, furtive nips, until he had consumed the requisite amount of liquor to start his day. Ron Levine, the teetotaler, the hypochondriac, typing away, his elaborate screening system up to protect the back of his neck from drafts, his various bottles ranged in front of him.

Pass Through Manhattan

Only Joe Morton missing. Ray sighed, and pushed his swivel chair away from his desk by expanding his paunch. He stood up, and walked over to Ron's desk. "How about Joe, Ron? Know where he is?"

"On a bat," Levine said promptly. "He cuffed me for a five spot last night."

"Oh, Lord. The Chief's on the warpath again. Why did you give it to him?"

"You know arguments always upset my gastric system," Ron said. "And Joe can get so very nasty when he has been drinking and wants money."

"Oh, nuts. Well—" Ray walked back to his desk, stopping to peer over the shoulder of a cub. "A man can't divorce anyone but his wife," he said automatically. "Just give her name and let the reader guess the relationship." It was a toss-up which were the most trouble to him, the ones who wouldn't work because they were too old or the ones who couldn't because they were too young.

The steam pipes along the wall were beginning to bang, the place was warming up. He took off his coat, and sat down at his desk. The Chief came in, saluting one and all with decent jollity, and went into his private office. The noise of an electric razor from there added itself to the growing clamor of the news room.

At eight o'clock the Chief had finished shaving, had sent out for his breakfast. Ray picked up the phone, dialed Joe Morton's number. But it was Don who answered. Ray said: "Don, this is serious. If you have to get a masseur in to rub your old man down, make him come in today. He doesn't have to work if he feels grouchy. Just show his face. The Chief's sore."

"I'll see if I can wake him, Ray."

Ray thumbed through a bunch of flimsy on his desk,

marked a couple of items: "More." The copy-desk chief, on his way to the water cooler, said: "Everything ready for the suburban except Page One, Ray." Ray nodded, jumped as the kid's voice in his ear said: "He isn't in his bed, Ray."

"Oh, Lord. Well—"

"But Ray, he never did that before. I've heard him brag, he's always made it home, no matter—"

"So've I. I'll call you back, Don. Don't worry." He hung up the phone, frowned, automatically initialed some stuff his assistant shoved across to him. Ron Levine, idle for the moment, was reading a novel. Ray yelled for him.

"Ron—Christ—Joe didn't get home last night."

Levine's white eyebrows mounted. "Ah. He never—"

"I know. Got any idea where he could have gone?"

"He was talking wild about what a wonderful boy Donald was. How he hadn't done right by Donald. But—" the white eyebrows contracted, the whining voice became official, the voice of a professional reporter reporting. "He bragged about the power of the press, saying that a good newspaperman could make black look white, and this was one time he was going to use his—er—self-deprecated abilities to make white look white. He said that this would also make a good feature story. 'I'm going in heavy for the Angel of Mercy,' he said. Does that make any sense to you, Ray?"

"Yeah, plenty. Thanks, Ron. And look, pass the word to Brawley. Whenever the Chief's in the room, look busy. He wants to make the place into a complete kindergarten."

"When I work, I work hard. In between—"

"Just try and make the in betweens when the Chief is in his office. It was about six-thirty when you saw Joe?"

"Nearer six-fifteen. But if the Chief does not think me an asset to—"

"Well, you know how it is, part owner and M.E., at the

same time. Thanks, Ron." You practically had to beg these guys to keep their own jobs.

He stared at the papers on his desk. Wire played up Hitler. Too damn much Hitler. His own department had a gas suicide for its best story. Financial wasn't even open yet, and Sports—

He sent a Joe Louis story over to the copy desk for a banner. City Editor, nuts. He was the managing editor and publisher, too, while the Chief shaved or ate, and also while the Chief took visiting aviatrixes—or aviatrices—out to lunch. The Chief had had a plumbing contractor in last week to see about putting a shower in his private lavatory.

He called over Mills, the most promising of the cubs. "Son, you said you wanted first crack at that job of doing the news on the op ed page?"

"Yes, sir. I reviewed books for the *Daily Princetonian,* and I've acted in several little theaters. I feel I'm particularly well adapted—"

"Don't want to be a reporter, huh? Want to be a reviewer, a critic. Don't like it in my department?"

"Not at all, sir, but—"

"O.K., O.K. Well, I don't pass anybody on till I know he's learned his business. I want to make sure you're a good reporter, a good city news man before I give you over to the white-tie department."

"Yes?"

"Here's an assignment for you. If you make good on it, the job's yours."

"I—"

"Find Joe Morton. He went off on a bat last night. You've got several leads. Your hottest one is the nurse who was in that bus accident yesterday."

"A hospital nurse?"

Pass Through Manhattan

"Listen, son. I said the bus accident. If you can't find a copy of yesterday's paper, how are you going to find Joe?" Ray reached in the big drawer of his desk for the old bottle, took the first aspirin of the day. "He was working on that story when he went off. He might have followed any angle of it. Or he might have started drinking at the corner here, said to hell with it."

The boy smiled.

Ray said irritably: "You're lucky if he did start drinking, because a newspaperman like Joe would think up so many angles on a story you'd be all week trying to find him if he was working. O.K. Get going. Need expense money?"

"No, sir. And thanks for—"

"Don't thank me. If you find Joe, you get the job you wanted. And don't let your uncle know Joe's been drinking." Ray whipped a finger at the Chief's office.

"O.K. And thank you, sir."

"Don't call me sir," Ray said. He watched the boy go across the office, then reached for the phone, dialed. "Don? Your father's O.K., just phoned in. He's got a hot tip on a political story, he's following it up." He hung up the phone as a waiter came out of the Chief's office with the wrecked tray.

Ray stopped the waiter with a thumb-wave, looked over the tray. There was a cup of lukewarm coffee left in the silverplated pot. He poured this into a glass on his desk, and smeared butter on an untouched roll, waved the waiter on. If that kid thinks he's started his father off on a bat, it'll be hard on him. And how the hell can you tell a boy his old man's just a plain lush, using any excuse to get cockeyed? How can you tell him that?

*　　　*　　　*

Pass Through Manhattan

PEGGY REILLY AND LUCY FARLEY were running a water test in the lab. They had completed chemical, were on bacteriological. Big Lucy squirmed over the microscope. "I don't see any sense in this, who's ever going to ask a nurse about drinking water?"

"Maybe in a small town," Peggy said dreamily. "Mary Nafziger said to watch it. She said they sneaked germs or chemicals into the water that you'd never expect to catch you."

"Well, if there's any typhoid b. in this, I'm crazy," Lucy said, writing negative on the blank. "You make the dysentery test, Peggy, my arms go to sleep using this silly little instrument. The only water I'm ever going to have anything to do with will be either frozen or lukewarm, anyway."

"What do you mean?" Peggy asked. She took her place on the stool, careful not to wrap her feet around the rungs and spoil the shine. Next week white shoes. No more ugly black shoes, blue dresses. All in white. All—

"I'm taking a job with the State," Lucy said. "I've passed the civil service, all but getting my pin here."

Peggy looked up from the microscope, her mouth open. "You mean—psych?"

"That's right. I take two weeks off and then I report to Matteawan. Hit 'em with an icebag, and pop 'em into a lukewarm bath, that's all I know."

"Oh, Lucy. I couldn't—they say you go—crazy yourself if you work in one of those places long enough."

"Ha," Lucy said. "But if you don't, if you get the extra certificate, you get double pay the rest of your life. And I'm a natural for it. I'm stronger than a lot of male nurses. What are you going to do, Peggy?"

"Nurse. Just nurse. I like clinical work, but if I can't get it, maybe I can get in the wards, or on private duty."

Pass Through Manhattan

"You're a honey for private duty, you've got that lady-like manner. Me, I'm just a workhorse. That's why I took up nursing. The boys at home used to bet each other they didn't dare kiss me. On account of I knocked a boy's tooth out once. And who'd want me in an office?"

"You're not so fat, Lu."

"I'm not fat at all," the big girl complained. "You can reduce fat, but this is all muscle. My old man ran a saloon and did his own bouncing, and my ma has twelve children. I was the twelfth, and she still did all her own washing and ironing and wouldn't use store bread. Baked it all herself. . . . Your folks had money, didn't they, Peggy?"

Peggy dropped a single drop of phenolphthalein on the slide, put the cover over it. "He was a doctor." Maybe it was the other girl's confidence, maybe it was the sword that hung over her. But suddenly she wanted to tell all about it. She'd never told anyone. Not about the last, the shameful part, but not even about when it was all bright and shining, her father waking her up at two, three in the morning to sit in the kitchen with him and drink milk, while he sipped slowly on a bottle of beer from the icebox and chewed cornbread sandwiches. "Don't tell the neighbors, Peggy, that I get you up at this hour. They'd think it scandalous, something immoral about the early morning. . . . I've had an idea, if they don't let me publish about things down here in the papers, I'm going to the A.M.A. convention and read it as a study, call it: Effects of Malnutrition on Communicable Diseases. That'll fix 'em."

"Let me make you another sandwich, Dad. I'll bet you didn't eat any dinner."

"Did so, boiled three eggs in the sterilizer and . . . People aren't like that. People aren't mean, murderers and child-torturers, Peg. They just don't think, won't think." Tugging at his wispy goatee while she slowly uncoiled her feet from under her nightgown, put them on the floor, holding her breath because of the shock when they touched the linoleum after being all warm from being sat on. "Man thinks he has to keep dirty, disease-breeding slums in order to make money, put it away for his children so they won't have to go live in dirty, disease-breeding slums. While, if he stopped to think, if there weren't any slums, he wouldn't have to worry. Eh? . . . Bring me the mustard, Peg o' My Heart."

And then, always: "But I know, I know, Peggy. Doctors know. Seen hundreds of men, women die, and they're all right. Nobody ever died mean, Peggy. There aren't any villains. People mean all right. You be a doctor, Peg, or a nurse, keep your faith in humanity. People are sick, they're all right. . . . If I was sure you were going to be in the medical profession, I'd rest easy in Purgatory."

"Dad, you're not—"

"Father McLarnine he does be sayin' so. Because I never get time to go to Mass. . . . No, I'm teasing you, Peggy. You're a good Irish girl, and I'll not worry about your faith in God, but no one but a doctor has any faith in Man. You—I've got to make them see it, uptown, Peggy. That they have to, must, tear these shacks down, put up a decent hospital down here, stop treating human beings like they were cattle. Just because they don't see 'em, won't look. . . . D'ya think I'd be wicked if I drank a second bottle of beer?"

"No, Dad, but drink it quickly, you don't get half enough sleep." Cold feet again, the heavy grained door of the ice-box swinging wide, her fingers chilly from handling, dishing up and uncapping the bottle of beer. Then back to her chair, blanket over her shoulders, fingers tucked in her armpits, feet under her.

Pass Through Manhattan

How old? Nine or ten at first, after Mother died. Fifteen when Dad died, hiring out as a mother's helper, room and board and work had all the time you're not in school, people mean to you, getting more work out of you than they would pay for, a year of college, and the other girls sniffing about clothes. Trying to make money hard, selling things, aluminum door to door, silk stockings, fitting corsets, hating the hard-eyed women who tried to cheat you and abuse you.

And then the night she was asleep in the cheap hotel in Ohio, worn out, and she had dreamed about sitting on the kitchen chair again. "So busy getting money they don't stop to think. . . . Rest easy in Purgatory."

She didn't know, wasn't sure she believed in Purgatory, in the Church, the way she ought to, though she went to Father Cardovic regularly for confession, and Mass every Sunday. But she was sure she had had the best father, the wisest man in the world for a father, and he had told her to be a nurse.

And it had come to her twice, when that horrid old man died in Cincinnati, the one none of the nurses would wait on because he was so crabby. But when he died, and the child with the red hair that died, too—so senselessly, it seemed—she had seen that plan of life, that inner goodness of people that her father had told her was there, and she knew, now, that he had been right. Without the faith in Man, that Dad had always talked about, sipping his beer, you were only half alive, and she knew no way of reaching it except by nursing.

"Mark dysentery plus," she told Lucy. "Amoebic dysentery. See, here's the reaction in the manual, and look in the microscope, the color."

Pass Through Manhattan

"I hate to look in microscopes," Lucy said. "I always have to close one eye, and you shouldn't do that."

Peggy laughed, pulling the slide out, taking the cover off it, and—a hand tapped her shoulder. "They want you in the superintendent's office, Miss Reilly."

*   *   *

MRS. LEMPE PLACED THE CLOVERLEAF ROLLS, one by one, in the box, resting them carefully on the waxed paper, careful not to spoil their smooth, floury finish. She closed the box, tied a string around it carefully, placed it on the top of the glass showcase just out of easy reach of the customer's hand. "And now?"

"I think that will be all."

"Eclairs is very good today. Just finished."

"Well—" the lady was fat, with the small mouth of a greedy eater. "They are nice looking. How much?"

"Forty cents the dozen. T'ree for a dime."

"I'll take six."

"Yes, madam." Another, smaller, box. Waxed paper, eclairs, one by one, each in its little frilled paper next. Another piece of waxpaper, tucked under so it would not touch, as they used to tuck Georg's sheets after the army doctors took his legs off, before he died, the last of Marie Vogel's brothers. "So, madam. And from the oven a nice loaf of homemade bread."

"Oh, dear. I—No, not today. Mrs. Lempe, I do declare, you're trying to ruin my figure."

Marie Lempe laughed politely and accepted thirty-five cents for the cash register. She continued smiling as the customer went outside, letting a blast of cold air into the hot little shop, smiled on as the woman passed between the window lettered HOME BAKERY and the WPA crew chopping up packed snow from the 96th Street pavement and loading it into a truck marked D of S.

Forty-five cents for three people's bread, the woman, her husband, their maid. A maid, and she had to go buy rolls outside. Ach, what a wonderful country. When Grace was married, she would have a maid just to cook the meat and vegetables and clean the house and make the bed, and she would buy her bread ready-baked. A real American wife, bridge all afternoon, never turn a hand except to stay pretty.

And Washington would have an office downtown, such as she had seen in the movies, all shiny desk and deep carpets, and pretty girls to whom he would say: "Take a letter, Miss McManus. To Mr. Morgan, Dear Pierpont."

Why not? Look out there, the WPA. Paid more than in Germany—even in the good old days—the government paid a German to go and get shot, killed, in France. And to do what, was the WPA paid? Why, to make things nice for other poor people, to make playgrounds in the park or clear the snow away.

It was worth it. Artur was a good husband, he was all right. Not like some of the Yorkville Germans, they thought they were in the old country, children must quit school as soon as possible and make money, wives must work. If she worked in the bakery, it was because she wanted to. Every week she put away a little for college for Washington.

He could not forget Germany, though, that Artur. He had left because a man could not make money, not, like her, because he wanted his children to be free, free from military service, free from people who said "peasants," and spat. If he could make money there, Artur would go back to Germany, especially now, when Herr Hitler made everybody feel it was noble and glorious to be German.

But not she. She would not go back to Germany, not if Grace could marry a Hohenzollern, or a Wittelsbach.

In Germany was everything worked out. You were a peasant in peacetime, so in war you were a private or maybe a sergeant. You were a Jew, so in good times you kept a store, in bad times you were a pig, and in wartimes maybe you could be a second lieutenant. You were of the nobility, so always you were boss.

But in America your mama worked in a bakery, and you could be a bank president. And you would not have to be ashamed of your mama, oh, no, you would have her picture with yours in the *Daily News* or the *Journal*, Banker Buys Mother Ermine Coat, Woman Who worked by bakery to give G. Washington Lempe a Columbia Education is rewarded by grateful son.

A man opened the door of the bakery, letting in another blast of icy air. It caught her down in the stomach there, like always. She would go to Mount Sinai, like that nice young American nurse said, and tell Artur she had been by Fifth Avenue. It did no harm to lie a little, the poor man, his head was full from such nonsense, she would humor him. And he was good to the children.

"Yes, sir?"

"Are you Mrs. Lempe, Mrs. Artur Lempe?"

"Yes, sir."

"My name is Brefogel, Mrs. Lempe." He laid a card on the counter.

Her first thought was about the children, maybe one of them had been bad in school. But she looked at the card, and it said Vanderbilt and Brefogel, Attorneys at Law.

"You shouldn't be working, Mrs. Lempe," Mr. Brefogel

said in a deep, sympathetic tone. "After your terrible experience Saturday. You had better go home."

"But, I feel all right, my job—"

"Your husband, Artur, is a very good friend of mine," Mr. Brefogel said, in German. "He asked me to come get you and take you home, he is worried about you."

"Well—"

But Mr. Brefogel was already pushing past her to the back of the shop, seeing the boss, explaining things.

Robert Seasongood Seligmann lifted his dark, almost ugly face from the papers on his desk. In his beautifully inflected New York accent he said: "Oh, yes, Tenbruye. I wanted to see you. Sit down."

John Tenbruye sat down in the chair opposite the boss's desk. He would not say "sir." This was the first time Mr. Seligmann had ever called him in, but Seligmann was no older than he, and it would not do to say "sir."

"More or less of a personal matter, Tenbruye," Robert Seligmann said. "I saw about that accident you were in. Nothing serious, I hope."

"No, I went on to the Squadron riding afterwards."

"You're a member of the Squadron, eh? An uncle of mine, Solomon Lehman, is one of the colonels or board of governors or something. I've never been much interested in military matters, though our little boy is in the Knickerbocker Grays. . . . Frankly," said the boss, smiling, "I'm afraid of horses. Still— But that isn't what I called you in for. I didn't know you knew Eleanor Castron."

John Tenbruye smiled.

"Did you know we—the Seasongood Trust, that is—had an equity in that old house she and her mother live in, on Orange Street?"

Pass Through Manhattan

"No."

"Yes, we do. My mother went to boarding school down at Morristown with Eleanor's mother, she was a Miss Cortlandt. When Castron—well, anyway, we picked up the second mortgage on the land. Rather complicated, since the first mortgage is in arrears."

John Tenbruye leaned forward. There was some sort of under-current to this.

"My mother read about the accident, was interested to see that you worked for us, that sort of thing. She occasionally reproaches Anne and me for not keeping in closer touch with Eleanor, but living in Westchester as we do . . ." Mr. Seligmann turned the papers on his desk over with his long, brown fingers. "You were in real estate before you came to us, that right?"

"Yes, sir." Oh, damn it.

"Well, if you could, through your old connections, do anything about that Orange Street property, I would appreciate it personally. And it would be of some value to the firm; the more we can liquidate for the Seasongood Trust, the more we have to invest for them."

"I see."

"That's all, Tenbruye."

John Tenbruye stopped outside Mr. Seligmann's office to wipe his face with a clean linen handkerchief. But the boss's secretary was looking at him strangely. He went out into the hall, and down it to the washroom. He soaked his face carefully, dried it on a paper towel, and leaned against one of the washbasins, smoking.

That was clear enough. Robert Seasongood Seligmann had spoken. Secure from his position—three hundred years in Wall Street on both sides of the family, a membership in the Spanish Synagogue, an estate on the Hudson which had been granted by Holland to old Levi Spinoza, and a wife whose family had contributed ambassadors and governors to both political parties—secure in all that, Mr. Seligmann had indicated that Eleanor Castron's husband would go farther in the firm than just an unpedigreed Tenbruye, one of the "wrong" Tenbruyes.

How happy this would have made him Saturday. But now.

Good God, the girl was unbalanced. She was—Inbreeding, that was it. There was a streak of insanity in all those old families. Look at the Social Register, how many women's maiden names were the same as their married ones. Incredible. Like Kentucky hillbillies, marrying their own cousins and—

Hot, blinding shame came flooding through John Tenbruye's head as he remembered that scene in his apartment Saturday. Took off all her— A more unprincipled man, a cad would have—

But he had kept his head. When she fainted on the floor without any— He had thrown her camel's hair coat over her, carried her into the bedroom, made her drink coffee until she was well enough to be taken home.

And thank God for that now, because he would have no trouble facing her mother, when he went over this evening to ask permission to pay his respects. His conscience was clear.

Yes, he had acted like a gentleman.

His secretary didn't announce the guy, but she followed him in, saying: "Mr. Firstin, I couldn't—"

The guy shoved her back through the door, and closed it. He said: "Hello, Jake."

Jack Firstin tried to place him. He'd seen the face before.

A cop, but what kind? One of the city cops who had taken him in on Rena's suit, or a State cop from the attorney general, or a G-man?

Bluff it out. "All our contracts are let out. You want to make it an application, you'll have to wait until we start our next building."

"Don't you remember me, Jake?" the guy laughed, pushing his hat back on his head. He leaned over, slapped the big canvas-backed book on Jack's desk. "Remember, I served the subpoena duces tecum on you to bring that along when the bond company failed." He took Jack's hands off the edge of the book, flipped it open. "Yeah, this is the one." He riffled through page after page of newspaper clippings, neatly pasted in, each one with a little label showing what paper it had come from. The cop flipped past grimy clippings of the first 96th Street building through all that public relations stuff on Greenwich Square and the Westervelt Hotel—stuff that had cost Jack Firstin more money in public relations counselor's fees than if he'd just bought advertising space—on through all about the bankruptcy of Firstin Management and Jack Firstin, Inc., the failure of the bond company, the alimony suit and the jail sentence—

"Golly, Jake, you figger publicity is publicity. If my old woman had me clapped in the hoosegow, I wouldn't put the pictures away wit' my soovenirs. Hey?"

The big hand had stopped, was looking at the tiny clipping from the Building Permits Granted Column. "First & Tenth Corp., huh? We should'a known that was you."

"You got it a warrant?"

"Me? Naw! This is a friendly call, Jake. Yeah, and here's all the stuff on that bus accident. That's what got us started. M' wife woke me up yest'day mornin', an' said me pitcher was in the *News*. They used the old one of you'n me—oh, yeah, you had it pasted up."

"I am a very busy man," Jack Firstin said. "What is it the attorney general wanted? This building is strictly on the level, every loan will be—"

"Aw, we already looked up the 96th Street Building. It's O.K. We just wanted you to know, Jake, you ain't got a chance to make a public offering of stocks or bonds in this State."

"Who said I was going to?"

"A little birdy. You got the signs, Jake, you won't stay on 96th Street."

"There are other States."

"There's an SEC, too. We told Washington."

"This is persecution. I could go down to Dewey and—"

"Dewey'd throw you out on your ear. Naw, get it, Jake. You put up your twelve-story jobs, and you're O.K. There's a shortage of good apartments, anyway. Maybe my wife and I'll move into your new one, we been living over on the river, on 99th, but that steep hill's pretty bad weather like this."

"I build good houses, no complaints from the tenants."

"Yeah, I'll say that for you. A cousin of mine's living in Greenwich Square right now. You never do gyp on the specifications, good sound houses. Why is that, Jake? Lotsa them builders useta bribe the inspectors and put up junk."

"That would be dishonest," Jack Firstin said. When the big man laughed, Jack jumped up from behind his desk. His froggy face was purple with wrath. "Gerouta here. You ain't got it a warrant, gerouta-here, you big, you big—"

Pass Through Manhattan

"O.K., Jake," the big man said and tilted his derby forward. The door slammed behind him.

Jack Firstin stood trembling a minute, then grabbed for the phone. "Get my lawyers," he screamed at the girl on the other side of the desk. Then he took a deep breath, the purple tide ebbed in his cheeks. "No, never mind." He had known all along that when the time came for the move downtown, he would have to be careful, hire a front.

His eyes filled with the tears of self-pity because the steel and glass hotel on Mr. Hearst's land down on 57th would never have Jack Firstin's name on the cornerstone. He was going to have a cornerstone made out of this new translucent glass block, too.

*   *   *

I'VE GOT TO GET OUT OF HERE. Pull out of this town before the weekend, or I'll go nuts. I just wasn't cut out to be a city boy, that's all there is to it. If I have to go down to Standard Oil and sign one of their three-year tropical contracts, I'm going to get out of here before I cut my—

Walk to the window, walk back. Turn the steam-heat valve one way, turn it the other. Lived in two dozen New York flats in my life, and I don't remember one where you could turn the steam heat off after the radiators got warm.

Try reading a book, try listening to the radio. Play *Washboard Blues* on the phonograph, *gotta get me gone from here, wash them dirty clothes all year* . . .

Turn the damn thing off. Go look at the window. Remember the clean snow, falling down on the park, white as cotton. Cotton eyebrows on Copper's brown face. She's not white now. Black and sticky. Look at that patch on the window sill, with the round depression in it where we kept the milk bottle. Black chunks of coal.

Pass Through Manhattan

Isn't that finance and industry for you? Good men and true spend their lives getting coal out of the ground, and Manhattan takes it, chews it up and spits it out in the air to make itself dirty. Oh, a little heat is absorbed in passing, but those little hunks of coal on my window sill are just as combustible as the finest anthracite in Pennsylvania.

Burns COAL Burns. But only a little of it. Most of it this city chews on and then spits straight up in the air to fall down on itself. It's an ill bird that—

Get my textbooks out and read up on coal mining. If I'm quitting Armstrong and Grainger, there's no knowing what kind of job I'll have next. Oil, coal, bauxite, iron. Copper, silver, molybdenum, lignite, the white silicaceous clays so valuable in pottery, precious stones.

Just give me a hunk of ground and I'll dig something out of it that somebody wants. Like the Southern boys sing on Saturday nights in Fair Play. *I'm a rambling wreck from G'o'gia Tech, and a helluva-nengineer.*

Well, I am the hell of an engineer. I am not, the good Lord knows, conceited about my looks, breeding or general knowledge, but I am a hell of a good mining engineer.

Or am I whistling to keep my pecker up? Trying to forget that I killed a man, a man named Ringgold, alias Copper. A bum off a ship and out of work. A man, in a town where men are far between and few in the slucies. *Give me my pick and shovel, let me dig, let me dig, let me dig.*

That's not right. I—

Armstrong and Grainger are tying the can to me. Shot off my mouth Saturday night to Mr. Makin, and now it's the blue slip for little Donald.

I won't starve. That is, in a way, the hell of it. I won't starve. Ray'll give me a job on a newspaper, or, without much trouble, Standard would let me tend a tank on Aruba or some place.

But without a mine, I'm no more good than a cowboy without a horse, a sailor without a ship. A sailor without a ship is a bum, a bum shoveling snow off a bunch of dudes caught in a bus. Shoveling snow for a chance to pass the hat.

No, Copper had said he didn't care whether he got paid or not. He was down in that snow because he had to be. Couldn't leave those people down there.

Just got sneakers on mah feet, workin' in the snow and sleet—

Cut it out, Don, stop it.

Don Morton brought himself to his feet, his clenched hand beating on the window sill, grinding little particles of coal dust into the side of his palm. He took off his coat, necktie and shirt and went into the bathroom, where he carefully washed his face and hands, dried them with minute care, and redressed. He got his overcoat and hat out of the closet and brushed them, started to put them on. He would go down to the Engineers' Club and start an argument with somebody about something. Something nice and technical, that would involve the bringing out of slide rules and pencils.

The phone rang when he had his hand on the front door. "Don Morton speaking."

Soprano: "Just a moment, Mr. Morton, Mr. Makin calling."

Then, tenor: "Hello, Morton. You know that proposition we were discussing Saturday?"

"Sure."

"Well, I think we have worked out your difficulties.

Pass Through Manhattan

Could you meet Mr. Grainger and me at the Lookout Club at—say—quarter of six?"

"Of course. I'm on salary, my time is yours."

"Oh, now, don't take that attitude, Morton. I'm really your friend, you'll be delighted at what I have to tell you."

"That's on Broadway, isn't it?"

"Yes. The penthouse over the Silver Building."

"Quarter of six."

Don hung the phone carefully back in its prongs. He stripped off the overcoat and hat and laid them on the chair near the door, went to lie down, flat on his back on the couch. A damn funny piece of business.

He had thought he was through, and now—

That "talk" with Makin at the Tsigany had seemed final enough. He tried to recall the exact phraseology, the terms, the—the nugget in the middle of all that waste of words, but all he could remember was Cowboy Connors' drunken moon face and the lashing whine of the gypsy violins.

It was queer that Makin would go on with it. If he remembered anything accurately—and he had not been drinking, of course—it was that he had refused to compromise his professional honor by testifying that the All's Fair ought to be kept open as a future source of iridium, which should close the deal, because that was all Armstrong and Grainger wanted out of him. Without his testimony, the mine would close, and he would be out of a job.

He might be a hell of an engineer, but he wasn't so good that A & G would put him on another mine after he had refused to favor them with a small bit of perjury.

He sat firmly down before his desk. He had helped his father and his father's friends work his way through college by corresponding for whatever paper Ray was on at the moment. Football games and dances mostly, but a good deal of interviewing professors.

He took a pencil and paper. A good reporter can recall the salient points of an interview at any time. He—

He began writing down what he had said, what Makin had said. One speech recalled another, by closing his eyes and concentrating on Cowboy Connors' face a whole chunk of stuff fell into the puzzle.

By humming the theme of the gypsy song another hunk came in, but it was Herb Lewis's silly poem about the horses being watered that— There had been nothing said, directly, but a lot of hints. About how smart Dad was, about—

Looked at one way, Don's whole attitude was of a man who wanted a better job, an office job, an executive job before he would give testimony not directly important to digging.

How to get ahead in the world.

Don laughed, tearing up the notes he had made. Well, it could be easily straightened. He wanted neither a desk job nor to commit perjury. But maybe he could talk them into giving him a mine some other place.

Quarter of six. It was now one. The best thing to do was to go downtown and see a few other people first, have an ace, or possibly a pair of aces, in the hole. Stone & Webster, Calumet, the Soviet people, the Guggenheim interests. Someone he knew, classmate or someone he'd worked with, at each one who would introduce him to the boss. He ought to—

But that was a bad thing for an engineer to do. He was still under contract to A & G, and officially not open to accept another job. And these damn money people all stuck together so, it would be almost certain to get around Wall Street and—

And maybe he had an overrated idea of his own importance.

But he would go nuts trying to stall till quarter of six. Four and three quarters hours.

He could go to a movie, but he didn't like movies, especially in the afternoon. If he knew a girl he could go call on her, maybe she'd think of something to do.

The trouble was, he hadn't bothered to scrape up new or old acquaintances this winter, he'd been busy taking courses and seeing his father.

While there were girls he had known in college and before, he couldn't, after all this time, ask them to kill an afternoon with him. You had to open up by taking them to a show or to dinner.

There was— He had an idea. He would walk down to Wall Street. Even if it was city air, a walk in it would be better than clogging himself up with this predigested steam heat.

Wonder how far it is? Twenty blocks to a mile. 96th to zero, four and four-fifths miles. Then below zero to the tip of the island—

He dug out his compasses and a classified telephone book with a map of the city in it. Mile and a half below zero, approximately. One point five plus four point eight equals six point three.

On a good trail a man could do four miles an hour. But snow and traffic, and looking in shop windows, plus the fact that he would have to wear a long-tailed overcoat, should slow him down to three miles. Two hours and six minutes.

That left him two hours and a half. But—wait a minute.

Pass Through Manhattan

Broadway, which he would follow, went across the Island diagonally. Therefore, a block on Broadway, unlike a block on Amsterdam or on a numbered avenue, did not equal, exactly, one twentieth of a mile. It was, instead, the hypotenuse of a right-angled triangle, the longest other side of which was one-twentieth of a mile. To determine the length of the hypotenuse, then, it was necessary to know either the angle which Broadway took at that point, or the distance from Broadway to the nearest vertical avenue . . .

*   *   *

HARLAN MCCRACKEN, EDITOR OF *Nightstick Stories* and seven other pulp magazines, picked up a Ms. off his desk. He read:

LUCKY BUMP

By W. Gordon Maxwell

First-class Detective York Mason crouched in a doorway. His black face shone with tenseness. Only an hour ago his number-one stool pigeon, Sniffer Sneigh, had come and said: "The Vermillion Gang are hiding in an old warehouse on Fourth Street."

So Detective Mason was here to get them. There were seven bullets in his army issue, 1917 Colt's Automatic Pistol, and he had heard that there were seven members of the Vermillion Gang.

So he could not afford to miss. When the lead started flying, when the slugs began to sing their deadly song over Fourth Street, every chunk of greased lead would have to count, for the Vermillion Gang didn't give a copper time to slip another clip into the old automatic pistol.

Pass Through Manhattan

There. A slim, vertical crack of yellow light—yellow as a mobster's heart, yellow as the name of the Vermillion Gang, yellow as the flash that blooms from a pistol when the slugs start flying—showed in the door of the old warehouse.

Detective Mason's purple palm slid the safety catches—both of them—off the automatic pistol—and his brown fingers tensed on the trigger until white showed at the knuckles.

The vertical yellow crack of light grew, and now it was no longer a crack, but an oblong. Then it was blotted out by the body of Chink Magee, the gangster who led the dope-peddling, child-killing mobsters of the Vermillion Gang.

But Detective Mason held the fire from his gun. He waited, waited, for he did not want to get Chink Magee alone; he wanted to wipe out the whole gang. Those had been the orders from H.Q., from the Big Cop himself.

One by one the seven members of the gang filed into the street. But still the oblong of light glowed. Good grief. An eighth mobster had added himself to the seven.

And a Colt's Automatic holds only seven slugs.

Detective Mason knew that he would have to get all eight. No man who trailed with the Vermillion Gang could be allowed to live.

Now was the time. Now the oblong panel of light was gone, and there were eight blodgy shadows ready for the cop's automatic to mow down.

Those strong brown fingers tensed. The lead flew.

One down. Two, three. Blood pouring into the gutters of Fourth Street like booze into the scuppers of a pirate ship.

But now the Vermillion Gang, three of their number

dead, were taking cover, were answering the fire of Detective Mason with more fire, fierce fire, lead-carrying fire.

Detective Mason felt something hit him below the floating ribs, hit him with the force of a baseball bat. If he hadn't been shot by gangster's bullets so many times before, he would not have known it was a slug that had gotten him; it felt like a blow from a mighty fist. Later the real pain would start.

But no time to think of that. A fourth member of the Vermillion Gang was down, a fifth, a sixth.

Two more, and only one bullet.

A flat-nosed profile showed itself in the gloom. Chink Magee himself. Detective Mason fired. But as the slug, the lead slug, left his automatic, something hit him on the head. He went down. He lay still.

When he came to, he was in a car. Something cold and sticky was running down his side. He did not need a doctor to tell him it was blood, his blood, the blood from the wound he had gotten from the mobsters' slugs back there on Fourth Street.

He had gotten six members of the Vermillion Gang, and the surviving two were taking him for a ride. Not that their gangsters' hearts grieved over their lost comrades. Mobsters were a dime a dozen. But the prestige of the Vermillion Gang, their "face" in Chinatown where they dealt in brain-destroying drugs, called for the death of the dick who had dared to oppose them.

All this Detective York Mason knew.

Chink Magee moved, and something metallic dug into Detective Mason's side. The familiar, friendly contours of a .38 Smith & Wesson revolver. Ah, if he could just turn and get it.

But his body refused to answer the commands of his

brain. The bullet that had creased his head! That slug had robbed him of his automotive powers. That was why Chink Magee was so careless. He knew Detective Mason was paralyzed.

Sweat broke out on the detective's brown face. He would—have—to—pull himself together. But he couldn't! He was paralyzed.

"Step on it, Dipy," Chink Mason growled at the other man. "We ain't got all night."

"With the dick in 'at shape, I wuz scairt to go over bumps," Dipy said.

"So he croaks?" Chink snarled. "Saves us a bullet."

In answer to the boss-gangster's command, the car picked up speed. Its motor whined, whined like a trapped mobster, whined like a lead slug from a Smith & Wesson .38 revolver. Ah, to make that move, to—

The car hit a chunk of snow left over from the last blizzard. Detective Mason's poor, wounded, creased head hit the top. Something went *ping!* in his head.

" 'At was a bad un," Dipy said. "See if'n it croaked the copper."

The boss-gangster slid his hand under Detective Mason's coat. And as he did so, York Mason knew that his locomotive powers were back. He could move! Hitting his head a second time had undone the damage.

Carefully, oh, so carefully, his hand crept up. It closed on the protruding butt of the Smith & Wesson. One brown finger slid the single safety catch off. Another closed on the trigger and pulled.

There was a roar, a splashing, yelling roar, there was the smell of burning cloth. Chink Mason was dead.

Dipy turned. "What's the idea of givin' it to the copper afore we got outa the city limits?" he asked. Then his rat-like face sallowed as he saw that it was the Law that held the gun now.

He went for his own gat, but he was too late. Another roar, another .38 slug, and he went to join his pals.

Detective Mason reached across Dipy's body and held the wheel of the car, guided it to the curb, where a call-box bulked on the side of a light pole. He staggered out of the car, dripping blood.

"Hello, Sarge? First-Class Detective Mason reporting. I got the Vermillion Gang. Some of 'em on Fortun, some of 'em here. Send the wagon. . . . Trouble? Naw. I had a lucky bump."

Harlan McCracken laid the story down, looked at the top. It said: "Exactly One Thousand Words." He yelled: "Gordie!"

W. Gordon Maxwell popped his head in. "Yes, Chief?"

"Good yarn, Gordie. You sure it ran exactly a thousand?"

"I counted it twice, and had Elise count it once."

"Seems more like eleven hundred to me, but you ought to know," said Mr. McCracken. "O.K., Gordie, put it through, ten dollars for you. Send it right out to the printers; we've got a thousand-word hole in the next issue of *Nightstick*."

"Don't I know it."

"Say, there's one thing. Why make your dick a nigger?"

"Oh, I thought it was kind of unusual, Chief. Lots of the readers may not know they have colored detectives in New York." He cleared his throat. "I met one the other day, he works at the 104th Street Station."

"It won't do," said the editor. "This magazine has to sell in the South." He took his pencil and crossed out, blackly, every reference to Detective York Mason's color. "Other-

wise it's O.K. Nice, colorful piece of writing. You ought
to try something for the slicks sometime, Gordie."

"I'm going to," W. Gordon Maxwell said. "Next weekend, I plan to—"

*   *   *

I AM A FOOL, I am such a fool. Living on my nerves, that's
what I have been trying to do, trying to get by on my
nerve. You can't do it, you have to have rest and sleep, and
good nourishing food. And you have to have someone to
love you. A girl has to have someone love her, or the whole
thing falls apart.

I should have come home after the accident, I knew I
was worn out. But because the house is always cold and
drafty, because Mother nags and worries all the time, because I wanted a nice supper, I went on to the armory and
then up to Tenny's apartment, and made a fool of myself.

Well, no harm done. He didn't take advantage of me.
Not that snot-nosed upstart. He looked at me, and didn't
want me. Or couldn't he want me? Is he a little, just a little, like those boys you used to see in Childs after dances?

Oh, Eleanor, say it. Queer, pansy, fairy, perverted. Don't
be so nicey-nice all your life. Homosexual. There.

Hell hath no fury like the body scorned. You acted like
a cheap little tart and it didn't get you anywhere, and
you're sore. Not that you wanted Tenny. You don't. Admit it, you don't.

Maybe you did some good, anyway. Maybe you got rid
of Tenny.

Because Tenny is a temptation, Tenny has been a temptation. Tenny is so— I don't know—he would take care of
Mother, put up with Mother. And that's a prerequisite to

marriage for me. Which means that I, Eleanor Castron, will die a spinster. No one I loved would be sap enough to put up with Mother.

Maybe I could get a job as a strip-teaser at Minsky's.

Giggling, Eleanor sat up in bed and pushed her chestnut hair back. Eleven o'clock of a Monday morning. If I had a job I would have been working for two hours.

I will get up and put on my clothes and go around to Lord & Taylor's and ask for a job. Saks Fifth Avenue. All the stores. Mother will just have to learn to get along on a salesgirl's salary.

But—can I stand behind a counter all day and then come home and listen to other complaints all evening? About my salary, about a Castron waiting on the nouveau riche, about Papa dropping all his money in the market, about the insolence of the weather, the butcher, the subway guards and God? Or will I go nuts? I think maybe I am going off now. That performance at Tenny's.

Oh, Lord, there's Mother coming up the stairs. I could duck back under the covers and pretend to be asleep, but—

Too late.

Mrs. Castron bustled in. "Does my little girl feel better? Did you have enough sleep?"

"Yes, Mother."

"Mother has some nice coffee ready for her little girl. Come downstairs, Eleanor, young ladies shouldn't have breakfast in bed."

Eleanor suppressed a frown. Mother making coffee was too much. All she did was mess up the percolator and produce a pot full of brown mud.

"And I have a surprise for you," Mother said. "Cousin Gray's coming to stay with us for a week."

Eleanor was so surprised she lay down again. "Gray?"

Pass Through Manhattan

"You remember your second cousin Gray from Delaware. He's a year older than you, they came to stay with us when he was eleven. You two played together so nicely."

"I don't remember very well."

"Cousin Charles, his father, was my first cousin. Charles Burroughs, his mother, was a—"

"What does Gray do?"

"He teaches French at Harvard. It seems there's some sort of meeting of French professors in the city, and he's going to be here a week. Harvard is having its spring vacation."

Oh, dear. Just two or three years ago, would I be tired. The colleges letting out for Easter and a dance every night, a date for tea every afternoon. And I didn't even know it until a French professor remembered he was a cousin of ours.

"Is Gray married, Mother?"

"No. He's wrapped up in his work, Cousin Charles says, he's never had any time for girls."

Eleanor said: "I'll be down and make some good coffee in a minute, Mother."

*   *   *

COWBOY CONNORS POLISHED BRASS on the captain's launch of the *Oregon.* Another half hour to lunch.

*   *   *

DON MORTON WALKED QUICKLY, easily, down Broadway. He climbed the hill up from the fault of 96th Street, and went south. Maybe his earliest memory was of the opening of the great Astor market from 94th to 95th, hundreds—or so it seemed to him—of stalls selling everything edible a boy could think of, and off to one side the first Mirror candy store, or the first candy store he had ever known where they gave away little lead toys, tiny fire-engines and motorcycles, horses, cups, dogs, with your change, a little handful of them. And the sign in the window had been built around real mirror, and that had seemed wonderful.

Now it was a movie theater.

The things he remembered. Winckelman's grocery store at 93rd, where they had given him a kitten once. The Standard Theatre on 90th, and the Adelphi on 89th—the former live actors, the latter movies in the old days.

Funny his father had always lived on 96th, his drifting, rootless father could never be persuaded to move more than a block or so from the 96th Street subway station. Had said, once, it was so Don could go on to P.S. 165 on 89th, but that didn't make sense after Don had graduated and gone to high school.

The neighborhood had changed, run downhill. New York was always changing. He had been happy once, as a kid, playing in Riverside and Central Parks, then, later, going on hiking trips over in the Palisades with other boys. Wonder if that little waterfall is still there, three miles north of Tenafly, a mile and a half in from the Alpine ferry road. Wonder if kids still eat burned potatoes and half-cooked steak by it? I could find it in my sleep, but it's twelve years since I left the Scouts at fourteen—

Funny I can't stand New York any longer. Born here. Played here, raised here. Do Westerners feel the same way about getting to New York I feel about getting away from it?

Can't you be a man till you cut, geographically, the ties that bind you to your childhood?

Pass Through Manhattan

Downhill now, all the way to 79th, where another fault falls abruptly away to the river. 86th, the little drugstore that used to sell us replacement for our chemistry sets. There was a pet store on the corner of 84th where I used to watch puppies playing. The same man is still in business further south, I saw him the other day, you couldn't mistake him. He looked like a red-headed Japanese.

Maybe Dad wouldn't move away because he thought Mother might come back. But that couldn't be it, she'd find him through his paper easily, he's had a by-line ever since before I was born.

Wonder what happened to Mother? Maybe she changed her name and is a character actress in Hollywood. I'd not know her if I saw her.

I could ask Ray or Ronald Levine any of these things. They probably know. Ron was Dad's best man, wasn't he? The Mayor married them, married the brilliant young newspaperman and the actress who, at nineteen, was a whizzing, sizzling success on Broadway.

And out of this union came me. The geniuses labored and gave birth to a mining engineer.

The Hotel Ansonia on 74th, where white-socked baseball players used to lounge in the sun, smoking cigarettes. We kids used to wonder about that, smoking cut your wind.

Now the cold wind up 72nd. Where the Drive cut in and ended. They have extended it now, run it south from there on stilts.

What's this all about? Saying good-bye to the city of your birth. You'll never cut the string. A mining engineer is tied to Wall Street as long as he mines.

But— It would be different, safer, to come back, a burly,

127

red-faced man in a big hat with a narrow ribbon, a Westerner staying at the Commodore or the Roosevelt.

The Armory used to be across the street there, from 68th to 69th. Dad bought me a book of riding tickets there, once, and when they ran out, Mr. O'Connor let me exercise horses free.

The first time I ever heard about Colorado, except a pink space in the map.

Tough, regular army private lifting a horse's mane, spitting tobacco juice, showing me a line of letters and numbers branded on the bay's neck. " 'At's a way they brand horses now, kid. Shows he come into the remount at Fort Collins. S'helluva way to brand a good horse. This 'un looks like he was more'n half Morgan. They got Morgan stallions at Collins, I served 'ere in my first hitch, before the war."

Then, a little boy, very anxious to show he had remembered all his friend had told him about horses: "I thought Morgans came from Vermont?"

" 'At's right, Donny, only the Army took a lot of 'em out to Colorado. 'At's wunnerful country fer horses, deep snow ina winter, big, thick grass ina summer. Got a place they call South Park, not a park at all but a great big valley, all green in summer. We rode across her oncet."

After he'd grown up, gone out on his first job—potash cutting in the Carolinas—he had lost all interest in horses. Guess he'd just loved the Armory because it smelled of manure and tanbark and horse-sweat, the good smells of the country, and not like the rest of Manhattan.

But now he was at 66th, threading his way through the mess that Columbus makes crossing Broadway to become Ninth Avenue, and he had passed the site of the old Armory. Torn down. Wonder what little boys who hate the city of their birth and don't know it do now? No doubt there are still livery stables and armories. But grown-ups didn't know about them.

The old Colonial, where a boy with pocket money could follow the acts down from the Riverside. Sophie Tucker. Eddie Leonard. Bert Williams, Ted Lewis, I even remember Eva Tanguay.

Where are they now? On the beach at Santa Monica, in the NVA home, dead? Nora Bayes, with her gorgeous white hair piled high on the top of her head.

Good-bye, good-bye. Next time I see you I'll be a red-faced colonel in a big hat, never going north of 52nd, or south of 40th except to go to Wall Street.

Going to have cocktails with Mr. Grainger. I have never met Mr. Grainger before except to be ushered into his office by Makin, allowed to hold the sacred Grainger hand for a minute.

Crossing Columbus Circle. I said, I'm goin' Souf, got the taste of sugar cane right in mah mouf. Got to—

Don went on along Broadway, through the 50's, past the shining automobile salesrooms, and then into the Times Square district, squalid, tawdry, catch-penny. His mind was turned off now, no memory could live in this neighborhood, no use recalling the simple, enthralling pleasures of a city childhood, no way to avoid facing the next encounter.

You're too sensitive a soul for a mining engineer, he told himself. Should have been a minor poet. By the laws of eugenics, you just barely missed that. A brilliant newspaperman, a great dramatic actress.

He remembered studying the Mendelian law in college, L'Abbé Mendel with his sweet peas and his white mice. The hot excitement of being about to discover the secret of life, then the loss of interest—which resulted in his having to be crammed by a graduate student before he passed a sophomore Biology—when he discovered that Mendel's fine law could not be applied with success to humans, because their ancestry was too dubious, their genes too numerous.

The professor saying: "How many of you can tell me the color of the hair of all your great-grandparents?" And one lone hand shooting up, Bobby Wilcox, the class genius and the class clown—a Negro.

Don had passed 42nd Street; the first half of his walk was ended. Soberly he returned to himself, Don Morton, Mining Engineer, about to call at his father's office.

*   *   *

ELEANOR CASTRON GOT OUT OF THE TAXICAB in front of the Orange Street house. Twenty dollars, she had made twenty dollars. And just when—

Oh, say it wasn't a summer, it was such a *pretty* swallow. Ten dollars would keep the grocer and the butcher quiet, five dollars would buy all kinds of ribbons and threads and ornaments to refurbish her wardrobe, and three dollars to Mrs. Finely to come and do her clothes over.

And out of the sky! But legitimately. Cousin Gray, dear Cousin Gray, blinking his blue eyes, and saying: "I want to have a good time while I'm here, Cousin Eleanor. I—to the deuce with the Romance Languages."

"Romance without the languages?" she had asked. Feeble, but something.

It had wowed Gray, though. Why, the lamb, the little woolly lamb, had nearly giggled. "Yes. I—I want to laugh and dance, and stay up all night and—do all the things you do, Cousin Eleanor."

"Why Cousin, Gray?"

Pass Through Manhattan

"Eleanor, then. I—when could you give me an afternoon? I want to get some nice clothes. A—a dinner jacket that doesn't make me look like a missionary."

The upshot of which had been, she had steered him to shops where she got commissions, and she had made twenty dollars. How too, too wonderful, how divine, she felt twenty herself, and not dollars.

He had finished paying the cab driver, was walking along beside her towards the steps, over the icy pavement. Sand gritted under her shoes.

She said: "Let's not go in yet, Gray. Let's walk to the end of the street and look down at the harbor."

He nodded. But she had to reach out and practically drag his arm to get him to give it to her. She didn't think Gray could have been out with many girls in his life. A vir—

No. She was going to have nice, clean thoughts all the time he was here. She was going to crawl out of the gutter she had been in the last few days.

There were more important things in life than sex. There were, there were, no matter what the intellectuals said. Let them wonder where the next meal was coming from for a while. Let them—

Honesty and gaiety and nice clothes were more important. And she was going to have nice clothes—if only a new sash on an old evening gown, a new artificial flower on a cocktail dress—and she was going to be gay if it killed her. She owed it to her little woolly lamb here, holding her arm so carefully, so as not to press his own arm against her body.

And honesty—

They stopped by the spiked iron railings. Below them the Heights fell away. A white floodlight hung from the mast of a ship, and men were busy unloading stuff in burlap-covered bales. The edges of the light, and the spotlights of tugs picked out ice floating in the harbor, the lights of Manhattan were bright across the water.

Now. If he said anything he was just an old stick, a dressed-up Harvard professor seeing how the other half lived. And if he didn't he was a—

Gray sighed and was still.

He was a woolly lamb.

The cold was biting through her thin slippers before she spoke. And then the words surprised her. "Gray, I have a confession to make. I wasn't doing you a favor taking you around to the shops this afternoon. That's how I make my living."

"Eh?"

"I'm a licensed shopper. You get a license from the department stores, they have an office you go to. I made twenty dollars this afternoon."

"How clever of you," he said. "And I thought you were just a—just a butterfly. Why, Eleanor, you're a business woman."

Honesty. She was going to have honesty with him, too. She was going to have everything!

He said: "But I can send you ever so much business. Single men, college professors, are lost in the big shops, you know." He laughed. "Jeff Grimes, he teaches Math and has the next apartment to mine, got into a store one time, and came home with a tweed suit in checks two inches square. He—he said the salesman looked like he needed his job."

"You're nice, Gray."

"But look here, Eleanor, you know, you don't have to spend all your evenings taking me around just because I'm a customer."

"I want to take you around, Gray."

"Or a cousin, either. Or because I'm staying in your house. There are meetings every night of the group, and—"

"I want to take you around, Gray. I'm going to love it. Let's go in and wash up and go to the St. George for cocktails."

"I'd hate to feel I'm putting you out, Eleanor, or—"

"And I don't get commissions from nightclubs and bars either."

He laughed. "Oh, I say, that is an idea. Why don't you call up—Leon and Eddie's or—or the Casa Mañana and tell them you have a sucker with five hundred dollars to spend and what sort of—sort of cut can they give you?" His laugh was almost bass. Tenny laughed in tenor.

"Oh, dear Gray, what have you been reading?"

She started up the block to the house. He caught up with her and this time he hooked his hand under her arm, almost hugged it. Oh, she thought as she put her latchkey in the door, I'm glad, I'm so glad I was honest with him. I'm out of the jungle, that awful, steamy hot jungle I've been in so long, I'm—why, I'm Eleanor Castron, the post-deb again.

She had the door unlocked, halfway open. She reached up with her free hand, and patted his cheek. "Hurry and wash now, Gray dear, we'll go to places where you won't need your dinner jacket tonight. They promised it for tomorrow."

"All right."

As he brushed past her, she was surprised to feel that he was trembling a little. Had no girl ever patted his cheek, or was it being called Gray dear?

Her mother came out of the drawing room. "That nice Tenbruye boy called, little girl." The look she gave Gray was sickening, *see how popular my little flower is.* "He wants you to call him up."

133

"Oh, nuts with him," said Eleanor, and ran up the stairs, unsnapping her placketed frock as she went.

*　　　*　　　*

PEGGY REILLY PACKED. Her mind was still too stunned to make plans.

*　　　*　　　*

AT QUARTER PAST FIVE John Tenbruye signed his mail, washed up, and got out of the office. His first intention was to go up to the Armory and see who was in the troop room; but then he decided he had better get something started about the Castron's Orange Street house. He waved at a cab, and gave the driver the address of John's Hungarian Grill on Maiden Lane.

The cab went up Broad Street without any trouble, but got bottled up in front of Morgan's, where Broad Street ends and traffic has to go through the narrow path of Nassau Street.

You wouldn't think there was any depression in Wall Street, from the way they swarm along here. No, sir, looks as active as—John shut his eyes as the driver nearly ran down a group of stenographers ambling happily down the narrow street.

The cab shifted to second, then into low, and inched its way along. The pimply, fuzzy faces of office boys were pressed against the glass, the taxi was swamped by under-paid humanity.

Old men, the leather cases of runners tucked under their arms, scurried along with their heads down into their collars against the blasting winter.

Pass Through Manhattan

They say you can learn a lot from those old boys, some of the brokerage houses and houses of issue gave the jobs to their old customers after a wave of holdups made them quit having boys. I don't know. Sounds like one of those things you can hear in the Street.

The taxi was going so slow now that the trotting boys could pass it. John Tenbruye leaned back and dreamed of the old days in Wall Street, the days when the first Tenbruye—who must surely have been at least a cousin of John's great-grandfather—had come over from Jersey and indentured himself as a clerk to a great Wall Street house.

The days when there were no cars, when a man drove his trotter to work or had his coachman drive him down behind a team.

The senior partners of the firm that old Loos Tenbruye wormed his way into had once ridden in chairs, carried through these very streets.

The Street didn't change so much. It was still a community, with its own battles, its own problems. Those fools in Washington thought they could treat it like a business, just any business, with its ethics and rules, but they would find they couldn't. The families of Wall Street each had its place in the Street, and no one had ever been articulate enough to express just what that place was.

Wall Street had its art galleries, its rare book stores, its favorite restaurants. No newcomer could ever get very far in Wall Street. Names like Jim Fisk and Dan'l Drew and Mike Meehan came and went, but the old names went on. Seligmanns, Lehmans, and two or three other Jewish families. Morgans, Roosevelts—the Emlen Roosevelt branch, neither the Theodore nor the F. D.—Reids, Doremuses.

Laugh at it, call it money-grubbing or gambling or the

fleecing of widows and children, but it wasn't. It was a love for an old neighborhood, an old way of life. For streets that smelled of spice and roasting coffee, streets that were narrow and crooked and unchanged since chairmen had been the cab drivers.

Why, these Southern and Western nincompoops of the SEC ought to look at the woodwork in some of the old houses, and they would know you couldn't smash a thing like that. The building that housed the American Banker, for instance, a man didn't need to be a college professor to see where the clerks had slept upstairs, where the partners had tasted coffee or felt cotton from the last China clipper—

And it was, by God it was, possible for him to get in. His name meant something, it meant that he could feel the rhythm of the Street.

There was the story of the du Ponts. Found themselves with millions of dollars' worth of factories and powder mills, and no man in the family capable of running them. What did they do? Sell out, or call in an outsider?

Lord, no. They found a du Pont who was not an heir, a descendant of a collateral branch who had made a success outside the business, and turned it over to him. And the greatest du Pont days of all times had followed.

Rensselaer—Whippy—Tenbruye was a marvelous amateur rider and steeplechaser. Cornelius—Nelly—Tenbruye got himself sued by chorus girls. All the other descendants of Loos Tenbruye were women or men over fifty.

And he, John, had as legitimate a right to the great name as they—

The hackdriver said: "Here y'are, boss—"

He paid the man, tipping him, not opulently, but well, and went into John's. Most of those Brooklyn Heights mortgages were owned by the insurance companies, and the insurance men stopped in here for a drink in the evening. He knew several of the real estate men for the big insurance firms from the days when he had carried a real estate broker's license.

No one else at Seligmann's would have known about that.

He would trade this property into something, and maybe Mr. Seligmann would run into J. K. Tenbruye or Lafayette Tenbruye at the club, and mention the incident.

Anyway, he was glad to do the job. A future banker ought to know all branches of New York money, brokerage, bonds, real estate. The Tenbruye Trust had the interest from ten million dollars to look after.

*   *   *

"NO, NO," ARTUR LEMPE SAID, kindly. "Leave the boots alone. Washington will polish them."

She knew he was trying to get around her when he put that name to the boy. "Washington is not a bootblack." But the fight was out of her. It was stuffy in the little flat all day, boring, and that pain in her side had come back. And with Artur fussing over her, she had begun to feel really sick.

"Then I will polish them myself," said Artur. He slid his hand into the black boot leg, caught up the polish can.

"No, no, first you must wipe the dust off."

"Ja, ja." He pushed her back into the chair, the boot heel pressing her shoulder. "So, easy. Sit still, rest, my poor Marie. Soon the doctor will be here."

She rolled her eyes, frightened. Had she moaned in her sleep, sometimes the pain was pretty bad from the side, and when you are asleep you cannot always remember to be still and not complain. Oh, her children, someone must look after her children. She—"Artur, if I die, promise me you will not take Washington to the old country."

"Now, now, Marie, you must rest. Let me help you to the couch."

"No, Artur, promise me."

"You are talking nonsense, woman, you will not die. You will see, the best doctor money can buy will soon be here."

"But promise me."

He dropped the boot on the floor. She craned forward automatically, but no, the damp polish had not stained her nice carpet. Artur sat down on the arm of her chair and put his hand around her shoulders, holding her. She laid her cheek against the hand that smelt faintly of shoe polish.

"You will see, dear Marie, everything will be all right. They cannot take poor people and herd them around in their dirty buses like cattle, let tons of snow fall on them, crush them, suffocate them, and not have a reckoning. They have done these things to you, they must take care of you."

Marie leaned back, her cheek against his hand. How many years was it since Artur had been so nice to her? She had almost forgotten, when she married him she had sworn to herself that she would be loving-sweet to him, she would not make him feel that she had married him just because he was coming to America.

And she told him that, she had been honest with him. But she would not keep reminding him, she had told herself, she would be nicer to him than a girl who married for love, because love can fade, but the memory of a sacrifice, a favor, lives forever.

Favor, what a silly word. Boon, grant, what did she mean? To bring her to where George could be born, a free man, with no military service ahead of him. Where George—not Georg Vogel Lempe, as she had planned, after her favorite brother, but George Washington Lempe—could rise to be a bank president, even President of the United States of America, for was he not native-born? And now, if Artur would only love her, let her love him as in the old days, it would be so wonderful.

"You must not worry, little Marie," he said. "Mariechen, do not worry. The money you have been saving for the college for Georg, all we make out of this lawsuit, it will go in there. You will see, it will be thousands."

"You like the children, Artur?"

"Yes, yes, they are good children."

There was a clatter on the stairs outside. Artur straightened up, got off the arm of her chair, coughing. He picked up the boot, carried it into the bedroom, shut the door. Then he went, stiffly, like a porter in a German hotel, and opened the door. And then he stiffened even more, saluted.

He started to give the old German army salute, but remembered in time and thrust his arm upright. "Heil Hitler."

"Heil Hitler," said the pale, blonde, bespectacled man who entered. Artur, with his free hand, signaled her to rise, but the blonde man waved her back into the chair.

"Rest, Frau Lempe," he said.

Mr. Brefogel came in, "Heil Hitler," and then a man in the old-fashioned beard of a German doctor, like the old king of England. "Heil," the doctor said, absent-mindedly. "Is this the patient?"

The other two men frowned at him. Then the leader waved a hand at Artur, who stopped standing at attention. "My wife, Herr Doktor."

"Does she speak English?" asked the doctor, contemptuously.

"Yes, Doctor, I am a good American," Marie said, before she thought. The leader and Artur and Mr. Brefogel looked shocked, but she thought she caught a twinkle in the doctor's eye. He said: "Then go in the bedroom and get ready to be examined."

She put the boot away first, then slowly took her clothes off, lay down on the bed, pulling a sheet over her. She called: "Ready, Doctor," and he came in.

He was a real doctor, she could tell that by the brisk, kindly way he examined her. When he finished, he said: "You ought to have electrical treatments for that, or it will be necessary to operate."

"Yes, Doctor?"

"But, unfortunately, my hospital is not equipped to give them. Dr. Friedenberg at Mount Sinai—"

"I have been to him."

The doctor looked startled. "Do you mind if I smoke, Mrs. Lempe?"

She held her breath while he lighted the cigarette; she was almost certain that the beard was going to catch. It didn't, however. The doctor puffed on the little white tube. "I shall have to have a colleague in, then. If the Friedenberg treatments did not help, my diagnosis must be wrong."

"Oh, but they did. I felt so much better, I was nearly cured . . ."

"Why, then—"

She didn't answer, and after a moment he was silent, staring off across the room. She followed his eyes, and saw he was looking at the picture on the wall, the one she had had to make Grace stop calling Charlie Chaplin.

"Yes," she whispered. "My husband."

The doctor lowered his head, puffing on the cigarette. He had never taken it out of his mouth. "I cannot advise you," he said, stiffly. "The ethics of my profession do not allow a doctor to give advice counter to the advice of a husband." His voice wasn't very convincing.

"But, Doctor, isn't there someone else, not at Mount Sinai, who—"

"What the devil," he growled. "We have the military leadership, the great engineers, we have Der Fuehrer. Must we have the best doctors, too?" He swung off the bed, the springs creaking as he rose, and stamped to the door. He crushed the cigarette out in the tray where she put her hair combings in the morning, and slammed the door into the living room.

Marie Lempe clutched the sheet around her shoulders and ran to the closet. She took out her old pink kimono, put it on, and went to the door, put her ear against it.

"Yes," the doctor said. "I can safely testify that shock is not good for a woman of forty. Especially a woman with an internal lesion. Quite so. The bus accident was not good for her."

"Ah, good." That was the strong voice of the blonde man.

"On the other hand," said the doctor, "it is not good for a woman in that condition to keep such a clean apartment and also work behind a counter every day. When I say she ought to rest, if I am asked whether she should have rested if there had been no accident, I shall be forced to say—"

"That you did not examine her before the accident," Mr. Brefogel said, quickly. "Anyway, you will not be asked, Doctor. That is in my department, leave it to me."

"Also," said the doctor, "the woman should have been under treatment long ago. I understand she was, Lempe, and you forced her to discontinue?"

"It was at Mount Sinai. I did not like the thought of those Jewish hands—"

"You will not be asked that, either, Doctor," Mr. Brefogel said.

"I wonder if you politicians know what you are doing?" the doctor asked.

There was the noise of a door slamming.

Mr. Brefogel said: "Everything is going swimmingly, swimmingly. We have a wonderful case, Mr. Lempe."

"My compliments to Mrs. Lempe," said the leader. "Heil Hitler."

"Heil Hitler," said Artur.

"Heil Hitler," said Mr. Brefogel.

The front door opened and closed again, without banging this time. Frau Lempe went back and lay down on the bed. She lay there several minutes, and then she was conscious of the door to the bedroom opening.

"Marie," said Artur. "Marie. Do you cry, Marie? Shed no tears. Think of the money for Georg's—for Washington's education."

"Yes, husband."

*   *   *

EITHER ONE OF THE PRESSES had a loose floor bolt and was vibrating, or Ray had taken too many aspirin. He uptilted the hundred-pill bottle that he had opened that morning, and counted the tablets, pushing them from one pile to the other on the grimy desk.

Ninety-two. Eight. And there had been three left in the little pocket box. He supposed eleven was enough to make a man's ears ring, he hadn't taken that many since the day the *Vestris* sank and him with no reporter in the office but the assistant drama critic and a sports cartoonist who had been a writer on the *Warrensburg* (Mo.) *Star-Journal* fifteen years ago.

Pass Through Manhattan

Well, the ringing would stop as soon as he had a drink, but it was only two and he made a policy of not touching the stuff before four.

If he felt like slipping all he had to do was look over at Brawley Smith. Brawley'd been taking little half-ounce sips regularly since eight that morning, and he was, as usual, getting a little high. By four Brawley would—according to schedule—tell the paper to go to hell, but it didn't matter because the paper would then have gone to bed.

Editor and Publisher and the deans of the journalism schools would say that times have changed, but liquor would always remain the newspaperman's chief problem. The cold, windy assignments, the drafty barns they used for city rooms, the irregular, nasty hours—though this applied more to the morning sheets—the fact that most of the people a reporter was sent out to interview were in no position to get mad if they smelled liquor—all these things made for drinking.

These kids didn't seem to have the trouble. But then, in these days of tight coverage and short stories, a newspaperman didn't need the genius that had prevailed in Ray's day, in Joe Morton's, in Brawley Smith's day. Look at Ronald Levine. He had ridden through these thirty years without ever falling back on liquor, he had sworn he wouldn't go the way of the great figures of their youth. And what it had fetched him to was an old-lady senility, a hypochondria that was destroying him with bromides and body-conditioners, evil-smelling sulphur compounds and nuxated iron, bromo-seltzer and anti-allergic compounds. Destroying him just as surely as liquor was killing Joe and Brawley, as rheumatism and disillusionment were killing Ray.

All of which meant that Ray was half wild wondering about Joe Morton.

Pass Through Manhattan

The front door blew gusts of air into the room, and Ray started to yell to whoever was holding it open to close it. Then he saw it was the Chief, showing off his city room to some friends. Two dames, smooth skins, fur coats, sheer stockings—

Ray shot an amused glance at the Garter Belt, where his fashion editor, his sob sister and his society gal huddled. The three of them were staring, enviously. Never was a girl didn't want nice clothes, and to hell with a good job and mental attainments.

Looking back, he saw the Chief's face crinkling up with the infantile, pink rage that so ill-became him.

Ray didn't have to look. He knew. But he looked anyway. Yeah. Brawley Smith was asleep, the rewrite earphones on his head, his feet on the desk. And, past him, Ron Levine was alternately spraying his throat with an atomizer and examining it with a mirror.

One of the women laughed.

All right. All right, Goddamit. He knew that the cubs called Ron and Brawley and Joe his trained seals. But they were a fine team. He snatched up his phone, said: "Brawley," into it, and watched.

He had not counted to eight before Brawley's feet were on the floor, his fingers on the keys of the typewriter. Ray said: "There's a rumor that Mrs. Roosevelt just crashed in a plane. Give me about a column of stall till we can get facts." Hot damn, look at those keys fly.

Fill your eyes with that, Chief. Show that to those soft-skinned milk bathers you been feeding lunch to while a better man than you—better, but no truer—gets out your paper.

He looked at the door, but the Chief wasn't watching. He

and his guests were shaking hands with someone. Ah, Don Morton.

Ray felt better. It had taken the four of them, and Frank McCabe—now dead—helping—to buy Don the sort of education he deserved. But they had produced, out of the mob of them, one man. One completely balanced guy. One young man who had everything—Ron's classic background, Brawley's poetic imagination, Joe's cynicism, Ray's common sense—and through the years they had watched the result of that grafting onto a native mathematical and engineering ability.

Look at that boy's manner. Hell, he could be President some day. In a pretty lousy world, wasn't he something?

Those dames were impressed. The Chief was impressed, too. Probably offering Don a job. He'd mentioned it Saturday. Well, not that boy. No newspaper jobs for him.

Don had gotten loose, was patting Brawley on the shoulder with that special, city-room pat that means: "Hi, boy, see you when you get through," was talking to Ronald, laughing. Now he was coming over.

Ray said: "Hi, son. How goes it?"

Don sat down on the edge of the desk. "Not bad, Ray. Just walked down from 96th and shook off the blues on the way."

"You with the blues? How come, I thought you were off to your sweetheart in a week."

"The All's Fair may have to shut down. The government's thinking of putting in a dam, cutting off our water. I've got a date with Makin and Grainger to talk it over at quarter of six."

"Grainger himself? You're flying high, boy. Stop by the Financial Desk, ask Paul if he knows where Grainger buried any bodies."

"No, thanks," laughing. "I've never been good at blackmail."

"Say, Joe said something about your worrying over that Ringgold."

"All over. Just a little childish weltschmerz."

"You sound like Ronald. That reminds me." He picked up the phone, called Brawley. "That rumor was quashed, Smitty." Across the room Brawley Smith went back to sleep.

Don said: "Where is Joe?"

"He's got some sort of tip on that Larney killing last week," Ray said promptly.

Don said: "Cut it out, Ray. When I called up, you said it was a political yarn."

"Well, that Larney story may lead into some pretty queer —He's on a bat, Don."

The Chief came by, on his way into his office. He patted Don's shoulder in passing, did not speak to Ray.

From a row of chairs along the far wall a heavy man got up, carrying a little black suitcase, threaded his way across the city room, went in after the Chief. His masseur, giving him his post-prandial rubdown.

"He hasn't done this in years, Ray."

"Not since your mother—not in a long time, no."

"Whatever happened to my mother, Ray?"

Ray shrugged. "In 1929 she was a big success in a music hall in London. The last any of us heard. But don't worry, Joe isn't still—"

"No, I suppose not. He—"

Young Mills stuck his head in the door and yelled: "Someone come help me."

Ray said, desperately: "Hey, go back to the Morgue for me, Don, and see if—"

"That my fath—is that Joe coming in?"

Ray looked at him with a hunted expression. "O.K. I just thought it would be easier for him if you weren't here."

"I'll stay."

Mills and the elevator man brought him in. He was in very bad shape; Ray couldn't remember seeing him that way for fifteen years. He struggled away from the men holding him, lurched, caught hold of the top of a City News ticker, and pretended to read the type pouring out of the typewriter in the glass case.

Mills came over, said: "Well, there he is, sir. My unc—the Chief back yet? He had a heavy date for lunch, I tried to time it so we'd get in while he was out."

"You damn cub, why didn't you take him home?"

"You said—"

"All right, all right. Don, how about—"

Joe Morton let go of the top of the ticker, came across the room with the pent-up speed of the top-heavy. Ron Levine half rose from his desk, Joe straight-armed him and kept coming. Ron took a mirror out of the top drawer of the desk and started examining the cheekbone that Joe had palmed.

Joe Morton brought himself up in front of the city desk, leaned on it. "Hello, old paper-seller."

"Hello, Joe. Where you been?"

"All right, well, all right."

"Where?" Ray said.

"All right, well all right, I'm a Guild man. Don, did it all for Don did it."

"Joe, you look like hell. Let me send you over to a Turkish bath and—"

"Man with a son gotta. Duties of a father. Mutual give and take."

Ray looked up at Don. "I'll send him up to a health farm I know. They'll—"

Joe Morton beat his yellow hand on the desk. "Listen to me," he roared. "Best damn— No. Not that." He coughed, furiously, his cheeks turning white. "Son killed a man. So what? All right, well, all right. Went to find out. Went to see nurse. Pretty nurse, very well all right pretty nurse, but no damn good. Blemish, serious moral blemish. No nurse." He snapped his fingers to indicate how little nurse there was. "Went to see sailors. Great experience. Slug me on a head, sleep all night in flophouse. But."

Ray put his hand on Joe's. God. Must be running a hundred and four. He picked up the phone, dialed a number out of the hundreds filed in his head. "Si? Send an ambulance over to the office, huh? One of my best men out of his head. Pneumonia, I imagine. He's a chronic alcoholic."

"But," said Joe Morton. "All right, well, all right."

"Brawley," Ray yelled. "Bring the bottle over." He didn't know whether a drink would do any good or any harm, but it might help.

Brawley Smith poured a shot of his cheap rye into a tumbler, shoved it into Joe Morton's hand. Joe's fingers closed around it, automatically, then he said: "Never drink alone."

Ray nodded and Brawley poured himself one.

"Straightened everything out," Joe Morton said clearly. "Found out, Ringgold justa bum. Nothing for Don to worry about at all." He fumbled in his pocket, flopped a snapshot out on the desk. "Ringgold."

Ray shoved the picture over to Don. Don looked at it, looked at his own fingers trembling. Copper's face grinned up at him, against a background of cargo booms and a net full of fruit coming aboard. Clean water and a Haitian mountain in the background and black men. Clean, oh, clean.

Joe Morton gulped the liquor. "Better," he said. "First today."

The Chief's voice said: "Well, do you call this a city room?"

Ray wheeled in his chair. The Chief stood in the door of his private office, a purple silk dressing gown around him. In the background was the masseur, in black trousers and white athletic undershirt, big muscles, hairy chest.

"Fire Morton and Smith," the Chief said. "And Levine, too." He pointed at Ron, painting his cheekbone with mercurochrome.

Ray said: "Joe Morton's sick, Chief. I've sent for an ambulance. Feel his temperature, he—"

"I didn't ask you for a bulletin on the state of Mr. Morton's health." The door slammed.

Brawley Smith helped Joe Morton to a chair, where he sat, his breathing loud over the clack of the tickers, the underground rumble of presses.

Don Morton was looking at Ray, the photograph still in his fingers. His eyebrows crawled up.

"I can get a job on the *Times*," Ray said.

"You weren't fired," Don pointed out.

"I quit. We've been together too many years."

"Including the time you all kicked in to bring me up."

"Forget it, Don. You paid us back."

"Can you get Brawley and Ron on the *Times? . . .* I thought not. You'll split your salary four ways until Joe gets out of the sanitarium or one of them gets a job. Which might be never. You'll—"

"You don't forget all the things that have happened in thirty years, kid."

"I'm about to get a raise out of Grainger. And I'll be around the East a while," Don said. "To help you. Maybe Ron could write a book."

"O.K., kid. Joe's passed out, and here's the stretcher, and you'd better get on downtown. And good luck."

"O.K."

Iridium, here I come. Maybe I can make a flying trip to the mines once in a while to find out why production isn't heavier.

PART TWO

Peggy reilly stood outside the door that said Ring and
Walk In. She raised her hand and put a finger on the bell;
then she stopped, and examined her new gloves very carefully. They were marron glacé, very smart; quite spotless,
nice fitting. I look nice. I look very nice. I have on my
best outfit.

She pressed the bell.

Thereafter there was nothing to do but walk in. She
found herself in a hall between two doors; one door open,
one shut. Presumably—since no one appeared, there were
no footsteps—she was to go in through the open door. She
did.

The room reminded her of her clothes. It was Office for a
Doctor, just as she was wearing Outfit in Which to Apply
for a Job. Slick maple furniture, very bright and as shiny
as her gloves. Smooth, easy-flowing draperies of a dove
gray not too far removed from the discreet tints of her suit.
Hooked scatter rugs and a ruffled white blouse.

Pass Through Manhattan

She sat down, her knees pressed tight against each other, her hands folded over her bag.

Nothing happened.

She became convinced that her nose was shiny, that her lipstick had smudged, and that her hat was on crooked.

Nothing happened.

She wanted to open her bag, take out her mirror and examine the wreckage.

Nothing happened.

Now, in April, the snows had melted, a few flies flew lazily about New York. One of these buzzed on the window pane.

Peggy Reilly stood up, laid her bag on the desk, and picked a magazine up off the waiting table. She walked to the window, pulled the drapes back, and killed the fly with the magazine. Then she had the problem of either leaving Dr. Wilcomen's magazine spoiled or ruining her gloves.

She had worked the problem out to the point where she opened her bag, took out a square of make-up tissue and wrapped the fly in it, when she was aware that the door through which she had come was closing.

Peggy turned, the encased fly held between thumb and forefinger of the right hand.

A very tall, very thin, man of about thirty in a spotless white jacket bowed to her and sat down behind the desk. His ears were very high set on the sides of his close-cropped head; his eyes had a slight slant, and were deep blue. He indicated the chair in front of his desk and sat back, making a steeple of his long, black-haired fingers.

Peggy cursed herself as she felt a blush coming on. She looked around, trying not to get a wild expression on her face, and finally put the fly in an ashtray. Then she went and sat down, pulling her skirt over her knees, laying the bag in her lap, folding her hands over the bag.

Dr. Wilcomen smiled, and reversed his locked fingers so as to show the people under the steeple. "You may smoke if you want to," he said.

"No, thanks, I don't—"

He made a steeple and pointed it at her bag. She looked down at her lap and saw that she had not refastened the snap after she had taken out the tissue; a package of Lucky Strikes showed gold and red and green.

She put a cigarette between her lips, forgetting to tap it, and Dr. Wilcomen unmade the church his fingers had become and lit a match. His arms were so long that he did not have to move his thin shoulders away from the back of the swivel chair.

He said: "I don't eat babies, you know."

She smiled.

"My name is Dr. Wilcomen."

"I'm Miss Reilly. I've come about a job."

"Yes. You hardly look pregnant."

She gasped.

Dr. Wilcomen said: "You don't know how nice it is to see a woman in this room who is neither nauseated, terrified nor a prostitute."

Peggy said: "It must—I mean, honestly, I am terrified."

"Ah, quite so. But not the sort of terror I mean. . . . The job pays fifty dollars a week, and all found. You will have days off only when convenient; which means when one of the other nurses—there are six—is available and willing to watch the telephone and the office. You will, of course, live in the house here."

"I—"

"Lest you misunderstand, one of your duties will not be

to sleep with the doctor. A man in my line prefers the opera or the theater for his leisure hours."

Peggy gasped.

Dr. Wilcomen laughed, suddenly, separated his fingers and laid both hands flat on the desk. "All right, Miss Reilly. The judicious use of the cold insult is the best antidote, I find, for female hysterics. I get so I use it automatically. You see—I got you so mad you forgot to be scared for a moment." He lit a cigarette. "Now—there are a couple of things. I don't like that name Reilly."

"I don't have to use my own name if—"

Wilcomen shook his head. "Not what I meant. Are you a Catholic?"

"Yes."

He said: "That won't do. You would have to confess to your priest what you were doing for a living, wouldn't you?"

Peggy said: "But anything said in the confessional is secret, the Father wouldn't—"

Wilcomen said: "It worries me, though. The Catholic Church considers this sort of work a direct insult, a sort of anti-Catholic activity."

Peggy said: "In that case—"

"On the other hand," Wilcomen said, "God knows I have enough trouble getting nurses who are clean, trained, and—shall we say—ineligible for more conventional nursing. And, I must admit, many of my patients have been Catholics."

Peggy said: "Yes. I know."

Wilcomen stirred in the chair. "Do you mind telling me how you come to join our little society of faintly malodorous practitioners of the medical arts?"

"I—I fell in love with a doctor in a Cincinnati hospital. When I was in training. I had to have a—an operation."

Pass Through Manhattan

Wilcomen chuckled. "You should have come to me. Dr. Wilcomen's Friday treatments are famous; why lose time from work? Sometimes I have as many as twelve patients Friday afternoon after the offices close. They all go back to work Monday morning."

"A nurse in training doesn't get from Friday to Monday."

He nodded. "A nasty situation. And then—"

"I enrolled at Mount Sinai, started all over again. I was in a bus accident, and my picture got in the newspapers. And—"

"Quite so, Miss Reilly. . . . Well, no matter. As I say, you will work here, answering the phone—emergency advice is terrifically important—overseeing things, and, above all, lending courage to young men—until such time as I can spare you to go out on cases. For that work you will get twelve and a half dollars a day."

"Yes, Doctor."

He said: "Go get your clothes and things, and come back. I'll have Jod—the colored man—get a room ready. And don't give this house as a forwarding address. Rent a post-office box."

"Yes, Doctor." She stood up, walked to the door.

Dr. Wilcomen said: "Miss Reilly . . . I am genuinely sorry for your trouble."

She turned, more startled than ever.

He said: "I mean it. I— Where most doctors my age have a copy of *If* on the office wall, I have that other great work of Kipling's—*Baa, Baa, Black Sheep*." He stood up, shook his coat down, split his handsome face into a smile. "I made the error of allowing a gangster to die in a ward. He was supposed to recover sufficiently to do a little testifying before he was electrocuted. . . . I'll see you later, Miss Reilly."

Outside, she walked slowly to the corner. Ahead of her a

taxicab stopped, and a fat, red-faced boy of about twenty-four helped out a girl who looked Italian. He put his arm around her, and they walked up the block, past Peggy. The girl's eyes were puffy.

Peggy waited until she saw them go up the stoop of Dr. Wilcomen's house. They rang and walked in.

*   *   *

MISS MORACCI SAID: "Mr. Corning would like to see you as soon as possible, Mr. Seligmann."

Bob Seligmann smiled at his secretary, and nodded. Then he went into his own office, hung his hat and coat in the closet, washed his hands in his private washroom, and sat down at his desk. The clock said exactly fifteen minutes of ten.

He spent the next five minutes skimming through the formulae in an article on "The Ecology of Tobacco Mosaic." He was—very anonymously—one of the world's leading students of the filterable virus, and much concerned with coryza. For some time he and the bacteriologist who had been working with him on stains had felt that there was a relationship, a similarity, between the metabolism of tobacco mosaic virus and that of canine distemper. This being true—

But his clock said ten minutes of ten. He closed the *American Journal of Botany* and put it in a special drawer. He pulled the first pile of mail towards him. Miss Moracci always put letters from the family first; it was entirely plausible for one of the aunts to conceal a buying order in a mess of verbiage about the shortcomings of a parlor maid, and if he missed the market opening, he didn't hear the end of it for weeks.

The aunts were vague, but they read the market page.

Pass Through Manhattan

Yes, by golly. Aunt Rosalie had asked Mr. Dey to see if he couldn't do something about the temperature in her hot-house—it being suspected that the gardener was stealing the cooking sherry—and he had told her to buy Steel on Tuesday, as—

Long years of reading the aunts' letters enabled Bob to wade through the cooking sherry and the steam in the greenhouse and come up with the order. He picked up the phone, told Miss Moracci to tell the floor-partner to purchase a hundred Steel outright and charge Miss Rosalie's account, and went on.

At five minutes of ten he finished the family pile, started on the customers' and important general, and exactly at ten, as the ticker on the corner of his desk started, he gave a quick glance through the residue of unimportant mail and offerings, and picked up the phone. "Mr. Corning. . . . Jase? Come on in, old man." The market, he noticed by the ticker, opened up a full half. "Miss Moracci, call the floor and tell Wagnalls to take any profits the Trust has shown since noon yesterday. Tell him I said he'll be able to buy back three-eighths to a half cheaper by one o'clock."

He lit a cigarette and leaned back, pulling the ticker tape out till it would reach him. He let it run through his fingers while he regarded Jason Corning, red-faced and beaming, coming through the door from the conference room.

"God," the senior partner of the firm said, "you brokers lead a soft life. I've been here since half-past eight."

Bob smiles. "How'd they go this morning?"

"Beautifully, beautifully. That little Cora Sue that I took to Aiken went the eighth in eleven-two."

"Congratulations, old man," Bob said gently. It must be good time from Jason's voice.

"And she's an April foal, too," Jason said. "Think of it!"

"It sounds like you have a winner, Jase. . . . What's on your mind? Miss Moracci said—"

"Oh, yes. Why, Bob, you know I never interfere in the way you run the firm. Damn glad to have you. Family only put me in here because I was the last surviving male, that sort of thing. I hate Wall Street, you know—"

"I didn't want to come in here, either, Jase. What's on your mind?"

The vague Corning said: "Oh, yes, of course, quite. Took that Reginia mare of mine over to Westie's, yesterday. You know Alan Westervelt?"

"Hudson Valley Insurance Company."

"Yes. Said something about giving our firm his firm's stock business, or something."

"An insurance company isn't exactly a firm, Jase. And it isn't allowed to deal in stocks. Yes, we have been doing some bond business for Hudson Valley. Why?"

"Westie—I took Reginia over to breed her to that Crash-along, y'know—said something about one of the Tenbruyes in our firm. I didn't know that."

"Sort of an experiment. He's really more of a real estate man than a stockbroker. I took him in to see if he couldn't bring us some of the John Street accounts—which he has, including Hudson Valley—and also move some of the Season-good Trust real estate for us."

"I see. Funny though. You'd think a Tenbruye coming into the firm would look me up."

Robert Seasongood Seligmann lit another cigarette. "As a matter of fact I don't think he's related to the same Ten-bruyes you are. But what was on your mind?"

"Well, Skippy Hazlett and Joe Pembrooke, and some of those fellows, want to charter a ship and go down to the Argentine. Ever since this Amor Brujo and a few like that, y'know, the Argentinos have been getting ahead of us. Want to buy stock, and study their training, and all. I'm thinking of going in with them. I'd take Cora Sue and Whitie—White Flash, y'know—and of course Morning Run and see—"

Bob crushed the cigarette out. "Your idea was to leave Tenbruye in charge of the Corning interests?" His voice betrayed no anger.

Jason nodded, relieved.

"I tell you, old man. The aunts are old, y'know. And I— well, to tell you the truth, Jason, I've thought of asking you to buy out the Seligmann interest in the firm." This with a smile.

"Bob! Why, Corning and Seligmann was founded in 1837. Over a hundred years ago."

"I know. But you see, Jase—old man—there hasn't been a resettlement for about fifty years. The Cornings still own three-sixths of the firm, the Seligmanns only two, and the Seligmanns—meaning me—do all the work."

"Well, y'know, I'd just be in the way. No head for figures or anything of that sort."

"Someone was asking me the other day. What's Morning Run done in the last few starts?"

Jason blinked. "One-fifty-two, nine furlongs, one-thirty-seven the mile and—"

"I think you'd make a fine broker, Jason."

"Oh, but I say—"

"After all, the morning breezes are over before the market opens, and you could be out at the track at three-thirty or a little later every afternoon."

"But what would I do in the winter?"

"No," Bob Seligmann said, "it isn't worth it. Anne and I can live on the interest of what we've got if we put our money into government bonds, and as the children grow older, we can reasonably expect to inherit from the aunts. As for you—"

"I can't live on three percent or whatever it is that madman in Washington's paying to—"

"No, you'd have to shut your stable down. But you could still go to the races, Jason."

Jason Corning said: "I— This comes as rather a shock, Bob." He turned and walked towards the window.

Seligmann studied the tape running through his fingers. He touched the switch on his desk. "Tell Wagnalls to sell that Steel of Miss Pereira's. Miss Rosalie Pereira." Three points was ample for Aunt Rosalie.

From the window, Jason said: "It wasn't my suggesting this Tenbruye, Bob? You didn't think that I don't trust you?"

"Of course not, old man."

"Just—well, a system of checks and balances, y'know. Two heads better than one. A man's not at his best training his own horses, y'know."

"Of course, Jase."

"You'll reconsider, Bob?"

Bob Seligmann smiled.

"I—you can't let us down, Bob. The Cornings and the Seligmanns have always stuck together, you know. And this Argentine business means a lot to me. Might even turn a profit on it. My stable's within an ace of making money, y'know."

"It always has been."

"Ha, ha, quite so. Well—"

"Good-bye, Jase."

The red-faced man left, waving his hand.

Bob Seligmann sat back, mopping his brow. His sensitive

dark face registered disgust for a minute. But—he had three sons. The firm would take care of at least one of them. Not just money, but the assured position of something your family had had so long. And with Howard in Corning and Seligmann young Peter might well be able to be a scientist. Already he could spot the paramecium in the little compound pocket glass his father had given him, which wasn't bad for a ten-year-old. . . .

"Get me Mr. Tenbruye, ask him to step in here. And tell Wagnalls to start buying back the Trust's industrials, but let the rails go till the last thing this afternoon."

So far as he knew, he and Penson were the first to try to get at filterables through starvation. What does a virus eat? "Oh, Tenbruye. Mr. Corning and I were talking about you this morning. We thought we ought to thank you for landing us that John Street business. It's not large, but it's the kind we like."

"Thanks, Mr. Seligmann."

"It'll be noticed in your pay, too. But—Tenbruye. I sent you up to John Street to do something about Mrs. Castron's property. How about it?"

"Well, Mr. Seligmann."

"Yes?"

"I have done something. I've gotten options on the houses on either side."

"Eh?"

"Now I'm ready to find a builder. They won't go into a one-lot proposition."

"In whose name did you accept these options?"

"My own, sir. I—"

"You'll transfer them to the firm. At once. Of course, I don't understand real estate, but it seems to me that—unless you have a specific builder in mind—you've gone about this in a peculiar way. You've given the owners of the other two lots to understand that Corning and Seligmann will liquidate their property?"

"Well, hardly, sir, I—"

"What builder did you think of?"

Tenbruye said, desperately: "That's why I kept the firm's name out of it. The only man really in the market for a good property is this Jack Firstin, the speculative builder, and—"

"Bring this Firstin in to see me. I am the responsible head of this firm."

"Yes, sir."

"I don't want it forgotten." *But what does a virus eat?*

*   *   *

DON SIGNED EIGHT LETTERS and pushed his way back from the desk. Five of the letters were requests for catalogues from mining machinery companies, one was personal to a classmate who was announcing his marriage, and the other two wanted to know why Armstrong and Grainger operations in Durango and North Carolina were falling off in production. He knew the answer—spring fever was a problem that could be solved neither by yellow-dog contracts nor by an industrial relations board—but as a field super he had always had to answer such letters from the home office, and he saw no reason why the time-honored custom should die.

His secretary came to get the signed letters and to hand him an envelope full of money; he had sent her over to the bank to get his semi-monthly pay check cashed. He counted the money, four hundred and thirty-two dollars and eighteen cents, and thanked her. As she closed the door after her, he walked to the window.

By craning his neck a little, he could see the tiniest corner of the upper Bay. A tugboat's searchlight played for a moment along the side of a freighter, even picked out the strange flag. United Fruiter, they had ships registered in the most unexpected South American ports.

From the way the flag was flapping, there was a good breeze out on the Bay. He started to open the window, but the first little crack let in such a gust that he pressed it shut again. Up here, on the forty-seventh floor, you didn't dare open the windows. Makin said they were going to have air-conditioning machinery installed before the heat of summer.

Behind him, his secretary cleared her throat. He turned, surprised to see her standing in the open door with her hat and coat on. He smiled: "Good night, Miss Cowan."

The hat, tall, pointed, faintly reminiscent of Merlin or the magicians in the Arabian Nights, gave her a personal touch that surprised him. During the day she took his footling letters and answered his phone and generally made a too-easy life even easier for him. He was aware, he suddenly thought, of a great many things about her, things that should be known only to her husband or brothers; that she wore garters with gold clasps, that it was necessary for her to take charcoal tablets after meals, that she was using a glycerin wash for her complexion.

He was aware—necessarily—of every journey she made to the ladies' room, and, from the length of the trip, whether she smoked a cigarette or not while there.

But he had not been aware, up to this moment, of that side of her personality which would cause her to select just that hat.

Pass Through Manhattan

The idea was a little repulsive. It opened a whole new side of Miss Cowan, what was the first name that a lower case vc on letters meant, whether she was engaged—or even married —and what she did with her evenings. It might, in the future, make him self-conscious of the gold-clasped garters that he saw when she crossed her knees to support the dictation notebook.

"You can go, Miss Cowan. I'm all through."

"Thanks. There's a Mr. Tenbruye outside to see you, Mr. Morton."

"Tenbruye?"

"Of Corning and Seligmann. But he says it's personal."

"Well—I'll see him, of course. And you needn't wait. Do you have far to go to get home?"

She started, it seemed to him, then smiled. "Another girl and I have an apartment in the Village. I take a local over on Greenwich Avenue."

"Well, good night." He went back to the desk and reached inside his coat for his personal check book. He wrote out a check to A. J. Cartwright, M.D., for one hundred and forty and no one-hundredths dollars. He was blotting this when Miss Cowan reopened the door and ushered in Tenbruye.

Don took a blank sheet of paper, folded it around the check, and put it in an envelope. There was no need to tell Dr. Cartwright that it was for two weeks' care of Joe Morton in the Cartwright Sanitarium. A psychiatrist ought to be able to figure that out for himself.

"Right with you, Mr. Tenbruye." Don stood up, holding out his hand. Tenbruye was shorter than Don, a little heavier. Hair that lay down without hair oil, black eyes.

Tenbruye took the hand, shook it. "You don't remember me?"

Pass Through Manhattan

"I'm afraid—"

"You saved my life." Tenbruye gave a nice laugh—not dismissing the debt, but not wanting to embarrass Don. A salesman, Don decided.

"Of course, the bus accident."

"I read in the *Wall Street Journal* a week ago that you had been appointed to the home office of Armstrong and Grainger, and I thought—as long as we're going to be neighbors—you might step out for a drink with me. That's why I called just at closing time this way."

"Nice of you. I don't know many people down here."

"I figured that. Put on your hat and let's go around to Robbins'."

"Just a moment." Don wrote the doctor's name and address on the envelope, shoved it in his pocket. "O.K." He shrugged into his heavy, expensive-looking ulster, and tapped his new hat square on his head. "Let's go."

"Our office is right downstairs," Tenbruye said, "on the forty-fifth floor."

"Stockbrokers, aren't you? I'm afraid I don't indulge."

"Oh, I'm not in that end. I'm more or less the real estate expert for the firm. You see, some of our largest accounts are really unofficial trust funds, the older members of the Corning and Seligmann connections."

It was the first time outside of a book that Don had ever heard the word connections used in that way. He had to say something; he was beginning to regret accepting Mr. Tenbruye's invitation.

"You handle the Tenbruye estate?"

"No. There are brokers from the senior branch of the family, you know, Doremus & Tenbruye, Tenbruye Read & Co. I'm descended from a cadet branch."

Me, I'm descended from a dipsomaniac newspaperman

and a somewhat flighty actress. I believe that I had grand-parents, but I'm not sure about it. "There's a Tenbruye Street somewhere around here, isn't there?"

"The Brooklyn Bridge wiped out most of it. What's left is just an alley with a blacksmith's shop at the end."

They were down on the street now, the cold wind coming up from the Bay, fresh despite the fact that neither man could have raised his arms over his head without making a previous arrangement with the horde of people pushing through the narrow sidewalks.

"It must be funny to stay so close to the tracks of your ancestors."

"Most people don't think of it. You're from Colorado?"

"No, I was born in Manhattan. Though hardly in the—er Tenbruye circles." Hell, that was an ungracious thing to say.

"There were some Mortons who had a dairy farm on Staten Island next to the first William Vanderbilts. Perhaps they're your family."

"Perhaps," Don said.

"And here's Robbins'. I'll be glad to get a drink. Chilly out."

The bar was so long that the end could not be seen. Men were elbowed up to it two and three deep. "They make a wonderful whisky sour here."

"I'll take a beer."

"Sit down and let me get it. I'm an old Wall Streeter, used to this."

The big room was filled with little bare-topped tables, around which men sat, all with their overcoats on, most of them wearing hats. Don sat down at one of them and shoved his hat back on his forehead. He felt a little foolish, and very sorry that he had so blithely come along. But hell, he'd had nothing to look forward to all evening except a restaurant supper and a movie. He'd seen all the movies he could stand.

Tenbruye came back carrying a glass filled with his own pinkish drink, a beer for Don and a plateful of little fishes and olives and things from the free lunch. He sat down: "Ein prosit."

"Your health."

The conversation died. Don said: "I'll get two more."

"No, I invited you to—"

"It's a challenge," Don said. "I've been sitting here studying that bar, and I think I see a weak spot in its defense."

He made it, got back, set the drinks down. "I wasn't man enough to go after the free lunch. A hard-drinking community, your Wall Street. Are all the bars this jammed at closing time?"

"Oh, Robbins' is quite the place to go."

Don stared. He had the vague feeling that this Tenbruye was kidding him, and yet it didn't seem likely that Tenbruye would go to the trouble of looking him up just to patronize him when he found him.

"You'll have to show me around some," Don said. "I swear I don't know a soul in New York. You know how it is when you've been away a while. I hardly feel like looking up boys I went to high school with, and the ones I knew in engineering college are scattered all·over the country."

"An engineering education is a wonderful background for Wall Street."

"I don't intend to stay here all my life."

"That reminds me of what F. D. R. said to Eleanor the other day—" He told it. Then, inevitably: "The New Deal has ruined Wall Street."

Donald contemplated the bar. "Has it? I was in Washington the other day. There was a hearing on some operations we're interested in."

"No doubt you came off the worse for it. Any firm with a Wall Street address—"

"No, we got what we wanted. The Army was on our side."

Tenbruye said: "Ah . . . Well—another one?"

"I don't think so," Don said. Then before he could stop himself, "I say, I was quite literal about being at loose ends. You wouldn't have dinner with me?"

"Why, I'd love to, but I have to run over and see the Castrons, the Orange Street Castrons, you know. Oh, but of course."

"Of course?"

"Eleanor Castron—she came out in '32—was in the bus with me that day. We were on our way to the Armory. Squadron A, you know. She'd love to meet you."

"Oh, but I don't—"

"I'll tell you. Let me get you another beer and I'll phone them. Eleanor might go to dinner with us, there was nothing definite. And especially if you want to meet some nice girls. The Castrons have entrée everywhere."

"But I—"

"Not another word, old man."

*   *   *

THE HOUSE THAT PUBLISHED *Nightstick Stories* among other literary productions paid its help and its writers on Tuesday. Munsey paid writers on Monday, Street & Smith Friday, and these pay days, together with the Popular Pubs, the Thrilling-Margulies outfit, Dell and the numerous minor pulps that paid off monthly, sporadically, or on publication, meant that a well-established action writer or assistant editor could get a drink and the loan of a dollar any night in the week.

Tonight was Tuesday and the W. Gordon Maxwells were giving a party. Gordie had stopped at Broadway and 96th and bought two quarts of sugar gin. Elsie had bought a dozen English mutton chops—the kind with a kidney wrapped in the middle—from the butcher on Lexington, promising to pay him on delivery, if delivery could be made after six o'clock. She had also tucked the loose ends of all the slip-covers back between the cushions and the frames of the easy chairs, and put into bureau drawers all the half-finished stories that were more than two weeks abandoned.

Jay Krinnel, a horror writer, had come uptown with Gordie. He stopped in the delicatessen store next to the liquor shop where Gordie got the gin, and bought a half dozen cans of pineapple juice. As an afterthought he also purchased a pound of assorted salted nuts. After that, they caught a bus across the Park.

When they finished walking the block down Fifth Avenue from where the bus had let them off, there were already lights blazing Chez Gordon. Someone was banging the piano. Most of the time the Gordons lived on the ground floor, as at present; their usual stay in a furnished apartment was about three months, if on the ground floor with no one but the janitor under them; or about a week if they became domiciled over a paying tenant.

Gordie held the vestibule door for Jay Krinnel with his elbow, and then set the package of gin down on the floor while he fumbled for his key. Eventually he found it and used it to lock the door; then he unlocked it again, held it open with his foot while he picked up the gin, and dropped the key into his pocket. He and Jay Krinnel went in.

John Harrington Young, editor of Lasso Yarns, looked up from the piano. "Hi, boys. Have a drink. There's a plate of ham on the kitchen table."

Elsie Gordon looked up from the typewriter in the corner, and said: "Oh, Gordie, pay John for the chops, will you, the butcher came early."

"How much?" Gordie opened the closet door and hung up his topcoat, being careful not to get the arm of the hanger into the hole in the lining instead of the sleeve.

"Either 2.31 or 3.12," Elsie said. "I'll find the bill."

Jay Krinnel dropped his overcoat—he wore no hat—in the corner, and carried the pineapple juice and salted nuts out to the kitchen. He took a dish out of the cupboard and dumped the nuts into it. After helping himself, mostly to cashew nuts, he put the dish down next to a platter of sliced Virginia ham. He found a beer hook, opened a can of pineapple juice and made himself a drink from it and from the half-empty fifth of good gin that he found on the drainboard.

Then he opened the icebox and put the pineapple juice in. A pink-wrapped package attracted his eye; he slit the paper, and found it was the mutton chops. A sales slip was wrapped in; he took this back into the living room. "Two dollars and thirty-one cents," he told Gordie. He handed over the slip. "Have a drink, Gordie."

"Thanks, I'll help myself," his host said, taking the slip. He went over to John Harrington Young, who was still banging the piano, and put the exact change in Young's pocket. Then he went out in the kitchen, opened the sugar gin, and poured some into two glasses, one for Elsie, the other for himself, and added tap-water to them.

Pass Through Manhattan

Elsie set the glass down next to one containing "good" gin and ginger ale and went on hitting the keys. Gordie read over her shoulder for a minute, muttered: "O.K.," and went out and ate a piece of ham. John Harrington Young stopped banging the piano, followed Gordie into the kitchen, and said: "That was a nice yarn of yours."

"Yes?" Gordie had his mouth full of salted nuts, and couldn't answer properly.

"The one about the lucky bump. With a little polishing you could have sold that to the slicks."

"What are you working on now, John?"

"A serial about ivory hunting in Africa for the *Saturday Evening Post*."

"You ought to make the *Post*, John. You're wasted on the wood-pulps."

"So are you, old man." John Harrington Young helped himself to a glass of the gin and ginger ale he had brought; Gordie took another snort of sugar gin and water. When John opened the icebox, Gordie said: "Oh, I want to pay you for those chops."

"You already did." John jingled his side pocket.

"That's right. I ought to cook them. Do you think we've got enough?"

"Six pounds ought to be ample."

"I'll put them on to cook. Do you like yours rubbed with mustard and garlic salt?"

"Anyway at all."

They both went back into the living room, arriving in one door just as Irv and Nora Shapiro burst in from the street. Nora, who did weird covers, yelled: "Irv sold a painting!"

Everybody stopped drinking his or her own particular version of alcohol. Irv Shapiro took a pinch-bottle of

Scotch out of the pocket of his neat, well-cut Chesterfield, and took a drink straight. The effect of this was interesting, as he nerved himself for a terrific shock, drank, and then relaxed, the shock having failed to arrive. The rest of them stared at him fascinated, as though they had never heard of liquor that could be drunk without either previous doctoring of the drink or subsequent medication of the drinker.

"It is a fact," Irv said. "The galleries just called up. They were just closing, and a guy in a big hat came in and wanted to buy *Sundown*, they had it in the window. Said it looked just like the view from his back porch in Idaho."

John Harrington Young said: "What was it supposed to look like?"

Irv Shapiro made a wry face. "Well," he said, drawling a little, "the funny part of it is—well—the lower half of it was a cover that Nora started for *Sexy Western*, or something like that."

"You know," Nora cut in, "those smutty action magazines down in Del—"

"Yes," Gordie said. "Garter-snapping on the open range."

"Flagellation," Nora corrected him. "The Western one is all about cowboys whipping girls with horsewhips. It's the adventure one that goes in for garter-snapping. The detective number is search-conscious."

"Go on with the painting," Elsie said, looking up from the typewriter.

"Oh," Irv said. "I was out of canvas. And Nora hadn't done much to the canvas, just daubed up the bottom. So I painted in the sky the way it looks over Jersey."

Irving took another drink and waved the bottle. "Have one?"

Nobody accepted, but his wife said: "Have you any

rum? I've found that Cuban rum doesn't give me a hang-over."

"I'll go get you a bottle," Irv said. "Give me some money."

His wife handed him two bills. "Get the Cuban *type* rum," she said firmly. "What are you writing, Elsie?"

"Confession," Elsie said tersely, "about a girl who never went out with boys, because she had a wonderful voice, and every day after school she went around to this old German for voice lessons. So he dies and she comes to New York to find another teacher, and all the ones she goes to want to sleep with her."

"Do they?" Nora asked.

"Some do and some don't," Elsie said. "That's what makes the story. I have to have it in tomorrow, it's on order."

"What are you getting?" Jay Krinnel asked.

"Two and a quarter."

"I'm going to take up confessions. You'd have to be Jesus Q. Shakespeare to get more than two cents a word out of pulps these days."

John Harrington Young and Gordie—the two editors present—said: "The American News is going to clean up the stands so we can get some good sales. Prices'll go up in the spring."

"Well, spring's here. Say, Nora, can I have the original of that cover you did for *Underground?*"

"Which one?"

"The hunchback releasing the jaguars and the gal tied to the post."

"Oh, did you write that?"

"Yeah."

"Ask Gordie. His boss is the editor."

"I'm afraid," Gordie said, "that's gone. The vice-president took it to hang on his yacht."

Irv Shapiro came back, carrying a bottle. He said: "I met this gentleman outside, he was looking for your apartment, Gordie."

Elsie looked up and said: "Tell him if he's from a lawyer named Rosenstein, we're not going to give him a cent till he lifts the garnishee off Gordie's salary."

John Harrington Young said: "But how can you keep from giving it to him if he's got a garnishee?"

Gordie said: "The law only allows one garnishee at a time, and there are three— Oh, hello, Mr. Ranulph."

Dead silence hit the room as Buck Ranulph walked in embarrassedly. His ten-dollar hat hung at his side, his coat of English tweeds was carelessly unbuttoned; he was the only man in the room who made as much as sixty dollars a week, and he looked it. But he said, with what composure he could muster: "I didn't know you were having a party, Mr. Maxwell, or I wouldn't have—"

"But it's swell, Mr. Ranulph," Gordie said. His ess sounds were very clear, as though he were having trouble with them. "This is Detective Ranulph, of the 104th Street Station," he told everyone. "We were in a bus accident together."

"Have you been subpoenaed yet?" Buck asked. "Someone's suing over the accident."

"No," Gordie said. "Let me get you a drink. I duck process servers so much, I wouldn't be likely to. Who's suing?"

"Some German lady. Lemke, or something like that."

"I don't remember her, do you?"

Buck accepted a tumbler half full of Scotch from Irv

Shapiro, and said: "Thank you." He said: "No" to Gordie's question, but Gordie was already gone.

Three women came in the front door. Buck swung his hat desperately at his side. Nora Shapiro said: "Here, Mr. Randolph, let me take your things," and guided him to the corner.

"Ranulph," he said.

"My name's Shapiro, Nora Shapiro."

"Do you write? Are most of these ladies and gentlemen writers?"

"Most of them, but Irv and I paint. I do covers, mostly weird, and he's pure."

Buck swallowed. "And which is Mrs. Maxwell?"

"In the corner, at the typewriter. She confesses. And the gray-haired guy with the round face is John Harrington Young, he runs Lasso Yarns, and writes adventure. Jay Krinnel, with the curly hair there, does mostly horror and an occasional weird. The thin girl who just came in is assistant editor on *Sagebrush Sweethearts*, and she sells some detective on the side. Her name is Myra McGrail. The fat one with her, Kay something or other, she works down at Street & Smith. The other girl is Lee Davids, she does novelizations, and she's been married three times in ten years, and hasn't bought a new suit of tweeds in all that time."

Buck gulped, and grasped the only phrase that he was sure could not be obscene. "What are novelizations?"

"Writing books out of movies for the fan magazines."

"But I thought movies were made out of books?"

"They are, but the fan-magazine readers like the story to stick closer to the movie. . . . Are you really a detective?"

"Yes'm. Third class."

"Swell. I think that's wonderful. I used to know a policeman, we lived next to him in Flushing, but I never knew a detective before. Let me get you a drink."

She left him, and the sweat broke out on his brow. He tried to join the nearest group to him, but John Harrington Young was dominating it, saying: *"Collier's* wants types, not characters, but they won't admit it."

Lee Davids said: *"Collier's* is hydra-headed, that's the trouble with it."

"So's *Liberty*," Jay Krinnel said, "and I never have any trouble selling it."

"I liked your last yarn in *Liberty*," Lee said.

Buck shook his head. He was a college, nearly a law school, graduate, but he couldn't understand a sentence these people said. And yet—

Myra McGrail took his arm, and said, "Hello, copper."

He said: "How do you do?"

"Do you write?"

He was phrasing an answer when Nora Shapiro skated by, stuck a glass in his hand, and turned her back, screaming at John Harrington Young: "Did you hear that that lousy boss of yours is going to bring out a line of reprints with second-hand plates?"

Buck gulped the drink. The rum slid down to join the Scotch, and he sighed.

"Well, I have written a little story, I brought it over to see if Mr. Maxwell would criticize it for me, but I didn't know this party—"

"Let's see it."

With some hesitation, Buck took three pages of typescript out of his pocket, handed it over.

Myra McGrail looked at it, said: "You type nicely."

"I had a public stenographer copy it."

She hefted it, peered at it. "A thousand-worder? They're

easy to sell, the magazines need them to fill in holes. . . . Go talk to Lee Davids, while I retire to the johnny with this." She went away.

Buck made a grab for her, but she was gone. And anyway, he'd been brought up in the belief that it was extremely dangerous for a colored man to so much as touch a white lady's elbow, and it was apparent that force would be needed to keep Myra McGrail from reading his poor little story.

He stood there, sweating, unable to leave because there was a mob between him and the coat closet, unable to join in any conversations, stumped. Gordie Maxwell rescued him with a drink of gin and water that nearly made Buck sick. Lord. When they found any of that in a Harlem apartment they poured it down the sink. It tasted like the stuff the Porto Ricans used to make during prohibition. But it surged around inside him along with the Scotch and the rum.

Mr. Maxwell was talking to him, something about the bus accident, and did he know that the man who rescued them was the son of Joseph Kolk Morton. He yessired and nosired, his eye on the bathroom door.

Jay Krinnel grabbed his left elbow and stuck a drink of gin and pineapple juice into his right hand. "Don't you agree with me that *Esquire* is the last refuge of the amateur verbal athlete?"

Myra McGrail came out of the bathroom, and yelled: "Can I borrow your mill, Gordie?" She disappeared into the bedroom, carrying the three sheets headed Buckingham Ranulph.

Lee Davids said: "You're just jealous because Harvey can sell *Esquire* and you can't."

Pass Through Manhattan

Much against his better judgment, Black gulped the new drink. This gin was better anyway. But when someone handed him a jelly glass with two inches of what seemed to be green chartreuse in the bottom, he put it on the mantelpiece, and went into the bedroom.

Myra McGrail was seated on the edge of the bed, her knees wide to support a cardtable with its legs still folded. On top of the cardtable was a typewriter. "How—" Buck began.

"You made the usual mistake of the beginner," Myra said, briskly. "You put two different plots into a short short. I'm cutting out one of them for you." She typed a moment, whipped the paper out of the machine, tore the first page of Buck's story up and replaced it with the one she had done. "The typing stinks," she admitted. "I'm used to my old Remington mill, I hate these portable jobs. Show it to Gordie, they're in the market on *Nightstick*."

He hesitated. She put the typewriter on the bed, strode briskly past him, and into the living room. Buck followed her.

John Harrington Young shoved a glass of gin and ginger ale into his hand, and said: "You better eat something, there's some ham in the kitchen. Did you ever try a Western?"

"You mean egg and onion sandwich? We call 'em—"

"No, a Western story. Did you know some of the most famous cowpunchers were colored? The first herd ever driven up the Chisholm Trail had two—"

Gordie Maxwell took Buck's arm, and said: "That's a swell yarn Myra showed me. We'll buy it at a cent, old man. Have a drink."

Buck shook his head mutely. He was a successful, commercial writer, but he was also sick to his stomach. He hurried for the bathroom door.

*　　　*　　　*

IN THE BIG FIELD devoted to the buffalo, *bos* or *bison americanus*, snow still lingered, patches of it in the crevasses of rock, a big patch of it—discolored by the city and by the buffalo—in the sheltered space uphill from the feed shed. The buffalo themselves looked moth-eaten and shabby, but Washington explained that they were shedding their winter coats.

"All mammals have two coats a year," he said. "They shed in the spring and fall."

Marie Lempe adored her learned son with her eyes. "My aunt near Ulm had a little white dog," she said. "He shed his coat all year. Always white hairs on everything."

From all over the zoo the snow was melting, the gutters of the neatly made white footwalks were running full. There was a fine, earthy smell of melting snowwater and manure and rich brown dirt.

Washington said: "There's the Rocking Stone."

"Maybe this year you can make it rock."

The thirteen-year-old boy ran up the little bluff on which the Rocking Stone poised, incredibly. Its huge bulk rested, apparently, on one tiny point, and the slightest touch would send it rolling down the hill. But it had been there, according to the sign, since time immemorial, and no one had ever budged it.

Each year, since early times when Marie had had to read the sign in her stumbling English to Grace, even, because the children were too little to read, Washington had hoped to be able to roll the stone away. Next year, he would say, next year I will be big enough. It would be a fine thing, he would have his picture in the papers, everybody in New York knew the Rocking Stone in the Bronx zoo.

Marie watched the boy, laughing, throw all his weight on the huge boulder. But it did not stir from its pedestal. Washington came running back to her, his face red from pushing and laughing at the same time.

"Maybe next year," Marie said.

He imitated her German accent. "Eat your spinach and your good cereal, and maybe next year, Washington."

"Where shall we go? Shall we eat lunch now, or later? I have lots of money, papa says I should sit in a wheel chair, but no, we spend it on, on—"

"Let's buy some peanuts and feed the elephants."

"Washington, it says do not feed or annoy—"

"But not the elephants, mama, you can feed the elephants. Remember I asked the man once, he said it was all right to feed the elephants."

But it took them a long time to get to the elephants. They kept passing such wonderful things, the polar bears—already looking sick from the spring, though there was plenty of ice and snow left in their den, it made you chilly to stand in the breeze after it had passed over their rocks—the reptile house, with its interesting alligators, its alarming snakes and, though Marie was sure they were no reptiles—its charming pair of tiny kinkajous.

She stopped a keeper in a blue cap. "These are not from reptiles, no?"

"Naw. The small-animal house was crowded, and I dunno, we kinda like to have them here."

"It gives mistakes to the children, that they should be in the reptile house."

"Aw, lady—"

Pass Through Manhattan

Then, because it was spring, they were both laughing, the flatfooted, somewhat grimy reptile tender and the workworn immigrant woman. Washington looked from one to the other, his eyes as bright and inquiring as the kinkajous'.

Suddenly the keeper opened the little cage, and took one of the tiny creatures out. It nestled on his shoulder, sticking its black muzzle into his neck, rubbing the fur of its brown neck against his, nipping at his ear experimentally.

"Want to hold it, son?" He handed it out to Washington, whose hands shook with excitement. The kinkajou, hospitably, washed the boy's nose, and Washington squealed with delight.

"Oh, mama, I want one."

"Papa wouldn't—"

The keeper said: "They're not easy to come by, lady. They come from Central America, and they gotta be kept real warm."

"I'd keep him warm, he could sleep under the covers with me every night, and when we went out he could get under my overcoat."

The keeper put the kinkajou back, saying: "That's a good boy you got there, lady," and walked away.

After that, nothing less than the lions and tigers could be interesting. They sat on the high platform opposite the cages and watched the big animals moving, the tigers incredibly big, incredibly brilliant in their coloring, the lions lazy, and, like the buffalo, mangy at this changing season.

The black panther was enraged by something. He leaped and tore at his bars, whirling through the air.

Marie was glad enough to sit there, to rest her feet. She had on her good shoes, not the ones she did housework in or had used to wear while standing behind the bakery counter. But the heavy smell of the cathouse made her head ache

a little, and when Washington began to fret, she rose will-
ingly enough.

They passed through the big, handsome house given over
—according to the sign—to Apes & Primates. There was a
crowd around one cage at the near end, and they stopped
automatically.

A tremendous, kindly, middle-aged colored man stared
out at Marie Lempe from between heavy bars.

Automatically she smiled. He looked understanding, sympathetic, it was a shame to keep this poor fellow locked up
that way. It made her nervous to be staring at him, although
the sign said he was a gorilla.

The chimpanzee that shared the big fellow's cage postured
and strutted, bowed and did gymnastics, but the crowd was
still, watching the immobile gorilla. The monster's flat nose
moved with the effort of his breathing, he sighed.

A colored girl in the crowd giggled nervously. The gorilla's liquid eyes rested on her for a moment, contemptuously. She stepped back through the crowd, and hurried
out, her gaily dressed boy friend trotting after her.

The gorilla stood up on his bowed legs and stretched his
arms. Then, slowly, he lumbered to the back of the cage and
through a small door, which he closed after him.

The crowd let out its collective breath, and began to melt
away, oblivious to the importunate posturing of the chimpanzee.

A little boy said in German: "But mama, the elephants,
let us see the elephants."

"Speak English, August. We shall the elephants now see."

"But mama, where are they?" The boy spoke English better than his mother.

Marie Lempe turned, to look at a woman near her own
age, in the late thirties or early forties. The woman was

better dressed, perhaps, but with a Continental touch. A greenhorn.

Marie said: "We are going to the elephants."

The woman nodded gravely. August and Washington sized each other up, and then, receiving some mysterious signal of friendship known only to children, they walked ahead. Marie could hear Washington explaining to August that he knew all the elephants by name. "We come here every year, sometimes twice. They have an African. elephant, too, you can't train those."

"That gorilla," the German woman said, "he was human, nicht wahr? But I hear that if he gets out, he kills you."

"Yes. You know," Marie said, "he reminds me from a chauffeur who used to buy rolls for his mistress, in a bakery where once I work. A schwartzer," she explained.

"To me, it is disturbing, these Negroes on the street. In Hesse, where we live, I have never seen a Negro except in the cinema."

"You are from Hesse? Cassel, oder Darmstadt?"

"Cassel."

"Me, I am from Württemberg, we are nearly neighbors."

"You do not say? I am homesick a little. I would not, to my husband, admit it, but the Rhine, it was so pretty in the spring." The stranger sighed. "And the Negroes, and the Italians on the street, they make me afraid. That ape—" She shuddered. "Perhaps it is true, Negroes and apes, they are the same."

"That is taught in the Fatherland now, yes?" But Marie didn't wait for the answer. Washington had run back to her, was demanding the money for the peanuts. She gave him two dimes, for a bag for himself and one for August. She looked around, saw a refreshment stand with some little tables set under a tree. "We will be there, Washington."

Pass Through Manhattan

The woman said: "Washington? Your son, then, was born in the United States?"

"Also my daughter. She is in Hunter High School going. That is the best high school in the city, only good pupils go there."

"August, he has had to drop back a year in school, because of the language. But the teacher, she says one year, that is very good to lose only one year. He will make it up."

"Would you join me in a cup of coffee, or maybe a Coca Cola? That is an American drink, very good."

"But—"

"Please. To drink coffee or Coca-Cola by oneself, that is not good."

The woman flushed, and Marie guessed that she did not have much money. It would, under the circumstances, be tactless to tell her how Artur had given her money to rent a wheel chair.

"Please. My husband, he will be so happy to know I have spoken with one newly arrived from Germany. Always he is homesick."

"But not you?" The lady had tacitly consented, apparently, to the Coca-Cola. Marie paid for two bottles, and they carried them to one of the little tables.

"No, always since the war, I wish to come to the United States. For the children. It is good here."

The other woman sighed. "But now I am here, I cannot forget. The pretty chestnut trees. Our friends. Even the little pastries with the coffee in the afternoon. You will think I am foolish. Your speaking of the bakery, perhaps, put the thought in my mind."

"They have good Rhenische pastries there. The owner and his wife, they are from the Rheinpfalz. Do you live near 96th Street?"

184

Pass Through Manhattan

"But yes, on 94th and West End Avenue. Cousins of my husband, they have so kindly sheltered us until employment we can find. My husband, he is a pharmacist and must pass an examination in English for to be licensed."

Marie said excitedly: "The good people from the bakery, they seek a woman. Until I come back it is, only, I was in an accident and Herr Lempe will not permit I should work, but—oh, but you are a lady, you will not stand behind a counter."

"Oh yes I would, I would, and think, if I was there, then you would be sure I would leave when you were well again, you would not be worrying about some stranger taking your job. Oh, I knew today, it would be a lucky day."

"Drink," Marie said, pointing towards the pop bottle.

The woman drank. "It is good."

"It is American," Marie said.

"Yes, I know. We shall like it here, when once— It is hard, you know. Where is the bakery?"

Marie told her the street number. "Between Broadway and Amsterdam. Not far from where you are living. Me, I had to come across town, we live in Yorkville."

"Yorkville?"

"Yes. . . . And tell them, by the bakery, that I said you would be good, my name is Mrs. Lempe."

"Lempe?"

The woman stared at the table top. Then she rose, her face flushed. "I am afraid you have made the mistake. My name, it is Frau Goldstein. I am—"

"Well? Oh, you mean—" Tears, silly, blinding tears, came to Marie's eyes. "That does not matter, really not. Are we not both— Oh, tell me, is it so bad in Germany then, so terrible?"

"Yes," the Jewish lady said, "it is."

Pass Through Manhattan

THERE WAS A STEP ON THE STAIRS, and the young man squashed out his cigarette in the overflowing ashtray. He got up and walked rapidly towards the two sliding doors that led to the hall. Then he stopped and looked at Peggy Reilly, neat and cool in her white uniform, her spotless white cap that was not even relieved by a black ribbon.

Peggy went on filing cards.

The cards were recipes from a kitchen filing set that she had found there. One of her predecessors, sleeping in between jobs, had advised her to take the cards and shuffle them between calls: "You've got to do something or you'll get more flustered than the men. And we don't keep any records or write any letters, of course."

Peggy said: "Just sit still. Mrs. Smith will be down in a few minutes."

The boy had chestnut hair that stood straight on end. He blinked at Peggy, and said: "Will she be all right? I mean—"

"Dr. Wilcomen has never lost a patient, or had any trouble. If he had, he wouldn't be here, buddy. Think it out."

The boy lit another cigarette. "Does it—does it hurt much?"

"It's over quicker than having a baby," Peggy said. "It will be all right, Mr. Smith."

"I sure hope so. We wouldn'ta done this, but, well, I only get eighteen dollars a week, an' Josie gets twenty-three an'— As soon as I get a raise—"

It was against the rules to sympathize. Any sympathy, and they went all to pieces. Peggy said: "I know. Fifty dollars would be only the beginning with a baby."

"Yeah, that's—"

There was another step on the stair. The buzzer rang under Peggy's desk. She stood up. "Mrs. Smith will be down in a minute. Now, the best thing for her is to walk at least a block before you get a cab."

"Yes, miss, yes."

"I wouldn't walk more than two blocks. And don't talk any more than you have to in the taxi."

"Yes, miss."

Peggy helped him into his coat. The smell of rank, cold sweat came to her nostrils. They all smelled alike, all the young men who waited and watched her file cooking recipes. The smell of fear—

The buzzer rang again. Peggy slid open the doors, shoved Mr. Smith out into the hall. "Good-bye. And if anything happens, don't hesitate to call up."

"No, miss."

Jod, the colored porter, helped Mrs. Smith down the stairs. Mr. Smith took her elbow carefully. But her eyes were shining with the shot in the arm Dr. Wilcomen always gave them to finish up on. Jod opened the front door, and they went down the steps.

The colored man went into Peggy's reception room and picked up the ashtray. Dr. Wilcomen came down the stairs on his heels.

"Wait a minute, Jod. You count 'em, Reilly?"

"No, I didn't have a chance," Peggy said.

The doctor took the ashtray from the colored man, rapidly counted the butts. "Sixteen," he said. "Even. That's another dime I owe you."

"Fifty cents, doctor."

"Wait a minute. There were two Joneses today, and three Smiths. Or was the last one a Smith?"

Peggy said: "Yes. All right, a dime off. Forty cents. But you're cheating me. There are always more Smiths than Joneses."

"I wondered how long before you'd catch on. The fair bet is the Smiths plus the Joneses against everything else. I'll take either side. . . . No more today, are there?"

"No. Dr. Vlecken is sending a Mrs. Wilson down at ten in the morning."

"Quite a number of Wilsons. . . . Jod! Bring me a high-ball. Have one, Reilly?"

"Yes, please."

Peggy opened the closet door, put her cap on the shelf. She dusted powder on her nose, and sat down on the edge of the desk, crossing her ankles. Wilcomen lounged on the settee, his long, white-clad legs stretched straight out in front of him. He said abruptly: "I've got nearly ten thousand dollars in the bank."

"Congratulations."

He waved a hand. "I just happened to think of it."

Jod came back in with the tray. He set it down next to Peggy and went out again, and she slid to the floor, mixed two drinks and carried them over to the settee. Wilcomen put up one bony hand for the drink, rested the other on the back of her knee, just under her skirt. His hand slid up and down, gently.

"You ought to wear silk stockings," he said lazily.

"I would if you'd get me a desk that wasn't so splintery."

He gulped his drink. "Get me another snort. And drink up."

Over the noise of the ice tinkling, the glass clinking, he drawled: "You change faster than anybody I ever saw, Mick. I don't think you give any more of a damn now than Cox, and she's been doing this twelve years. When I think of you two weeks ago—"

She brought the second round of drinks back and sat down next to him. He slid over till his head rested on her shoulder, and took half his drink down in a gulp. "Let's get drunk and go to bed together, Mick."

Peggy didn't move. "No sale," she said. "I don't mind a little light feeling when you're tired, but that's all."

"God, you're tough, Mick. What's the matter with you?"

"I wanted to be a nurse," she said, "and what did I get? I've lost my religion, I've been kicked out of two hospitals, and I've had an abortion."

"Stop talking shop."

She stood up, letting his head slide down the leather back of the settee. He shoved himself back with one foot on the floor until he was flat on his back. He watched Peggy mixing herself a third drink. "You seem to be taking me up on the first half of my proposition, anyway. Save some for doctor."

She brought him his drink, and dodged the arm that groped for her. "Can I have tonight off? Jordan's coming in."

"Oke. I sure like you, Mick. Why won't you—"

She sat down on the desk again. "Because I won't. Anyway, if you could get that at home, you'd never go out. It isn't good for you."

"Hell, kid, I'd just as soon marry you. Why not? I'd save your salary."

She put her glass down. "Would you? Would you marry me and throw this up?"

"What the hell would we do? Ten thousand dollars is a lot of scratch, but it wouldn't last forever."

"We could go to one of the Latin-American countries. They need doctors and nurses, we could start with a small clinic, and have our own hospital in a few years. You've got your degree, and they aren't going to care whether you ever interned or not. And I—"

"You could be a nurse. That's the hell of an idea."

"Why?"

"I don't like bananas. That's all they have in Central America, bananas and monkeys. I don't like monkeys, either."

"All right, then Labrador or Alaska."

"I don't like pemmican. I'm very fastidious. Nuts with it, Reilly. I'll tell you. I'll grow a beard and disguise myself as a veterinary."

Over the rim of her glass she said: "Skip it."

"Come on out with me tonight. I'll take you to a movie and pinch your thigh in the more important moments."

"You'd better do something about yourself. You'll be making passes at the patients next thing you know."

He made a face. "That isn't funny. Mix me another drink and I'll stop talking dirty."

"That's because I beat you at it and—"

The front doorbell rang and opened. Wilcomen swung up, and started for the door into the back hall, but Jod had left the sliding doors open and the unshaven man saw them. He pushed in. "Miss Margaret Reilly?"

"Yes."

"Welcome to the big city." He slapped a paper into her hands and was gone.

Wilcomen stood over her, his face white as a sheet. "You dirty little Irish double-crosser. What Sinn Fein sell-out is—"

She opened the paper, took a quick look at it, and laughed. "One on you, Doc. It's that bus accident I was in. They want me for a witness."

He snatched the paper from her, read the first few lines. "I thought—"

"I know what you thought. You'd better get out of this

line of work, Wilcomen, it's giving you the jitters. I wonder how they found me."

"They can always find you," he said gloomily. "Look at me. They can't get me, because to do it they have to have a stool pigeon for me to operate on, and how the hell would they find that? And every patient I get is sent by a reputable physician. And I pay five hundred dollars a month for protection. And still and all, I know it's only a matter of time before—"

"Quit and let's—"

"Aw drop it," he snarled. He walked to the door quickly. "I'm going out. You stay here till Jordan checks in and make sure the phone's switched to her room. That next to the last one this afternoon might hemorrhage."

His feet drummed on the stairs as he trotted up. But when he reached the first landing that had the operating room and his bedroom, he slowed to a walk, almost a funeral crawl.

Peggy heard the door of his room slam.

*   *   *

JACK FIRSTIN LOWERED HIS MASSIVE BODY down into the red leather chair. He said: "So you have examined it from A to Z?"

Mr. McCransten nodded. "If I were you, Firstin, I wouldn't let any grass grow under my feet. I'd snatch up this Seligmann offer tonight."

Jack shrugged. He brushed his knees off, fastidiously. "But maybe I don't want I should build in Brooklyn."

"Brooklyn Heights is a pretty fine locality. Some wonderful old houses over there."

"Drek. Always you hear how fine old houses were. Did

they have steel girders, did they have re-enforced foundations? Drek, that's all. Not over four stories would they have stood up. . . . For why should I have to build in Brooklyn?"

"Listen, Firstin. This is the opportunity of a lifetime. Seligmann, think of it. A chance to work the name of Seligmann into your promotion material."

"Since when is it so good to be Jewish?"

McCransten shook his head. "It isn't that. It puts you beyond the district attorney, the attorney general, Washington. There's not a one of them would dare say that Corning and Seligmann would countenance a crooked deal. The administration in Washington is leaning over backwards to avoid antagonizing business, and they wouldn't dare open their mouths. Robert S. Seligmann is related to a lot of influential people. He's—"

"But from this building we would not be selling stock."

"Of course not. A straight cut-up. Corning and Seligmann buy in the option on the outside lots, and take stock for their clients' interest. I can get you a building loan that will satisfy the Starrett people. And the bank's willing to give you a mortgage on the strength of the Seligmann interest. They're anxious to get some of that Wall Street money into New York real estate, there isn't a bank in town hasn't got a few frozen acres."

"But Brooklyn, you say Brooklyn, it makes the tenants think Flatbush."

McCransten said: "But that's your specialty, Firstin. Think what you did with Greenwich Square, it was a Mick slum. Think what you did—"

"Wait a minute," Jack Firstin said. "I got it. Lissen. Modern materials that should express the spirit of old New York. Dutch modernistic, huh, what was it they called them these old Dutch lords or sirs, or something? Maroons, or—"

"Patroons."

"Yeah, it should be pat—Patroon Arms? No, it stinks. Lemme think."

He finished the job of closing his eyes that his fat cheeks had started. In the lobby of the Architects Building, that's where they were, he had seen them on display. Hollow concrete, finished in a light blue. Dutch blue. Sure, from that building on East 79th he had built, he had used Dutch Deal —no, Delft—tiles in the kitchenettes. A whole building like that.

And always clean and shining. This tile, now no sandblasting to eat away your good stone and get dirty again right away anyway. Just a hose. No cracks to start erosion, and no bills from Nicholson and Galloway to rebuild stone. Always blue and shining, up there over the harbor.

"I will start it a new residential section so it becomes common to live on Park Avenue," Jack Firstin muttered. His body moved uneasily.

McCransten said sharply: "You'll have to have a name that reminds people of Corning and Seligmann. That's the point. So when these crackpot visionaries relax the security laws a little, you can say on circulars that you were the builder of—of Seligmann Square, or Corning Arms or—"

"Tenbruye Place."

"Eh?"

"From Corning and Seligmann, their young man is named Tenbruye. I should name the building for him, and he will serve on my next board of directors." Jack Firstin grinned wisely, the grin of the ghetto boy who knew something the Scotch lawyer didn't know. "Seligmann, what kind of a name is that? Can you rent apartments to Hitler and the Klu Klux with a name like Seligmann? Tenbruye Place."

"Sounds all right to me."

Jack Firstin nodded. On nice days the water in the harbor was blue, and it should be such a blue in the brick. "Hand me your phone."

After a few minutes he said: "Hello, Mr. Tenbruye. I am ready, maybe we talk business . . . Yes? Yes? Well, then at four. I'll make it a date." He hung up. "It should be good, Mr. Seligmann himself wants to see me."

McCransten said: "Watch him. Robert Seligmann is no fool."

"Is there anything crooked in this deal?" Jack Firstin stood up. "Good-bye, McCransten, I got to go over to the Architects Building. . . . Oh, by the way, this ain't nothing, is it?"

He smiled when he saw the look of horror on McCransten's face at the sight of the legal paper. That was the way he had felt when the process server had given it to him.

Then McCransten laughed. "No, it's nothing. They want you for a witness about that bus accident. If you're busy, I can arrange to have you send in a deposition instead."

"That's what I thought." The blue in which the subpoena was wrapped was the same color almost as Delft.

*   *   *

SPRING WAS COMING IN FULL BLAST up the harbor, and though it was nine o'clock at night, you didn't need to button your topcoat to stand against the railings that overlooked the harbor from Brooklyn Heights.

Eleanor said: "You ought to have a girl, Don."

He chuckled. "That's a nice remark. What do you consider yourself?"

"But I'm in love with someone else."

Pass Through Manhattan

Below them the stevedores finished unloading a ship, and floodlights began to go off. A tug hooted.

"Not Tenbruye?"

"Certainly not. John Tenbruye is a—a—"

"He's all right."

"How would you like him to kiss you?"

Don laughed. "Well, now, I can't say that that's what I've been waiting for."

They both giggled, hanging to the railings. Don took his hands down, wiped the rusty moisture off them. "There's a fog coming down the river. That's from the snow melting up in the Catskills. Smell it. We get that in Colorado in the middle of summer sometimes, the snow never melts on some of those peaks, you know. Maybe we'd better go inside."

"I'm not cold. I like it out here. Do you like New York any better, Don?"

"Well, you can't like or dislike a thing like New York. In the line of work that I'm in, it's the only place to be. The money's here and the banks. A man has to stay close to them."

"But I thought you were a mining engineer. Shouldn't you be where there's a mine?"

"That's all right when you're a kid. But there's no future in being out on the rim when the power comes from the hub. Tenbruye's got the right idea. A chap told me the other day that Tenny's going to be one of the most important men in the Street in five years."

"Thank God we live on the Heights, is all I have to say. . . . Do you remember when I first met you, you were worrying about that man who was killed getting us out of the bus?"

"Yes."

"I just wondered if that was going to come up in this lawsuit. You've been served, haven't you?"

"Yes. No, the suit hasn't got anything to do with Copper. With Ringgold, I mean. It's one of the passengers, a German woman."

"Ringgold, I remember the name in the papers. Why did you call him Copper?"

Don stared down through the railings. It was impossible how people grew up all of a sudden. Just a few weeks ago he had been a moonsick calf worrying about a bum, just because the bum had an attractive face, a pleasant voice. Worried his father into—

Eleanor said: "What are you laughing about, Donald?"

"I like the way you call me Donald. Oh, I was laughing about my father. He's in a sanitarium, you know."

"Oh, that's terrible. I'm so—"

"Don't be sorry. He did what he wanted to all his life, and he got just what was coming to him. Let me take you in, Eleanor, I have to get up early in the morning. If I don't, that Makin gets in and reads the mail on my desk before I can."

"And if you're first, you read the mail on his desk, I suppose."

"Doing anything tomorrow night?"

"I thought I might run up to Boston for a few days. Tenny's selling our house, and the bank said they'd give me a little advance."

"Oh. Well—give me a ring at the office when you get back."

"I'll see you at the trial if I'm too busy between now and then. You'll be sitting with Tenny."

"What? Oh, yes, I suppose so. He's the only person involved I know, except you. You remember, he looked me up when I was transferred to Wall Street."

"Trust him not to overlook a contact."

"It's the way to get along." He smiled. "Good night, Eleanor."

"Good night."

Donald waited till the heavy door of the old house closed after her. Then he walked slowly towards the subway station at the St. George.

Passing through a dark stretch of sidewalk, he suddenly heard a voice singing. "Load your cotton high up in the baler, market's waitin', don't you—"

The almost childish words, the minor tune, cut through a brain that was thinking about Makin and Mr. Grainger, and the North Carolina operations. Before he knew it, Don had vaulted the stone railing of an areaway, dropped to the paving.

A voice said: "I ain't doing nothin', Misteh, I—"

Don struck a match. The face that quivered close to his was Negro, and elderly. It was ashen with terror.

"Where'd you get that song, eh?"

"Boss man, I *always* knew that song. All the folks know that song in Georgia. I ain't doin' no harm, just—"

The colored man had been pawing through ashcans, looking for anything of value, presumably. Don handed him a quarter and got out of there.

Makin was getting old, didn't know the first thing about checking up.

Here was the St. George. The subway station was downstairs, but Don went straight ahead to the bar. "A spot of whisky."

The stuff still tasted awful, but it produced the desired

effect, it took the chill out of a man's bones. He went on to the subway.

*   *   *

ARTUR LEMPE WAS IMPRESSED. In the big office building of which he was heating superintendent, there were offices as fine as this one of Vanderbilt and Brefogel, there were, in fact, offices even finer, but he knew what they cost. Plenty. For a corner location like this, you paid as much as five dollars a square foot, this office of Marie's attorneys must cost more just for rent than Artur made in a whole year.

And the neat Amerikanische girls passing back and forth, they do not work for you for love, either. And the young men, each one probably a Herr Doktor in his own right, there must be a dozen of them.

He shifted his derby hat to the other knee and sat up straighter. The lady at the telephone switchboard promptly smiled at him. "I'm sure Mr. Brefogel will see you in a minute, Mr. Lempe. He's in with Mr. Vanderbilt just now."

Vanderbilt. Artur rolled the name over in the back of his mind. A rich name, an influential name. One of the finest families in New York.

Nevertheless, he wished they would see him. As it was, he would have no time to eat lunch, and if they did not hurry, he would be late getting back to the building. Twelve to one, that was the time he allowed himself off, although, considering his position, there was no one to tell him he could not have longer.

It would not do to have Vanderbilt and Brefogel, attorneys at law, think that he was a janitor, a furnace man. His furnaces provided the heat for ten thousand people, he had two dozen men under him.

198

Pass Through Manhattan

Perhaps he could say to the young lady that it was all right, he could wait, but he would have to call his assistant. The trouble was, what could he tell Mike after he got him on the phone? Everything was automatic, with thermostats, he could not very well tell Mike to make sure and repair anything if it broke. That would sound childish, amateurish. He—

A buzzer sounded on the young lady's switchboard, and she flipped a switch, said: "Yes, Miss Malone— Yes." She turned halfway around on her chair. "You can go in now, Mr. Lempe. Mr. Vanderbilt will see you."

"But it is Mr. Brefogel—"

"Mr. Brefogel is with Mr. Vanderbilt."

Artur bowed. Aha. They recognized a man of importance. Mr. Vanderbilt himself wanted to see him. Artur straightened his neat little striped tie, smoothed the felt of his derby, and marched in the direction the young lady nodded.

Another young lady opened a door, bowed him in. That was right. Formality and dignity, that was the way to run a business office.

Mr. Brefogel was standing by the biggest desk Artur had ever seen. Bigger even than the desk of the president from the bank that had its headquarters in Artur's building.

The Landesbundfuehrer himself lounged in a big chair next to the desk. At sight of him, Artur halted and threw up his hand. "Heil Hitler!"

The national leader made a negligent gesture. "Heil Hitler," he said.

The man behind the desk made a little face, as though he were spitting. He was short and fat, and looked something like a frog. "All right, all right. You're Arthur Lempe?" His voice was high and whining, like a sick child's.

Mr. Brefogel said quickly: "Yes, Mr. Vanderbilt, this is Lempe."

"Let the man talk for himself, can't you?" Mr. Vanderbilt complained. "Speak up, Lempe, you talk English, don't you?"

Artur nodded. "Yes, sir, I have been in this country since 1920."

"All right, all right. That's good." Mr. Vanderbilt pursed up his mean little mouth again. "That'll go good with a jury."

The Leader said: "I tell you, Mr. Vanderbilt, I am opposed to this idea of a jury. How are we going to—"

"All right, all right. Maybe we won't need a jury. But what you going to do if we get a judge like Levy?"

The Leader said earnestly: "We can ask a mistrial. They can't do that to—"

"The devil they can't," Mr. Vanderbilt said. "This is the greatest Jewish city in the world. And Vanderbilt and Brefogel don't like to lose cases, do we, Brefogel?"

"No, Mr. Vanderbilt. Of course not," Mr. Brefogel giggled.

Artur could not take his eyes off Mr. Vanderbilt's face. Surely, he was a—

"What are you goggling at, Mr. Lempe?" Mr. Vanderbilt asked. "Don't you think I'm pretty? Would you like me to grow a little black mustache like Charlie Chaplin and—"

"Mr. Vanderbilt," Mr. Brefogel interposed.

"All right, all right. But I have to talk to this man, don't I? Don't I have to know my clients? Maybe Limpy here has some ideas about juries. What do you think of juries, Limpy?"

"Lempe, please, counselor. I do not like juries, no. They are not neat. What is it the man in the street knows about law, about justice? A learned judge, that is what you should have, a man with knowledge from the great universities."

"Well, blow my nose," Mr. Vanderbilt squeaked. "The little fellow's a philosopher, a little deep-thinker. By God, I've been practicin' law forty years, and I haven't learned any more about juries than that. Talk up, Limpy, talk up. So that's what they teach you in these Nazi meetings, huh? What line of business you in, Limpy?"

"Is this necessary, Mr. Vanderbilt?" The National Bund Leader was nervous.

"Hell, yes. Why, blow my nose, the man's a gem, a gold mine."

"I am a heating superintendent, Mr. Vanderbilt."

"Yeah? You don't say? What's that, like a janitor, a furnace man?"

"I have twenty-four men under me, I have charge of all the heating in the Blacktower Building. Nine furnace men, three oilers, three electricians, seven repairmen, a night superintendent, and an assistant superintendent."

"Yeah? Well, it takes all kinds to heat a house, huh?" Mr. Vanderbilt waited for Mr. Brefogel to get through giggling. "Now, tell me, Mr. Limpy, how do your principles apply to your kind of work? I mean, now, you say if we do away with juries, how it would make my work easier, and I'm damned if I don't think you're right. How's this Nazi business gonna help you?"

Artur's eye lit up. He said: "That is a very fine question, if you will permit me to say so, Mr. Vanderbilt. By the offices in my building, we have thermostatic control. This you understand?"

"Sure."

"So if it becomes too hot in an office, all they have to do is wait, the thermostat takes care of it. But no, you cannot make them wait. They throw up the window, bang. The office, soon it gets too cold. They throw down the window, bang, and they call up and make us raise the thermostat, they say we are making them to freeze to death. Is this right?"

"Isn't he a jewel, Brefogel? No, that ain't right, Limpy. But what are you gonna do? If everybody knew as much about heating as you do, why would you have a job?"

"In Chermany," Artur said, "it is that when a man is an expert, everybody must do as he says. In Chermany, it would be against the law for to throw up the windows without the permission of the heating superintendent. Would be against the law for to crowd into elevators all at once when the elevator superintendent says no. Is it not so, Herr Landesbundfuehrer?"

"Yes, that is so," the Leader said. "But if the learned counsel will take up the business we want to see you about, I am sure that you want to get back to your important position."

"I don't know whether I'd like a Nazi government or not," Mr. Vanderbilt said. "Sounds like there'd be a lot of litigation, but not much you could do with it after you got it. What do the lawyers do, huh?"

"They work for the government," the Leader said impatiently.

"That's out," Mr. Vanderbilt said decisively. "Governments don't pay anything at all. All right, all right. Now, Limpy, what we wanted to see you about was to get you to sign this paper. While you were here, I wanted to talk to you, see what kind of a witness you were gonna make, and I'll say, it's been well worth my time. Now, you just sign this paper, and that's all we need."

"Please," Artur said. "First I read."

Pass Through Manhattan

The Landesbundfuehrer said: "It is not necessary."

"Oh, yes it is," Mr. Vanderbilt said. "You can get into trouble filing a complaint the complainant hasn't read. G'wan, read it, Limpy. If there's anything you don't understand, just ask me."

Artur picked up the paper. This seemed all right. Yes, Marie had not cooked him a meal since the accident. She had not taken care of his clothes. She had been unable to go to work. Yes. That is—

A phrase caught his eye in the next paragraph. "Please, marital functions, what is that?"

Mr. Vanderbilt told him.

Artur laid down the paper. "Please, learned sir, I cannot sign that."

"Ain't it the truth?"

Artur said: "We have children. They read, perhaps, the papers. It would not be nice they should read such things about their mother and their father!"

Mr. Vanderbilt squealed. "Where d'they think you got 'em, from a stork?"

"Please, Herr Landesbundfuehrer, could I see you a moment?"

The Leader looked at the lawyer and shrugged. Then he rose lazily from his chair, straightened the spectacles on his straight nose. His cheeks were rosy and clean, a fine, handsome man. "May we use your office, Brefogel?"

"Certainly."

Mr. Brefogel's office was not so impressive. But on the wall, with other diplomas, was one from Bonn. Mr. Brefogel had studied in the Fatherland, as well as in Harvard and Dartmouth.

"Well, Lempe," the Leader said with distaste. "What is it?"

"Please, gnädige Herr, that Mr. Vanderbilt."

"Yes?"

"I do not trust him. I am afraid, perhaps he betrays us."

"So, you do not think me competent to pick a lawyer for you?"

"Oh, no, no. It is that—I do not think his name is Vanderbilt originally. I think perhaps he is ein Jude."

"Oh, is that what troubles you?" The Fuehrer laughed. "Yes, you are right, Lempe. Quite so. But see—" He reached into his pocket, pulled out a book. It was beautifully bound in real black leather with gilt on the cover like an old-fashioned Bible. "You see, here in *Mein Kampf* it says, until we come to power we must use all means to our holy end."

"Oh. I see—"

The Landesbundfuehrer—the most important man in all America—put his arm around Artur's shoulder. "You are a good soldier, a clever Nazi. But in court, Brefogel appears."

Artur hesitated, but only for a moment. The Leader had winked at him. He, Artur Lempe, was in the very center of the holy movement, in the very confidence of the National Leader. "I sign," Artur said.

*　　　*　　　*

WHEN THE CAPTAIN DISMISSED THE TROOP, Sergeant John Tenbruye took his horse around the ring a couple of times at a slow canter. Some of the men were setting up jumps, a number of the horses had already gone down, but he just cantered around, thinking.

There was the usual crowd of girls and women in the balcony. Troop B was holding a reception in its room. He, along with the other sergeants, had been invited, but he decided, suddenly, not to go. He turned his horse down the ramp, and put him up, with only a perfunctory rubdown. Setting a bad example for his men, but he was tired.

Pass Through Manhattan

There was a mob in his troop room, bottles of liquor had been taken out of the lockers, somebody offered him a Scotch. He drank it, chatting with a couple of his troopers and the second lieutenant of their troop, but he couldn't get his mind off something that had possessed him.

When he finished the drink, he said good night, shrugged into his uniform overcoat, and left.

The short walk to his apartment reminded him, for some reason, of the snowy afternoon he and Eleanor had been in the bus accident. The weather wasn't the same. It was dark, but ten o'clock at night in April was hardly six in a blizzard.

He had had a narrow squeak that time. He had come within an ace of what Eleanor had so dramatically offered. The finish of his career, that's what it would have been. Because he would have had to marry her. It was all right to marry her. It was all right to seduce servant girls and waitresses, but a gentleman could hardly betray a lady of his own social métier.

Why, only the day after that incident, he had considered going to Brooklyn Heights and proposing. To oblige Mr. Seligmann. Ha!

He stood between the elevator and his own door, thinking. Never occurred to him before; that bus accident had been the turning point. If Seligmann had not seen the item about it, he would not have turned over the Castron house to him. And it was the Castron house, the visible evidence of Corning and Seligmann's confidence in John Tenbruye, that had enabled him to go up to John Street and land those three accounts, including the juicy Hudson Valley-Westervelt business.

For a while he had hoped for some business out of Don Morton. The *Wall Street Journal* had made it sound as though Donald Morton had been put in charge of Armstrong and Grainger's investments. That had fizzled out. Several evenings wasted. Still, he occasionally got a tip from Don, and Don had—ah, yes—distracted Eleanor Castron.

She had been looking for a husband, that was it, it had hardly been a week before she had told him she was engaged to that dry-rotted cousin of hers, that professor. Wonder if that lasted, or if she dropped him for Donald? Better stay away from there, she's a man-eater—Inbreeding.

Old Jason Corning, John thought as he unlocked the door of his pied-à-terre, had summed them up. "Thing to do would be to have some good public schools, like the ones in England. Fella was tellin' me, they give you the eddication we get here in the first two years of college. Plenty for a gentleman, and what's the use eddicatin' a bunch of rotters? Eh? Spending good money to support these college professors that are trying to start a revolution down there. Don't tell me!" Old Jason roared. "They won't be satisfied with anything short of a revolution. Well, 1940'll show 'em."

Taking off his overcoat and what he called his tunic, unstrapping his spurs and putting his boot-heels into the jack, Tenny continued to smile, fondly. Old Jason was a character, all right.

An inspiration hit him. He would have his section give a dinner for the old boy. A regular, bang-up, three-kinds-of-wine dinner, and let old Jason tell them about thorough-breds. All of Tenny's troopers were horsey enough not to be bored, and the sort of half-mock, half-serious deference they gave their sergeant would be a good thing for Jason to see.

Wonder if the old boy would like it if I called him Uncle Jason. Or maybe just Jason. Don't want to make him feel his age.

But that gnawing, itching worm kept on. He pulled a silk

bathrobe in the Squadron colors around him, and began pawing over the bookcase. In a book called *Men of Millions* he finally found what he wanted.

A time had come in the life of the financial community when a Tenbruye could make his way rapidly, the "old" New York families—those that had had money for three generations—bitterly resented the predatory raids of such crude men as Astor and Drew.

But more bitterly did they resent anything that distracted their attention and their time from their pleasures, their country estates and their fast trotting horses.

So that the word soon got around amongst the Rensselaers and Cortlandts that there was a young man—a quite presentable young man—ready to handle such mundane affairs as the stealing of railroads and the watering of stock, and that, furthermore, young Tenbruye was quite good company.

When he refused to name his first locomotive the *Loos Tenbruye* and unveiled it instead as the *Nicholas Rensselaer*, he had found the right road to success. The next year he married old Nick's daughter, and banked his first million.

That was it. That was, by God, the thing that had been troubling him all day.

John Tenbruye looked at the pretty little crystal clock over the mantelpiece. Only ten-thirty. He thumbed through the telephone book, dialed the number of the Hotel Jacques. "Mr. Firstin, please. . . . Hello, Firstin, this is Mr. Tenbruye. Say, I've been thinking over your very flattering offer today, and I've decided to ask you to change it a little. I think the building ought to be named after old Mr. Jason Corning. I know he'd like it. . . . Yes, Firstin, Corning Heights would be good. . . . No, I'm sure, Mr. Seligmann won't mind. I'll still be president of the company if you want me. I know Mr. Corning would not care for anything that active. . . . All right, good night, Firstin."

He hung up the receiver, lit a cigarette. Then he dialed the number. "Hello, is Mr. Corning there?—Oh, Mr. Corning, this is John Tenbruye. I've just come from a conference with Firstin. . . . No, I frequently have to transact business at night, I don't mind. Well, I'll tell you. Mr. Corning, the poor fellow was in quite a dither. Took him an hour to come out with it. Wants to name his new building after you, and didn't have the nerve to ask you. . . . Yes, I know you don't care for publicity, Mr. Corning, but it would be a big favor to do Firstin. He's had a hard time you know, the Federal government nearly wrecked his business and if you . . ."

While he listened to his own voice droning on, John Tenbruye got his bankbook out of the drawer of the telephone table. Twelve hundred dollars saved up. He had been waiting to take a flyer, but—

Corning was giving his consent. "And another thing, sir," Tenny said. "I've been wondering, I've been pretty successful in the market, and I've got a little money to play with. How much could I buy a horse—say, a two-year-old—and race him for a season for?"

Corning really went on a long ways that time.

"Well, sir, it would be mighty decent of you to let your trainer handle him. But I've only got twelve hundred dollars to drop on it, and maybe I'd better wait until next year. After all, we don't have our boyhood dreams come true all at once."

"Boyhood dream, eh?" Corning's voice was gruff. "Every young fella used to have a race horse. Nothing like it. I'll tell you what. Could you get over to my flat about four tomorrow morning? I'll take you out to the farm and show you the string. Perhaps there'd be a two-year-old there would take your fancy. Not that I'm tryin' to sell you a horse, y'know."

They both laughed. "I'll be there," John Tenbruye said. "But I'm afraid I won't sleep all night for excitement." He laughed boyishly.

"See you then."

Tenny hung up the phone, his eyes shining. He mixed himself a very weak highball. Oh, dear Lord, let that horse turn out to be a bum, let me lose my twelve hundred dollars. Please, Lord, let that happen so old Jason Corning will feel he's got to make it up to me.

Maybe the firm name would never be Tenbruye & Seligmann, but it might be Corning, Seligmann & Tenbruye. And if his first son were named Jason Corning Tenbruye, they could call him Corny so everybody would know where the Seligmanns stood.

In the middle.

*   *   *

RAY SHOVED BACK THE PASTE POT and the scissors, shoved his pipe and tobacco tin into his pockets, and stood up, yawning. The clock stood at two-fifteen.

"Good night, boys."

"The boys"—his fiftyish, sixtyish contemporaries—grunted, and nobody's head turned as he stepped off the edge of the copy desk and walked to the hat tree. He put on his suitcoat and overcoat, carried his hat.

The night city editor saluted him. "How's it goin', Ray?"

"You can't say that being on the rim of the copy desk is hard work, kid."

"There'll be a rewrite spot open for you pretty soon."

Pass Through Manhattan

"I think there's going to be one on the *Times* if this paper doesn't need me."

The elevator carried him downstairs, he went out the back way to John Bleek's. The barman saw him coming, and slid him an old-fashioned, without soda. "How's the weather out?"

Ray said he hadn't noticed. He had just finished his first drink, was about to order his second when the front door opened. Oh, God. The managing editor of the *Mail*. The pink-cheeked, weak-minded Chief.

Ray would have headed for the backroom, but it was too late. The Chief said: "You can always find newspapermen in here at any hour of the night. It went on right during the prohibition period, if the law had attempted to close this place, the morning uptown papers couldn't have—" He saw Ray, and gulped.

Ray smiled sourly at the party of slummers behind the Chief, and said: "Hello. And good night." He started for the door.

One of the ladies with the Chief was a little lit. It didn't become her well-groomed fat, or the wrinkles in her neck, but she was, anyway. "Ooh, are you a newspaperman, too?"

"Too?"

The Chief said: "Now, really—"

" 'Cause I just love newspapermen."

"Give me your phone number and I'll send a couple up sometime."

He pushed through them to the street. There was a light drizzle falling on 40th Street. Hope to hell it isn't raining in Brooklyn, and me with a half-mile walk after I leave the subway. Hope— Someone was calling his name.

The Chief stood in the doorway of John Bleek's, reluctant to take his dress clothes into the rain. "Oh, Ray. A minute."

Ray walked back. "Yes?"

"Couldn't we bury the hatchet?"

Ray shook his head. "Why? I'm doing all right, I'm on a better paper than the *Mail*. And you must be happier being the boss in your own office than you were with me there."

The Chief said: "Couldn't we go have a drink together? It's damned chilly here. . . . To tell you the truth, I'm not entirely satisfied with the *Mail*. What would you say to being managing editor?"

Ray's eyes jumped. But— He looked down at his hands, spotlessly clean because the rubber cement they used on the copy-desk erased the dirt away. It also pulled most of the hair off your hands. He said: "The M. E.'s office would be a wonderful place to spend my failing years."

"Well—er—"

Ray laughed. "I get it. You'd still be publisher, and keep the office."

"We could partition off the southwest corner of the room, where the—"

"Oh, nuts. Let's go back and have that drink—"

In the bar, Ray excused himself and went to phone his wife. Poor, patient Helen. He said: "I probably won't be home at all, dear. Take a room at a hotel some place over here and get a nap. If I can."

She said: "Poor darling. If you do get home, there's some marvelous head cheese in the icebox. What is it, a fire or a crisis in Europe or—"

"I'm negotiating to go back to the *Mail*. If I cinch it, I'll have to get out the paper tomorrow, and maybe work on the *Trib* tomorrow evening till they find another copy-desk man."

Pass Through Manhattan

"How about Brawley?"

"I don't think he'd do. I'll call you in the morning."

"Not before nine, darling. I've had a headache, I'm going to sleep late. Good luck."

"Thanks." There was no use asking her what she wanted him to do. She didn't care. She read the *Daily News*, and thought the standard-size papers on which Ray worked were all equally dull.

She was not extravagant, and not much interested in saving money, so that any living wage was satisfactory. Her friends, the wives of storekeepers, police lieutenants, real estate agents, didn't know the difference between a copy-desk reader and a managing editor, so no glory he could acquire would trickle through to Brooklyn.

If they'd had children . . . But they hadn't had. Ray had his own theory about that, too, a theory sufficiently interesting to propound over beer at thirty, but probably without scientific basis: that metropolitan life had a sterilizing effect on the great middle class. That the exacting, finicky, meeching details of running the wealthy's empire—of bossing or intimidating, or recording the physical labor of the lower classes in order to report to the profit takers—was—being sterile in itself and producing nothing—sterilizing in effect.

He went back to the table. One of the Chief's inevitable ladies said: "Which one is Lucius Beebe?"

"He isn't here yet," Ray said. "He shows up about three-thirty. You'll know him when he comes in."

The Chief said: "Want to talk business, Ray?"

"Sure. I hire and fire my own men, and I run everything except the editorial page. You can have it."

"That's—"

"And you build yourself a penthouse on the top of the building and decide policy from there. I'll not attempt to run a paper with a superior officer on the same floor with me."

"Really, now—"

"Take it or leave it. There's Beebe, Mrs.—"

The lady told Ray her name. He didn't listen. He was admiring her. She was the final personification of the sterility of Manhattan. Although she had breasts—you could see the upper curve of them quite clearly—and haunches, and all the rest of the equipment, you could not imagine those breasts filling with milk, that pelvis—so carefully girdled that it could probably break without interfering with the lady's walking or doing the rhumba—you couldn't fancy that pelvis cradling a living, kicking child.

No, this was a machine designed to titivate polite, discreet desire without any aftermath. She wanted to meet Beebe. Well, nothing more appropriate.

He led her to the bar, she was given a cigarette from the heavy gold box with the jeweled lid, she was given a Scotch and soda. You had to admire Beebe. In John Bleek's in the afternoon, he would drink beer. Thereafter, in the fabled, fancy dives he wrote about, he would move serenely, drinking vintage wines at the Hapsburg House, ale or Dutch beer at the Tavern or Dinty Moore's, champagne at night clubs, Martinis at 21, and so on. Always the proper drink, and the proper amount, and end up at Bleek's again, with a Scotch and soda.

He led the lady back to the Chief. He said: "Chief, you ought to go down to 63 Park Row, and see the penthouse the Pulitzers used. Up under the Dome. It'd be a swell thing if you could buy the old dome and move it up to our building."

"That's right, Pulitzer ran the *World* from the roof,

didn't he. . . . It's a deal, Ray. Who do you want for city editor?"

"I'll see. Haven't made up my mind yet. . . . I have to be on my way. I'll be on deck tomorrow—this morning to get out the second edition."

As he moved away, he heard the Chief say: "Wonderful, these old-time newspapermen. Don't need sleep at all."

Poor little rich boy. He didn't like horses or speedboats or whatever it was that his cousins and club mates liked. He liked newspapers and workingmen. The latter, of course, in moderation and subjection, but still he liked them. But the paper that his family bought him wouldn't run right for him, and the newspapermen wouldn't take him to their bosoms. Still, Hearst had been like that, and look what *he'd* done. And Roosevelt, except he liked politicians instead of reporters—

At the Western Union office on Broadway, Ray asked for Nick. The forty-year-old, unshaven telegraph boy lounged up from the bench. "Move my stuff from the *Trib* back to the *Mail*, will you, Nick? It goes in the old publisher's office, I'm to be managing editor." He sent a wire to Brawley Smith, telling him to report to work, another to the chap who had gotten him the job on the *Trib*, asking to be relieved.

There would be no trouble on the *Tribune*, people would go out of their way to keep in with a managing editor.

As he composed a wire to Joe Morton, it occurred to Ray—for the first time—that success had arrived. He was a managing editor, the highest job he could aspire to. Knowing nothing about purchasing or advertising, he would not do as a publisher, an editor was a front job, window dressing. He had reached the top of the ladder. He asked the telegraph clerk for a glass of water and took three aspirins.

JOSEPH KOLK MORTON
CARTWRIGHT COUNTRY HOME
PORT WASHINGTON L. I.

JOE THEY FOUND OUT THEY COULDN'T RUN
THE MAIL WITHOUT US. GET WELL AND
COME BACK YOU WILL FIND ME IN THE
M.E.'S OFFICE.

RAY

His nurse could read it to Joe in one of his more lucid moments. That took care of two of them. Ron Levine was book editor on an extremely elegant weekly magazine, run by another of these rich boys who didn't like yachting or spectator sports. It would blow up at any minute, the stock market was falling and the family of the publisher would put the pressure on. No doubt the Chief's family were responsible for Ray's being rehired, they had told him to take up chorus girls or something cheaper than a newspaper so very deep in the red.

It was really raining now. Ray pulled his shabby collar up around his ears. A sprinkler came up Broadway, spraying water out in hard streams that washed the filth of the night into the gutters. The driver had on a sou'wester and slicker against God's water, but the water from the sprinkler hit the curb and bounced, dampening Ray's trouser legs.

A taxi coasted along behind the sprinkler and Ray flagged it down, gave the Morton address on 96th. Leaning back against the cushions, he fought down an impulse to sleep. He had to think up some kind of a crusade. With a trust company some place putting pressure on the Chief to drop the *Mail*, it would be necessary to have action and have it now.

Pass Through Manhattan

Ray squinted through the rain-spattered stretches of Times Square, pretty well deserted now. Then, at 49th, there were the dance halls, ten cents a dance, that's what they pay me.

North, north through the automobile belt. No lotteries, no contests, no coupons. Dave Stern had tried to bring the *Post* back that way, and it hadn't worked. Give away an automobile with every copy, and you get a bunch of people too busy riding around to find time to read your paper.

Maybe that's a wise crack. Columbus Circle. First metropolitan story I ever covered was a Columbus Day meeting of Italians here. Angle? Columbus and Mussolini. Christ, no. Mussolini was dead news against the more flagrant intelligence-insulting of Hitler. And with every paper in New York taking a swing at Hitler, he wouldn't hop on *that* band wagon.

Passing a good news center now, the sector where the Filipinos congregated, had their employment agencies and their dance halls. The big, fat, blonde girls who went with the Filipinos were always getting involved in something pretty gruesome, murders and stabbings, dope, rape and prostitution. A guy could dig up a crusade here, but the trouble was, nowadays, people had to have pix, and these blowsy tarts didn't raise indignation with their photographs.

Past 72nd, where the men who hoped to lay down the sort of fortunes that would enable their descendants to have newspapers and literary magazines and racing stables kept their mistresses. Why? What made such truly individualistic activities come together to form a colony?

Ron ought to write a book, the *Bawdy Iconography of New York*. Who sleeps with what on which streets. Include famous murders, block by block, since murder always had a sexual base, as suicide had a financial one.

Pass Through Manhattan

Except holdup accidents and gangster killings. And pretty often, if you pushed far enough, the holdup man was trying to get dough to do something about a woman—pick one up or impress or hold one already met—and the gangster was trying to make a showing before some moll. A guy could eat without resorting to violence.

North through the Steam-heated Ghetto to Joe's. How often he'd made this ride, along a Broadway grown a little brighter and cheaper each year, to 96th. How many flats Joe had lived in in this downhill neighborhood. Why, Don's childhood was tied into every flat and apartment house for a block or so around the 96th Street subway station.

Here we are. . . . Ray paid off the driver. He hadn't thought up his crusade yet, but—

The sleepy colored man answered his ring downstairs, dragged him up in the old water-power elevator that whined protestingly. He rang the Morton bell, waited, leaning against the heavy, rough-surfaced brown wall paper. A couple of generations of people had worn a greasy slick band along the paper at elbow level, delivery boys had drawn pictures and messages around the bell. He pushed it again.

Don Morton, in pajama pants, opened the door, his hair tousled. "Oh, Ray."

Ray felt a stab in the heart that had nothing to do with aspirin or coffee stomach. The kid looked so damn young with his hair that way, his eyes half closed. Wonder if Don remembers when I used to take him over to Brooklyn to spend the night, while Joe tried to hold his pretty wife by dragging her around to cabarets.

Ray, who made his living from words, wondered what had happened to the word cabaret, and said, "Hi, Don. You can start packing." He lounged into the living room, dropped

217

his coat and hat on a chair, stretched out on the couch. "You can go on out to Colorado."

Don said: "What's the joke, Ray?"

"Better go put a bathrobe on, it's chilly."

"Too hot in the apartment. What's happened?"

"I'm back on the *Mail*. Unconditional surrender. Managing editor, with a free rein. I'll put Joe on the payroll tomorrow, his salary can pay his expense at Cartwright's till he's ready to come back."

"I can take care of Dad, Ray."

"Let the paper do it. He was on a story when he got pneumonia."

"He was trying to catch a silly bogey man that got his little boy scared, he's got D.T.s, not pneumonia."

"Sometimes it's hard to tell where one begins and the other leaves off—Anyway, you can go back to your precious All's Fair and let Joe look after himself for a while."

"Want a drink, Ray? . . . I've hired a man to run the All's Fair. New Mexico School of Mines boy named Dibrell."

"Fire him."

"He's doing all right."

Ray looked at his watch. Five o'clock. "I'm going to catch some sleep. Get me a blanket. What the hell, Don, go on and find another mine then. Start one. Joe and I'll be rolling in dough."

"I don't think it would be strategic for me to step down back into the field after being New York operations manager of Armstrong and Grainger."

Ray sat up. "What? Say that again."

"If I resign my present position to take a job as a field super, they'll say I'm limited, no good except to boss a mine."

Pass Through Manhattan

"Well, son, are you? Is anybody ever any good doing something he doesn't want to do?"

Don said, sulkily: "I'm an engineer, not an evangelist or a newspaperman. I can't throw words around with you. Skip it. It's my life."

"Sure, sure. It's your life. If you want to spend it in Wall Street, instead of out in the mountains, hell, spend it there. Get a paunch, get a skin like a frog's belly—oh, no, I forgot, you'd naturally stop at the club every evening and get sun-ray treatments. I've known a lot of sons of bitches in my time, but no worse ones than the boys who sit around Wall Street letting better men go out into the country and make fortunes for them."

"When was the last time you were out of the city?"

"We're not talking about me."

"Let's, though. Who was it who said a managing editor, because of his job, had to be out of sympathy with the men who actually got the paper out? Sour grapes. The first time you get a crack at the job, to hell with the reporters and rewrite men and correspondents. You're going to be the boss. Let them stand around in the rain waiting for stories that you'll take the credit on. Let them—"

"I'm an old man. It's a choice between going on up, or starting downhill. Either I'm an executive or a copy-desk man. You're young, you could—"

"I could run my own life and see that it doesn't get into the blind alley when, at your age, I have to get a job as night watchman at a mine I used to run."

Ray stood up, waddled over to his overcoat. "I give up. But don't think you're fooling me. You've got a girl some place in the city. Well, hell, go sleep with her and get it over with."

"A hell of a lot you know about it."

Ray shrugged into his coat. "Well, if she isn't that kind of girl, marry her, then. There are worse things. If she really loves you, she'll live at a mine head happily."

"You're all wrong, Ray."

Ray looked up, and began to grin. "I detect a certain note of uncertainty in your voice. Oh, Lord." He began to laugh. "Didn't you know you were in love till I told you? Why, son, men don't change as fast as you've changed. Just a few weeks ago, you were worrying about that chap you called Copper. Ringgold."

Don sat down on the edge of the sofa, said: "That was kid stuff, field-boot stuff. I'm growing up, Ray. Maybe having a syndicate of fathers kept me young too long. Or maybe it was staying in the field."

"Don't forget, son. You know why you worried about him so? It was because you and he, of all the people involved in the bus accident, were outdoor men, men who had been out in the United States doing things instead of sitting around New York ordering them done. You didn't have anything in common with that busload of passengers then, you don't have now. The only two reasons for wanting to stay in this town are money or a girl. Think it over."

"Money. The field engineer does the work, the Wall Street man takes the dough. That's life, and I'm making the only sensible choice."

Ray rubbed his hand through what was left of his hair. "Go make a pot of coffee, son, I've got to go to work. I'm too tired to sleep, now."

"Yes, Uncle Ray."

"You haven't called me that in twenty years."

Sitting on the sofa, his clothes damp and moldy against his middle-aged skin, Ray felt better than he had in weeks. Out in the kitchen the boy was humming some sort of a wild tune, all minors, like nigger music. Sadder than hell.

Don had denied it, but—

Ray wondered who the girl was.

*　　　*　　　*

ELEANOR CASTRON PUSHED AND PUSHED, and finally the trap-door opened and she climbed up on the roof of the Orange Street house. Coal dust gritted under her feet as she walked, and oily smoke from the Bay drifted across with a hot, rich smell. The spring sunlight was comfortable enough; she dropped the triangular pillow and the old steamer rug against the foot of the chimney, and walked around the roof.

She hadn't been up here for years. Not since she was twelve or thirteen, or whenever it was that she had used to have those dreams about going crazy. Well, modern literature had answered that one; all little girls, or anyway lots of them, get that feeling at that time.

There were the brass bolts in the roof where, they told her, her great-grandfather's telescope had stood. The second Captain Castron had not followed the sea like his father; he had had the title Captain through courtesy, since he owned a dozen fast Atlantic steamers. But he had been close enough to the sea to climb to this roof on Brooklyn Heights and see his own ships come in, by himself.

Books also tell us that the scions and heiresses of the old New York families are all nuts from inbreeding. Maybe I am crazy. I would rather be crazy and be put away in a nice, safe asylum than be the way I am. Because I am either crazy or I am a—a harlot. A tart. A prostitute.

I thought I wanted to marry Gray. But I don't. Oh, God,

221

I don't. And I can't marry him feeling the way I do. I could do a dirty trick like that to Tenny, but not to dear Gray. Not to the Gray who was so wonderful for the week he lived here. And so awfully, frightfully damn dull in Boston.

Gray's marvelous in action, but I can't be the proper faculty wife for a French professor in Harvard. I just can't. No fun, not even a little giggling in the halls. All look out, here comes a professor's wife, careful, Eleanor, that lady over there looks like the Dean's cousin.

I want to have fun. I wish there was a war. I would be wonderful at entertaining soldiers on leave. Why couldn't I have been born sooner?

Or I could go out to Nevada, I hear they still have dance halls and—restricted districts out there. . . . I wonder if you get the money first or afterwards? The money is a good idea, when a man pays cash, he knows he's paid up and no more to worry about. I don't mind the—the sex part of it, it's what comes after, the meet-my-friends, the do-you-think-your-aunt-will-like-me.

Maybe I do mind the sex part. Maybe there's something wrong with me. Isn't it unusual for a girl my age to be a virgin?

There hasn't been a virgin over twenty in any book I've read for years.

Books. Books. Marching up and down again. Books, books—

When is life going to start for you, Eleanor Castron? When are you going to give in? Because, listen, my fine filly, nobody gets everything she wants in this world. You and Gray could have summers and Christmas and Easter and maybe even weekends through the school year to be silly and gay and gentle as he was when he came down here.

Pass Through Manhattan

And if you haven't got the nerve to take the dullness with the fun, you don't deserve anything.

No doubt, my friend, girls in dance halls and—dance halls don't have all fun, either. Though men are so nice when they're not talking about business. When they're not worried about getting ahead. When—

The tricky sun was getting behind more and more clouds over towards the Bayonne shore. Eleanor stood up, beating her slacks clean, and picked up the pillow and blanket. Something made her look up, and from high in the wall of the St. George she saw a pair of binoculars flashing at her. Somebody must be awfully hard up to watch a girl decently clad in slacks lie on a roof.

But quite consciously, deliberately, she waggled her hips as she walked across the roof. If whoever it was was that bored, that was the least she could do to help out. . . .

The phone rang while she was in the tub. Don Morton. "Want to go out and paint the town a little, Eleanor?"

"Oh, yes."

"How was Boston?"

"Dull. Just frightfully dull."

He said: "That's too bad." But she detected—he wasn't trying to conceal it—a jubilant note in his voice.

"Look," she said, "come over from the office, I'll give you a cocktail here and you can wash up. I want to run around town all night, baying at the moon."

"O.K.," he said, laughing. "I hope there's a moon."

She hung up the phone still smiling, and then frowned as she heard her mother calling down the stairs.

"Eleanor," her high, ladylike voice was hardly equal to the distance, "that awful Mr. Firstin who's tearing the house down called up. He wants to see our cellar. Will you take him around, I've got—"

"Yes, Mother, sure." Maybe Mr. Firstin would want her. On the cellar floor, with the mice and the cockroaches.

She giggled at the idea, having seen Mr. Firstin's face once. But she'd bet there was no nonsense about Mr. Firstin, he'd leave a five-dollar bill in the top of a girl's stocking, and never give the incident a second thought.

Well, at least a two-dollar bill.

*　　*　　*

BUCK RANULPH SHUT HIS OFFICIAL MEMO BOOK with a snap and headed for the front door of the hall. Uniformed patrolmen, both white and black, were letting the people out in small groups; on the street, mounted cops were hustling them away. No congregating on the public streets.

An aged and completely black man with the peculiar walk of the West Indian sailor who did not put on shoes till late in life, pulled himself ostentatiously away from Buck. "Look out his fyce, chappies. Look out his fyce, the black cap'n what sells his ryce for a peeler's wyge."

Or, at least, that's what Buck thought he said. Some of these monkeychasers were almost incomprehensible. Buck shrugged, he was used to being denounced at the tail end of these interminable meetings about colored rights.

Say someone followed him after one of these meetings. A group of bravos, to beat him up. And by the mud on one of their shoes, the detective spotted the man as one of a group who had held up a paymaster out in the country that afternoon, men who were just using the meeting for an alibi.

Too rough. He'd polish on it a little and take it down to Mr. Maxwell for criticism.

Buck went into a cigar store, put his slug into the slot,

said: "Police business," and gave his name and shield number to get the lucky slug back. He got Lieutenant Ralfs at headquarters. "Ranulph. The meeting went off without violence."

"What did they decide?"

"They're going to concentrate on the milk companies. Fifty jobs from Sheffield's, fifty from Borden's."

"What's their plan? All pay their milk bills on the same day the way they did the light company?"

"No, everyone in Harlem is going to buy milk from one company one day, the other the next. They won't decide which company until eight o'clock the evening before, when they have one of those ministers toss a coin."

Ralfs, of the Sedition Squad, laughed. "Gotta hand it to you niggers, you can think up some of the damnedest things —well, that's all, Ranulph. You didn't get any proof that they're Communist-inspired, did you?"

"No, sir."

"Well, if you do, I think maybe there'd be a permanent spot for you down here at headquarters and a first-class rating. I'll turn your report in to the milk company, but they probably had someone there themselves."

Buck said: "Yes, sir" again and rang off. He bought a package of cigarettes in the store, trying to flog his brain into creating a story. He had sold three to Gordie Maxwell, but they were all shorts, fifteen hundred words and less. Still, thirty-seven fifty was not bad earnings in a business he was just learning.

He wanted to try a long one, though, about forty-five hundred words. If he could begin to sell those with any regularity, he could quit the cops, and live some place where his color wouldn't matter to anyone any more than it seemed to Gordie Maxwell's friends. This was the first business he had ever heard of where a Negro seemed to be on the same level with a white. In fact, there was no reason why editors should even know what color he was, a writer doesn't have to see editors.

And it was a snap for him to think like a white detective or a cowboy instead of like a Negro. He guessed he was white-minded.

All right, Ranulph. A good opening. A mass meeting. Tapping feet behind the detective as he went home. Footsteps that faded, stopped when the dick stopped, resumed when he walked. Then—a shot in the dark. Yellow flame splitting the night. The detective falls, pretends to be dead. The crooks creep up on him. He rolls on—

No.

That would end the story right there. Frustration is suspense. For a forty-five-hundred-word yarn, the detective must make two attempts to capture or kill the crooks, and be foiled each time. On the third he succeeds. He—

Mass meeting, footsteps in the night, yellow—

Buck Ranulph became aware of footsteps behind him, became aware of the fact that they had been following him since he left the cigar store. He dropped his hand to his gun, turned.

A soft voice said: "Hello, Buckingham."

"Who's that?"

A tall, tigerish-looking mulatto with the pale cream skin of a Buddha stepped into the light. "Remember Bert Williams?" he asked. "Who dat say 'who dat' when Ah say 'Who dat?'" The bright skin shook his head, natty under a felt hat the color of his skin. "A great comedian, even if he did burlesque his own race. Why, Buckingham, you remember me. Harold De Bruliere. We were classmates at N.Y.U."

"Oh, hello, Harold. What are you doing these days?"

Pass Through Manhattan

"A little of this and that, old man, a little of this and that. I saw you at the meeting, and followed you up to renew old acquaintance. Will you join me in a libation to the old class days?"

"I'm not much of a drinking man. I'll have a beer."

The taller man fell into step beside Buck, said: "This way, then. Are you familiar with Joe Jones' Jowl Joint? Good, solid race cooking.

They moved through the Harlem street together, two tall, well-set-up, well-dressed professional men. There was a certain ridiculousness about the relationship of one man to the other, they were racial counterparts; De Bruliere was three quarters white, Buck three quarters Negro.

Joe Jones' Jowl Joint was on 131st, a corner store made over into an imitation slave cabin of the old South. Slabs had been nailed to both the interior and exterior walls to give the appearance of logs, and plaster did for moss-and-mud chinking. In the center of a U-shaped counter three cooks in white caps slaved over a half-dozen frying pans each, and the girl who served as cashier had wrapped a brilliant red bandanna around her straight-end hair, tied it at the top in imitation of the traditional Mammy.

A huge picture of Lincoln dominated one wall, but, in respect to the changing politics of his customers, Joe Jones had hung an almost equally large lithograph of Franklin D. Roosevelt on the other.

The place was bright, noisy, cheerful, and clean, considering the fact that the frying pans kept the air greasy twenty-four hours a day.

Harold De Bruliere chose a booth by the wall, told the slim Mammy who came to take their order: "Two beer and ears." She went away.

Buck examined the menu. Cracklin's. Chitlin's. Our Specialty, Pig's Jowls and Black-Eye Peas. Fried Mississippi Catfish like Mammy Used to Fix, our Catfish are flown daily from Missouri by TWA, The Lindbergh Line. Deep-Fried Pig's Ears, served with drinks, all you can eat for a quarter. Without drinks, 15¢ a plate. If You Are Not Satisfied, tell the Manager. Joe Jones, Inc.

The girl brought them two huge plates of crisp ears, the fat still sizzling on them. She set cold glasses of beer in front of each man. Harold De Bruliere held a pig's ear in a paper napkin, snapped off a piece and washed it down with beer. "S'hot."

Buck salted his own plate, blew on an ear, nibbled it. The beer was cold and good. He said: "What are you doing these days, Harold?"

"Oh. I'm playing around with politics a little. Are you still on the police force?"

"Yes. I'm thinking of resigning, spending all my time writing."

"Writing, eh? I've done a little of that myself, the *Amsterdam News* has used two of my articles. What sort of writing were you thinking of?"

"I've been pretty successful with detective stories, sold three this month to the Bullet Group, no doubt you know them. I think I'll concentrate on the pulps till I get a little stake ahead and then make a try for the smooth papers."

"White magazines, eh?" De Bruliere bowed. "Congratulations, old man. I've never even tried anything but the race press. Of course, there's no money in it just now, but I think there's a great future."

"I don't exactly see why a colored American should want different reading matter from—"

"Don't you? My dear chap, psychologists teach us that the reading of fiction is an escape, a sublimation. How can a

Negro boy sublimate himself into the place of a white hero?
. . . You admit that you would not be allowed to have a
Negro hero?"

"No. But I'll tell you what I do do. I don't say he's white,
either, and I think of him as colored, and—"

Harold De Bruliere said, sharply: "Please, Ranulph. I get
angry enough with white people who don't know any better, but I should think you'd dislike the appellation colored
as much as I do. It carries the implication that we are
lumped—together with the Orientals, the Filipinos, the Indians and so forth—into the general group of subject races.
We're not, we have our place as Americans, but the race
has to throw off the apologetic attitude—"

Buck said: "What kind of politics are you working on?"

Harold De Bruliere raised his eyes from the plate of pigs'
ears. He said: "We won't discuss that, Ranulph, as long as
you're on the police force. It's information that might embarrass you. . . . Now, wait a minute. Let me order two
more beers, and get to the point of why I picked you
up. . . ." He stared at the table while the girl was getting
them the beers. She came back with fresh ears, carried the
cold ones away. De Bruliere said: "I knew you in college.
The life of a Negro in college is not always happy. But
somehow, I look back on it as a good part of my life, and
you were my friend. That's why I'm saying this. You say
you're going on with your writing, and that's fine. That's a
load off my mind. I wish you were writing something else,
something that contributed more to the race, but that is
none of my business. This is: *we're* rising in Harlem, here.
The bloodless revolution, if you want to call it that. *We*
pay our taxes and cast our votes, and as such we have the
American right to be represented. We're not going to do
business with companies that don't employ Negroes. We've

already come to terms with the phone company, the utilities, with Woolworth's. We're not going to pay taxes to support an anti-Negro police force."

"Do you know how many Negroes there are on the force?"

"Yes, I do. And I know what kind. Stool pigeons. Blackface stooges for the Irish comedians downtown."

"Mayor LaGuardia—"

"Yes, I think he's with us. He certainly isn't as against us as Tammany is. But the police force isn't run by the Mayor. It always lags behind, confident the old bosses will get back in, and in the meantime, there is civil service. You're a marked man, Ranulph. Harlem doesn't like to see you at meetings, taking your reports."

"I'm a sworn police officer."

"You're a salaried, civil-service stool pigeon. If the police want reports of our meetings, let them send white cops, or cops in uniform. It annoys my people to see you pretending to be one of us. We're breaking no laws."

"If you advocate revolution you are."

"We don't. We advocate using economic capitalistic methods to get our fair share of what the capitalists owe us."

"You don't mean to pretend, De Bruliere, that there aren't Communists in your movement?"

"Of course there are. There are also Baptist and African Methodist and Episcopal ministers. Even the Catholic priests of some of the West Indian churches are in with us. Call them revolutionaries, Communists?"

"I've got my living to make, Harold. I went into the force because it pays sixty dollars a week, and I don't know any way a Negro can make that much doing anything else. But —I see your point. Listen. Make it easy for me. Start pointing me out at meetings as a police officer. That would ruin my use as an undercover man without giving them any chance to put me off the force. You say your purpose is jobs for col—Negroes. Do you want to start by losing me my job?"

De Bruliere sipped his beer, ate a whole ear. "Son, you're on. I told you I've gone in for politics; well, a politician needs friends. You can help me. Some day I'm going to sit in Congress."

"I'm sure you will, Harold. I think it is my turn to buy a beer for us." Buck ordered. "Which party do you belong to?"

"We don't follow parties any more. We vote for the living man, not for Abraham Lincoln or against Jefferson Davis. But I hope," De Bruliere said, "that I can go to Congress on the Democratic ticket. So the Louisiana representatives will have to shake hands with me when they want my vote in a caucus."

Buckingham Ranulph was silent. "I guess my folks were from Virginia," he said. "I never think about it much."

"I'm trying to forget it," De Bruliere said. "Here's to N.Y.U., Buck."

*　　　*　　　*

PEGGY REILLY CAME OUT of Father Cardovic's little church with her face white, her hands clenched. Ohhhh.

She was damned, eternally damned now. If she were run over or in a bus accident, her soul would go straight to hell. She had lied in confession.

Oh, our Father which art— No. She had no right to appeal to God any more. The Blessed Virgin would turn Her lovely face away from Peggy's plea.

When Father Cardovic had asked her if she had anything more to confess, her tongue had been tied. She had shaken her head no, and left the confessional with a false absolution on her head, and the most heinous crime of all unconfessed. Murder. Daily, frequent murder, she had been aiding the murderer of unborn children, the thwarter of the Holy will, and she had denied it to the Father.

You could be excommunicated for that. Oh, the awful tolling of the bell, the casting down of the book.

To a horrible secular crime she had added a worse religious one. She had falsely obtained absolution.

Peggy turned back. She would run back into the church, throw herself at Father Cardovic's knees, and tell him all. It was not too late.

But Dr. Wilcomen's face came between her and the church. She had promised him. She had— And then she had followed her training, if you only got inside the church, God would help. . . . Shuddering, she hurried to Fifth Avenue and climbed to the upper deck of a south-bound bus. She sat on the very front seat, and cried, the tears rolling down her face unchecked. The church had not helped her. God had not helped her. She was beyond all help.

*   *   *

DON LOOKED AROUND THE HUGE OFFICE. "Boy, this is something. You'll have to get some new clothes, Ray, to live up to this."

"Wait'll I see if I can pull the old *Mail* out of the red. In the meantime, I'm saving my salary."

"What are the prospects?"

"Good. I've got Brawley out trying to see if he can't dig me up a good white-slave crusade. That's the stuff to build circulation on, and he's the boy to get it. I wish I had Joe here."

"Cartwright says he can come back next week."

"I know." Ray shoved his paunch body back from the desk. "How are your affairs, Donald?"

Don laughed. "I want to ask you a question, Ray. Just how important is sex?"

"Oh, hell, the whole world revolves around it. If there's anything you find out in this game, that's it."

"You put me on something the other night. I never thought it might be a girl that was wrong with me."

"Sure. It usually is. Especially at your age. Put it up to her yet?"

"No. I'm not sure yet."

"Well, try seeing if she'll just roll in the hay with you."

Don shook his head. "She's from one of the finest families in New York," he said, stiffly.

Ray lay back in his highly upholstered mahogany swivel chair and roared with laughter. "Oh God, oh God," he said finally. "That's the best I've heard in years. Good grief, boy, is that what they teach you in Wall Street?"

Don said: "Newspapermen don't get any money, they never get to meet anybody but murderers and cops, they have to work like hell. They take their compensation in thinking the rest of the world's stupid."

Ray said: "Your father is a newspaperman. I'm one. Your old man—yeah, I know what you think of him—is a better man right now, flat on his back in a private booby hatch than you or any other sniveling Wall Street parasite will ever be."

"Don't get sore. I was just quoting you."

The editor chuckled good-naturedly. "Don't mind saying it ourselves, but we hate to hear it from outsiders."

Don sat down on the edge of the desk. "When did I get to be an outsider?"

"You're turning into one. You've changed more in the last few weeks than anyone I've ever seen. Wanting to give up your profession to sit in an office."

"Field supervision is part of engineering. You've got the layman's idea that an engineer is a guy in field boots bossing a bunch of pick and shovel men. Do you think the big engineers sit on a pile of mud watching dirt moved?"

Ray said: "I'm not as stupid as you think I am. The big engineers stay out in the field till they get big enough to head their own projects. They don't quit and take book-keepers' jobs.

"Without financing there wouldn't be any engineering. It—"

"How about the WPA? Son, you're of age. Maybe that girl's bothering you. Make up your own mind. You've got the yen; if you don't know what to do about it, go to a doctor. If you want a telephone number—"

"Ah, go to hell. I notice you jumped at this chance to make money. Well, I've got my chance, too. I'm making more money now than any guy in the field for us. I'll make more as soon—"

"As soon as you put the knife to Makin, who got you into the office originally. Good Wall Street tactics."

Don said: "He had to get me into the office. They needed my testimony in that iridium business."

"I wondered if you remembered that," Ray said. "A hell of a fine basis for a career—perjury and treason to your country."

"Governments have frequently been wrong. I could explain to you that that dam would have been a mistake in any event. But you wouldn't care for that. Newspaper talk. Black is black, white is white, and to hell with subtlety.

Pass Through Manhattan

You sit here trying to dream up a crusade to sell more papers and then you have the nerve to call me a liar."

Ray said: "Did you go to all the trouble of coming up here to tell me what was wrong with my profession? I knew it years ago. Do as I say, not as I do. We've been friends too long to fight, now, kid. The first time I saw you you didn't even have diapers on, because your parents had forgotten to buy any. In fact, now that I remember it, I went out and bought your first pants for you in a shop on 97th Street. I'm not sure that Joe ever paid me back either."

Don said: "Are you all through?"

Ray said: "No. When you get yourself tied up into a knot in that dirty business you've gotten into, Joe or Brawley or Ron or I will dig up some dirt on some mine owner and blackmail him into letting you run his mine. How do you like that?"

"So long, Ray."

Donald swung on his heel and fumbled his way through the door and out into the news room. He collided with Brawley Smith, who caught his arm, and said: "Hi, capitalist."

"I've just been hearing about the evils of my ways from Ray."

"The thwarted uncle, that's what Ray is. I suspect him of putting gold dust in my liquor. Say, if you want to see the old boy light up, come back in. I've got a wonderful crusade for him. The abortion racket. Did you know there are at least two thousand illegal doctors in this city?"

"Oh, nuts," Don said, and took his arm away. He stumbled across the news room, his eyes blurring. Hell, was he going to cry like a kid, blubber in the streets? Say that he had lost his last friend, say that—

All his life, Ray had been closest to him of anyone. When he was a kid, Ray had treated him like an equal, when he grew up and wanted to talk something over, Ray had always leveled with him. And now the old boy had turned preacher. Run out, just when Donald—

Stepping out of the corridor downstairs, Don shrugged. He was grownup. He didn't need anyone to tell him what to do. And if he did—

Ray's new job had gone to his head, that was all.

*　　*　　*

DENNIS COSTI LOOKED AT THE BIG MAN with what he knew was well-concealed distaste, and handed over the monthly check.

The big man said: "Thanks, Your Honor." These men always called you Your Honor, which was, at least, better than being called Counselor.

"That's all right," Judge Costi said, "always glad to help the club along. Baseball bats for the neighborhood kids, you said?" Sometimes it was Christmas baskets, pretty soon it would be to help children get confirmation dresses and suits.

"That's right, Your Honor. Can't do too much for the kiddies," the well-padded gent said, rising. "The boys of today are the—"

"Voters of tomorrow," the judge said. He was sorry after he said it.

"Ha, ha. Yes, sir, that's right, I guess. You haven't been around to the clubhouse much lately, Your Honor."

"No, the calendar's been pretty crowded. I start a new case tomorrow, and then I hope to get away to the country for a week or so."

"Well, you picked a nice time of year for it." The big man shook hands. Dennis Costi walked him to the door, pumping the well-manicured hand. "Hope you get a good case, Your Honor."

"I hope I get a short one."

"Yeah, I guess so. Anybody from our district?"

"Well, in a way. The defendant's the City of New York. A bus accident."

"Sock it to 'em, Judge. We're gonna throw those Fusionists outa City Hall at the next election, you weaken 'em up for us now. Ha, ha. I'm jokin', of course; I know you're the straightest judge on the bench. My friends the newspaper boys say you write the best decisions, too. So long, Your Honor."

"Good-bye."

Dennis Costi shut the door of his chambers firmly behind the ward boss's broad back, and went over to the window. His chambers faced north, towards the new white buildings of the city and the long, tomb-like State Building. Below him, on the courthouse steps, all the riff-raff that attaches itself to litigation congregated, cheap lawyers, bondsmen, professional medical witnesses, process servers. Trash, trash.

His brother was the one who had it easy, running the big warehouses of Costi & Company, the import and export firm their father had founded. Even though the firm was not doing so well—Dennis knew to his grief—it paid its president a salary as good as a Supreme Court judge's. And it was better to deal in olive oil and sardines and nice little tubs of pickles than in political deals and the unhappy, nagging wails of the public in litigation.

Dennis Costi sighed and went back to his desk. He picked up the pleas in this matter of Lempe *v.* the City of New York *et al.*, and sighed. A nasty case. There was no hope that it would be a short one, either. This business of inability to fulfill marital duties was impossible to either prove or disprove, and it would mean endless, stupid parades of doctors across the stands, the clearing of the court of women, all the mess in the world. He shoved the pleas away from him again, leaning back in the chair, lighting one of the Italian stogies his brother brought up from the warehouse. The rank, twisted tobacco put out smoke that filled the room, and—

He reached for the phone. He would call up Sylvester at the warehouse and have lunch with him. There was really no reason to go studying this Lempe business, plenty of time for that while the jury was being drawn.

Oh, no. Sylvester wasn't fun any more. Sylvester had almost a phobia that Mussolini's sole purpose in the world was to ruin Costi & Company, and it was pretty hard to get Syl off the subject, or to keep from getting on it yourself. The salad at lunch was almost certain to start Syl off. The quality of the olive oil was a personal insult to Syl's standing as an honest man; he seemed to feel that no one but he knew that the Spanish war had ruined those olive groves from which comes the bland Spanish oil so necessary for blending with the stronger Italian.

Whereas the Japanese—

Dennis Costi smiled at the cigar, but there was no real joy in the smile. Nothing seemed to be much fun any more, and once the world, New York, had been such a bright place.

Wonder if my kids have as much fun as Syl and I used to. My, we had fun. Snowball battles in the back yard of the old house on 68th, skating down Central Park West or on the Mall, playing basketball in the smelly old gym at the McVurney School. Even going to church was fun, because we belonged to both the Irish and the Italian congregations, and we could make a sporting proposition about which Sunday School was going to get the most treats.

Pass Through Manhattan

The time I picked Father Lynch and Syl picked Father La Cresta, and we got to go on a picnic out to Karatsonyi's Landing and they got a trip to the zoo. I teased Syl till he got mad and chased me all down the back yards between 67th and 68th, me going over the high board fences like a cat, and Syl stopping to throw stones and hunks of dirt at the seat of my pants every time I got up on a fence.

There was never anybody more fun than Sylvester Costi, but not any more. Well, I guess I'm just as bad, complaining about the stupidity and lack of education of the lawyers who come before my bench with their bad grammar and their sneaky manners.

I'll be irritated all through this trial because everyone will insist on calling Mrs. Lempe Mrs. Lemke, and every time they do it it will sound like someone scratching on a window.

Well, the old man wanted one of his sons to be a judge, and I was the younger. Too bad he didn't live to see me elevated way up here, he was so happy when I was appointed a magistrate.

If I'm a good boy and don't get fresh to that fat lout that just left here, I'll go to the Court of Appeals pretty soon. The top of the profession Pa chose for me.

His face softened, thinking that he and Syl had been very good sons, anyway. Ah, the days of my childhood. Papa with his silver hair and his fine mustachios, always smelling of wine and just a little garlic. Going down to the warehouse on Saturdays on the Ninth Avenue L, and Pa so proud of us, his sons: "Real Americans. Dennis, he's gonna be a judge; with a name like that all the Wops and Micks both'll vote for him."

Making themselves sick eating the samples, the workmen so proud that the boss's boys came back to the long sampling room where the wine tasters worked around their big, circular tables. One time we drank a whole fiasco of Chianti.

For years, when I grew up, I had the idea that was why people used fiasco the way they do; because of something like what happened to Syl and me, post-fiasco.

Ah, damn Mussolini. I'm as bad as Syl, thinking that Europe's been used up as a way of making my brother bad company for me.

Dennis Costi wiped his hand across the fine bright blue eyes that were his mother's heritage to him, and reached for the papers in Lempe *v.* the City of New York.

"And that the said bus did then proceed along 96th Street, despite the exigencies of the weather and the hazard to life and limb thus—"

You would think a man like Vanderbilt would employ a clerk who could spell. And exigency! No meaning at all in there. Even if old Vanderbilt was a guttersniping old shyster himself, he could hire lawyers with education.

Vanderbilt makes five times what you do every year. Ten times.

Oh—

Dennis Costi shoved the papers away, and picked up the phone. "Get my brother, will you?"

He threw the stogy into the cuspidor provided for all judges by the benevolent State of New York, and fumbled another one into his mouth, reaching for matches. The phone buzzed. "Syl, how are you, boy? Say, listen, I'm not doing anything and starting tomorrow, I'm going to be tied up on a long, nasty case. Let's get in my car and go down the island to Canoe Place Inn or some place and get drunk on Chianti. A whole fiasco, Syl."

Pass Through Manhattan

The older brother said: "Why, I'd love to, Dennis, but there's a rumor going around that Hitler and Stalin are going to sign some sort of treaty with each other."

"Oh, hell, man, they can sign it without you, anyway."

"That's all very well to say, Dennie, but in God's name, what will that do to me? Whatever Hitler does, Mussolini does, and for all I know they may be planning to give Spain back to the Communists, just when I've finished a good contract with Franco's people that would see us all on the road to recovery." Sylvester sounded as though he were going to cry. "I had a contract for every bit as much Spanish oil as I needed, and now it will be all shot to hell; they may even swap it with Russia for some of that Amtorg stuff. I—"

"Ah, Syl, have a heart. You can take care of it in the morning."

"Oh, you've got a salary from the State; the only thing worth being nowadays is a bureaucrat. I've got to get out and scramble for a living, lie awake nights worrying how I'm going to keep Costi & Company open with nothing to import or export."

"I'm too tired to fight with you. But if I had you in the back yard of the old house on 68th, I'd teach you who was a bureaucrat."

Syl laughed. "Anyway, come down and have lunch with me."

"Not I, Sylvester. I don't want Mussolini with the soup, Hitler with the spaghetti and Franco with the cheese. I think I'll go to a burlesque show."

"Good-bye. Say, if any of your connections can guess which way Roosevelt would react—"

"No, Syl."

He hung up the phone and wiped his lips with a fresh

linen handkerchief, holding the stogy in the left hand. His secretary came in with a bunch of papers. "Habeas corpi," she said.

He grinned behind the handkerchief. Miss Winters was a graduate of Wellesley and the Harvard Law School and she never let you forget it.

He signed the orders automatically. There was no use reading them, since, if the police had the prisoners, they ought to take them to trial, and if they didn't, the court orders did no harm.

But a name out of the newspapers caught his eye. "What's this?"

Miss Winters glanced at it. "Oh, yes. He was leading a demonstration against a Nazi mass meeting. He's the Communist leader, you know."

"My brother says the left hand is about to find out what the right hand has been doing. Leave chaps like this in a pretty pickle, won't it?" Dennis rapped the paper with his knuckles and signed it. "And by God, they claim a Jewish policeman picked him up. Isn't law and order wonderful, Miss Winters? Isn't everything a mess?"

"Why, Judge Costi, all these papers are in order, I'm sure I—"

"I wasn't criticizing you, Miss Winters. You're the finest secretary I've ever known."

When the door closed behind her, His Honor threw the stogy in the cuspidor, and lay back in his swivel chair, staring at the handsome ceiling. It blurred before his eyes.

*   *   *

MARIE LEMPE TRIED ON THE BLACK DRESS that she had bought with the assistance of the lady from Mr. Vanderbilt's office.

Pass Through Manhattan

It was going to be hot, but Mr. Vanderbilt insisted on a black dress.

Well, it had been a nice summer. It had been nice, not having to work in summer when Washington and Grace were out of school. Soon after the trial would come Labor Day, and then they would start their education again, their good American education. But it had been nice, she and Washington had been every place in the city. To Staten Island on the ferry, and to the zoo and the Aquarium and all the museums.

Now comes the trial. For herself, she would rather it had been in the spring, since she had to wear this black dress. And it would be hard talking about snow in August in New York.

But it had been a real summer, the finest she had ever had. Artur so full of loving-kindness and even Grace willing to take time to go to Klein's with Mama and buy nice little dresses for school.

There had been some trouble with Artur about Klein's, he did not like the name, but when he found out about the prices, he said maybe it was right to take advantage of Jewish cupidity.

She got out the garnet brooch Artur's mother had given her when they were married, and tried it. No, it was old-country, greenhorn stuff.

The phone rang. She answered it. "Hello? . . . Oh, yes, Frau Goldstein, hello. How is the bakery?"

"Oh, business has been a little slow, the hot weather. So tomorrow starts your trial?"

"Yes. Soon it will be over. I am sorry, Frau Goldstein."

"Oh, I think maybe I have a position, with a dentist in the Bronx. And Herr Goldstein, he is ready for his pharmacist's examination, we will be all right. How is the pain?"

"It is nearly gone. The doctor says after next week I do not have to come back, just to take the medicine after meals."

"I am so glad. That is the doctor by Mount Sinai?"

Frau Lempe giggled. "Yes. But Artur—"

"I understand." Tactfully, she did not add that she would never be likely to meet Mr. Lempe. "Maybe on my day off I come down to the courtroom and see if perhaps you cross your legs for the judge."

They both laughed. "I think maybe the trial will be over before then; Mr. Vanderbilt wanted it now because he said the jury would hurry to get away for Labor Day."

"Well, good-bye and good luck, Mrs. Lempe."

"Good-bye, Mrs. Goldstein."

PART THREE

THEY HAD BEEN AWFUL GREENHORNS when they got off the boat on that day in 1888. The Weintraubergs couldn't know it, but what hit them in the face, what whipped through their thin clothing, what had nearly kept the boat from crossing from Ellis Island to Manhattan was the beginning of the Blizzard of '88 that made New York history as the worst snowstorm that ever banged the rocky city.

That crooked labor agent who had opened the office in Memel had had his walls covered with pictures of fruit trees and banana bushes, and the Weintraubergs had given away all their heavy clothing, their sheepskin jackets and caps to neighbors in the ghetto. They had gotten through the ocean-crossing by staying in the big immigrant cabin, along with the rest of the mob that had been assembled at Kishinev by the agents.

When little Moishe whimpered every time the door to the deck was opened, Papa would take him on his lap, the caftan smelling of the wood fires of home, and tell him of how the sun always shone in the new land, it never rained. Mama would shake her head and say: "How then does it give water?" but Papa never listened.

Finally they had to pay one of the stewards to give them three extra blankets. Mama shook her head over this, the dollars had been expensive to buy, but Papa said it was all right. In America they would give you a free farm, it was a fine thing, all you had to have was money for the stamp on the document.

Moishe wanted to know if the stamp would have a picture of the Czar on it, and that made Papa laugh. "No, it would have a picture of George Washington." Then it blew up rough, every few minutes the propeller on the boat would come out of the water and the immigrant cabin would shake and shiver. So they were two extra days getting to New York and Papa took some of the money and bought food from one of the stewards because what they had brought with them was all gone. Never mind, Papa said, soon they would have their farm and grow everything they ate themselves. In the old country, it was not allowed Jews should own farms.

Then there was Ellis Island, but Moishe, who had not been sick at all on the boat got sick to his stomach as soon as they stepped ashore. He was sick all the time at Ellis Island, he was still sick when they got off in Manhattan and walked around in all the snow.

Because it was such a bad day not many runners were hanging around the dock, and Papa could only find one who spoke the same kind of Lithuanian Yiddish he did. He told them where to go to get a room, plenty of their people there. They started walking up town following his directions; for a dollar he had written the address on a card in

Pass Through Manhattan

American for Papa to hold in his hand. But the snow got worse and worse and there didn't seem to be many people on the street and Mama said maybe the boat had gotten turned around and taken them to Siberia, she didn't see any banana trees.

They nearly froze and it got dark. You couldn't see your hand two feet away from the base of the street lamps against whose posts the snow was piling up two and three feet thick. A lot of the lamps went out.

The runner had told them there would be a sign in the window of the house they were to go to, he had drawn the sign on the card Papa carried. After a while they would stop and look at the card after each street light. Then Moishe saw the sign in a window:

ROOMS FOR RENT

and the number over the door was 312 just like the card.

But Mama said she had seen a lot of numbers the same, it was the name on the lamp post at the corner that made the difference. Moishe sat on Papa's shoulder and held the card up, yes it was the same as the sign, HOUSTON STREET.

So they went into 312, and the woman didn't understand them at all, but Mama kept pointing at the sign, and Papa held out money, and finally she took them to a room that didn't have any furniture or blankets or anything. But there was a stove there and the woman loaned them two blankets and had her red-headed son bring them a big pile of broken-up wooden boxes to burn in the stove. The boxes had American writing all over them.

The storm lasted two days, but Moishe and the red-headed boy went out and bought food, and all the people in the house loaned a little furniture, a chair here, a couple of plates there.

Moishe found out the boy's name was Daniel. When Moishe picked up the word "eggs" from listening to Daniel, Daniel was just as proud as if Moishe was his own brother. He called Moishe Michael.

Mama died that winter, and the people in the house were all nice to Michael. It was not till a year later that he learned that they should have gone to 312 East Houston Street instead of West, and that they were the only family on the block who weren't Irish. But by that time he was going to public school with Daniel, not parochial school because Daniel's people, like most of those on the block, were North Irish Protestants. Michael didn't know that meant "Christians" until a few months later.

When the teacher asked Michael his name, he didn't understand. Daniel said it for him, but Daniel had only gotten a vague idea of it, and the teacher wrote down Vanderbilt, which she had heard of, and which did sound a little like Weintrauberg.

Papa must have been the only Jewish ditch digger in the city, too. Lots of times contractors didn't want to hire him, but the Houston Street gang regarded Papa as their luck, they felt it was distinctive to have him with them, and they always got him on.

But Mama dying, and the other ladies on the block always sick, and never enough to eat made Michael Vanderbilt and Daniel Sheridan swear that when they grew up they would never be poor. They never were, either. Daniel was one of the biggest sewer-pipe contractors in the city and Michael was one of the biggest independent lawyers. Daniel was an alderman for a while, but then he quit holding office and became a big man in the Old Guard of Tammany Hall.

Pass Through Manhattan

Maybe it was a lucky blizzard after all, Daniel used to say, and Michael—this was when they were both over fifty —would say, maybe that steamship agency that started them off for Kishinev wasn't such a liar after all.

*   *   *

"TAKE A LETTER TO DIBRELL at the All's Fair," Donald said. He watched Miss Cowan with interest. He had found out an interesting thing about her; her boy friend had given her, about two weeks before, a pair of blue elastic garters that resembled rural armbands. When she and the boy friend were on the ins, she wore the garters; when they fought, she went back to the old gold-clasped ones. He had pieced the origin of the blue elastics together from overhearing guarded phone calls: "Yes, I've got them on. I wore my blue beads to match— No, silly, I haven't got them around my neck; you know where I've got them." Miss Cowan was not a pretty girl—her cheek bones were too low, giving her a sulky look; and she did not have a good figure; but her legs were all right, and it was apparent to Don—who had plenty of time to study her—that she did her best to call attention to them. Eleanor, whom Don had told about the elastics, said they probably were armbands; that fancy round garters had not been made in years.

"Dear Dibrell," Don said. "Your last tonnage report was very disappointing; Mr. Grainger himself commented on it. Mr. Makin and I both feel that you have let things go slack at the All's Fair. New paragraph, Miss Cowan." The phone rang. He picked it up, said: "Morton speaking."

A familiar masculine voice said: "Is Miss Cowan there?"

Don handed over the phone, said: "For you."

When she leaned back, he saw it was the gold clasps today. Unbidden a picture came to his mind of a couple squabbling in a vestibule. No, she had an apartment with another girl; probably they took turns, one girl and her date went to a movie while the other couple used the room. Two daybeds and a table, probably, and a gas or electric plate in the bathroom to cook dinner on. But better than making love in vestibules. Walking late at night you saw them, a couple in every other doorway on some streets, pressed close together, whispering or just standing—

He had been doing a lot of walking at night. Couldn't sleep for some reason. Maybe he ought to take up handball or squash, but the dusty, linimented air of the gymnasium choked him—

Miss Cowan said: "Don, I'm taking dictation, I'll call you back," and hung up.

Don said: "Same name as mine, eh?"

"Yes. 'Let things go slack at the All's Fair, new paragraph.'"

"As you know," Don dictated, "at your suggestion we provided the pressure hoses with Southern California fire nozzles, it being your idea that the men could adjust the backspray over themselves, and thus keep production at peak through the hot weather. These nozzles were a considerable expense to Armstrong and Grainger, and we do not find that they have repaid us in ore gotten out. New paragraph, Miss Cowan. Old man, you have put Mr. Makin and me in a bad spot; it is up to us to explain to Mr. Grainger. So please see that this week's tonnage is higher than last. With kindest personal regards, etc."

Miss Cowan made a flourish on the notebook. "Yes, Mr. Morton."

"Archibald, at Tehachapi, Sonora, Mexico. Dear Archibald: In re your letter about the dropping off of free gold in your concentrates, believe you are quite right in not stirring up trouble. With the Mexican government taking the attitude it has towards American industry, any inquiries made on the spot might result in collectivization of the whole property. New paragraph. I have passed the matter along to our Mexico D.F. representative, Señor Hernandez, and in due course a government detective will come into your picture. I think this, while slower and more expensive, will be best in the long run. Put that in code, Miss Cowan, and shoot it off airmail. I suspect Archie's clerks of a little double-crossing."

"Yes, Mr. Morton."

Don handed over a mimeographed paper. "Send this to Collister, at Sierra, with a note: Dear Collister. This was read at the last meeting of the American Society of Mining Engineers. What do you—"

The phone rang again. Miss Cowan made a dive for it, her face reddening. "Mr. Morton's office. Yes, Mr. Grainger, yes." She rang off. "Mr. Grainger wants you right away, Mr. Morton."

Don said: "Finish that note to Collister, What do you think about this? I'll sign 'em when I get back." He stood up, tapping his heels to straighten his trouser legs, pulling down his vest, brushing off the shoulders of his coat. As he reached the corridor door, he could hear Miss Cowan already dialing her number. He stood in the corridor a moment, the door held open a crack.

She said: "Don. How many times have I told you not to call me during office hours? I'll call you when Gladhand is out and—"

Don walked away quickly. An eavesdropper hears no

good of himself, and that's a fact. So he was Gladhand to the girls in the office. And Makin was Fishface, he knew that. Gladhand.

Of course, all girls in offices had nicknames for the bosses. It—

But Gladhand. Don Morton, the contact boy. The super-dooper salesman. The pain in the neck. He—

He rapped on Mr. Grainger's door. "Ah, Morton. Have a seat."

Don sat down, startled, a little excited. It was the first time Grainger had summoned him without Makin being present. Grainger shoved over a box of cigars, his long, mottled fingers holding the edge of the porcelain-lined humidor like a claw. "Cigar, Morton?"

Don took one, bit off the end, held a match for Mr. Grainger, then lit his own, making all his movements as much like the boss's as possible.

"Morton," Grainger said, "what do you know about the Matagordo chain of mountains?"

"They run along the backbone of South America," Don said. "Through about three countries. They're largely unexplored, I believe."

"Mineralogically—"

"Oh, the parts that have been explored have shown traces of gold," Don said. "So far as I know, there are no commercial operations, though. For one thing, nobody is entirely sure which country owns which part of the Matagordos."

"Quite so, quite so," Grainger said. "Now, I'll tell you something you don't know. The particular part of the Matagordo foothills known as the Lacrimas has been put under a three-way mandate. For five years. Whatever income it brings in in that time will be divided among the three countries, and the rulers of those countries are extremely anxious to get going. Bids will be opened in Washington in a month. Well, Morton. Armstrong and Grainger, acting on a report from an explorer and geologist named Shattuck—you know him?—are going to bid forty percent. We keep sixty percent of all the gold we take out, in other words. The mandate boards get forty. I believe we'll get the contract."

Don frowned. He could have sworn the old man winked at him. Bribery, corruption, Washington stuff.

Donald said: "Even the foothills of the Matagordos are pretty damned inaccessible. You'll have to fly machinery in there, take concentrates out by plane. What did Shattuck say he thought the ore would run?"

"High. From forty to seventy-five dollars a ton. Not under forty, though."

Donald was silent for a moment. There was a joker here of some sort. Old Grainger never made a mistake like that in his life. He said: "You get about a six months' season if we start right now, go right through to the rains. In any South American operation, governments change, you've got to pay for your pioneering the first season. But the low Matagordos are hellish good places for insects. Sleeping sickness, yellow jack, and, of course, malaria. What did Shattuck have to say—"

"Shattuck died after his return. Some form of embolism."

Don lowered his eyelids, squinted at the boss. "Your whole first season would go into insect control. Of course, with planes it's fast, but it's also expensive. Mr. Grainger, unless you've got a joker in here, I'd let the thing go."

"Joker?" Grainger turned his icy eyes on Don. "Joker?" Donald met his gaze coldly.

"Young man, Armstrong and Grainger never turned back because of fear. This firm was built on risks. Now, I want you to get me two good young engineers to go into the Matagordos. A mining man, and a construction man. I leave it to you to estimate how many foremen we'll need; I assume native labor will be best."

Donald nodded. "How about a sanitary engineer and a doctor?"

"Think over the medical aspects of the operation and give me your best thoughts on the matter," Mr. Grainger said. "And—er—I shall do the same. We shall want the least expensive plan, with, of course, the proper amount of peace of mind for the engineers."

Don stood in the door. Grainger's eyes bored through him, Don dropped his own. "Quite so," he said. His voice was brassy in his own ears.

*   *   *

FROM THEIR ROOM IN THE TOWER of the hotel, you could see a cloud of dust that hung over one part of Orange Street. That was their house, that was where the Polish and Italian housewreckers were tearing down what was left of the Castrons of Orange Street. The boss of the job had told her when she went to watch them that her "grampa" had built too well; it was a tough job, he'd lose money on it.

Good-bye, Orange Street, good-bye. Eleanor moved around the room, straightening things. The phone rang.

"Oh, Elly dear, this is Mother. I'm going to have dinner and go to a movie with that nice Mrs. Frenstrar, you know? I hope you don't mind."

"Not at all, Mother." Taking Mother out of that house had sliced ten years off her shoulders. She was gay as gay could be.

The room was on a corner of the tower, windows on

254

three sides. Eleanor walked away from the window that faced on Orange Street. But the next window showed her the harbor, tugs moving, wisps of smoke curling up from tugs. The water shone a brassy blue that made her feel hotter than ever. The third side was just Brooklyn.

She sat down facing the one solid wall, with its doors that led to the little hall and the bedroom. She—

Call up Donald, call up someone? She—

She started walking around the room. Men in torn, dirty undershirts tearing down the Orange Street house, ripping out the big oak timbers, sweat pouring down their hairy chests. Men on the decks of tugboats tossing ropes, the muscles across their backs moving like ropes or snakes in a bag. Men in the packed downtown streets, moving under the L tracks in little mobs, narrow-eyed, their thin flanks pressing a path through the crowd, getting into the subway—

She—

Eleanor stood up, jerked the shades down abruptly. The one on the window facing the harbor tumbled down on her head.

Her eyes filled with tears, standing there, one hand to her cheek, tangled in the crackling folds of window shade.

The Castrons of Orange Street were in storage. Portraits of short, red-faced, chubby men in blue clothes, and brass buttons, paintings of thin women, the twelve Currier & Ives prints: *The Castron Clippers*—all these were in storage in a huge, windowless building.

These were the dead, but the living had been put away, too. The last of the Castron women, she and her mother, were locked away here in this square tower room. Stored as impractical, useless—

No. Ah, no. In dying, in giving up, she, Eleanor Castron,

had done one last, final decency, one gesture worthy of the people who had sat for those paintings.

"Gray. I was decent to you, Gray. I could have ruined your life, too, but I didn't."

She began to feel more cheerful, even hummed a little. She could call someone up. Maybe Donald, or Tenny—

But her eyes were still tender, her lips still smiling. "Dear Gray," she murmured. Yes, she would call up Don and get him to take her out.

*   *   *

"GOT TO BE GOIN'," Jason Corning said. He held up his hunting-case watch, so they could all see it. "Three o'clock. Just got time to make it, got to be going, you know. A wonderful evening, my boy, wonderful. No, don't you chaps get up, don't want to break up Tenny's party."

John Tenbruye felt old and tired. His eyes had gravel in them, his throat was like sandpaper. Looking down the table, between the ranks of the corporals and troopers of his section straight into Old Jason's bloodshot eye, it occurred to him that he was the only sober one there. He leaned back, took a deep breath.

Old Jason would know he was a man of parts. A Burden, a Whitney, the Lehman twins, and a Cortlandt were among the men at his table. His, John Tenbruye.

"Don't want to break up Tenny's party," Old Jason said. He pointed to one of the waiters from the caterer's. "Get my hat and coat."

"But I'm going with you," Tenny said. "I want to see Linda breeze this morning."

"Iron man," Old Jason said. "You've got to be down at the office by nine."

Pass Through Manhattan

"What's sleep when you can see your own filly do her first eighth?"

Maybe Corning would pass out in the limousine, and he could get a few winks in. He had an appointment with Firstin that he wanted to wash up before the market opened. And—God—he had to appear in court that afternoon, that bus business. Well, Morton would be there. Wanted to see Morton. Rumor around the Street that Armstrong and Grainger were closing a deal in South America, Corning and Seligmann might like a small piece of it. Gold stock was an easy sale these days.

Now they were leaving, yells of "So long, Tenny, so long, Sarge," nicely bred young men being polite to their host and to an older gentleman despite the somewhat startling amounts of liquor they had consumed.

Down through the echoing halls of the Armory, the troop-room door shut behind them, barring out the noises of the party from which the host and guest of honor had departed.

Mr. Corning's chauffeur struggling to his feet, out of the limousine, his uniform collar unhooked. "Cheer up, Demmy," Mr. Corning said. "We'll be in bed by nine. This young man has to go to work when we get back from the Island."

"Yes, sir."

Deep in the back seat of the car, legs stretched out, the smooth motor taking them down Park Avenue. Somewhere on the slick surface of the Queensborough Bridge Tenny fell asleep, didn't wake till it was dawn and they were parked at the race track among a handful of other cars.

Demmy handed him a pair of binoculars, and climbed back into the car to sleep again. Rubbing his eyes, Tenny followed Old Jason's broad back through the mist towards the Corning barns.

A stable boy told them Misteh Mac was in Cora Sue's stall.

The Irish trainer was belted into a trench coat, though it was already turning warm. Chin down against the high neck of his sweatshirt, Mac was watching the boys put an exercise saddle on little Cora Sue's bay back. "All right," he said. "Take her out. You, Tony, take her all the way around the track, easy. Stay behind that chestnut."

Mac turned, acknowledged the owner's presence. "We're breezin' that Linda filly," he said. "The chestnut."

"How d'you think she'll go?" Tenny asked.

"I dunno." Mac pointed at a colored boy. "Get this stall cleaned out afore Cora Sue gets back."

The colored boy's eyes filled, his lower lip wabbled. "Well," Mac snapped, "I'm not gonna give 'em the signal fer five minutes. You better hurry if'n you want to see her breezed." The boy flew at the pitchfork leaning outside.

Mac turned on his heel and walked towards the track.

The mist was up now, the sky was still hazy in patches, but you could see clear around the track. Someone was working horses down the Widener chute, and two big gray jumpers went around and around over a short hurdle course, going so evenly that they looked like a horse and a mirror.

All around the track different stables were working. Far over on the other side, near the clubhouse, Tenny saw a red horse that might be Linda. He said: "Is that my mare over there?"

Mac didn't look. "She's a red filly," he said. "What we call chestnut."

Old Jason nudged Tenbruye. "Don't talk to Mac," he

whispered. "He doesn't like to be talked to when he's work-ing out the horses."

Mac had turned his fat back square to them, and was asking one of the assistant trainers about a movie he had seen the night before. "Me, I go fer that Miriam Hopkins. I'd walk clear into N'Yawk to see her," Mac said. "She's comin' to the RKO next week, and boy, you don't want to miss her. . . . You better go up to the three post, Joe."

The assistant trainer walked away up the track. Mac held his hand up, and Tony brought Cora Sue in. Mac put his hand on the bay neck. "Yeah, she's warm. How's Linda?"

Tony said that Slivvie was having trouble holding her.

"Go back of the three about a hunnerd feet. When you pass three, let 'em go." Mac raised his arm, gave some sort of signal to Joe, took his stop-watch out of his pocket, and said, grudgingly: "When Joe waves they're off. When they pass here, they're finished, Mr. Corning."

Old Jason took his stop-watch out.

Mac looked at Tenny, said: "Gotta watch?"

"Not a stop—"

"Here's one."

The two fillies were back a quarter of a mile away from them. Mac dropped his arm and the boys let their horses come up into a little, gentle hand-gallop. The tiny hooves thudded and thudded, or maybe it was Tenny's heart, and then Joe's handkerchief had waved and the three watches clicked and the little chestnut turned into a flash of red fire, fighting to pass the more experienced bay who had gone off like a shot at the word.

Cora Sue was leading, but Linda came up, and up, and it seemed like minutes passed and they were even with Mac and the post, and the watches clicked, and Linda had passed just a little bit ahead of Cora Sue, not much, but a nose.

Pass Through Manhattan

John Tenbruye looked down at the watch in his hand. "Eleven and—" he began. Mac hit him, hard, in the face, and vaulted over the rail running down the track.

"What?" John Tenbruye said stupidly. "What—"

Linda was down, lying on the track, her head under the bottom rail, her legs kicking. A half-dozen exercise boys had stopped their horses, were sitting on her, the reins of their own horses straight out behind them.

John went over the rail after Mac, pushing his way in. He told somebody, gravely: "I'm her owner."

Mac looked up from running his gnarled hands over the chestnut. "Get the doc."

"What is it, Mac?" Old Jason asked.

"Think it's just her hip," Mac said.

"Just—"

"Aw, shut up, will ya—"

The vet must have started early, he was there. He kneeled beside Mac, his hands busy. "Hip," he said finally. "Dislocated."

"How about it?" Mac asked.

"Pull her shoes, put her on grass. Turn a cold hose on her back ever so often. She's all right." The doctor walked away again.

Tenny watched him go. Mac stook up. He said: "All right, Slivvie. Take her head in your lap. Hold her down, boys, till we can cut that rail, and we'll get her up."

Slivvie sat there, tears making furrows in the dust on his face. The older Tony, holding Cora Sue's head, said: "Aw— I done—"

"All right, kid," Mac said. "They're just fillies, there's gotta be some bouncing around. G'wan, walk Cora Sue out, she didn't mean to do it. Walk her cool, and tell that swipe to give her her mash."

Someone had brought a saw, was taking the rail away from over Linda's head.

John Tenbruye said: "Then it isn't serious?"

Mac said, "Naw. I was afraid it was her leg fer a moment."

Tenbruye said: "That's swell. Look, she did eleven and a—"

"What difference does it make?" Mac asked. "She'll never race."

"She won't—"

"But she's all right for breeding. Where's that— Oh, there you are." Mac put his hand on a young man's sweatered shoulder. "You Goddamned buzzard," he said affectionately to the young man. "This is the horse's owner here."

The young man said: "My name's Van Slyke. I'm getting up a little breeding farm down the island. I'll give you fifty dollars for your little mare."

Linda struggled to her feet, stood on three legs and the toe of the fourth.

"Fifty dollars?" John asked.

Van Slyke reached in his pocket. "Here—"

"Oh, take her," John Tenbruye said. "She's yours."

"Well, thanks." Van Slyke went down the track very slowly, Linda limping after him.

For the first time since John Tenbruye knew him, Mac smiled. "You paid fourteen hundred for her, didn't you?"

"Twelve."

"Well, better luck next time." Mac walked away, shouting at a colored boy to shake a leg, you guinea.

Old Jason said, gruffly: "Sorry, m'boy. Dreadful end to a fine night. I—I—"

Tenny was happy, happier than he could remember ever being. Twelve hundred dollars to be a junior partner in

Corning and Seligmann. Boy, oh boy, oh boy. He said: "Uncle Jason, you couldn't help it. Please forget about it."

"Feel like it was my fault. Look, let me make Cora Sue over to you, or—"

"Uncle Jason, I loved that Linda," John Tenbruye said with a boyish earnestness. "I'm afraid I won't feel like owning another race horse for a long time. . . . I've got to get into the office. Firstin's coming in to see me at nine about the Corning Manor."

"Yes, yes, of course. Wish I—"

"How about meeting me for a toddy at five, Uncle Jason?" John asked. "If some things develop today the way I think they're going to, I may be able to tell you how to make some money."

As he walked away, towards the cars, he heard old Jason's gruff voice saying: "Real thoroughbred, that boy."

John Tenbruye walked faster, but not fast enough to escape hearing Mac growl: "It wasn't his hip, was it?"

But it didn't matter. He was free from Mac's insults, he could always plead heartbreak if Jason wanted him to get another horse.

* * *

ARTUR LEMPE COULDN'T UNDERSTAND. Marie and he had been there on time, the young Irisher for the city had been there, Mr. Brefogel was there. And then Mr. Brefogel had gotten up and asked for a postponement.

Not so was it in the new Germany, wrongdoers were punished at once. They had injured Marie, they must pay. What, then, was there to wait for?

He had sent Marie home to take off her courtroom dress, too hot was it to wear black, and here he was, changing into his overalls. All the valves must be taken down and cleaned, right after Labor Day they sometimes had to turn on the heat for a few minutes every day.

Artur Lempe blushed, remembering the day in 1929 when a September cold snap had caught the building he had then run with half its pipes down. Ach! Luckily, Indian summer had come along in time to save them.

Now, in July and August, the interior pipes were prepared, cleaned out, reinsulated if necessary, the boilers chipped, furnace points cleaned, and so on. With these big furnaces, sometimes the whole crew could spend a month repairing the flues alone.

Then, in September and in June, all exposed work could be done. There was hardly a rental so small that it did not have two radiators; one could be taken down and its inlet capped while the other was ready for use.

Is this, then, the work for a janitor? Ten thousand people worked in the heat provided by Artur Lempe. The offices for every kind of factory, of magazines, of shipyards, were in Artur's building. And he, Artur Lempe, saw that the brains that ran America were kept warm.

Dressed in his neat, stainless overalls, Artur took the elevator to the eighteenth floor. He had told Mike to have three men working on the offices from that big fruit-growers' association, they liked plenty of heat there, best to have it done early.

On the service elevator landing Mike had set up a temporary plumbers' shop; Artur's idea. Why crowd the elevators that should be for the tenants with radiators and plumbing? Bring the tools, the portable plumbers' furnace and the dies and all, up with you in the morning before the tenants arrive. Then you can work all day on one floor.

Pass Through Manhattan

The elevator operator said: "Thought you was in court today, Artie?"

"Postponed. My counsel asked for a postponement."

"Zat so? Mike'll be glad to see you. When I stopped at eighteen last, he had used up all the Amurrican cusswords he knew, an' was startin' on the Cherman ones."

The elevator stopped at eighteen, Artur got out. Automatically he stepped over to the little furnace first, adjusted the flame. Always Mike set it for too much gasoline, like it was going to be used for a blow torch when all he wanted was to melt a little lead.

Mike himself was bent over a radiator, a short one, swearing.

Artur said: "What has happened?"

Without looking up, Mike said in German: "That dirty ten-thumbs of a Harold put the valve in cross thread." He gave a heave. "It is going to be impossible to get it out without—"

"Where is Harold?"

"I put him to carrying radiators. Norwald is taking them down for me, and those two incompetents over there are cleaning." He jerked his sweaty chin towards the corner where two workers looked up at the boss, grinned, and went on working.

"I will take charge of this. Get Harold."

Mike straightened up, a hand on his back. "O.K., Artur. I'm glad you're here. Oh. Did you win the case?"

"Postponed. Mr. Brefogel asked for a postponement. Our case is not yet prepared."

"You'll win," Mike said, and took his lean, long frame through the door to the tenants' corridor.

Artur selected a fourteen-inch Stillson, carefully adjusted it to grasp the stem of the valve without crushing. He fitted a piece of pipe to the handle of the Stillson, and bore down, gently. The valve moved with a little, wailing noise of stripping screws.

Mike came back with Harold. "Here he is, boss," he said in English.

Artur straightened up. "Now, Harold. In the fitting of valves, great care must be used. I will show you now what must be done. Take hold of the pipe, so—" He took the young man's hands, fitted them around the extension. "Now you must bear down—no, easily, easily—so. And a little more—so."

The valve came out. Artur tapped it out of the Stillson, removed the pipe that he had used for a lever from the handle, returned Stillson and pipe to their racks on the work table.

Harold shifted from foot to foot.

Artur took a fountain pen flashlight from his pocket, showed Harold the stripped threads. "You see? Completely ruined. Now, is necessary you remove all these threads, with a hand file. Then rethread the stem. Afterwards, fit a female thread to it with this brass collar here—see? Then ream out the aperture on the radiator, fit in the collar, and all will be well. It—"

"Aw, nuts," Harold said. "Whataya think I am, a convict? Ream the radiator, sure, and get a valve with a bigger stem. A little valve like that—"

"It is worth more than a day's salary, Harold. You can fix it in a half a day. That is right."

"Lissen, this is a big building. They c'n afford a new valve. Fer Gawd's sake, I useta haf to do that sort of thing when I was a boot in the Navy, but I bin a watertender. 'At's convict stuff."

"You will do it, Harold. By rights I should make you repair the damage you have so carelessly done on your own time, but we will, this time, write off the extra time to education. You will make a good heating superintendent, Harold."

"Yeah? Well, how would you like to take your valve and shove it up your Dutch—"

"That is all. You will do as you are told."

"I quit."

"It is up to you. We pay good wages. Only yesterday, I had an application from the second engineer for a freighter for your job."

"Let him have it. I'm a white man. Bet he's Dutch."

Artur took a pad from the cubbyhole of the portable work bench, wrote on it, first consulting the time over the door. "You will take this to the employees' entrance and be paid off."

Harold refused the slip. He stared at Artur a minute. He said: "Well, now—"

Artur stared back at him, still holding the slip. "If you apologize—"

"O.K.," Harold said. His face was red. "Sorry, teacher. I—"

"Then start cleaning the stem." Artur handed him the file.

The corridor opened and Mike came in pushing a radiator. He wheeled it over to the two cleaners in the corner, said: "All right, I will help clean. Ward, you push the wheelbarrow," and effected the transfer. He went out again, followed by Ward pushing the cleaned radiator.

The service phone rang. Artur picked it up. "Mr. Lempe speaking."

The oiler on duty at the hot-water furnace said: "A Mr. Brefogel wants you to call him right away."

Pass Through Manhattan

"O.K." Artur stepped to the elevator, pressed the button. Behind him the little, whispering noise of the small hand file went on as Harold cleaned away the ruined threads. "Be careful now, Harold, take your time," Artur said, and got into the elevator.

As the door closed, Harold threw the file to the composition floor. "The dirty Dutch slave driver," he told the cleaner in the corner. "I know what's been going on here."

"Take it easy, Harold," the cleaner said.

"Him and that Mike, holding Nazi meetin's on their lunch hour. Wonder if th' owners know that?"

"Take it easy, Harold," the cleaner said again.

Ward pushed another radiator through the door that Mike held open for him.

*   *   *

ON THE TABLE NEXT TO THE CHAIR where Peggy usually placed the men who waited for Dr. Wilcomen's patients, there was a cedar-lined box; one of her duties was to keep it filled with cigarettes.

Wilcomen had emptied these out on the table, was busily engaged in making a log cabin out of them. "Did it ever occur to you that I look like Lincoln?"

Without looking up from her magazine, Peggy grunted: "No."

"Well, maybe you're right. . . . What cha readin', Mick?"

"Nothing." But she heard him sweep up the cigarettes, dump them in the box, and rise to his long height. He came over, leaned one hand on her shoulder.

"*The Annals of Tropical Medicine*, September, 1939. . . . What's the idea, Mick?"

"Nothing."

"Oh, hah. Still thinking about the happy, happy life we could lead in the tropics, cutting haws out of the Indians? Or do you cut out haws?"

Peggy didn't answer.

"Really, Mick, it wouldn't do," Wilcomen said. "I'm making money hand over fist. There's no money in the tropics. And you don't like fruit, yourself."

Peggy looked up: "Sooner or later your hand is going to slip. See how much good your money does you then."

"It will buy me cigarettes in prison."

"Doc! Don't—"

"Oh, all right, Mick. Just when I thought you were developing a sense of humor— What are you doing tonight?"

"Not going out with you."

"You're missing a great opportunity. Garning will be in tonight, she can watch the phone. I'm going to take a room at a hotel uptown, get into bed, and drink champagne. Did you ever drink ice cold champagne in bed?"

"Certainly not," Peggy said. But she smiled a little.

"Come on along and I'll make it a double bed. Or even twin beds if you'd rather. Of course, I don't guarantee to stay on my side of—"

The front doorbell rang. With a flirt of his bony hands Wilcomen disappeared into the reception room, behind her desk; Peggy straightened her ribbonless cap and waited.

A chubby young man and a thin young woman came in. "We want to see Dr. Wilcomen."

Peggy looked them over. Neither seemed the hysterical type, though the boy had been drinking. "If you'll have chairs? Whom shall I say?"

"Mrs. Robinson. Dr. Bleeker sent me."

"Yes, Mrs. Robinson." Peggy stepped through the door into the back room. Wilcomen, in a fresh white jacket, was throwing a pencil up and catching it. "Hysteria?" he asked. Peggy shook her head. "Nausea? . . . Then send her in, Mick, send her in."

Peggy stepped back into the reception room. "Dr. Wilcomen will see you now." Mrs. Robinson went through the door, which Peggy shut. Mr. Robinson took a cigarette.

"Would you like something to read?" Peggy asked.

Mr. Robinson shook his head. "I never read. I'd like to talk, though. You must see a lot of life in a place like this."

Peggy didn't answer.

"I'm a writer," Mr. Robinson said. "Boy, what a lot of material you must have. I get paid—"

The buzzer under Peggy's desk went off. Startled, she jumped up, went into the reception room. Mrs. Robinson sat opposite Wilcomen, completely dressed. "Please take Mrs. Robinson upstairs and prepare her for an examination. Take a blood test, and a Wassermann spinal; a sample for urine analysis, and a basal metabolism. Now, if you'll come back—let's see—Thursday, Mrs. Robinson, we'll have the results and we can—"

Peggy stood there. There was no equipment for any of those things upstairs. "You had better take a coagulation test, too, Miss Jarvis," Wilcomen told Peggy Reilly. "I'm afraid you're going to be rather full of holes, Mrs. Robinson, but I don't like to take any chances. When you city dwellers have babies, it is sometimes serious."

"But all this is unnecessary," Mrs. Robinson said. "I know I'm pregnant. I had an analysis made at a drugstore and—"

"Well, exactly," Dr. Wilcomen said. "Now it is a question of what we do next."

Mrs. Robinson said: "But I want to know how much it is going to cost. We only have fifty dollars—"

"Erhm," Wilcomen said. "Well, these examinations will

cost ten. But then you have at least six months before the baby arrives. If you could save ten dollars a month, we could do the trick. Twenty-five dollars to me for delivery and another twenty-five for prenatal care. A semi-private room would cost—"

"But, Doctor—Dr. Wilcomen—I can't have the baby."

"How do you know you can't? That's what the examinations are for."

Peggy backed up against the wall. He wasn't drunk, either. He never drank till after the last patient had gone.

"I mean, we can't afford, a baby would ruin—"

"You should have thought of that sooner," Wilcomen said. "I'm sorry."

"Isn't there anything I can do?"

The doctor smiled. "You seem a sophisticated young woman. There are various medicines, quinine and ergot and so on. No doubt you've tried them. Outside of that—"

"Couldn't I—couldn't you?—I mean—"

Wilcomen stood up. He went over and patted Mrs. Robinson on the back. He looked like a picture out of a calendar, the young doctor. "I'm not a murderer, my dear. No doubt there are such doctors, but I don't happen to know any of them—"

"Oh." Mrs. Robinson stood up. "Then I won't bother you—" Peggy let her into the reception room. Mr. Robinson stood up. "How much?"

"I'm sure the doctor won't charge you, under the circumstances—" She watched them out the front door. Then she turned. Wilcomen was in her reception room, teetering on his long legs, smiling at her.

"Oh, Doc, oh, Carl." She almost threw herself at him, pressing her lips against his. "We're going to, are we going to—"

"We're going to drink champagne first."

"I love champagne." Her hands felt the hard muscles along his shoulder blades, hugged him to her. *Oh, Blessed Virgin. I thank Thee that—*

Carl Wilcomen's voice was suddenly harsh. "No," he barked. He twisted away from her, his bony fingers squeezed her shoulder, dragged her to the window.

"Look," he snarled.

Across the street the Robinsons were talking to two men. They might well have been detectives; they looked flat-footed.

"Oh. You—"

"Sheridan warned me. The politician."

"Oh. Doc, I thought for a minute you—"

"No," he said. "But you know, I was quite pleased with things. I was going to kill two birds with one stone, use it to get you to—"

"You don't have to tell me. Why did you tell me?"

"I dunno," he said dully. He turned away. "Make me a drink, will you? Maybe there had to be one person I hadn't lied to yet. Maybe—I dunno, Mick."

"Carl," she said. "Carl. I still like champagne."

*   *   *

MR. VANDERBILT STRETCHED HIS SMALL, warped body around in the big swivel chair, trying to get comfortable. "Well, blow my nose," he whined, "haven't you gotten us into a mess, just? Where is he, do you know? Where is he, I asked you?"

"I don't know," Brefogel said, dully. "Just gone."

"Well, find him, find him," Mr. Vanderbilt squeaked. He bounced up out of the chair, looked out the window. "Nice weather out, pretty weather. Think I'll get the car and go for a drive. Think I'll ask O'Farrell to go along. Nice young man, bright young man, if he is a spike. Dan'l was saying just the other day, too good a young man for the Corporation Counsel's office. Yes, yes, get him on the phone, ask him if he wants to go riding with Mr. Vanderbilt."

"Mr. Vanderbilt—"

"Yes, Brefogel, yes?"

"I'll find him, Mr. Vanderbilt. And if I can't—"

"Yes, Brefogel? Blow my nose, man, speak up."

"Lempe has three thousand dollars."

Mr. Vanderbilt bounced back into his chair. His eyes were like little beads. "Yes? Little Limpy saved three thousand dollars, eh? Well, get it out of him, get it out of him. This is a highly important case, Brefogel. Can't afford to go running around without a refresher. If this nasty Leader fellow can't pay us, get Limpy's money."

"But how about this other charge up in New England?"

Mr. Vanderbilt looked like a little gnome huddled behind his desk. "If Limpy can retain us himself," he said, finally, "we never heard of this feller that's disappeared, we never heard of the Nastys, we don't know a thing about this feller embezzlin' money up in New England. Straight open an' shut case. Limpy's wife was hurt, Limpy sues."

"But Mr. Vanderbilt," Brefogel said. "We can't possibly win the case. You know that. The Bund was paying us to prosecute it for propaganda purposes, not so Lempe could get damages."

"Quiet," Mr. Vanderbilt squeaked. "Quiet, you fool, we're lawyers, ain't we? Think we're gonna get inta the middle of a case and then find there ain't anyone to pay us? Think I want that papist Costi investigatin' us, sayin' we're Hitler agents? Well, blow my nose, a lawyer's all right as long's he got retainers and refreshers. A lawyer's all right so long's he gets paid. It's when you can't show who was payin' you that you get disbarred."

"Yes, sir. I'll get in touch with Lempe right away."

"You do that. You do that, Brefogel. And if you get one more client in here that embezzles the money that oughta go to me, I'll get me a new partner. I'll get O'Farrell, the dirty Dublin rat," said Michael Vanderbilt.

* * *

DRESSED IN A PENCIL-STRIPED BLUE twill worsted suit, Ray sat on the shoe-shining stand in the lockerroom of the Newspaper Club and watched the colored boy bring a lustrous glow to his black calfskin shoes. From time to time he took a puff on the Corona that he held breast-high and a little out so it wouldn't drop ashes on his clothes—

The boy finished and Ray handed him a quarter. Then he slowly walked towards the swinging door, the Negro scurrying ahead to hold the door open, and out into the lobby that overlooked Times Square. He stood at the window, gazing down at his city. He was pleasantly aware of the bustle behind him, of the fact that he was, at the moment and for the day, the most important member of the club; the man who had shoved a newspaper into that tiny circle of metropolitan dailies that made their own living.

There was no job in the newspaper business too big for the man who had brought the *Mail* out of the red. He and Roy Howard—

You could always pick up a New York paper that was losing money, and every few years the cornstalk geniuses, the men who had made phenomenal successes in the Middle West and the South, tried it. And every ten years or so

273

someone succeeded. Patterson, just after the war, had constructed the *News;* Howard had pulled the *World-Telegram* together in the early thirties out of a dead *World,* a moribund *Telegram;* and now the *Mail.*

The man of the moment, the big shot of the decade, walked to the door. "My guest here yet?"

"No, sir, Mr. Morton has not arrived."

"I'll be in the bar."

He was halfway through the bottle of imported beer when Donald came through the doorway. Ray raised one hand, and the boy smiled and came over. "Hi, Ray."

"Donald, how are you? Try a bottle of this, it's very good here."

Don nodded at the bar boy, sat down behind the long thin table.

"How's Wall Street?" Ray asked.

"How should I know?"

"Have you got a broker, Don? I want to tuck away a little of my money. Take a flier."

"Tenbruye of Corning and Seligmann. He—"

The old gleam came to Ray's eye. "Wait a minute. . . . John Tenbruye. East 94th Street. Right?"

"Sure."

"One of the passengers in that bus yarn you covered for us?"

"That's right. He looked me up when the financial sections ran the item about my being appointed to the home office."

Ray smiled. "A customer's man. Your father comes back this week, Don."

"I know."

"I'm putting him in charge of our new Saturday Section. Sort of a modified Sunday Supplement. It may lead to big things, Don. I hope to make another *This Week* or an *American Weekly* out of it, sell it to papers out in the sticks for an insert. The big money's in national advertising."

Don sipped his beer. "Good beer, Ray."

"Czechoslovakian. Or was. God knows what it is now. You're not trying to change the subject, are you?"

"Well, you know Joe. That's more of a job for Ron, it seems to me. Joe's always been a newsman, he won't like being an editor. He won't like feature work either."

"He's unreliable," Ray said. "With the *Mail* going good, I can't take a chance on Joe. Unless you could straighten him out."

"Make him sign the pledge?" Don shook his head. "I've got a good deal less influence with him than you have. What have you put Ron at?"

"He's in charge of the opposite editorial page. Doing a damned good job, too. Brawley's chasing crusades for page one."

"You're a loyal friend, Ray."

"I've tried to be," Ray said. "That's what I wanted to see you about. I—I was a long time coming up, Don. Thirty-odd years. I don't think success can make a man forget thirty years, but I don't know. It changes every man. . . . The *Mail* was a mess, but I kept it alive with the peculiar genius of Joe, of Ron, of Brawley. But chiefly Joe. Now it is a paying paper. I can afford the reporters, so-called, to give me adequate coverage. I can cover a news item as thoroughly as any evening paper in the city. I don't need them any more."

"I see," Don said.

"No," Ray said. "You don't see. A punk can be successful, and his old friends don't mean a thing. But I'm no punk. I'm an old man, really. I will not throw my old friends out.

But—on the other hand—the *Mail* means a lot to me. I've never had any children, and maybe I'm a little queer. You used to— Let that go. Say the *Mail*, the new *Mail*, the successful *Mail*, is my baby. If Joe comes back and threatens it, I don't know what we'll do."

Donald said: "I've never heard anyone talk just like that before."

"You never will," Ray said. His voice got fierce, hot. "I tell you, I'm the oldest man who ever achieved a success like this one. Old enough to say with my mouth what other men only think with their subconscious. Don, there isn't anything about success and failure I don't know. And I'm not going to kid myself. Not ever. If the price of success is hypocrisy, I won't pay it. But that's the one thing I won't do."

"Then if Joe threatens the *Mail*—"

"I'm making big money. He'll never starve. But he won't louse up my baby."

"You're clear. You're explicit. I'll try and warn the old man. You'll be down to meet him?"

"Probably not. That's the clearest way I know of telling him times have changed. . . . Let's go eat and you tell me about your career."

They strolled through the club. Publishers, managing editors, newsprint-company executives were glad to see Ray; times had indeed changed. The man of the hour.

They ordered lunch. Ray said: "What's Armstrong and Grainger up to, Don?"

"We're going into the Matagordos. Know them?"

Ray smiled. He liked to be asked if he knew unusual things. He had the fine memory of the top-flight editor. "A man named Shattuck, Roland Shattuck, explored them about two years ago, as I remember. He died shortly after his return, of a disease similar to the one that killed Theodore Roosevelt in 1919. Right?"

"Right. This is off the record, of course. A. and G. are about to make an agreement with a three-power mandate to take the gold out of the particular part of the Matagordos called the Lacrimas."

"Well, swell," Ray said. "You going to be in charge?"

"From New York, of course. No, I'll hire someone to go in with the crews."

Ray busied himself with his foods. "You know," he said, "I'm going to turn into the sort of stuffed shirt who eats so much rich food at lunch he has to work out in a gym every afternoon. . . . You're gaining weight, Donny."

"We'll play handball together, Ray. . . . Or was that a sly crack?"

"You won't get sore? . . . Why, Don, I've known you since before you were born—literally. I knew the elements that went into making you. Christ, I know more about you than's decent. And just like Joe, you're no editor. You're a reporter. A field man, in your business."

"Back on that again?"

"Always. This Matagordo thing sounds like the McCoy. Adventure, hard work, romance."

"Fever. Indians, salt pork."

"Gonna send a man to do something you're afraid to do yourself?"

"I had to do that sort of thing to get where I am."

"You'll have to do a lot worse things to stay— Skip it, kid. What do you think of the National League?"

*　　*　　*

BUCK RANULPH WALKED up the dirty chipped-stone steps of Centre Street. The battered pensioner at the information desk looked at him inquiringly; Buck smiled to himself. I don't look like a cop. And why should I? I'm a member of the bar and the author of eight published stories.

He walked up a flight and through the iron bars to the Detective Bureau; he knew his way, all right. He went into a room where a half-dozen plainclothesmen sat at desks. One of them looked up and said: "Hello, Ranulph."

"Th' lieutenant in?"

"Go right in."

Lieutenant Ralfs was leaning back in his swivel chair, his feet on the desk. "Hello, Ranulph, what brings you down town?"

"I'm a witness in a civil case. It was postponed."

Ralfs swung his feet down to rest on the only other chair in the room. "What can I do for you?"

"I want to get out of Harlem, Lieutenant."

The lieutenant screwed up his meaty face, ran a hand through his silvery hair. "Well, take it up with your sergeant."

"Yes, sir."

"I'd stay there, though," Ralfs said. "You know how it is, the taxpayers object to nigger cops in the white precincts. Unless you want to put in for traffic."

Buck didn't say anything.

Ralfs said: "Well, what the hell do you want?"

"I was admitted to the bar last week. I've had several stories published in magazines. I thought maybe there'd be something for me in headquarters."

The lieutenant said: "You dinges are smart, aren't you? Whyn't you concentrate on police work, instead of on stuff outside the department, like being a lawyer and a writer or doing fancy French dances or something?"

Pass Through Manhattan

"Have you been satisfied with the work I've done for you?"

"Hell, no. Every shine in Harlem's got you spotted by now. You're no good to me any more."

"I see. You told me—"

"Well, want to make something of it? Wanta file a complaint with the commissioner? I told you there'd be a regular job on the squad here for you if you turned up the ringleaders that have been making all this Harlem trouble. You didn't. Now there ain't even any use you're going on, since they all know you. You musta been talking, Ranulph. You musta shot off your mouth and they got on to you. Why didn't you try a little harder? You have to get on committees and things to find out anything."

"Well—"

"They seem satisfied with you up at 104th. Stick to it, do what your sergeant tells you, that's the way to get ahead in this department. And don't try and show off."

"Yes, sir." Buck turned to go. But the lieutenant wasn't through.

"I'm against educated cops. You think you're too good to chase fifty-cent whores and milk-bottle crooks. We don't need lawyers; leave that to the district attorney's office. Go out for a record of lots of arrests and information, and you'll make a cop yet."

"Yes, sir." He'd get out of the department. Write out his resignation today. The Civil Liberties Union or the Friends of the American Negro would send him south to defend Negroes. Or maybe Gordie Maxwell could get him a job as an editor. No. Probably they wouldn't like him working in an office with white men and women. He'd work real hard on his stories and—

Pass Through Manhattan

He saluted the lieutenant and turned on his heel. Cheap, lousy, blustering jackass of a lieutenant. Probably only got through grade school by snitching on the other kids. Or maybe by twisting their arms till they did his homework for him. A shield and some muscle, that was Ralfs.

Buck was halfway out the door when the lieutenant called him back. "Wait a minute, Ranulph. You really want to settle down and be a copper?"

He would tell the fat white slob to go to hell. Take his sixty a week with him. Buckingham Ranulph could wear the rags and patches of his race with more honor than the tailored tweeds bought by being a stool pigeon. He—

"Yes, sir?" he asked.

"Sit down, Ranulph," the lieutenant said. He swung his feet to the floor. "Sit down. I'll give you one more chance."

Buck sat down. He hated the feeling of pleasure he got from having the white lieutenant offer him a chair. But there it was and what could he do about it?

"This is an easy one," Ralfs said. "And if you pull it, you'll be raised to first class. No fooling this time. You might almost say this is your first important case. . . . Now, there's a dinge up in Harlem named Harold De Bruliere. As far as we can find out, that's his own name, maybe his old man made it up. Niggers love fancy names. We got pretty good information, Ranulph, that this guy is a Bolshevik."

Buck didn't say anything.

"Anyway, he's a trouble-maker from way back. We wanta get him. You see?"

"What's the charge?"

Ralfs laughed. "That's up to you. Didn't I tell you he was a trouble-maker and a Communist? Them guys are all free-lovers. Maybe you could sock it to him for sleeping with a girl under sixteen? I'd like a bomb charge, but they're pretty hard to get these days. Now, can you get this De Bruliere?"

"Well—"

"It'd be a soft touch for you. You went to college with him, I got it all down here. He'd trust you. Now, my idear is, I'm gonna get you broken back into uniform. I'd kick you off the force, but I don' wanna cost you your pension time. You're sore, see? And the first thing you know, you'll be De Bruliere's right-hand man. You get the dope, and we sock it to him."

"Well—"

"C'mon, Buck. I'm giving you a second chance, and they'll tell you down here Jimmy Ralfs don't do that very often. Pull yourself together. Don't you wanta be a success, don't you wanna make something of yourself?"

"I'll try it."

"You don't wanna say that. Say I'll do it. That's the way to get ahead."

*　　*　　*

IT WAS GOING TO BE A HOT DAY. Klompoos's men, pulling the Castron house down, would slow up, climb off the scaffolding for drinks of water, buy beer for their lunch and be dopey after it. No skin off Jack Firstin's nose. A straight bid Klompoos had made on the wrecking, with a time set, it was Klompoos's worry.

Only maybe they should finish early, and the foundation contractors could get in there and start the caissons for Corning Manor. Now, with this heat, no, they would not finish early.

No skin off the nose of Jack Firstin, only you would think they would want to get through early. It would be nice to see the foundations building, strong and solid and good, concrete and steel down to bedrock, down to the firm hard bedrock of Brooklyn Heights. Steel would be going up soon, so's at night, just before the sun went down, you could maybe half close your eyes and see how she would be finished.

Jack waddled to Broad Street, flagged a taxicab. Corning Building Corporation was paying him a hundred dollars a week, he should ride the subway on a hot day. "I want to go to Brooklyn Heights, Orange Street." He sat down, pulling at his trousers, which were already sticking to him.

The cab headed up Williams Street for the Bridge. Then over, onto the Brooklyn Bridge.

Jack leaned forward, panting a little. There, right there, sometime, soon, would be Corning Manor, framed like in an art gallery in the steels of the Bridge. Blue, and the steel that was red usually, and then blue water and the mica in Brooklyn Heights rock—

His head swam with the glory of it, with pity for himself because the wreckers were slow, so slow.

Someday a company that would do everything from wrecking to renting. No sub-contracting, no commissions to Wall Street houses for bond selling, no waiting for brick and concrete and steel men to get off their fat *tokases*.

The Firstin Construction Company? The Firstin Building Company. Rent from the Company that Built Your Home.

And one of those smart-alecky press agents like he used to have. A downstairs show window on Fifth Avenue, and they could put stuff in the window. Like those hand-made wooden dowels from the Castron house, next to a big rust-proof steel rivet from Corning Manor.

Then his own company should build it, the Firstin Village. A whole cross block and three up-and-down blocks with bridges across the streets. Maybe he should find it a politician who could fix up to be alderman in case the city didn't like it the bridges should hang over the traffic? Maybe—

But not Firstin. Not the Firstin Village. These three failures would come up and people would not rent in Firstin Village.

He would get him a front. Young Tenbruye now, he would be good. One of the finest names in Manhattan, and yet a man could do business with him. He had the look around the eyes of a fella you could do business with. Tenbruye Building Corporation—

Maybe better he should tell McCandless to leave clause 13a out of that first mortgage. Maybe better to pay the interest on the bonds on Corning Manor straight and honest. Three per cent less profit that way, but if Seligmann saw that clause 13a would make the mortgage no good if he foreclosed—

Not time for a killing yet. Not—

The taxi stopped in front of the wooden cover Klompoos had put up to protect the sidewalk from falling debris. Jack Firstin climbed out painfully, and went up the wooden steps to the wreckers' office. Just like he thought, the men were dragging around, no pep. They would never be done in time for concrete to be poured before the first. They—

Three men were tugging at the bracings on a twelve by twelve that had supported the first floor. Big. Not D.F. or O.P.

Oak, by God. Imagine a dope like old Castron, putting in oak twelve by twelve for a three-story house. For why hadn't he gone on up, built the first twelve-story house in the world, when he had such a foundation? And now, so solidly built, you had to almost pay to get it wrecked.

Pass Through Manhattan

That twelve by twelve now, good lumber, good like the day it was put in. It—

Over the doorway, a wooden beam over the doorway like in Spanish or California building, out on Long Island. No weight it would carry, why not? Carved Corning Manor—

Jack Firstin ran down the steps of the job, stumbling on the rough wood. "Easy, don't wreck that beam. I buy it from you."

*   *   *

ROBERT SEASONGOOD SELIGMANN picked up the phone. "Ask Mr. Tenbruye to step in when he gets a chance." Then he leaned back in his chair, rubbing his eyes. Dull. He felt dull, logy. Turning in his swivel chair, he could see a wedge-shaped piece of the sky over Jersey. The sun was setting red. Evening red and morning gray, sets the traveler on his way—

He would get the station wagon out tomorrow morning, load the boys in it and drive up to the farm. There might still be some ducks left in the marsh, or if not they could take the springers out for a little upland shooting. Jackson would know where to get the birds—

"Miss Moracci. Get Jackson up at the farm for me."

His blood began to pump through his temples. The cold wind blowing in off the Sound, all the smells of fall, and the color showing in Peter's rather sallow face as he raised his little shotgun, Howard's sturdy back trudging ahead of him, John laughing at the dogs. The swift ripple and drag of the water from a rising duck's legs, or the solid whir of a grouse's wing—

Those ring-necked pheasants we stocked in the spring ought to be shot into, break up the coveys, and Peter can

284

bring his compound glass. A world of fine specimens in a fall rainwater pool, in stumps.

We—

John Tenbruye opened the door and came in. He took the chair opposite Bob's desk and crossed his knees; he lit a cigarette.

The blood stopped pumping through Bob Seligmann's temples and he felt the cold chill of warning. He looked at Tenbruye's narrow face with no more dislike than he felt for the set of *Standard Statistics*, for the fountain pen stand or the Poor's Manual or the telephone that were the tools whereby he made his living.

"Ah, Tenbruye," he said. "I wanted to know how our—er—real estate department is doing."

"You received my memo about the second mortgage."

"Yes. Was it necessary to commit Corning and Seligmann to quite so large a share of the second mortgage?"

"Money's tight in the real estate business. We had to give the title company some assurance we were really standing behind Corning Manor."

No sir. Not even a Mr. Seligmann.

Bob said, slowly: "The firm appreciates your starting this real estate work. As the years roll on, we are more and more in the position of trustees rather than brokers. There was something— Oh, yes, Tenbruye. Aunt Susan wants to come to town this winter. Will you find her a nice apartment some place in the East Sixties? There is just herself and her maid, Annie."

"I won't have time for quite a while, Bob. Maybe you'd better have a regular real estate broker handle that."

Bob, by golly. "Well—all right, Mister Tenbruye. I think that's all for the evening."

He watched Tenbruye out, pressed the buzzer. "Mr. Corning's account, Miss Moracci. Jason, of course. . . ."

He turned the papers over. It— Yes. Ten thousand shares of J.C. on full margin. Yes—

He leaned back in his chair. He hated to do this. But Peter's eyes came across his memory, Peter peering into the little compound glass. Peter, who could be a great scientist and still maintain his social position, if his father left him the Seligmann money. And that couldn't be done unless there was the interest in Corning and Seligmann to give to Howard. John would get his mother's family money, he—

It would have to be done. If you were going to be a business man, be one. There was nothing more despicable than those Wall Street pinks who apologized for making a profit out of brokerage or banking.

Bob picked up the phone. "Give me an outside wire, Miss Moracci." He opened his little pocket notebook, laid it beside the phone, dialed a number. "Uncle Frasier? Bobby. I'd like it if J.C. was down tomorrow. Way down. I think you would make money on it, Uncle Frasier, it may be quite a movement. . . . Yes, sir, and thank you. Drop around some evening, and play a hand of cribbage with Anne. You know we're in town for the winter." "Jock? Bob. How's about helping an old room-mate out and selling that J.C. your firm's been holding? I'll let you have some Acme Paper five under the market if you'll liquidate— Done, then. I'll send you a memo. . . ." . . ."Cousin Raoul? Corning and Seligmann's likely to find itself up the creek tomorrow noon if J.C. doesn't do a bit of falling. Help a chap out?" "George? Bob Seligmann. Got a little tip in exchange for that very helpful information about Explosives. There's going to be a big selling movement in J.C. tomorrow. I can guarantee that Suler and Newman, Fayette and Lefevere,

and the Bursary crowd are all selling; Corning and Seligmann are hopping on, and I thought you ought to know. . . .
No trouble at all, old man. Glad to pass it along."

He broke the outside connection by ringing Miss Moracci,
stood up. Wash up, stop by the club on the way home. If
anybody asked him what he knew, he might give them the
J.C. tip.

Corning and Seligmann could make quite a bit of money
tomorrow on the bear movement in J.C. Were sure to. He
wrote out a selling order, dropped it in the box. Now . . .

The phone rang and Miss Moracci said: "Here's Jackson,
Mr. Seligmann."

Bob said: "Oh, Jackson. I just wanted to tell you, if I
can't get up this weekend maybe you ought to shoot into
some of those coveys and break them up. . . . That's right.
Don't forget now."

When he had hung up the phone he went into his private
wash room and cleaned up.

*　　　*　　　*

MISS WINTERS CAME INTO HIS CHAMBERS and stood in the
doorway. Sun slanting down the city made a beam that hit
her right on the cheekbone; she stood there, all dark, dark
serge suit, man's brown shirt and blue tie, and then the
brilliantly lighted cheek, its thin skin made transparent to
show that the Wellesley graduate did have blood in her
veins.

For a moment Miss Winters was beautiful, and Dennis
Costi looked at her gratefully. "Yes?" he said. In the ordered
wastes of Miss Winters' brain the judge spoke first; an
officer in the army of the law recognizing a private.

She moved, so that the light flooded her whole face, and

287

was no longer beautiful. "Mrs. Lempe to see you, Judge Costi."

"Well, show her in, show her in." Dennis waved at his desk. "I'm not doing anything. What are you waiting for?"

"Er, hm, I—"

"Speak up, woman, speak up."

"I was wondering about the ethics? Shouldn't a representative of the corporation counsel's office be present when you interview the plaintiff in a case pending before your court?"

Dennis stared at the girl. "Justice," he said, "is the giving to each man his due. Anytime a taxpayer wants to see me, justice demands, nay, cries, that that right be granted. Show Mrs. Lempe in, Miss Winters."

In the interval while the door was closed he slid open the big drawer of his desk, stole an automatic look at himself in the mirror lying flat there. He smoothed his silvery hair, straightened the black tie with a little silver stripe, and stood up to receive Mrs. Lempe. Marie Vogel Lempe, femme covert, East Ninety—

"Ah, good afternoon, Mrs. Lempe. And what brings you all the way down from Ninety-fourth Street?"

"Good day, Mr. Judge." The little woman stood damn near at attention opposite his desk.

He walked around the desk, held a chair for her. "Sit down, madam."

"After you, Mr. Judge."

He placed a benevolent hand on her shoulder, pushed her down. These Germans!

"Thank you, Mr. Judge, Your Honor."

He took his own chair. "Just call me Judge, or Judge Costi, or Mr. Costi if you want to. In court you call me Your Honor out of respect to the bench I'm sitting on.

Pass Through Manhattan

Now, Mrs. Lempe, I presume it is about your case you called."

"Yes. Mist—Judge Costi."

"Quite so." Dennis threw a sop to Miss Winters. "You understand, you know, you mustn't ask any questions that would tend to give you an idea of how I would decide the case. Outside of that, if there is anything I can do—"

"It is about our attorneys, Mr. Vanderbilt and Mr. Brefogel."

Dennis sat up, his interest rising. God, if Mike Vanderbilt had stepped out of line, he would fry him in oil. And the judge who nipped old Vanderbilt could have anything in the state. Governor: Sheridan—which meant Vanderbilt and vice-versa—had the Protestant bloc and the disaffected Catholics tied up in the Hall. Break Sheridan, and the Hall would be solid for Costi—

"The case is held over till Thursday, this week."

"Yes. It is money they want."

Careful now, Dennis, careful. This might be a trick of that dirty Orange crook, Dan Sheridan. It might— "After all, Mrs. Lempe, it is customary for lawyers to want a fee." Especially Vanderbilt.

"But we were given to understand it would cost nothing. Now they want Artur my husband should give them a thousand dollars. We work hard, Judge Costi, for our money, I must be sure— It is for our children we save, I want them to go to college, like American children, and—"

Easy, boy, easy. "Please, Mrs. Lempe. Let's marshal our facts in an orderly manner, as it were. You say Mike, you say, Vanderbilt and Brefogel were going to take your case for nothing?"

"It was from the Bund to be paid. And now, you understand, of course, the Bund cannot pay, and Mr. Brefogel, he says Artur must. But Judge Costi, we must not our money lose."

Dennis Costi said: "Wait a minute, madam. I am, after all, a simple man, and things are coming a little fast for me. Now, the Bund cannot pay?"

"Because the National Leader, he has taken the money. Or so they say. In New England he is arrested for—"

"Yes, yes, I read it in the papers."

"Of course, Artur," Mrs. Lempe said, "says this is the prosecution of the Jews, what they do to the National Leader, but I do not this man's face like, Judge Costi. I—"

"Mrs. Lempe, sit still." Well, this is what I get for being a good boy and going to Mass every week. I think I'll put a five spot in the poor box on the way home, and maybe St. Jude would like a candle or so.

Miss Winters came in in answer to the buzzer, and Dennis said: "Your book, Miss Winters. Mrs. Lempe, this is my right bower, Miss Winters. She is going to make a record of this so—er—we can study it at our leisure."

"You look things up in these big books, jah?"

"Yes. We—er—look things up in these books."

"In America, is so wonderful. Big judges they are so kind to poor women, as to duchesses."

"Surest thing you know, Mrs. Lempe. Now . . . You are a Nazi?"

"No, Judge. I am good American woman. I bring up my children to be good Americans, too, they are named Grace Coolidge and George Washington so they will not forget. But Artur, he is sad for the Fatherland, you know? Never can he forget, never. Once, when we first came by this country, I think, so soon as Artur he gets a good job, he forgets, but no."

So he is the Nazi, eh? Dennis Costi thought. "Vanderbilt and Brefogel, they are the regular attorneys for the Nazi party—the—whataya call it—the German-American Bund?"

"That I do not know, Judge Costi. But first the Bund pays all, the Leader tells Artur, I am hurt, it is right the city should pay, the Bund sees we get justice. Now, Mr. Brefogel says Artur must give him our savings, he has gone to great trouble, we must pay him. I do not understand."

"Does Mr. Lempe know you came to see me?"

"No, Judge Costi. Artur, he says this is because Mr. Vanderbilt is a Jude, the Leader does not understand. Artur says the Leader did not know Mr. Vanderbilt was a Jude, when he find out he makes everything all right. He says he will not pay Mr. Brefogel until the Leader, or at least the Korps-Hauptmann tells him so."

"Never trust an Irishman or a Jew," Dennis muttered. "Mike Vanderbilt's the only Irish Jew I ever knew. . . . How did you happen to bring suit?"

"Well, I was by the bakery working, and it was snowing. So—"

Miss Winters started to say something. Dennis got there first. "No, no. Don't tell me about the accident. I mean, when did you decide to retain Vanderbilt and Brefogel? Did they come to you or did you go to them, or—"

"After the accident, I went home. There was on the bus a nurse from Mount Sinai, she gets the doctor to look at me, and so I go home and—"

"No, no. You mustn't tell me about the accident. You may still want to go ahead with the case, you see, and— Well, anyway. When did you first hear of Vanderbilt and Brefogel? Put it that way. You're getting all this, Miss Winters, aren't you?"

"In the bakery the next day comes Mr. Brefogel. He says from Artur he has orders, I must go home, lie down, from the bus I am—"

Miss Winters gasped. Dennis said: "Please, Mrs. Lempe, don't tell me when you first felt ill, or anything about it. So it was Artur who retained the lawyers. He didn't consult with you first?"

"No, not first. After he tells me, he is at Korps meeting, and the National Leader is there. And they talk about why Artur is late, he tells them I am in bus accident, and the National Leader says, because the driver is a Jew, the city must pay."

"Because the driver is a—" Dennis shook his head. "You got that, Miss Winters? Go on, Mrs. Lempe. No, wait. Did you believe this?"

"I do not know about law. Artur, he believes it. It is written in the book they give him, the Jews are incompetent. He says, it will be easy to show this driver he takes drugs, or—"

The woman stopped. Dennis Costi reached out and patted her hand. He said: "You didn't believe this, Mrs. Lempe, did you?"

"No. By America, all peoples is the same. And in Chermany, in the old days, I know Juden, they are just like you or me. I—I do not know. I have friend, Frau Goldstein, she comes lately from the Old Country. She says all things there are bad now, it is not like the Bund tells Artur."

"Well, of course, Goldstein. She's a Jew and you're a German—"

"I am not a German," the little woman cried. "I am good American. I think this is a dirty thing the Bund makes and Herr Hitler. But I am a wife, and Artur has been good to me and—"

Pass Through Manhattan

"Don't cry, Mrs. Lempe, please don't cry," Dennis said, in distress. "Oh—Miss Winters, why don't you go have a good talk with Mrs. Lempe? Make a transcript of it and strike out everything that might prejudice my impartiality if I ever have to judge this case, and give it to me. And Mrs. Lempe, where does your husband work?"

"He is heating superintendent, the Blacktower Building on—"

"Yes, I know. You go wait in Miss Winters' office, now."

Dennis rose to watch her out of the room, Miss Winters held the door, Miss Winters came back.

"How about it?" Dennis asked. "You think we can nab Vanderbilt on it?"

Miss Winters said: "He's a pretty clever man, Judge Costi. But— Did you ever hear anything worse?"

"Yeah," Dennis said. "I've heard a lot of worse things. I kind of like that Mrs. Lempe, don't you?"

The lady lawyer said: "She's a dear. I'll go talk to her."

"Good."

Left alone, Dennis Costi locked his hands over his stomach and beamed. He—

Well, damn them, the church-defying, bishop-persecuting Fascists. He was going to strike a blow for liberty, for democracy, for Americanism. Dennis Costi, by God, bowed to no dictators.

Then he chuckled at the picture of himself as a knight in shining armor. Well, there was nothing dubious about any battle in which Mike Vanderbilt was on the other side.

And those dirty Fascists. He hoped he could strike a blow at Mussolini while he was at it.

*   *   *

Pass Through Manhattan

"A VERY PROVIDENTIAL THING," Mr. Grainger said, "that Dr. Bastable showed up just now. Just the man for that Lacrimas operation, Morton."

Donald smiled non-committally. The yellowed whites of Bastable's eyes were due, he supposed, to a life in the jungle with all its diseases and privations; the trembling of Bastable's fingers could be caused by malaria. It was too bad to dislike a man because he had been ill; but you couldn't exactly cotton to Bastable on first blush. Those tremendously long, bony legs, that snakelike bald head, the thick lips that the man kept moistening were not attractive; face it, they were not pretty.

"Dr. Bastable knows the Matagordos as well as any man alive," Mr. Grainger said. "And he's done good work for Armstrong and Grainger in the past."

"Went through the Lacrimas foothills in '32," Bastable said. "Crummy bunch of molehills. Was lookin' for white Injuns, y'know?"

"Did you find them?" Don asked.

Bastable rolled his eyes at Don. "Haw. Never do find white Injuns. 'F we ever did find 'em, be out of a job, what?"

"Well," Mr. Grainger said, "you and Morton work out the details, Dr. Bastable. Let us off easy now, old man. When do you think you could start?"

"Got m'quipment all together, eh. Just need time to buy a few groceries, see a bit of li'l ol' N'Yawk," Bastable said. He licked his lips. "Chap gets hungry for a bit o' white meat, y'know?" He chuckled.

"Morton, you show Bastable around a bit, eh?" Mr. Grainger said. "Armstrong and Grainger will pay the bill, Bastable. We don't find you in New York very often."

"Damn good city to be shown around in," Bastable said.

Pass Through Manhattan

"And I'll bet this young fella here knows some good spots. Got a lively eye on him, eh, Grainger, what?"

"Well, boys will be boys," Mr. Grainger said. "Er—have a drink for me, will you, er, Donald? Gotta show Bastable we appreciate his—er—rare and unusual abilities."

Donald stood up. "O.K., Mr. Grainger. Come on, Doctor." He led the way back to his own office, musing, ill at ease. New York had not been so wild for him that he felt entirely competent to show anyone a hilarious and breathtaking time; it was dubious if Dr. Bastable would enjoy—say—a musical comedy with a good dinner before and a drink after. "Got a few letters to get out," he told the explorer. "Be with you in a minute."

Miss Cowan was talking over the phone. "All right," she said, as Donald opened the door. "I'll see him, I'll go—I'll call you back."

Donald put a hand on her desk, leaned on it to read the memo pad: "Any messages for me?" There was a name on the pad, Dr. Wilcomen, and an address. One of Cartwright's associates? Had his father started off on the train—

But Miss Cowan said: "Nothing for you, Mr. Morton."

"All right, let's get these letters out. I won't be a minute, Doctor."

Bastable said he'd wait in Miss Cowan's room, folding his bony length into a chair. The magazine he picked up whispered from the shaking of his fingers.

Don got behind his own desk, dictated two purchasing orders, a covering letter for a report to the Mexican government on the high-grading in Tehachapi, some other routine stuff. "That's all," he said, without looking up. "Get those typed, I'll sign them before I leave. Try and keep Bastable in your office, I've got a couple of phone calls to make."

"Yes, Mr. Morton." Miss Cowan stood up, dropped her notebook, knelt to pick it up. She had on the gift garters.

Standing up again, she put a hand on the desk, her lips sucked in. "You don't look well, Miss Cowan," Donald said. "Anything wrong?"

"Everything's fine, Mr. Morton. I'm all right."

"Well, you know if you feel seedy or anything, take a day off."

"I'm a little—a little tired. Maybe I'll take Friday off and get a good rest over the weekend."

"You do that. Get those letters right out, will you?"

He waited until the door closed, then called the *Mail*. "Ron Levine. . . . Well, then, give me Brawley Smith. . . . Brawley? Donald. Listen, I've got to do a little company drinking."

Brawley's deep voice said: "Take a bottle of milk of magnesia first and—"

"No, no, Brawley. Joe gets in this afternoon. I don't want to meet him; I've got this tropical tramp on my neck who says 'Let's have a drink' every two minutes, and I don't want Joe taking him up on it. I know Ray isn't going down to the train, and I want to be sure somebody's there to meet Joe; will you slip down to the Long Island station and meet the 5:11 and tell him about me?"

"Sure," Brawley said, "only meeting someone who's coming in on the Long Island is kind of like giving a Bon Voyage basket to a girl taking the subway. What'll I tell him about you?"

"Oh, I have to go over to Stevens and interview a couple of seniors who may come to work for Armstrong and Grainger."

"Oke."

Don rang off, flipped the switch for another outside call,

and dialed Eleanor Castron's hotel. He had the first number halfway around the dial when Miss Cowan, on the other side of the ground glass door, let out a little muffled yell. Her figure and Bastable's bony silhouette jerked across the screen of the door, the man's fingers talon-shaped.

Don dropped the phone into its cradle and stood up, pulling his vest down automatically. He got across the office fast, checked himself and calmly opened the door. "Miss Cowan, would you come in a minute?"

He shut the door behind her, said: "He bothering you?"

"I'm sorry, Mr. Morton. I should be able to handle a man without—"

"Christ, why? That's not part of your job."

The girl said apologetically: "Oh, you get used to it in New York." She rubbed her shoulder. "He took me by surprise, is all."

"I'll keep him in here," Don said. He was mad because he was having trouble meeting the girl's eyes; she was better than him, she didn't have to entertain scum to keep her job, she— Damn it, he was going to blush.

He opened the door. "I'm all through, Bastable, come on in. We'll have a drink." There was a bottle of Scotch in one of the drawers of his desk, visiting engineers expected it. He herded Dr. Bastable into the room, shut the door, mixed two drinks with water from the thermos carafe provided by the firm. "Your health."

"And yours, sir." Bastable swallowed half the drink, made a face; he added Scotch from the bottle, swallowed the other half, and poured himself a straight jigger. "Go ahead with your work if you want to."

"No, I'm through." Cautiously: "I have one more phone call to make."

Pass Through Manhattan

"Go ahead. . . . That's a nice little piece you've got doing your typing out there. Dandy legs, you know."

Don let the doctor have what he could make out of a smile, and took a deep pull at the highball. Whether he liked the taste or not, the only way he was going to get through this evening was on liquor. But, damn it, he'd have to have some more disguised potion than Scotch and water. His throat gagging, he dialed Eleanor's hotel again.

"Miss Castron. . . . Hello, Eleanor. Say, I'm awfully sorry, I won't be able to make it tonight. I've got some business that I have to—"

Bony fingers closed on his hand, took the instrument out of it. "Eleanor? Don't you believe the young fella. He's got to entertain me, 's what he's got to do. You his girl friend? . . . Ah, ha! Bet you're a lovely girl, too."

Donald reached for the phone, his head tight with anger. Bastable's bony face leered at him, and Don felt his fist clenching, swinging. He dropped it. Company business, company date. To hell with the company and—No.

"I'm just an old tropical medico," Bastable was saying. "But I know how to show a girl a good time. Don't you have a friend, Eleanor?" His deep laugh rattled the diaphragm of the phone. "Well, I know a saucy little piece. We'll let her take care of Donald, what, and you and I'll paint the town. You know André on Lafayette Street? Meet you there for a drink in a half an hour. You'll know me by the hat-check girl on my lap, what?" He rang off, laughed at Donald's tense face. "Don't look so angry, old man, I won't take your girl away. I like my evenings to last, old Doc Bastable he takes his time, like they say. No harm takin' a nice girl around till about two, things don't get hot till then. We'll drop her back at her home, good as new, and then we'll really step out."

Pass Through Manhattan

"All right," Donald said.

"Let the old doctor use your phone," Bastable said. "This the way?" He twirled the dial, humming. "Joan? How are your bedsprings, old dear? How they hanging, eh? . . . Sure, this is old Doc Bastable, the old man with the cast-iron belly. Got a piece of chicken for you, old dear, young engineer with the fuzz still on the—peach, as it were. Eh, what? . . . Meet us at André's as soon as you get your breeches on, then, Joannie. There'll be a hot time in the old town tonight."

Humming to himself, he hung up the phone, poured another slug into his glass. "You haven't drunk your drink, young fella. Cheer up. We're out on the town tonight."

Don took another swallow of the drink. "O.K.," he said, "let's go."

"What's the matter, you afraid I'll scare your girl friend?" Bastable snorted, reached out, grabbed the lapel of Don's coat. "Don't be frightened, young fella, I know how to treat a nice girl. But they're none of them as nice as you think they are, and don't you forget it. Hot stuff, my boy, hot stuff."

In the outer office, Miss Cowan said: "Good night, Mr. Morton." She had her hat and coat on. She pulled the top sheet off her memo pad and tucked it into her pocketbook. "I'll close up and turn the lights out."

"Good night, Miss Cowan," Don told her.

Bastable turned in the door, waved a finger at Don's secretary. "Y'oughta eat more red meat, young lady, y'look anemic. Take an old doctor's word for it."

Miss Cowan nodded, and went about straightening the office for the night.

*   *   *

Pass Through Manhattan

PEGGY REILLY KEPT HER HANDS IN HER LAP to keep the girl from seeing that her fingernails were biting into her palms. "I'm sure that Dr. Wilcomen will be here on Friday," she said. "And if Dr. McGrey has examined you there really isn't any need for worry. Four o'clock Friday afternoon."

The girl crossed her legs, showing gold-clasped garters that seemed grotesque after the strained anguish of her face. "Four o'clock Friday," she said. "All right. But you're sure the doctor will be here, I don't understand why he didn't—"

"He must have been held up on a call," Peggy said. "Your appointment was for a quarter of six, and it's only seven now. But you'll have to go, I have to close the office," or go crazy. "See you at four, Friday, and don't worry."

"Maybe it would be better if I came at quarter of six again tomorrow, and made sure?"

"The doctor," Peggy said firmly, "has appointments all day tomorrow. Good night."

The girl stood up, dabbing at her nose with a powder puff. "And you're sure I'll be able to go back to work Monday?"

"Quite sure," Peggy said. She went around the desk, started propelling the girl towards the door by patting her shoulder. "Good night, Miss Brown." She shoved the girl out, snapped the lock on the door, and leaned with her back against it, letting out a long, shuddering sigh. Had the name been right? Miss Brown, or was it Miss Smith or Jones or Robinson? Or who, who—

Old Jod shuffled in from the pantry, his face black above the white coat. "You eat now, Miss Reilly?"

"Yes. If it's ready. No, wait a minute, Jod. Fix me a plate and put it in the oven. I'm too tired to eat yet."

"Doctor back yet? I din' hear him come in."

Pass Through Manhattan

"No, no, Dr. Wilcomen isn't back yet. You can have the evening off, Jod, I'll wash up after myself."

The old man shuffled away again. I'll wash up after myself. I'll clean up the mess I've made. Not even a satisfactory office nurse for a malpractitioner. *For the sins we do two by two we must pay for one by one.* Dad used to have me read that to him, it was one of the poems in the red leather Kipling I used to read to him while he lay on the old black leather couch in the office, with his eyes covered, resting.

Dad, Dad. Carl says I've got a white-coat fixation, I'm still in love with my father and that's why I keep falling for doctors. But, Dad, I couldn't help it. Not hardly any of it, except maybe George in Cincinnati. Haven't I been punished enough for that? Why should God in His wisdom go on heaping punishment after punishment on me?

She went to her desk, opened a drawer she had not opened in weeks, and took out her beads. Hail Mary, full of Grace, Hail—

There was a noise, more of a scratching than a knocking on the front door. The rosary fell to the floor; Peggy bent, picked it up, tucked it between her breasts.

She breathed a short prayer and went and unlocked the door, her head back, her lips straight and untrembling.

Carl Wilcomen, M.D., lurched in and went backwards against the door, panting as though he had been running. Peggy closed, locked and bolted the heavy front door.

"Hello, Doc," she said.

His voice was an animal moan in his throat. "You bitch," he said. "You dirty— Get me a drunk."

"You are a drunk," she said. "And just call me Mick." Good Peggy, nice Peggy, your voice is just as gay as ever. You're all right, Reilly. She took his sleeve in her hand and guided him into the reception room. The coat sleeve was gritty and filthy under her fingers. She had to push him backwards to make him sit down on the divan; his legs sprawled out in front of him, his hands were weak and groping on the leather seat.

He'd had himself a time. Those dark eyes were bloodshot now, and vacuous; the crisp dark hair tangled and as filthy as his coat.

Peggy went into the back office, put together a dose of aromatic spirits, and soaked an office towel with lukewarm water; she went back in, held his matted head on her arm and poured the dose down him; then she mopped his face gently, ran the towel over his hair, and got her comb from her desk.

Carl Wilcomen sat relaxed, panting.

She made him take his coat off, rolled up his shirtsleeves, got a basin and washed his hands and wrists. She knelt, proud and efficient, took off his shoes, raised his feet to the divan. She put a pillow behind his neck. "Take it easy, Carl. You must have been having quite a time."

"Go on, go on," he said. "Go on, give me hell."

"What for?" she asked lightly. "Boys will be boys. Everybody goes on a bat now and then."

"You? You go on bats? You're pure white linen all through."

"Sure I am. Want a cup of soup?"

"Naw. Aren't you going to give me hell?"

"Forget it. I'll help you to bed."

"Thought about you all day. Staying here, staving off patients, quieting hysterical li'l girls an' avaricious old hags, holding the fort. Rock of Gibraltar in a white uniform."

"That's not bad," she said judiciously. "That's pretty hot."

"With no ribbon on your cap," he said. "They wouldn't

give you a ribbon for your cap. Not good enough. You're
a—"

"I'm anything you say I am," Peggy said. "But you're going to bed."

"Damn you, damn you, damn you," he screamed. "You're
so Goddamned good. What did you have to go to that hotel
with me for? Huh? I was doing all right. I was getting
along fine. Had ten thousand dollars in the bank, didn't I?
Doing all right. Simplest operation in the world. Nothing to
it. You just take a—"

"All right, Dr. Wilcomen. Time for bed."

He slumped over, his head on his chest. A shiny rope of
saliva drooled out of the right corner of his mouth, threat-
ened his already soiled shirt; Peggy wiped his mouth with
the damp towel.

About six feet one, a hundred and seventy pounds. One
flight of stairs. If you pressed on the spine, just above the
lumbar region, the semi-comatose patient will move his own
feet to a certain extent.

She knelt on the divan, dragged Carl's arm around her
neck, and turned, pulling so that they both came up at the
same time, his left wrist in her left hand, his weight on her
shoulders. She put her right arm around him, pressing the
spine with the sharp point of her elbow. It worked. He at
least balanced so that she only had to carry about half of
him. She was drenched with perspiration when she finally let
him fall on the big bed in his room.

"Be a good boy tomorrow," he said. "Dr. Wilcomen will
work swiftly and with precision and clear the docket up to
date."

"Sure he will. Lie still, you big lug." She stripped his
clothes off, pulled half the white coverlet over him, and got
a basin and sponge, warm water and alcohol from the

operating room. She got a clean pajama jacket from the dresser and worked his arms through the sleeves, buttoned it; she did not bother with trousers. Then she opened the bed on one side, tucked the loose covers tight against the doctor's long body and rolled him until he was on the sheet; stripped the covers off and remade them over him with square, firmly tucked corners.

She worked fast now, cleaning up the dirty clothes, the basin and sponge. She adjusted the shades so that the light would not strike his eyes at dawn, but so there would not be too much gloom in the morning; put a glass of water, properly covered, next to the bed; went back downstairs and got a magazine from that day's mail, took its cover off, and placed it next to the glass of water.

She went to the door and turned to have a last look at the room and the patient.

Carl Wilcomen lay with his eyes wide open, so still that terror struck for the moment before he spoke. His voice was a little cracked but no longer hysterical.

He said: "Don't you want to know what happened?"

Peggy shook her head. "In the morning, Carl. Go to sleep now."

"I'm not your patient." His head moved on the pillow, a trace of the old, faun-like smile crossed his lips. "You forgot the cigarettes, Miss Reilly."

"I'll get them." But when she hurried back with matches, ashtray, cigarettes, he was frowning again. "Take that uniform off. I can't talk when you're wearing that phony uniform."

"Don't you really think you'd better sleep now?"

"No. No, I want to get this off my chest." He lit a cigarette. "Go on."

Pass Through Manhattan

In her own room she put on a gray flannelette robe over her slip, ran the powder puff over her face. On second thought she untied her shoes, stepped into sheepskin slippers. When she got back, the doctor was just finishing his cigarette. He still looked calm.

He said: "Sit down on the edge of the bed and hold my hand, Peggy."

She couldn't remember his ever calling her Peggy before.

"Ever since I ran out this morning," he said, slowly, "I've been trying to get drunk. You know what's the matter, kid? I'm in love."

There were black hairs growing on the back of his hand. She smoothed them with a finger tip and said: "And I reminded you of her? I'm sorry."

The hand she held tightened on hers. She didn't look at him.

"I couldn't get drunk," he said. "It kept wearing off. I guess that's a trick that takes practice. I want to marry you, Peggy."

Still not looking at him, she said: "You asked me before."

His laugh had no humor in it. "Sure. Sure. I wanted a girl to sleep with, and if she wanted to marry me, what did I have to lose? I couldn't ask just anyone to come live in this house. . . . No, this is different. I'm willing to quit the racket if you'll marry me. Last night you—you're lovely, Peggy. I don't want to ask you to wait for me to get out of prison sometime or to go with me, or to take it on the lam. And that's the only end to this business. You know that."

"Yes."

"I want to come clean with you. I don't consider what I've been doing a sin. I know you do. But I don't see that

305

it's any crime to help out girls who couldn't support their babies if they had them. Only—the law's the law—and—being in love makes it different."

Peggy said: "I'll marry you. You don't even have to quit if you don't want to. But if you think marrying me will make you forget the girl you're in love with—"

"You dense Irisher," he said, beginning to laugh, "I'm in love with you. My God, you had to go to bed with me to make me find it out. That's a hell of a start towards respectability. That's—"

"Don't start talking like that again. You mean it, Carl?"

"Of course I mean it, sweet."

She bent her head and kissed him, without passion. "All right, Carl. I'll go to Father Cardovic tomorrow and confess. He can marry us day after tomorrow."

"I'm not a Catholic."

"He can marry us in the office of the rectory. If you agree to bring the children up Catholics."

"Kiss me again, you sweet Mick. . . . Lord, I feel almost coy at the idea of children. . . . I'm so tired. We won't have to go to the tropics, either, kid. I've got a cousin who has a little hospital out West. It's not big, but it can give you a license, me a chance to finish my interneship if I have to. We'll take our money and open our own hospital—" he yawned—"in some mining camp or desert town, and we'll do fine. Maybe we'll even have horses with saddlebags full of medicine. We can leave right after the wedding."

"I've got to appear as a witness in that bus-accident thing."

"I can get Sheridan to fix that. All they want is a deposition from you."

"You go to sleep now. I'll turn the light out."

"Lie down next to me a minute."

Pass Through Manhattan

She lay down on top of the covers, pulling his head over onto her breast. He sighed and snuggled down like a baby, and after a moment she pushed the flannelette gown aside so that his forehead rested on her skin above the slip. Moving cautiously, she turned the light out; Carl Wilcomen was already asleep.

*　*　*

A NEW START. When the train came out of the tunnel, a new start would begin for Joe Morton. No more drinking, no more gloomy introspection. He would hit the old ball and get out stories that would make Don proud of him. Might even knock off the Pulitzer prize this winter, he'd been runner-up a couple of times.

They would make the *Mail* as important in the evening field as the *Times* in the morning. The four of them pulling together, plodding Ray, literary Ron, tough Brawley, and the brilliant, dashing Joe Morton to lead them. Four guys who knew more about the newspaper business than anyone in the country; they couldn't miss.

Why, now that he had quit fighting the booze, he'd show them. President Congratulates Journalist. Joseph Kolk Morton, brilliant newspaperman whose exposé of espionage brought about the current Senatorial investigation, is shown being received at the White House by President Roosevelt.

Espionage, by God. This Hitler-Stalin pact would cause trouble in Europe surer than snakes. Boy-Ed and Von Papen in the last war would be repeated over here, and he, Joe Morton, would have the jump on the rest of the boys.

He—

The train was slowing. He'd have to tell Don he wouldn't have dinner with him; get right ahold of Ray, ask for Brawley for an assistant, and start getting lines to the Communists and the Nazis. Let's see, I did a favor for Browder's secretary once and—

The train had stopped, suburbanites filled the aisles. Through the window he could see frantic lines of home-bound commuters. No chance of getting a redcap in this mob.

He swung his suitcase down from the rack himself, his muscles working fine. That Dr. Cartwright was all right. Joe felt like a two-year-old, hadn't felt this well in years.

Jostled and pushed by the boaring commuters, he took pleasure in pushing back, using his new strength. Why, he could have run up those long stairs to the level carrying the heavy bag, if it wasn't for the horde streaming down the stairs.

Wouldn't be anybody at trackside, naturally, any New Yorker knows better than to try and meet the 5:11 from Port Washington. He'd told Ray and Don to meet him in the little sandwich bar upstairs.

At the top of the stairs he set his bag down, took a dutiful twenty breaths that he didn't feel he needed; Cartwright had warned him about overdoing it at first. Then he went over to the waiting room, shoved in, looked at the sandwich bar.

Brawley Smith got up from one of the tables and said: "Hi, Joe. Have a beer?"

"No, Brawley. I'm off the stuff."

"Beer isn't liquor. Just food."

"Where's everybody?"

"Ray couldn't make it. He's waiting at the office for you. He said you'd understand."

"Oh, sure."

"Ron had to go to the can for a minute. He'll be right back."

"Don?"

Pass Through Manhattan

"No, Ron Levine. Oh, yeah, Donald called me up. He's got to run some errands for his firm tonight, make a speech or entertain a customer or something. Said he'd see you in the morning."

"Oh, sure."

"The kid's been working hard. Guy I know told me Donald was one of the coming men in Wall Street."

"Well, I guess he couldn't take a chance of offending his boss. I've been a big expense to him, but that's all over. From now on, I'm going to hit the ball, and hit it hard. You ought to go out there, Brawley, that man Cartwright is a genius. He'd have you straightened out in no time."

"I don't want to get straightened out. I like being the way I am."

Ron Levine came from the direction of the men's room, waving a gloved hand discreetly. "Hello, Joseph. How are you?"

"I'm O.K.," Joe said. His two friends fell in on either side of him and they walked towards the cab stand.

"Tell me, you must have had a chance to talk to the doctors out there," Ron said. "Have they made any experiments with metafin injections to build up resistance to colds?"

"What kind of medicine?" Joe asked, dourly.

"Not medicine, metafin."

"I don't know."

"Some morning you're going to wake up and find yourself embalmed, Ron, all the stuff you put into yourself," Brawley said, leaning back in the cab. "It's all very well for you to talk, but I've never been robust. If I didn't look after myself, I'd go just like this." Ron snapped his fingers. "The *Mail* office, driver."

"Sometime between stories, you ought to go out to Cartwright's," Joe said, peering out the window at the dispersing garment center.

"Oh, but I'm not reporting. Haven't you seen the *Mail?*"

"No, they don't let the patients have papers. I picked up a *Times* at the railroad station, they hadn't gotten their evening papers for some reason."

"I'm editor of the op ed page," Ron said. "I have my own little masthead."

"That's swell. You like that sort of thing; it would drive me nuts . . . What did you say, Brawley?"

"Nothing."

"What was it Don had to do? If it's a speech, I could cover it. Give him a start, looking over at the press table and seeing his old man sitting there."

"The connection was bad," Brawley said, "I couldn't get it clearly."

Joe felt an icy fist punch him in the belly. "The kid isn't drunk, is he?"

Ron said: "You know he doesn't use the stuff any more than I do. In fact, I taught him how to fake drinking with vermouth and things."

"I just thought maybe—"

"No," Brawley said, "it seems to have skipped a generation. Was your old man a drinker, Joe?"

"Hell, no. He was a Methodist bishop, and strict as all get out. I ran away from home when I was fifteen."

"Some of those religious guys can be poison. I remember one old duck I used to run into when I crossed with the Ford Peace ship," Ron said. "He wouldn't sit at the next table to me if I'd had my gentian bitters. He said they had alcohol in them."

"Ron Levine, the walking pharmacopoeia," Brawley said. "The vade mecum of drugstores." The cab stopped in front of the *Mail* office; Ron and Brawley climbed out and walked into the building, leaving Joe to pay the cab and bring his bag.

When he joined them, Brawley said: "I'll be up in a minute. Sure you won't join me, Joe?"

Joe snapped: "No." He and Ron climbed into the elevator. The operator said he was glad to see Mr. Morton back; his look was curious, Joe felt like inviting him to smell his breath.

Well, he had been somewhat less than discreet back there last spring, when he had banged in and out of this building. But he had been a sick man, Cartwright had told him so. Nearly died of pneumonia. Now he had a new start—

The kid at the entrance desk was new. He said: "Good evening, Mr. Levine," and went on reading his funny paper.

"Ray's in the Chief's old office now," Ron said. "The owner's built himself a nest on the roof."

"Like Pulitzer?" Joe asked, grinning.

"More or less like Pulitzer," Ron laughed. "My office is over there, come see me when you get through with Ray. Maybe we could have dinner together."

The news room was nearly empty; an evening paper doesn't have much to do after five thirty. A young man was sitting outside Ray's door; he stood up. "Mr. Morton, isn't it?"

"Yes."

"I recognized you from the picture on the wall in there of you and the Chief on the old *Globe*. Go right in. I'm Peabody, the Chief's new secretary."

"O.K., Peabody. Say, call the Morgue, will you, and ask them to send around everything on the German-American Bund and the Communist Party."

"Yes, Mr. Morton."

Joe went on in. Ray was reading the opposition, *World-Telegrams* and *Suns* were all over the room. He threw the paper down. "Hi, Joe, boy, you look in the pink. I'll have to try Cartwright myself."

"You ought to, Ray, the man's a genius." Joe put his hat on the edge of Ray's desk, sat down in one of the luxurious red leather chairs. "Nice little nook you've got here, Ray. The *Mail* doing well without me?"

"It's in the black, Joe."

"The hell it is. Congratulations, Ray. You know I haven't seen a paper in five months, and Cartwright edited my mail considerably. Avoid excitement. Why, that's wonderful, Ray. I'll bet you've had some fine offers."

"Sure. The Hearst interests are after me to take over a block of their papers. But I'm sticking with the *Mail*, Joe. It's my baby. I was telling Donald the other day, I'm a little goofy about the *Mail*."

"How is Don?"

"Wasn't he down at the train?"

"No, he called Brawley and asked him to explain. He had to work at something or other. I guess Cartwright's fees have kept the kid's nose pretty well to the grindstone, Ray, but that's all over now." Joe held out his sunburned hand. "Not a shiver in a carload."

"Swell, Joe. . . . You want a job, I suppose. You want to come back to the *Mail?*"

"Where else, Ray?" Joe asked. Good God, had Ray turned into a stuffed shirt? Was he trying to give Joe Morton the boot?

"I hoped you would, boy. We can use you here. . . . I've got an office all ready for you, right next to Ron's. You two can share a secretary for the time being and—"

Pass Through Manhattan

Peabody came in, and handed Joe two big folders. "The 1939 envelopes on those, Mr. Morton. I'm having the folders for the last ten years brought to my desk."

"All right, swell, Peabody, and thank you." Joe waited till the boy had closed the door, and said: "Come, come, Ray. What do I need an office and a secretary for? It's nice of you to want to—er—feed my vanity, but just a desk with the other reporters is all I need."

Ray said: "You're promoted, Joe. You're not a reporter any longer. What's that you had Peabody get for you?"

Joe said: "Material for a hell of a big story. I had one of the old Joe Morton hunches coming in on the train. . . . See what you think of this, Ray. Remember I've been out of touch, but I picked up a *Times* out on the Island. Hitler and Stalin signed a pact, is that right? Pretty startling news. So— We shoot for the local angle, and what do we get? A bunch of Yorkville Nazis and Union Square Reds who have been at each other's throats for three, four years are suddenly allies. Follow me so far?"

"They're not," Ray said. "I had Brawley look into that. Stalin is trying to prevent a war. He still hates Fascism."

"So that's the line the Comintern handed the boys and gals, huh?" Joe chewed his mustache. "Good, good. Say that's a lie handed the party members and the Bund members till they can be lined up. Now. Those lice in the Ogpu and the Comintern high-ups, the rats that do Hitler's bidding, they're going to want to clean out all the American officials of their parties who stand in the way of a peaceful coalition."

"Jeepers. You got— Joe, you're on the trail of something. I'll have Brawley cut into it first thing tomorrow morning. You can get a bunch of disgruntled radicals and Nazis to give us statements, and the first thing you know, we can be bawling about the possibility of political murderers stalking the streets of New York. We can—"

Joe said: "Wait a minute, Ray. Where does Brawley come into this? It's my hunch."

Ray waved a hand that was clean of the news-ink and paste that Joe associated with Ray's office hours. "You'll hardly have time to do any story-chasing. You've got a big job ahead of you, Joe. I want you to start a Saturday magazine for me, something good enough to syndicate for an insert like *This Week*. The *Mail* wants to chase national advertising, and this is the way to do it. We're news in the business, and papers all over the country will want a little piece of luck or genius or something that put the *Mail* on the paying side of the ledger. It's all yours, Joe. Name on the masthead as editor. You can build it into something as important as *Collier's* or *Liberty* if you put the old Morton touch on it."

Joe smiled: "Good old Ray. You never let your friends down. That is certainly swell of you, boy, to cook up something like that for me. But I think I'll let it go. I've been a reporter too long to turn into an editor now. I'll leave that to you and Ron. Me, *I'm* going to chase my little E. Phillips Oppenheim story, and—"

"I don't need any reporters, Joe," Ray said.

It all died in Joe. He could feel his shoulders slumping, his arms going slack. "You're kidding, Ray."

"No."

"You're sore because I turned down your fine offer. I'm not ungrateful, Ray, but I thought you, of all people, would understand how it is with me."

Ray said: "Try and understand how it is with me. I'm the head of that rarest and most valuable thing you and I ever heard of—a paying metropolitan daily. I can't take any chances of—" He stopped.

Joe said: "I see. You want me in the office where you can be sure I'm working. Where my secretary can phone you if I have a rum cake for dessert at lunch. Sure. Your conscience would hurt you if you threw me out, so—to alleviate your feelings,—I, Joe Morton, have to be turned into a stuffed shirt like you. Well, you can go to hell, Ray. The name of Joseph Kolk Morton still means something in the newspaper business."

Ray said: "All right, you asked for it. You get out chasing stories, you'll get excited and overworked, and in a week you'll be back on the booze again."

"I'm cured, I tell you."

"If you don't overwork. You forget that Cartwright is a friend of mine. He gave you a reduced rate because of me. I called him up this afternoon and got the dope. Overwork, and you're back on the liquor, and you're all through this time. This is the third strike coming up."

"It's a foul ball."

Ray got up from behind his desk. He walked to the drapery-hung window, looked out at the lurid sky. He talked over his shoulder. "This may be a bitter pill for you to swallow, Joe. But you're man enough to take it. Your son is in a mess. The State Department is investigating Armstrong and Grainger right now. That's information I got confidentially, and I don't dare pass it on to Don, because Don would give it to the firm. Grainger doesn't suspect a damn thing; he's been pulling wires in the banana countries so long he doesn't realize that times have changed; Washington doesn't like American firms, banking or engineering, monkeying with our neighbors. I tell you this, Joe, to let you know what's up, and for another reason: to show you how much I trust you, what a fine regard I have for your integrity. I know you won't tell Don, won't sell out your paper for your son. Don's a big shot down there now, the guy who does Grainger's dirty work. He took the office job because he wanted to pay Cartwright. Maybe he would throw it up if he thought he would never have to support you in a sanitarium again."

"You're leveling, Ray?"

"I'm leveling, Joe. I always have, with you."

"And Ron and Brawley and Donald. Yeah. The little white father." Joe stood up. "I'll level with you. If I have to be tied to my desk the rest of my life, I'd about as soon be dead. But maybe I'd be better off that way. . . . Where is this office?"

"Right next to Ron's. I'll show you. It's a nice office, Joe. You'll like it."

"Like hell I will, but come on."

*　　*　　*

DENNIS COSTI CAME OUT of Mayor LaGuardia's office grinning. The last words the Mayor had said were: "As one Wop to another, Judge, give 'em hell for me." They were off. His politics and the Mayor's were different, but you could count on the Little Flower in a pinch. Maybe that was because LaGuardia was such a fine publicity-getter himself, he never minded someone else pulling a big stunt; Fiorello would top it tomorrow.

Walking under the windy arch of the Municipal Building, Judge Costi found himself still grinning. That was no way for a judge to go around the city; he wiped the smile off. Boy, wait till Sylvester heard about this. Wait—

Someone called his name and title, and he stopped, turning. Young O'Farrell from the Corporation Counsel's office. "Judge Costi, I was just on my way over to your chambers. The Mayor called me."

"Perfect. We'll have to work fast, before the Bund gets wind of this and leaves these poor little Lempes holding the bag. You bring your case with you?"

O'Farrell thumped the papers under his arm. "Of course, I have suspected all along this was a Nazi plot, but I didn't see how I could introduce that into the trial and—"

"Yes, yes. Don't talk about it now, the case is still pending before my court. We have to throw it out before it's legal for me to discuss it with you."

"I'm truly sorry, Your Honor."

"Forget it. A man from the District Attorney's office is going to meet us at my office. There's one thing, O'Farrell, a favor I want to ask you."

"Anything, Judge."

"If it's at all possible, I want Arthur Lempe not to find out it was his wife tipped us off. I'm an older man than you, O'Farrell, and I've found it never is a good policy to cause family difficulties."

"You can certainly count on my co-operation, Judge Costi. By the way, we can count on you for a week from Friday, can't we?"

"A week from Friday? I'm afraid—"

"You're going to speak to our sodality. I'm on the committee."

"Oh, yes, of course. Well, here's the courthouse. After you—"

Miss Winters looked up, smiling, when they came in. "Mr. Cruikshank of the District Attorney's office called up. He'll be right over."

"Good, good. Give O'Farrell here a copy of your transcript, Miss Winters, and get Vanderbilt and Brefogel on the phone." Alone in his chambers, he combed his hair, and picked up the phone in answer to Miss Winters' buzz. "Mr. Brefogel, Judge Costi."

"Hello, Brefogel. Listen, you're the man in charge of this Lempe case, aren't you? Or is it Vanderbilt?"

"Well, Judge, we're both interested in it. A good case, from a lawyer's point of view, absolutely clear-cut. We—"

Dennis Costi found himself grinning into the phone. "In that case," he said, firmly, "you both better get down here as quickly as possible. It won't be necessary to have a paper, will it, Brefogel?"

Brefogel said: "Well, Your Honor, I'll come down but I'm afraid Mr. Vanderbilt—"

"Is after all a sworn attorney, and an officer of the court. I can issue a paper, but—"

"I'll try and persuade Mr. Vanderbilt—"

"In an hour, then. Or sooner."

Dennis rang off. Lord, this was fun. He rang for Miss Winters. She came in, said: "Mr. Cruikshank's already here. He and Mr. O'Farrell are going over Mr. O'Farrell's brief and transcripts and—"

"All right. Tell you what I wanted to see you about, Miss Winters. You a betting woman?"

"Well, I like to put two dollars on a horse now and then," the Wellesley girl said breezily.

"Bet you a quarter Daniel Sheridan is the next man to ring us up."

"Taken," she said. "You just came from the Mayor, didn't you? My bet would be a newspaper."

"I'm going to call Lempe," he said. "Tell Cruikshank if I can't get him, I'll want the D.A.'s office to arrange for the patrolman on the beat to find him. I figure speed is important. And, of course, when Mrs. Lempe returns, it's the first time she's been here. She'll be back in an hour?"

"Right, Judge."

The phone rang. Miss Winters answered it, smiled, and handed it to the judge. She fished in the pocket of her tweed jacket, laid a quarter on his desk and went out.

"Well, Dan?"

"Dennis, old boy, how are you?"

"As usual, Dan, as usual. Nice to hear from you."

"Yeah, yeah. Say, Dennis, you know me, I'm blunt. As one Irishman to another, what's going on about Mike Vanderbilt?"

"Oh, Dan, it's just legal stuff. A layman like you wouldn't understand."

"Sure, I get you. The reason I asked was, Mike and I had a date to play some golf this afternoon, and I wondered if you'd mind putting whatever this is off till tomorrow? Mike didn't want to ask you, but I said Dennis would understand, old Dennis isn't the kind to get a swelled head just because the Hall elected him to the bench. Is it O.K., Dennis?"

"Why, Dan," Judge Costi said, "it's all right with me, but I don't think I can accept the responsibility. But if you've been counting on this game—"

"We have, Dennis, we have—"

"Then have Vanderbilt send me down a waiver of his rights and I'll see that he gets full protection."

"Waiver of his rights?"

"Immunity and the privilege of an attorney. If it's necessary to appoint counsel for him, I'll try and make it his own partner, Brefogel."

"Why, Dennis, I didn't realize it was so serious. I—"

"I'm sure Mr. Vanderbilt can straighten it out, Dan."

Dennis Costi rang off, grinning. There was a terrible temptation to call Sylvester and do a little bragging about what he was going to do to the bums who had messed up Europe; but the judge restrained himself.

Now— He buzzed Miss Winters to send the young gentlemen in.

Cruikshank was of the new, Princeton-Harvard type of assistant district attorney you got under the Republicans. They liked to refer to themselves as "career men" which simply meant that they would cheerfully forego the elephant for the donkey if they got a crack at a good Washington job. Dennis grinned, wondering how Cruikshank and O'Farrell were making out together; O'Farrell was the perfect type of young Tammany man, Sunday school class, sodality, clambakes and all.

"Gentlemen," Dennis said. "As you know, we are considering the dismissal of a case of which Mr. O'Farrell is the defense attorney. Inasmuch as there have been well-founded evidences of illegality, I have sent for you, Mr. Cruikshank, since your office will prosecute everything beyond and outside of simple contempt of court. . . . However, until the attorneys for the plaintiff arrive, I do not feel we should discuss the case. All I want of you at present is to know if there are any witnesses I can summon for you."

O'Farrell said: "If it pleases Your Honor, the interne who attended the bus passengers told me that a nurse from his hospital had been talking to the plaintiff. She said—"

"No, O'Farrell. Please don't tell me what she said."

"I could use her, Your Honor. To prove that the plaintiff was not injured—"

"You've talked to her yourself?" the judge asked, frowning.

"She was discharged from the hospital, and I've had a

little trouble finding her. The process was served on her to appear as a witness, but I didn't have a chance—"

Cruikshank sniffed at such carelessness.

Judge Costi said: "If you want her, I'll sign a paper for special expenses in bringing her here in a taxi and so on."

"Very good, Your Honor," O'Farrell said.

Judge Costi pressed the buzzer. Miss Winters came in and got her orders, and he signed his name. She said: "The Lempes are already here, Judge Costi."

Dennis nodded. Miss Winters went to the closet, got out his robe. He said: "I won't need that."

She said: "I would put it on, Judge Costi. Germans—"

"Quite so. You've sent for the court reporter? And I want that young engineer that dug the bus out. We may have to establish that there *was* a bus."

"Yes, sir. And I just heard the door open. I imagine that is Vanderbilt and Brefogel."

"Good," Dennis Costi said. "Then, gentlemen, I'll meet you in the courtroom, as per my brilliant secretary's suggestion that the panoplies of justice are likely to be important to—er—our subject."

Alone in the chambers, he opened the big drawer of the desk. He gave the mirror a perfunctory glance, and then got out the folder containing the pictures of his wife, his children, his sainted parents, and Sylvester. He glanced through them, reached further into the drawer, and got out his beads, and asked the intercession of St. Denis that justice might now be done.

*　　　*　　　*

ELEANOR HAD HARDLY SEEN DR. BASTABLE before he had handed her a Bacardi to drink, and she had hardly drunk the Bacardi before she knew that he and she were going to hit it off all right. The hard, thin lines of his face were appealing to her after all the soft, nicey-nicey boys she had been going with all her life; she thought he was the first man she had ever met.

Donald Morton, the little sissy, was shocked by some of the things Doc said, but she wasn't. After all, they weren't children.

The dinner was good, she must remember this place.

Joan, Dr. Bastable's girl, was beautifully dressed, but a little loud. When the waiter brought the coffee, she said: "You boys have a brandy, while Elly and I go powder our noses."

"Noses?" Doc roared. "That's good, Joanie."

"You go powder your nose, too," Eleanor told him, tickling the top of his bald head. She followed Joan, giggling to herself at her own wit. She missed the knob of the door marked Ladies, and Joan caught her elbow. "Take it easy, pard," Joan said. "You've got a long evening ahead of you. You don't want to get plastered now."

"I didn't drink any more than you did," Eleanor said.

"No, but I winked at the waiter. Here we are. . . . Nancy, Eleanor here got a little over herself. You better give her something."

"Yeah, Miss Joan, sure will," the colored woman said. "Just you sit down, Miss Eleanor, we fix you right up. I ain't seen you in here before, have I?"

"No, this is my first time."

"There ain't no better place in the city," Nancy said, mixing stuff in a glass. "Heah, drink this. . . . We got judges and police inspectors and all rich politicians in heah eve'y night. You feel better?"

"Yes, I do," Eleanor said, gasping from the stuff that had

322

seethed around in her stomach before settling down to its work. "Thanks a lot."

" 'At's all right. Maybe you lose parta yo' supper now, but with the figgers young ladies want these days, that's all to the good. Right in there, dearie."

When she came back, Joan was sitting on the couch, smoking a cigarette. "Sit down, Baby. It won't do the boys any harm to wait a few minutes. . . . Cigarette? . . . Been out with this Donald boy much?"

"Oh, yes, often."

"Hm. He seems a little slow. He's been nursing two drinks all during dinner."

"You want a powder for him?" Nancy asked over her shoulder, as she wiped out the washbasins.

"No," Joan said. "No. . . . I tell you what, Eleanor. Let's change over. Old Bastard's liberal with the drinks, but he's a little slow on cash. Y'know the type? Let's change over, that's usually good for a double tip. Just before we leave them, I can get Old Bastard alone and get sore at him for running out on me all evening, and you can go to work on —Donald, is that his name?"

"All right," Eleanor said. She was mad at herself for being so stupid. A smart girl should have spotted Joan right away. She felt scared. Oh, but it was all right. Donald would have explained to Bastable, and they could have a laugh afterwards.

Joan stood up, straightening her girdle. "Nancy, I'm a little broke. You mind—"

"Not at all, Miss Joan," Nancy said. "You'll be in for cocktails tomorrow afternoon, or the day after at the latest. You see me then, too, Miss Eleanor. You might need yo' cash tonight. You girls have any trouble, Miss Joan, Corky is running those movies up his place. You know the ones."

"Yeah," Joan said. "They're all right for putting life into a party, too, but I'll bet Old Bastard's seen them."

"Shum to him again," Nancy said. "He's done it with yuh before, too, but that ain't stoppin' him, is it?"

"You're cute, Nancy," Eleanor said, and went out with Joan. She was quite sober, and highly amused, and she didn't have to do anything she didn't want to, did she?

Doc was playing a tune on the glasses with a toothbrush handle when they got back. Joan plucked her arm. "We'll play a double shift," she said. "You take Old Bastard and tease him up. I'll go to work on Donny-pants. See? Then shift back when I give you the sign, and get some money out of Donny right away. Then we can shift again for the cleanup."

"All right," Eleanor said.

"You got a room?"

"Of—oh, no."

"Make it the Metropolis, then. I don't ever take them to my place, either. . . ."

"What you girls cooking up?" Doc asked.

Eleanor gave him a bright smile. "Don't you wish you knew? Where did you get the toothbrush?" He didn't rise when she slid into the chair next to him.

"Always carry one," Doc said. "Carry all the equipment for a one-night stand. Wanta see?"

Eleanor didn't know what he meant, but she gave him a slow look. "I can guess."

"You're a hot one," Doc said. "Oh, you're a downy old bird, eh?" Under the table his hand closed on her thigh, plucked one of her stocking supporters and let it snap against her leg.

"Cut it out," she said. She reached under the table herself

and hit him lightly in the pit of the stomach with her fist. "I want a drink."

"Stop," he roared, "I like it . . . Waiter!"

Donald was leaning across the table, trying to get her attention. Though she had been sober when she left the little girls' room she felt giddy again. "Eleanor," Don said. "We have to go."

"Why?" she said. "I'm having a good time."

But his face, serious, intent, familiar, spoiled her fun. He was a pretty good guy after all and—

"Excuse me, Doc," she said. "I have to talk to the boy friend a minute." She made a point of pressing her thigh against Doc's as she rose. Doc was still yelling for the waiter.

Donald led her over towards the phone booths. "Listen, Eleanor," he said. "I'm awfully sorry about this. I'd never been here before, I didn't know."

"Why, it's a lovely place, Don."

"I'm afraid you're a little—innocent," he said.

She made her eyes wide. "Why, what do you mean?"

He didn't blush, and her liking for him increased. "It's a house of assignation," he said. "Doc was telling me. Tell you the truth, Eleanor, I never knew they existed outside of books." He was laughing now. "You slip out and go up town to some hotel bar—say the Madison—and I'll get away and join you in fifteen minutes."

She laughed with him. "Why not a hotel room? If we're going to sin."

He caught her hand. "It would be all right with me, kid. But not when we're drunk, and not with that Bastable."

She caught her breath. From some place in the restaurant a table exploded into laughter, and she let him hold her until it died down. "That a proposition, Donald?"

"A proposal," he said.

There was just a moment there when she might have— But she was sober. Not in a mining town, any more than in a college town. And not with any one man, always and always, talk, talk, talk—

"I'll file it," she said lightly. "Oh—and Don. Let's go on with them. Let's see life. We don't have to do anything we don't want to."

He said: "Well—" But she walked away from him and sat down next to Doc again. His hand promptly caught her thigh under the table and she leaned towards him. A bony hand went around her shoulders, and the Doc started whispering in her ear, and there was a drink in her hand.

A long time later she looked across the table. Joan looked exasperated, Donald angry and a little disgusted. "Gotta go to the johnny," she said.

Out in the ladies' room she lit a cigarette. "Give me one of those powders, Nancy. They work all right?"

"Well, they wouldn't make no bull bust no cee-ment stable, but they sure make him try."

Doc had ordered champagne by the time she got back. She slipped the powder to Joan, and nodded her chin towards Donald.

And a very pretty chin it is, too, she thought, as she sat down again, and said to Doc: "Tell me another." She had never been more sober in her life.

*　　*　　*

THE DESK LIEUTENANT SAID: "Dismissed," and Buck Ranulph turned on his heel, and walked out of the station house. It had been a warm day, but for some reason the order had not come through to take their blouses off; he felt worn out from walking a beat from eight to four in a cop's heavy uniform, carrying a daystick, hand-cuffs, notebook, watch and gun.

His feet hurt, but he hurried towards his apartment on 137th. Get out of this blue prison and put on cool white linens and go have a beer at the Liberian Roof Gardens was all he could think of. The panama hat with the red and blue hatband and white socks, a red and blue tie on a light blue— no, light blue shirts were the kind he had to wear all day these days. A plain white shirt. All white but the hatband and the necktie.

He ought to stay home, and work on a story for Mr. Maxwell, but the truth was, he was too tired. Once he got used to patrolling a beat, he'd be able to work nights. Or when the weather got cooler. Next month he was due for the four to midnight and it would be cooler, he could work all day.

He turned into the brownstone stoop of the house in which he rented the second floor front, and unbuckled his blouse. He shoved his blue cap back on his head, and trotted up the stairs, twisting his necktie loose as he ran. He dropped the coat and cap and necktie on the couch, turned on the bath, stripped off his gun and belt and handcuffs, and finished undressing.

There was some gin in the cupboard, and he thought for a minute of sending the landlady's little boy out for lemons and ice and having a Tom Collins, but the Roof Gardens would be cooler, and linens no more confining than a bath-robe. He was getting out clean underwear when there was a knock on his door.

Buck scooped up his uniform and underwear and tossed it through the curtain to the bed alcove. He shoved the gun into his desk, on top of an unfinished Ms., slipped into a pongee bathrobe. "Come in."

Pass Through Manhattan

Harold De Bruliere entered. "Hi, Buck. Saw you leaving the station, but I thought I would wait until you were out of your uniform." Harold shut the door and sat down, pulling up the knees of his trousers. "Frankly, there is something about the blue garb of the New York Cossacks that disturbs me."

"I was just on my way to the Liberian Roof Gardens for a beer. Come along."

"Buckingham, I am not that sort of politician. Don't Roof Gardens charge a minimum of a dollar?"

"My treat, Harold."

"Which I accept with pleasure." Harold got up, started walking around the room. "*The Only Two Ways to Write a Short Story. Trial and Error. Writing as a Career. If You Want to Write.* Man, man, you've taken up fiction a thoroughly serious way, haven't you?"

Knotting his tie, Buck nodded. "Yes, I have. Want to borrow any of those books?"

"I might, at that. When I have a little more time."

Buck turned with his coat half on. "You up to something?"

Harold grinned.

Buckingham Ranulph—Patrolman, 1st Class, N.Y.P.D.—slid the rest of his way into his coat and walked to his desk. He sat on the side of it, and put his hand on the pull of the drawer. "You hot, Harold? You on the lam?"

"Please, Buckingham," De Bruliere said, "you are a university graduate. When you get excited, you forget yourself. 'Are you hot,' or 'You're hot,' is ever so much better than the—er—Gullah diction, 'You hot?'"

Buck still didn't open the drawer. "I asked you a question, Harold."

"There is no warrant out for me. I have committed no

328

new crime, except my constant one of failing to help our white masters keep my people in subjection. More omission than commission, eh?"

"That's all right, then." Buck opened the drawer, took the gun out, and tucked it in the special shoulder holster he had had made in his vest. He unbuttoned his badge from his blouse and pinned it in the leather case that had once held the blue-and-gold badge of a detective; the larger silver shield prevented his buttoning the case.

"Really," Harold said, "do you always go armed that way?"

"I can be tried for stepping out of the door, on or off duty, without my badge and gun," Buck said. "All cops must carry both at all times. Even at a wedding, I suppose. Let's go."

"All right. You look very nice, Buckingham. Where did you get the tie?"

"The tie and hatband are a set," Buck answered. "I got them at the Harvard Haberdashery on 131st and Seventh."

Harold made a face, going through the door first. "An ofay store," he said. "We're boycotting them."

Though it was five, there was no abatement of the August heat. Every stoop, once they left Strivers' Row on 137th, was brilliant with the colors of Negro clothing, with shiny dark faces; several houses had rigged awnings over the doors. The fire department hydrants had been turned on to make lakes in which black and mulatto children splashed happily; Lenox Avenue was thronged with groups under each tree, each store-awning.

"Harlem in August," Harold said. "Hell on Sunday. Why won't they at least give us room to live in? What do you pay for your apartment, Buckingham?"

"Sixty a month."

Pass Through Manhattan

"Downtown on West End or Central Park West, or even Madison and Lexington, you could have a modern three-room housekeeping apartment for that. In Yorkville the Germans get a five-room walk-up flat for what our people have to pay for the privilege of sharing two rooms with another family."

"The Federal government is building model houses—"

"But not enough, and they got a yellow-dog clause in the lease. You know that? There's a clause in those leases that the occupant will not make more than so much a week. They're a guarantee of cheap labor, a sop thrown into the scale of the so-called open labor market."

"Can't the white people do anything you like, Harold?

"No," De Bruliere said. "No, not for my people. What we do and get we got to do and get for ourselves or it'll have strings on it."

"The Communists are white."

"They're white-dominated," Harold said. "I'm no Party-member. I use them to get what they'll give me." He laughed. "They're hard to find these days. That agreement with Hitler makes them a little self-conscious. They gotta wait for the Comintern to tell 'em what to say."

"Remember Jesse Owens and the boys in Berlin?" Buck said. For the first time that day a genuine laugh was born in his throat, gurgled out.

"Oh, Lord, that was wonderful," Harold agreed. "Here's the Liberian. You want to go back and tell my shadow I'll be here about two hours?"

"Your—"

"You aren't a very good policeman," Harold said, "if you didn't notice that we were being followed. Commissioner Valentine and Lieutenant Ralfs of the Alien & Sedition squad, or whatever it is, have done me the honor of putting a shadow on my tail. From eight in the morning," he said, standing under the canopy of the hotel, "until eight at night, it's a white man in a brown suit. From eight at night until eight in the morning, it's a brown man in a white suit. Both suits need pressing."

Buck looked back at the crowd. In a throng that was a hundred parts dark to one white he had no trouble in picking out the cop; a man he didn't know. Probably brought over from Brooklyn for the job.

"Yeah, I see him. He can't follow us up, the Roof Garden is closed to whites."

"I know," Harold said. "Come on."

They went up eighteen stories in the elevator, got a table out on the roof that overlooked Harlem clear up into Morningside Park. Buck ordered beer and shrimp cocktails, told the waiter they'd have dinner later. . . .

"You like being in uniform?" Harold asked abruptly.

Buck said: "No. But—"

"But after I got people to point you out at all our meetings, they kicked you off the detectives. We owe you something for that, Buckingham; they're using white men now. It makes it easier, somehow—"

"O.K." Buck sipped his beer. Maybe that Brooklyn dick hadn't recognized him. Maybe. But Ralfs would give any shadow of Harold's a picture of Buck. Well, he could say he had been trying to get in with De Bruliere, like Ralfs had said, but it hadn't worked. They wouldn't put a cop on a committee.

When this heat lifted, he'd really hit the old typewriter, and write his way right off the force and up to glory. He could live on fifteen a week. And there was no goal in writing barred to a colored man. The Pulitzer prize committee—Harold was saying something.

"We owe you a little for letting us get rid of you that way. You want to help your people some more?"

"I dunno. I'm well known to the cops, I—"

"You wouldn't have to appear. I just want you to meet my committee."

"Well—"

The service door to the kitchen needed oiling or something, it hung for a moment, each time a waiter passed through. Looking at it, Buck saw a white face among the blacks in the kitchen. Harold's shadow.

That Ralfs knew everything. He would, somehow, know if Buck turned Harold's invitation down. To accept would be to please both Harold and Ralfs; to decline would arouse both their suspicions.

"When?"

"Tonight, while my guard is being changed. We'll leave here right at eight."

"O.K." Buck felt like a load was off his mind. "I'll order supper."

*　　　*　　　*

THE JUNIOR PARTNER of Corning and Seligmann smiled blandly at the senior partner and said: "Jason, I've got some good news for you."

Jason Corning sat on the edge of his chair sullenly, like a schoolboy sent for by the principal. "Eh?"

"You can make that trip to the Argentine after all."

"How do you figure that, Bob?"

Bob Seligmann took a long pale cigar out of the humidor on his desk. He bit off the end, squeezed the cigar here and there to make it uniformly porous, and lit it carefully, taking the last puff with the match a good inch below the tobacco. He took three long, unhurried drags, and held the cigar a few inches away from his eyes to see how the ash was forming. Then he put it back in his mouth and spoke around it. "Oh, the firm made a little unexpected money yesterday; no reason why it shouldn't advance you five thousand. That was what you needed, wasn't it?"

Jason Corning's red face got redder. "Well, as a matter of fact—you see, Bob—"

"Come, come, Jason, what's the trouble?"

"Well, I had a little bad luck yesterday. I was going to—er—brace you for a bit of a loan today in any event; I don't quite see how I can get through the quarter without it."

Robert Seasongood Seligmann took the cigar out of his mouth and gave what he hoped was a ringing laugh. "Oh, Jase, Jase, at your age. And after all the years you've been around the tracks. I thought you'd sworn never to put more than fifty dollars on a horse again."

Jason Corning stood up. "It wasn't a horse. The truth of the matter is, Bob, I've been playing the market a bit."

"The market? You mean the *stock* market? Why, Jase, I'm sorry. I suppose that was the result of my telling you I was thinking of retiring and leaving you to run the firm. I'm truly sorry, Jason." Bob let that sink in a moment. "Oh, well, forget it, Jase. We really cleaned up in J.C. yesterday. I'll loan you another five out of my own account, you can pay it back a thousand a quarter."

Now, quiet, Bob, and let that sink into Jason's fat head; it takes a moment to penetrate.

"Thanks, Bob, decent of you. Fine thing to know I can always count on good old—Bob, did you say J.C.? You made a killing in J.C. yesterday?"

"Why, yes." Bob puffed on the cigar to keep his lips from curling up. He hadn't thought he would enjoy this as much as he was.

Pass Through Manhattan

"But the bottom fell out of J.C. yesterday."

"Fancy," Bob said, pulling a pile of letters towards him, "your knowing that. I didn't know you followed the market, Jase." He puffed. "Letter from your Uncle Nate, Jase. Please buy twenty thousand dollars' worth of Liberty Bonds and put them in his vault, and will we send a boy up to Kauffman's and get him a dozen buggy whips. Now, what in the world does he want a dozen buggy whips for?"

"They use them in training those American saddlers he breeds," Jason said absent-mindedly. "What does he need twenty thousand dollars' worth of Liberty Bonds for? The old boy's ninety, and he hasn't been able to spend more than half his income in any one year since 1900. . . . Robert, just how much do you know about young Tenbruye?"

Bob was rapidly filling order slips from the directions in the letters. "He's a good real estate man, and we need one; I never had much flair in that direction. Don't imagine he knows much about stocks and bonds. Of course, Tenbruye isn't his real name."

"It isn't?" Jason had turned from the window; Bob could tell by the shadow shifting on his desk. But he went on working without looking up.

"I don't imagine so; at least your cousins never heard of him." He reached out and pressed the buzzer for a boy; the boy came in, and Bob pointed at the order tray. The office boy was halfway out the door when Jason Corning said: "After you've delivered those, bring me a Social Register, will you?"

Bob glanced at the clock. It was all over now. He said: "Ten minutes before the market opens," and started reading the dramatic page of the *Times*.

There was silence in the office except for Jason's heavy tread, muffled by the thick carpet. Up and down, up and down. Bob felt a moment's pity for his partner; it must be humiliating to be disclosed as a child, when your hair was gray and your body thickened with time. For Tenbruye he felt no pity at all; Tenbruye had deliberately sat in to a game whose rules were plain and clear; no mercy could be shown to a Wall Street opponent.

The ticker started warming up; the market would be open in a few minutes. Bob stepped over and read the sheets of the Dow Jones news ticker, ripped the last one off, and clipped it on his rack. Then he sat down again, letting the exchange ticker tape run through his fingers, ready for the always significant opening transaction.

Jason cleared his throat: "Bob, just how far are we committed to the Corning Manor deal?"

"Up to and including putting up most of the money for the second mortgage. We couldn't get out of building Corning Manor now." Did Jason not realize his mind was as transparent as jelly? There was really no need for him to speak; Bob knew in advance what he was going to say, always, on all subjects except thoroughbred horses.

The boy, released from the pre-opening rush, brought Jason his Social Register. Bob heard the heavy hands turning the pages.

The market opened with Paramount up a quarter. Funny thing to open with. Steel unchanged, McCormick off an eighth, Loew's up a half, NYC off nearly a point—

His eye still on the tape, Bob called their floor clerk. A chance to liquidate a little more of that movie stock the DaSousas had taken in part payment for real estate. There was going to be a little flurry in movie stock this morning. He would be glad when he saw the last of that stock; motion picture companies were bad things for a firm like Corning and Seligmann to fool with; the earning sheets and reports were incomprehensible, your proxies were valueless to trade for cash or information or proxies of other companies. He gave the order, looked at his watch, and kept an eye on the tape. It took four and a half minutes to execute the order; he glanced at the Dow Jones news to make sure the exchange ticker was not late, and had a complete picture of the market; there was a flurry around the specialists in movie stocks, his floor partner had been delayed two good minutes in getting to the center of it and having his order booked.

He repeated the order. This time it took six minutes; he was taking the proportions of a tiny boom. Nearly every movie stock was up a fraction to two. He redoubled it, and the order went through in two minutes, at an eighth less than opening; the boom had served its purpose—letting someone unload something—and died. Bob figured rapidly, and smiled with satisfaction. He had halved the DaSousa holdings, after waiting nearly a year, and done it at a point and an eighth higher than he had resigned himself to take.

Eleven o'clock. An hour of trading done. The order clerk came in with the slips for transactions consummated; Bob checked off the list he had started with. Everything taken care of but Nate's Liberty Bonds; the floor partner would take care of them at the first lull.

All necessary transactions washed up. He might step over to the Exchange and relieve the floor partner; he had a membership of his own, a luxury, since he didn't spend twenty hours a year on the floor, but he liked to get out there occasionally and get the feel of the market.

Bob lit a cigarette, reached for the Dow Jones board which the boy, passing through, had straightened. His mind digested news, automatically correlating it with dividend dates and current prices; he began the rough mental sketch of a transaction he could swing in Little Steel if he were on the floor.

He hooked the Dow Jones board back up, blocking in details. The management of Republic would undoubtedly have a pool to bolster, since—

Jason Corning cleared his throat and brought Bob back to earth. "Oh, Jase. I'd forgotten you were there."

"The man's an impostor," Jason said belligerently. "I don't understand, Bob, how you could be taken in so."

"What man?" Bob asked gently. Really, Jason was getting senile.

"This so-called Tenbruye. This upstart you have taken into Corning and Seligmann."

Bob said: "Oh, Tenbruye. I thought you liked him."

"He's an upstart. He's working under an alias. He—" Jason Corning rapped the Social Register, "is not even mentioned in this book as a junior."

"Look under Dilatory Domiciles," Bob suggested.

"I hardly expected flippancy from you, Bob, in a matter concerning the good name of Corning and Seligmann."

"Jason, I'm busy. You know the market requires all my attention from ten till three; if you have anything against John Tenbruye, go fire him. You're the representative of the senior branch of the firm."

"I—I fire him? I didn't hire him, Robert."

"All right," Bob Seligmann said. "As a favor to you, Jason, I'll see him at three and give him his regular two weeks' notice."

"Thank you, Bob."

"You know, Jason, anything like that is no trouble. Corning and Seligmann is here to make money for the family, and for you. It is your firm. . . . On the way out, will you tell Miss Moracci to have Tenbruye in here at three."

"Yes, Bob, I will." Jason went out, still muttering "impostor" and "charlatan" under his breath.

*   *   *

THE HOUSE WAS DARK, the phone disconnected, the front door locked and bolted. A truck had come from a second-hand furniture store and the man had given Carl seventy-one dollars for the furniture; the operating tables and professional equipment had been crated by old Jod, and shipped West to Carl's cousin.

Peggy, in a black dress, stood in the kitchen counting things on her fingers. The tickets were in her bag, on the table with her light traveling coat; the suitcases were at the Grand Central Station, the trunks checked. The rent was paid till the expiration of the notice period required in the lease. The light and gas men had been there and turned the meters off, received their final checks.

She called Jod and gave him a month's pay and the bonus she and Carl had decided was right. He said: "Thank you, Mrs. Wilcomen. And I sho hope you and the Doctor have a happy life out in the West."

"Maybe we'll send for you, Jod, when we have our own place."

"I'll come, ma'am, even if I got me a job driving Mr. Vincent Astor's horses."

"Good-bye, Jod." Peggy shook hands with the old man, and called: "Carl. Carl!"

He came trotting down the backstairs. "Almost forgot my rabbit's foot." He waved a charm, its base set in silver.

Peggy laughed until tears came into her eyes. "Rabbit's foot. You fool, Carl, you."

"Why not?" he asked. "I met you, didn't I?"

"Thanks, sweet." She put her arms around his neck and kissed him as hard as she could.

"Hey, you're embarrassing Jod."

"When he comes out West, we'll call him Uncle Jod, and then he won't be embarrassed."

They shook hands with the colored man again, and Peggy opened the back door. "Let's go, Carl."

"No hurry. Why don't we go out the front way; the alley's full of broken boxes and things."

The laughter died in Peggy's eyes. She looked at the floor. "People keep trying the front door."

"Oh." Carl made a big point of adjusting his necktie. "I should have kept my appointments. I—"

"It's too late now," Peggy said. "All the equipment's gone. Let's go, Carl."

Old Jod picked up Peggy's coat, Carl's coat and little overnight bag, and scurried ahead of them through the alley. Hanging on to Carl's arm, Peggy followed.

Peggy looked up and down the block quickly. No girls at the door. It would be too bad for Carl to run into one of the women who had been trying the door all day and turning away puzzled when they found the place deserted. But she had confessed, the priest had blessed their marriage, and you had to make a clean break. They couldn't have left town with a possibility that a case might take a turn for the worse later. This way—

Jod had set their stuff down, was running to the corner for a cab. As he went off, a taxi came from the east, seemed to be slowing. Peggy called: "We've got one, Jod, come back," and the cab stopped.

A man stepped out; she had never seen him before, but

she knew the type. Her heart went cold and chill and hard
in her breast. She stepped in front of Carl.

"Miss Margaret Reilly?"

She nodded.

Carl said: "She's Mrs. Carl Wilcomen now."

She caught Carl's arm; she knew he was about to hit the
cop. "No, Carl—"

The officer frowned. "Well, if you were Miss Reilly,
you're wanted in Judge Costi's court, right away. . . . Say,
don't look so scared, Miss. It's that accident you were in,
the Lempe case."

Carl said: "My wife already gave a deposition. We were
married yesterday, we're on our way to a train—"

"Well, gee, mister," the cop said, "I'm sorry. But this is
important; they sent me all the way up from the D.A.'s
office in a cab. Say, lissen. You go on down to the court;
the D.A. told me they'd only need Miss Reilly—I mean, the
missis—a little while—and I'll go on up to the railroad station
an' get your tickets changed for you till a later train.
They'll do it for me, on my badge."

"Well, that's nice—" Carl began.

The cop grinned. "We don't often get expense money
like this; watch me take a taxi up to the Grand Central."

Carl handed him the tickets, and the cop walked towards
the subway, still grinning.

Carl said: "Get in the cab, Peggy. It's just that accident
case—"

"I know," she whispered into his neck. "But I'm scared.
Oh, Carl, why didn't we go right from the church?"

"They'd have brought us back," he said. "If they wanted
us."

*　　　*　　　*

Pass Through Manhattan

THIS AMERICAN JUSTICE was beyond understanding. First everything is in order, the facts are marshaled, it is all clear like mountain water. Then your lawyer asks for a postponement.

Next he says you must give him the three thousand dollars which were to take you and Georg home to the Fatherland; but why should you pay out money when your case is good and soon the city pays you?

And then, with every thermostat in a building of ten thousand workers down for testing, comes a man with a badge to take you to see the judge.

Artur, carefully changing to his street clothes, could not understand any of it. But he knew his rights. He would ask the judge. I am a hard-working man, he would say, the heating superintendent from a big building. What is this nonsense, is this orderly? The judge would tell him. A judge in a case so important as this was a big man. From a judge you get justice.

He did not speak to the officer who had come to take him to the court in a taxicab, because the officer was not a big man; he needed a shave, his clothes were unpressed. The taxicab was a waste of the taxpayers' good money, too; the subway was close, right in the building, and faster.

This, then, was the court, the judge on his bench all correct, the lawyers before him. There was Marie, looking afraid. Artur went and sat down next to her, patting her hand. "Do not fear, wife. This is just a formality."

The judge was speaking: "The court sits. Mrs. Lempe, in the matter of your suit against the city for damages caused to you by a bus accident, this court has entertained a motion that the case be thrown out, since—it is charged—you did not bring suit to receive justice but to promulgate political propaganda, possibly treasonable. This hearing will be informal, and preliminary; there is a representative of the District Attorney's office present, and a transcript will be sent to the Federal District Attorney."

Artur blinked and sat very still. Mr. Brefogel arose and said that he wanted to know what charges had been filed against whom.

The judge said: "There have been no charges filed. But as a court of law, and a branch of the Court of the State of New York, it is this bench's duty and privilege to maintain order and honesty among its officers, the attorneys admitted to the bar of the State of New York. Therefore, Mr. Brefogel, for purposes of this hearing—and only that—you can consider that the defendants are you and your partner, Mr. Vanderbilt. Will Mrs. Artur Lempe please take the stand?"

Mr. Vanderbilt raised his squeaky voice: "May it please Your Honor, this is highly illegal. This woman and her husband may have charges filed against them as a result of this hearing; they are foreigners, not familiar with the language, and they are unrepresented by counsel."

The judge said: "Since this is a hearing, we can later entertain motions to strike out of the transcript any unconstitutional testimony, such as that of husband against wife. The purpose of this hearing is merely to find the truth; surely you can have no objection to that, Mr. Vanderbilt, Mrs. Lempe?"

"The learned judge maintains this is a hearing to investigate charges and rumors that we have attempted to use his court as a pulpit for political doctrines," Mr. Vanderbilt said. "I maintain that it is the judge who is playing politics; I want that put in the transcript."

"It is in, Mr. Vanderbilt," the judge said, "and so will be the Court's remark that you are in contempt of court. Sit down, Mr. Vanderbilt. Mrs. Lempe, please take the stand."

Marie was shaking so that Artur had to push her forward a little. A man in blue was making her put her hand on the Bible and swear.

Artur found he was perspiring. But no. The Korps-Hauptmann, the National Leader, all those big men had assured him that, while he was helping the Cause, he was also only asking for his rights. He had done nothing dishonest. Still, it was true that an American who had done what he had done in Germany would be beheaded. But no. This country was not like that. This was a democracy, and—

Artur mopped his face and sat back, turning over in his mind what he had just thought. This country was not like that. This country was not like that, this country was not like that, like that, like that.

It was funny that he had been thinking in English, like that, like that. How would you say it in German, dieses Land nicht—

No, it would be better German to turn it around and say, in Germany things are different. Bei das Vaterland—

What nonsense, what child's drooling was he now speaking? Marie was all through, she was coming back to sit down and he had not heard a word she said. My dear God, had she accused him? Marie loved America. Marie had only married him to come to America, she had told him so. Now—

The judge was calling a Miss Reilly to the stand. A pretty American girl. Who was she?— "Miss Reilly, the Court wants to thank you for coming. I understand you have had a change of name, you are now Mrs. Wilcomen? Congratulations."

What manner the judge had. So smooth as cream, so educated. A big man. To be a judge you had to read hundreds from hundreds of books, and remember them, too. How could a man do that?

"Mrs. Wilcomen," the judge said, "you were, at the time of the accident, a nurse in Mount Sinai Hospital. Is that right? And at the time the bus crashed into the snowbank, or whatever did happen—yes, I saw you, Mr. O'Farrell, I realize we do not yet know what the bus did—we have Mr. Morton here to help tell us if necessary—you were talking to Mrs. Lempe, there."

The young lady said: "Yes. I gave Mr. O'Farrell a statement about it, and Mr. Brefogel cross-examined me."

The judge said: "Yes. I have a copy of that, here. It merely states that Mrs. Lempe told you she had been ill, and then in the cross-examination, Mr. Brefogel asked you if you had at any time examined Mrs. Lempe, and you said you had not. Correct?"

"Yes, Your Honor. Is that all you want from me? My husband and I want to get to a train, we—"

"Just one more question from me, Mrs. Wilcomen. Did Mrs. Lempe tell you why she had stopped having treatments?"

"Yes, Your Honor," the pretty young American girl said. "She was undergoing the Friedenberg treatment that is given only at Mount Sinai, and her husband made her stop because Mount Sinai is a Jewish hospital and he is a Nazi."

"Hearsay," Mr. Brefogel was shouting. "Unsubstantiated—"

"All right," the judge told Mr. Brefogel. "Mr. Lempe, please sit down—" Artur did not know he had been standing. "Mrs. Wilcomen, you are aware that you are under oath? Quite so. Now, the statements you have made are not guesses or reconstructions? They are your clear, unshadowed memory of a conversation?"

"Yes, Your Honor."

"That's all," the judge said. "Mrs. Wilcomen can go. And thank you. I see no reason why this Court should not now sit as a magistrate and entertain a charge from the District Attorney of—"

Mr. Vanderbilt was on his feet. "May Your Honor please. I wish the privilege—the constitutional privilege of cross-examining Mrs. Wilcomen."

"Granted."

"Mrs. Wilcomen, you are the wife of Carl Wilcomen, known as Doctor Wilcomen?"

"Yes."

"It is true that Dr. Wilcomen has been practicing in New York City for some time without being a member of the county medical association?"

This was getting too confused for Artur. A court of justice is a courtly place, an orderly place. This has nothing to do— Ah. The judge had said so.

"Mr. Vanderbilt, the business of the defendant's husband need not now concern us. An attorney of your standing knows this is not pertinent."

"I will revise my question. Since leaving Mount Sinai, you have been employed as office nurse for the man you are now married to?"

"Yes."

The judge was asking Mr. Vanderbilt what this had to do with Marie's case. Right. A good judge, like a judge should be, not like it must now be in Germany, where there was one law for Nazis and one for—

Mr. Vanderbilt was yelling: "The matter under investigation is whether my client attempted to use the courts for political purposes. I wish to prove that the court itself is a political star chamber, that its only witness is an abortionist and the wife of an abortionist, paying blackmail to the political party of which our persecutors are members. I wish—"

Artur Lempe found himself on his feet; he was shouting, too. From some place far away he heard his voice saying: "Your Honor, please, I have no part in this. The lady speaks the truth, do not listen to lawyers."

But so did the lawyer. Donald lowered his eyes, realizing that he had gone green, that a court attendant was staring at him curiously. My God, what people!

You rescued people from suffocation, you dug down into the snow and pulled them back to life as surely as any doctor ever delivered a child, and they—they—they plan to use the incident to turn your country over to Hitler.

Or they quit a good hospital to go to work for an abortionist. That tall quiet guy sitting there, the one with the close-cropped black hair and the nice smile, he must be the doctor.

If there was one profession an engineer could look up to, it was medicine, and what kind of doctors do you meet in New York? Bastable and this Wilcoming or whatever his name is.

Cut it out, Donald. Trouble is just that you've got a hangover, and you had a hard time at the office, with Miss Cowan out sick. Just take it easy.

Wonder if Joe gets these hangovers every morning. If he does and goes on drinking, nothing will cure him—

The little Nazi was talking again. The words came through a blur.

"I wish a Bible. I wish to put my hand on the Bible."

Then the court was silent, everyone was listening to him, to Artur Lempe. He said: "Please, I wish to swear that I will tell the truth. So you will believe me. I am for ten years heating superintendent from one big building; there they will tell you that Artur Lempe speaks the truth."

And the learned judge said: "Mr. Lempe, take the stand. If you can clear up this matter, the Court will be obliged." Just as though he, Artur, was so good from a judge. So it is in America, one man he is like another man, brothers.

Artur swore on the Bible, and said: "It is like the lady said. My wife, she is good wife from me, but when she gets sick I will not let her go to Mount Sinai Hospital, because it is Jewish. This is because I am National Socialist, I listen to the Korps-Hauptmann when he says that the Party is going to make things right, so a man knows where he stands. But now I know better. Now I know, when a Nazi is in trouble, the Korps-Hauptmann does not come to court, the Landesfuehrer—what you call National Leader—does not come to court; they leave the little man to see it through by himself. They call themselves officers, soldaten, but it is not thus an officer does; an officer stands by his men."

The judge was stopping him. "Mr. Lempe, was it your idea that your wife sue the city?"

"No, learned Judge, Your Honor. The National Leader tells me to do that. What a leader says, I do; it is right and proper that men who know should lead. You are a judge, you must know about justice; if you say it is a crime to make politics from a bus accident, I know I am wrong, I should be punished."

Mr. Vanderbilt and Mr. Brefogel were yelling at him, but he looked at the judge. The judge said: "If those two men cause any more disorder, I want them put under arrest. Go on, Mr. Lempe. You went to the meeting the night of the accident, although your wife had been in it. Then you did not think her seriously hurt?"

Pass Through Manhattan

"No, Your Honor, learned Judge. It was the National Leader who—"

*   *   *

JACK FIRSTIN IDLY DREW CORNICES on a piece of scratch paper while McCransten talked in circles. "Jack, you can leave clause thirteen a out of that first mortgage if you want to. I'm perfectly willing to admit that it may make Corning and Seligmann readier to finance a second building if they get a good first mortgage. But, Jack, I'd wait till they mentioned it."

"Oh, sure, I know," Jack said, moving his heavy body. "In business it is every man for himself, they got lawyers good like you, McCransten. Only, for me, the profit is not so much now, either way. I want it they finance me another building."

"Well, you know how these old firms are. They may decide it's too much trouble. They make money in a hundred ways, all you have is real estate and building. And then where are you?"

"I'm where Corning and Seligmann ain't running around the city saying Jack Firstin is a gyp."

"After three bankruptcies, I should think you wouldn't be so sensitive. I should think—"

"Education you got, McCransten, building sense you ain't got it, or why should you be working for me. Huh? Me, Jack Firstin, I know what a good name is worth; Corning and Seligmann, they—"

McCransten's secretary came in and said: "Mr. Tenbruye is outside, he wants to see Mr. Firstin."

Jack said: "You see? Now they find out about thirteen before I got it a chance to be honest. McCransten, I get me another lawyer, you are— Show the gentlemen in, miss."

348

Pass Through Manhattan

Young Mr. Tenbruye came in. What a gentleman! Such clothes, and how he wore them so you would know he was from A Number One American upper crust. If he was front man for them, what buildings they could put up, they would reach the sky. The Tenbruye name, and Mr. Tenbruye to see the bankers, McCransten to write the papers and him, Jack Firstin, to put up the buildings and do the real thinking. Such—

So there was a Santa Claus.

Mr. Tenbruye was saying: "Mr. Firstin, I have decided to sever my connections with Corning and Seligmann. As the —er—other party to the biggest deal I engineered for them, I wanted you to be the first to know."

Fired? Fired, maybe. Gents that looked cold like that Mr. Seligmann did not like it their young men should have such a look you could do business with them like Mr. Tenbruye had. Or quit? "What is it you do now, Mr. Tenbruye?"

"I haven't made a decision yet. Of course there is always Tenbruye Sons, but, frankly, I prefer building and real estate to banking. I shall look around a while—"

Jack Firstin cleared his throat. A Santa Claus, that's what there was. "Mr. Tenbruye, would you consider it to go in with me?"

"I might, Mr. Firstin. I'll be frank with you, I hoped you'd say that. Together we could go far."

"Let's make it a deal." Jack stuck out his hand. Tenbruye Tower would be taller than Al Smith's Empire State. A hundred and fifty stories? Why not? The Manhattan bedrock could carry it.

"Now," Mr. Tenbruye said, "there is a question of clause thirteen in the first mortgage, Mr. Firstin. I've been meaning to call your attention to it, but I'm glad I didn't. We'll need money for our next building, and why shouldn't Bob Seligmann pay for it? He's got plenty."

Looking at young Mr. Tenbruye, Jack knew he had been fired. And he was out to get Corning and Seligmann. With that look from the eyes, Jack was glad he was not Mr. Seligmann. He was glad Mr. Tenbruye did not feel that way about him.

He would have to be careful with his new partner. But why not? Should he be a fool and put a knife in the back of his front? Ha!

*   *   *

EVERY TIME HIS HEEL hit the pavement it said: "Copper, Copper." And he thought he had forgotten. He thought— Good God. What had he been thinking of? He had nearly sent a couple of engineers down into the mosquito-ridden Lacrimas on a bill of health put out by that Bastable.

Told himself Bastable was an M.D., he would clean up the place. Hell. Bastable would park himself with the bhutas at the seaport, and never go near the Lacrimas. Bastable, Bastable, Copper, Copper.

I wanted to forget you, Copper. Wanted to forget how I killed you. For what? A bunch of Nazis and an abortionist, John Tenbruye and a—

God, what a hangover I have. Copper, Copper. You and I were better men than the whole bunch of them, we were working men and now you're dead, and what the hell am I? A contact man, a gladhander, drinking with Bastable and a couple of whores. Drinking all night and going home with that girl of Bastable's. Wonder where he and Eleanor went?

What the hell difference does it make? I know what they did, wherever they went. Mooning around after Eleanor all those months, and what she wanted was a Bastable. Hell,

Pass Through Manhattan

I'm no better. No better, no better, running errands for Armstrong and Grainger, sending men to do things I wouldn't do myself. Killed a good working man, a man who knew how to bend a rope or drive a timber, for a bunch of lousy parasites and a woman who tried to make Nazi publicity out of it, out of Copper's death.

The courtroom scene and the indescribable scenes of the night before came into his mind. He put out a hand and steadied himself against the side of a building. There was a gyp builder in the bus, that's when I first got worried, gypped people out of their savings. Hell, he was the pick of the lot. Tenbruye, Eleanor, the Nazis, a—

My God, what a busload. It's a wonder the fault didn't settle again and pinch them to death. Crush the whole damn bus between a few billion tons of schist and grind 'em into roach powder.

But any busload in this God-awful city would be as bad. A hunk of oreless, unfarmable rock covered with one tenth of a nation. What could you expect except that they'd be trying to make a living off the other nine tenths? First principle of life is self-preservation. The Isle of Parasites.

Something Ray said banged into his mind. The only reason to stay in New York is to make money. If you don't want money more than you want anything else, get out.

But once I was part of the other nine tenths, the ones who support this crawling rock of parasites. Copper and I. And now—

Gotta go look for Copper. But Copper's dead. Copper's dead, but not so dead as I am, living on a dead man's chest. Living—

Go see Ray. Go see my old man. My God, those people in that courtroom.

*   *   *

Pass Through Manhattan

PEGGY WAITED IN THE SECRETARY'S OFFICE while Carl was in talking to Cruikshank. Oh, Carl, Carl dear, I wanted to save you and look what I did. We had our tickets, too, we were on our way. And then this. Then this.

But it isn't my fault. All I did was take a ride in a bus. To get my hair waved because I was going to graduate. Going to be Margaret Reilly, R.N. And now I'll be number something or other. Or do they give us numbers in the women's prisons, is it just the men who get numbers?

Carl always keeps his hair cut short, it won't make so much difference in his appearance. He'll look— Oh, Peggy, you're getting hysterical, like those boys who used to wait in the office. Pull yourself together. You are a nurse, if there is no ribbon on your cap. You are as much of a nurse as if they had given you a dozen ribbons. And nurses do not get hysterics.

She smoothed her skirt, sat up straighter under the gaze of the District Attorney's secretary and the half-dozen seedy looking men who were waiting to see Mr. Cruikshank. She even put a little, professional smile on her lips, and then was glad because Carl came out.

He returned the smile and she rose, took his arm. There was no policeman with him, they could go. Maybe it was all right after all. But the arm that she held was tense, tight, the muscles as hard as marble under his sleeve. It must have been bad for him. Poor darling. That nasty little district attorney must have given him a raking over. Poor Carl. He would never in his life learn to bow his head. Oh, she didn't want him to. Tell them all to go to hell the way her father did when he nearly starved the two of them for the truth about his district's unhealthiness, when he fought the whole city for the lives of his patients.

Pass Through Manhattan

They were out in the hall now. She said: "Carl, what did he—"

His voice was strained. "Wait'll we get outside. I can't talk in this place. Let's get outside."

I guess we look all right. I guess we look like an honest young couple. I guess we don't look so very different from the way we looked just a little while ago coming out of the marriage license bureau just across the square down there. But people smiled at us then, why not now? How have we changed?

On Lafayette Street Carl said: "Let's get a cup of coffee." But when they were seated in the little restaurant, the coffee steaming up into their faces, their knees touching under the white-topped table, he didn't touch his coffee. He said: "It's all right. We can leave town."

"Oh, Carl, I'm so glad. He gave you back our tickets?"

"What do you think he did? He couldn't hold us. They didn't have any more on us than ever. No witnesses. Only a remark shouted by a little shyster lawyer in a courtroom— Say, that Dutchman was swell, wasn't he?"

"I didn't hear him. All I could think of was, it was the first time the word had ever been used about either of us. I— The word made it worse."

"There'll be no indictment. They have to have a witness, and they can't get one now any more than before. And there's Sheridan, the politician I paid off for protection. I think I'll go up and punch his teeth in; it must've been him that squealed to that Vanderbilt."

"Oh, don't bother about him, Carl," Peggy cried. "Forget him. We'll be free of this city forever. Let's go to the station and sit till the next train for your cousin's, and then get on it and sit till it pulls out. Oh, I'm so happy. And I thought I'd wrecked you again."

"My cousin?" he asked. "My cousin's? Don't you understand, Mick? We can't ever go to my cousin's now. They won't indict us, but they won't lift a finger to keep all that out of the newspapers. It's a privileged court record, that Cruikshank said. We'd wreck my cousin now."

"Oh, Carl."

"Well, let's go and turn our tickets in," he said. "Might as well get our money back. We'll need it."

She held his arm till they had paid for the untouched coffee, till they had gotten into the cab, till it started uptown. Then he pulled his arm free from her grasp, roughly, and her heart stood still. He was through with her. But she wouldn't blame him. She was nothing but bad luck, all the way through. She—

Ah! He had only removed his arm so he could put it around her. She whispered: "I'm sorry, Carl. I love you so."

"It wasn't your fault, Mick. Forget it. How could it have been your fault?" His face bore down, kissed her while the cab ran on and on through a misty forest of bliss.

"But Carl, what will we do? Where will we go?"

"I dunno. Something will turn up. There's Labrador or your spig countries. We can find something to do."

"We could—" she gulped, "we could—open up the house again. Just so I've got you."

"Hell, no," said Carl Wilcomen. "That's no business for a married man." He began to laugh. "We're not licked, Mick. Hell, together we can take the tropics like Grant took Richmond. We're unbeatable, Mick, together."

Oh, Blessed Virgin, Mother of God, I thank Thee. . . .

*   *   *

Pass Through Manhattan

ELEANOR CASTRON HAD A HANGOVER. She had a hangover with pink lace insertions, and polka dots. She had the hangover to end all hangovers.

But she had twenty dollars some place. Where—where— She found it fastened to her girdle by one of the stocking supporters. How long has this been going on?

She showered and dressed very carefully, put plenty of perfume behind her ears, and walked out into the hall. Wonder where Mother is? Probably tried to wake me, and couldn't. I was sure soused to the ears when I came in. Wonder if Mother saw the twenty bucks?

Eleanor began to giggle. She walked into the living room and took a shot of whisky, left the jigger glass on the table. Ahhhh. Warmth spread through her pounding head. She felt better already.

She got the suitcases out of the closet, began to pack. She took all the stockings in the drawer because she wouldn't remember which were hers and which were Mother's. She folded her lingerie and her clothes in neatly, no use getting wrinkled. There.

Write a note to Mother? Nuts. It was too much trouble with her fingers still feeling as though bugs were crawling over them, and, anyway, the bellboys would tell her she had walked out with her suitcases, so Mother would know she hadn't been kidnaped. And anyway, what could she say?

She took another shot of whisky, and picked up the phone. "Send a boy up for my bags." While she waited she poured a third shot, then left it there. Too much would be bad.

The bellboy. She said: "Take my bags down to a taxi."

"Going for a trip?" he asked.

"What's it to you?" she inquired. "You carry the bags and I'll do the thinking."

His eyes widened in amazement.

"O.K., I just asked." He went past her to get the bags, walking too close to her, brushing against her. She stepped away. A little punk like that. He had a nerve. She could get men, not little boys still wet behind the ears.

But she gave him fifty cents when he handed her into the cab. She settled back on the seat.

The driver said: "Where to, lady?"

"I want to go over to Manhattan. It's somewhere near police headquarters, I don't remember the exact address. A restaurant called André's."

"O.K., toots. I know it."

Free, free, I'm free at last, and I didn't have to ruin Gray to do it.

*   *   *

LIEUTENANT RALFS SWUNG HIS FEET off the chair next to his desk, and waved a red hand at it. "Sit down, Ranulph. Waddaya know?"

Buck Ranulph resisted an impulse to dust the chair off before he sat down. "Nothing much." He cleared his throat. "Nothing very definite." He felt tired, heavy. The heat, he supposed, though a formal rejection slip from Gordon Maxwell crackled in his pocket, and he had been up all night with Harold De Bruliere. Those two things were bad enough, but to be ordered down to headquarters when he finished his shift was worse. He was tired, discouraged.

It was obvious that he was through as a pulp writer. His last five stories had not sold, but he had gotten polite notes from Gordie Maxwell with each one; in fact, on the first, Gordie had had him into the office and invited him to rewrite the yarn and try again. Now he was down to sending printed rejection slips, and Buck knew what that meant. Finished.

"Well," Lieutenant Ralfs said, "if you don't know nothing, why take up my time?"

"I had dinner with Harold De Bruliere last night," Buck said. That far he could go, since Harold had pointed out Ralfs' white shadow following them.

"Yeah?" Ralfs said. He sounded uninterested. "Did he tell you what his racket was?"

"Oh, he's working with anyone who can help Negroes," Buck said.

"What's he get out of it?" Ralfs asked without looking up from the papers he was signing.

"A living, I suppose. He didn't say."

"I'm busy," Ralfs said. "Come back when you know somethin'. I hear they're transferring ya to Brooklyn."

Buck, halfway out of his chair, stopped. What Ralfs meant, of course, was that Ralfs was putting the pressure on. Transfer him to Red Hook, say, where every dock walloper with a couple of drinks too many would take a pass at a Negro cop. And so, out of the department for being unable to maintain order on a beat. The old toboggan.

That was all right. That would settle it. He was a valuable man. All he had to do was to tell Harold de Bruliere he was off the force, and he would have his choice of three or four jobs. He might even get one that paid as high as fifteen or twenty a week.

But he would starve in pride. He would not have betrayed his race.

Supposing he couldn't take it? He had never ridden in a Jim Crow car, never even seen one. He had never been south of Philadelphia in his life. Supposing he failed in the work the committee would give him, what then? He couldn't write. He couldn't go back on the cops. He couldn't have white clients, certainly. And the committee would see he didn't have Negro ones, not in Harlem. He—

"De Bruliere took me around to meet his committee," he said.

Ralfs dropped his pen. "Yeah? You mean the gang behind all this damn' trouble up in Harlem? Whata they plan next?"

"They didn't say," Buck said. "They wouldn't, you know, the first time they met me."

"Ah, hell. Takin' up my time wit' crap like that."

"But I can tell you who they are," Buck said quickly. "There's the Reverend Killain who has that church on Lexington and—"

Ralfs' pen scratched busily. "Good work, kid," he said. "Mebbe I can fix ya up with a little extry money if ya keep this up. . . ."

So I'm a stool pigeon. I would like to see De Bruliere make sixty a week. And I'm going to get more. If a man plays his cards right, he can even get to be a sergeant detective, first class, and then he won't have to be a stool pigeon. . . .

*   *   *

JOE MORTON LEANED ACROSS THE BAR, and asked the bartender: "Am I drunk? I ask you, am I intoxicated?"

"Of course not, buddy," the bartender said soothingly. "Of course not."

"Then give me another," Joe said. "I am demonstrating something. You see before you a man who is demonstrating that he can take his liquor—or leave it alone."

"Sure you can," the bartender said, pouring Joe a drink

out of a bottle of diluted whisky. "Here y'are. Two bits."

Joe put the quarter on the bar with a ring. "They think I'm all through. Think liquor's got me licked. But it hasn't." He spoke without the slightest trace of a lisp, his hands and legs were steady. But his eyes burned fiercely.

"I've got a son," he said, "and three friends."

The bartender wiped the bar in front of Joe for a minute while he gazed steadily into Joe's eyes. Finally he said: "That's more than most people have."

"And I've been away several months," Joe said. "Quite a while. A long time."

"Take it easy, Mac. Just take it easy," the bartender muttered. He moved down the bar, waited on two customers and stopped to exchange a few words with a fat man reading a racing form in front of the cashier. Then he came back.

"And my son never even came home the first night he was back. I mean, the first night I was back," Joe cried.

"Boys will be boys," said the bartender. "You remember how it was when you was a young fella."

"And my friends," Joe cried. "My friends—give me another drink—my friends wanta put me on the shelf. Want me to edit a Saturday magazine."

"My friends want me to manage the Yankees," the bartender said, too low for Joe to hear. He went back down the bar to the fat man. "How about that lush up there, boss? He's beginnin' to talk like he's full of snow."

The fat man got off his stool with a sigh. "I'll try and get rid of him. If he argues with me, hand 'm a Mickey Finn."

The bartender went back, slowly, so that the fat man got there first. The fat man said: "Mister, I think you've had enough, and just to prove it, I'll buy you one on the house and then you go home."

Pass Through Manhattan

"You know who I am?" Joe asked. "I am Joseph Kolk Morton. That's who I am. And they're trying to put me on the shelf."

"Why, it'll be a pleasure to buy you a last drink," the proprietor said. "Finkie, one for Mr. Morgan on the house, and then he's going home. That right, Mr. Morgan?"

Joe fastened his fingers around the jigger glass, gulped the straight whisky. "I thank you. And now you'll have one with me. We'll make a night of it, and show those boys. Tomorrow I go on the wagon, just to prove I can take it or leave it alone."

The fat man said: "I've had enough," and nodded to the bartender. The bartender reached under the bar for the Mickey Finn.

* * *

GUESS I LOOK ALL RIGHT, the elevator man didn't stare at me. Everything turned sour and lousy inside of me, but I guess I look all right on the outside. Oh, God, I feel so cold inside me, feel frozen. Sweat pouring down my face, and inside I'm freezing to death.

Ray was out at his desk in the city room, behind the city editor's desk, putting together the five-star final or the eight-star final or something. This is my final, the finale of Don Morton, erstwhile engineer, E.E. What does erstwhile mean, what—

Brawley Smith at his desk, banging it out, Ron had a light in his office. Go talk to Ron, he's in no hurry, his page has been made up for hours. "Hello, Ron." My voice sounds just like ever. Pull myself together.

Ron said: "Hello, Don," with that special smile any of the three of them always had for Don. Never noticed it before. These old boys love me. The only son any of them ever had. Ray says the work sterilizes you. Always thought that was just talk. Know what he means now. Mustn't scare Ron, give him dyspepsia.

"Ron, I've come to say good-bye."

"Going on a trip, Donald?"

"Going back to the mines." Make a joke. "Back to Siberia."

"The All's Fair?"

"No. I'm through with Armstrong and Grainger. I just told Mr. Grainger what I thought of him, I don't think I'll ever work in one of his mines again."

"Well, good. But you ought to get another job in New York," Ron said. "If you live in mining camps all your life, the food will ruin your digestion." He pushed his chair back from the desk. "That was my error, Donald. As a young man, I didn't pay enough attention to what I ate. I would just snatch a bite at the corner beanery, and now I'm paying for it. I'm a very sick man, Don, and I would hate to see you go the way I did. If you do have to go back to the rough sort of life you used to lead, eat mostly canned foods, and avoid beans. I've got a prescription I will have made up for you and—"

"I'll get it later. Where's my father?"

"Joe? I haven't seen him. Maybe Brawley—"

"I'll ask Brawley."

The familiar patter of Ron Levine was settling in a way. A little warmth was coming back. "Hi, Brawley. Where's Joe?"

"Haven't seen him." Brawley Smith tossed back his heavy crop of whitening blonde hair. "Say, I see you ran into my friend Wilcomen today."

The ice re-formed. "Yes. Do you know him?"

"Chased him for a week, trying to expose him. Too smart for us. We're giving that case today a big play, you see my story in the last edition? Big picture of you."

"My God, Brawley, wasn't that a busload I saved. Nazis, abortionists, embezzlers, customers' men—"

"Quite a load. Of course, those are the ones that stick out. I was checking the list out of the old story you wrote. There were a lot more. There was a sailor named Connors. And that colored detective; the morgue shows he got his lawyer's license after you pulled him out of the bus. Jack Firstin—"

"An embezzler—"

"Yeah, but he and Tenbruye, the other guy you saved, are going to put up one of the finest buildings in New York. Give jobs to hundreds of men. Y'know," Brawley said, "I called them this afternoon to get statements about the Lempe case. They'd just gone into partnership, and neither of them knew the other had been in the bus that day. Funny city, New York."

"A stinking, crazy city."

"Hey, kid," Brawley said. "Been out on the town? You look like you got the jumps. Why, Don, I wouldn't live any other place. More going on here—why, those people were all doing something. Or most of them. And there was some sort of hackwriter, a guy named Maxwell; he may turn out to be another Shakespeare. Why, everybody who amounts to something lives in this city; it damn near runs the world."

"I want to run my own life. I don't want to run the world."

Brawley Smith shrugged. "You'll never amount to anything that way."

"I don't want to." The ice was cutting his stomach. But

he couldn't tell Brawley about it. Brawley's idea of a good time was four murders and a rape. "Where's Joe, Brawley?"

"I dunno. Ask Ray; there goes the presses, the last edition's rolling."

Donald walked slowly across the room. In the ordered madness of a newspaper office, the hot revolt of a little while ago seemed crazy. He couldn't tell anyone about it; they'd laugh. If they laughed, he'd kill them.

"Hi, Ray. Where's Joe?"

"Just a minute, Don, while I get my coat. I thought you'd be showing up."

"Eh?"

"That's right, you've been down on the Lempe thing all day. Joe's off again, Don," Ray said out of the corner of his mouth. "Let's go look for him."

"I don't want— All right, Ray."

They rode down in the elevator together. No use telling Ray. Ray would say I told you so. Ron had his digestion, Brawley his stories, and Ray his maxims of how to live life. If he told Ray, Ray would want to know if his girl had thrown him over. And there was just enough truth in that to make it hard to talk about. A picture of Bastable's bony hand crawling over Eleanor's shoulder in André's crossed his mind, and he shuddered.

"What's the matter, Don? Armstrong and Grainger working you too hard?"

"I've quit them, Ray."

Ray was all right. Ray just looked at him, and said: "Good. I thought you'd get onto them sooner or later. What are you going to do?"

"Head West, I guess. If I can't get on as an engineer, I'll swing a pick."

Pass Through Manhattan

Ray said: "Maybe you're right. I'm tied up here. Let's go. There's only about four bars he could be in—"

They turned their backs on Broadway and Times Square that sent pink shadows of themselves fighting against the brilliant red of a Jersey sundown. Ray stuck his head in Bleek's; they hadn't seen Mr. Morton. They tried the bar downstairs at the *Mail,* the one nearest the *Times.* No Mr. Morton. They found him in front of a little dill-pickle joint near Eighth Avenue. He was hanging on to a lamp post and being sick.

"Gawd," Joe Morton groaned. "I'm dying."

"You must have gotten a Mickey Finn," Ray said coldly. "Come on."

Joe swung his arm. "You two. You Judases. Donald, not meeting me, not coming home all night. You, Ray, trying to make a feature editor out of Joseph Kolk Morton. Put me on the shelf. Enough to drive any man to drink. You dirty—"

For the first time that he could remember, Donald called Joe Father. "Father," he said, "I've come to say good-bye. Maybe forever. You hear, or are you too drunk?"

Ray said: "Don—"

"If you want to know where I was last night," Don said, "I was crawling in hell's own gutter, doing the job I had to take to support you while you took the cure. Last winter I killed a man covering a story you would have covered if you hadn't caught cold when you were drinking. Snap out of it, Father, I'm through. You're on your own, from now on."

Joe said: "Don. Donald—"

"All right. I love you, and I used to admire you. But it's time we both got some self-respect. I'll write to you."

He turned on his heel, walked east as fast as he could.

There was a hundred dollars in his pocket; plenty to buy a ticket to Denver, and to hell with all of them. Back to working for my living.

Behind him, Ray said: "Come on, Joe. I'll get you to a Turkish bath. That's quite a man we got there."

*   *   *

OVER IN THE CORNER under the bridge lamp, Elsie was working on *The Confessions of a Los Angeles B Girl.* Gordie read the *Evening Mail* with interest, digesting everything he could find about the final tremor from the bus accident he had been in. What a story, what a yarn—

The *Post* would buy an article from a passenger in that bus. Or no, he would write it into a story. Sure, he could sell that to the *Saturday Evening Post* and be started in the slicks.

As soon as he finished the filler for *Nightstick* that he had promised the boss by tomorrow—